"You are flushed with the heat of your bath, Rhonwyn. It is very becoming to you," he told her. "Are you coming out of the tub soon?"

"How can I when you are standing here, my lord?"

Reaching over the edge of the high wood tub, he put his hands beneath her arms and quickly lifted her out of the water, setting her down upon the floor. He drew a deep breath of pleasure.

With a gasp of both surprise and shock Rhonwyn snatched at the drying cloth and covered her nakedness. "That was unfairly done, my lord!" she scolded him.

"Has no one ever told you that all is fair in both love and war, my lady wife?" His eyes were burning a hole in the cloth.

"There is no love here, my lord, so we must be at war," she declared, "and you will find I am no easy enemy. . . ."

A MEMORY of LOVE

BERTRICE SMALL

IVY BOOKS • NEW YORK

An Ivy Book
Published by The Ballantine Publishing Group

www.ballantinebooks.com

ISBN 0-345-43518-4

Manufactured in the United States of America

First Trade Paperback Edition: July 2000
First Mass Market Edition: December 2002

10   9   8   7   6   5   4   3   2   1

For Cora Alexandra Small,
when she's old enough

A MEMORY of LOVE

Wales 1257

Prologue

The prince lay atop his lover, groaning and sweating his pleasure. The child, standing at the head of the bed, watched impassively. The prince's eyes met hers.

"Go outside, Rhonwyn," he said.

" 'Tis raining," the child whined.

"Then take your sheepskin and lie quietly by the fire, lass," he replied. Beneath him the woman moaned softly, shifting her hips suggestively as her impatient ardor grew.

"I want to sleep with my mam," Rhonwyn said stubbornly.

"Nay, lass," the prince laughed softly. "Tonight I sleep with your mam. Now make your bed by the fire. If I have to get up, I'll beat you. *Go!*"

Finally cowed, the child did as she had been bid and lay by the fire, wrapping herself in the warm sheepskin. She hated it when the prince came to their cottage. Then her mother had no time for her or her baby brother. The prince was their father, her mother had told them. They owed him their love and their allegiance. Without him they would starve. She and Glynn must always remember that.

Her brother was already asleep by the fire, his thumb in his small mouth, his dark lashes brushing his rosy cheek.

She loved Glynn more than any other person on this earth. He did not prefer the prince to her as her mother did. Yet when Llywelyn ap Gruffydd came to their cottage, he always brought his children gifts and greeted them lovingly. But I still don't have to like him, Rhonwyn reasoned silently to herself.

She heard her mother cry out, and the prince's deep voice said, "Christ's bones, Vala, no one feeds my itch like you do!" And then her mother laughed her husky laugh.

Rhonwyn's eyes closed at the sound, and she slept at last. There was no use in trying to stay awake. The prince would remain the night.

Part One

Rhonwyn 1258–1270

Chapter One

The late spring rain was heavy and chill. Some of it was seeping through the roof where the thatch was worn. The fire had gone out the day before, and the two children did not know how to restart it. They huddled together to keep warm. Their mother's body lay on the bed amid a pool of blood that was now congealed and blackening. The stench in the cottage had already numbed their nostrils, even as the cold had numbed their fingers and toes. The wind suddenly howled in mournful fashion, and the smaller of the two children whimpered, pressing himself closer to his elder sister.

Rhonwyn uerch Llywelyn focused her brain again as she had these past two days. How was she to save Glynn and herself from certain death? Their mama was dead, birthing the prince's latest child. Their cottage was isolated from any village, for decent women would not tolerate the prince's whore and his bastards. The old crone who had helped Vala in her two previous births had not been there this time, because this time the child had come too soon. *Much too soon.*

They needed to be warm, Rhonwyn thought sleepily. How did one start a fire? If only it would cease raining. Perhaps they could walk and find another cottage or village—but whatever a village was for she didn't really know, having never left the hill on which she had lived her whole five years. Rhonwyn hugged her three-year-old brother tighter against her when he whimpered again.

"Hungry," he complained to her.

"There is nothing left, Glynn," she repeated for the tenth time. "When the rain stops we will go and find food. If we leave the cottage now, we will surely die." They were apt to die in any event, Rhonwyn thought irritably. If she could only start a fire to warm them, the gnawing in their bellies might not seem so fierce. She hadn't meant for the fire to go out, but when her mam began screaming with her pain, Rhonwyn had taken her brother from their cottage so he would not be frightened. They had gone out on the hillside to pick flowers for the new baby. But when they had returned their mother was dead, and the fire was out. Not even a lingering coal remained that Rhonwyn might coax into a warm flame as she had often seen her mother do. Then the rain had begun. It had rained all night and into this day, which was almost over.

Suddenly Rhonwyn's ears pricked up at the sound of dogs baying in the distance. The noise grew closer and closer until it was directly outside. The door to the cottage was slammed open, and Llywelyn ap Gruffydd was outlined in the fading light of day. He stepped quickly inside, his eyes sweeping about the room. Seeing his children huddled together on their pallet, he asked them, "What has happened here?"

"Mam's dead," Rhonwyn answered her father. "The new baby came too soon."

"Why wasn't the midwife here?" he demanded.

"Who was to send for her? And where is she? Mam was screaming and screaming. I took Glynn and went outside. When we returned Mam was dead. There was no fire. No food. I didn't know what to do. I didn't know where to go, or I would have gone. Our mam is dead, and you and your rutting have killed her! She would not have died but that you put another baby in her belly."

Startled at the venom in the child's voice, he looked down at her, seeing his daughter for the first time. It was like looking into a glass but for her coloring, which was Vala's. She didn't like him, he knew. Her green eyes glared angrily into his. He would have laughed but for the seriousness of the situation. Rhonwyn was certainly his get and every bit as intense with her anger as he was.

"I'll make a fire," he replied. "Go outside and look in my saddlebag. There is food in it. Do not mind the dogs." He turned away from her and began to prepare a new fire. Seeing his small son staring at him, half fearful, half curious, he said, "Come here, lad, and I will show you how to make a fire so you will never be cold again."

The little boy crept from the pallet and came to stand by his father, watching fascinated as ap Gruffydd gathered a bit of kindling together and drew a flint from his purse. Using the blade of his knife, the prince stroked the flint until it sparked, and the kindling caught light. Glynn's eyes were wide with amazement, and the prince smiled, reaching out to ruffle the boy's dark hair. Ap Gruffydd added wood to the fire until it was blazing merrily, and the chill began to dissipate.

The man stood and handed the flint to his son. " 'Tis yours, Glynn ap Llywelyn. Now you know how to make a fire, but only in the fireplace for now, eh, lad?"

"Aye, Tad" came the reply, and the prince smiled again. It was the first time the child had called him father.

"So, you know I am your sire," he said.

"Mam said," the child answered simply.

"She did not lie, God assoil her sweet soul." Now the prince's attention was drawn back to his dead lover. She must be buried, although no priest would say the proper words over her. It didn't matter. God would have Vala uerch Huw because she was a good woman. He would not condemn her to a fiery hell because she had been Llywelyn ap Gruffydd's leman. He wished now he had married her, even though she had had neither wealth nor powerful family ties to recommend her. At least his children would have been legitimate. Well, he would formally acknowledge them. That would please Vala. He should begin to consider marriage, he thought. He was well past thirty and had nought but his two wee bastards to carry on his name.

Rhonwyn had reentered the cottage. She took bread and cheese, making small pieces for her little brother. Seeing the flint, she said, "What's that?" She picked it up and rolled the quartz in her hand gently.

"Give it back!" Glynn shouted at her. "Our tad gave it to me. It makes fire."

Rhonwyn shrugged and handed him back his prize.

"Was the baby born?" ap Gruffydd asked his daughter.

She shrugged. "I don't know," she replied, shoving bread and cheese into her mouth. "I didn't look."

He nodded, understanding. He would have to look. "Has the rain stopped yet, Rhonwyn?"

"Aye."

"I'll go and dig a grave for yer mam," he said.

"Put it where she can see the sunset," the little girl said. "Mam always liked to watch the sunset."

He nodded and went outside. Taking the shovel from the side of the cottage nearest Vala's garden, he sought for a westerly direction. The storm had gone, and the skies were clearing now. Finding the right spot, he began to dig. What was he to do with his children? he considered as he worked. While there was a truce between him and the English for now, there was still no place he really called home. Besides, it would be far better if as few people as possible knew of these two little ones. Even bastards had their relevance. They could be exploited by his enemies or used to cement treaties. Particularly as he had no other children. He had been faithful to Vala, for he had little time for his own amusement. Besides, there had never been a woman who pleased him like this descendant of the Fair Folk had.

The earth was soft with the rain, and he was able to quickly dig the grave. Setting the shovel aside, he went in to fetch the body. Vala's face was at peace, although her body was stiff and contorted. Between her outstretched legs, amid the black and thickened blood, he saw the child. It would fit neatly into his palm, but it was perfectly formed. "You would have had a sister," he told Rhonwyn and Glynn. "Get me a basin, lad, and you, lass, put on a kettle of water to warm. Your mam and your sister will go to their grave clean."

A sister, Rhonwyn thought sadly. She had wanted a sister. Mam had talked about names. Huw after her father if a boy. Gwynllian for a girl. Rhonwyn dipped the bucket into the water barrel by the corner of the cottage and then filled the iron kettle, swinging it over the fire to warm. Then she went to the cupboard and took out a pristine length of cloth, bringing it to her father and handing it to him wordlessly.

Ap Gruffydd smiled almost imperceptibly. There was a grim look in his eyes. He remembered how Vala had begged him for the cloth, how many years back? If she or the children died, she had explained to him, they would have a clean shroud to be buried in. He had laughed at her macabre request, but then he had assented and brought her the cloth. She was alone here on this green hill with her children because she had chosen to belong to him, thus eschewing respectability and the company of her neighbors. No one would help her in a time of trouble. She understood that and accepted her fate because she truly loved him. He should have married her, he thought again. Her father had held a small bit of land and was free. Oh, he would make a dynastic marriage eventually, but it was Vala he had loved. *Would always love.*

Ap Gruffydd spent the next hour bathing the body of the woman he had adored. He washed the barely born infant Vala's body had pushed forth. The bloody bedclothes on which she had died he burned. Then he tenderly wrapped the cold body in the immaculate shroud, tucking the baby into her embrace. Her limbs were so stiff it had been difficult to do so, but he knew that was how she would have wanted to be buried.

"Come and say farewell to your mam." He beckoned his children.

He saw Rhonwyn hesitate just a fraction of a moment, but then she took Glynn by the hand and came to him. He kissed his lover's icy lips a final time, and the children followed suit. Rhonwyn reached out and gently touched the baby's tiny head. He would have sworn for a moment that there were tears in her green eyes, but then she turned her hard gaze on him.

" 'Tis all your fault, Llywelyn ap Gruffydd," she told him. "Now what is to happen to Glynn and to me with our mam gone? Who will care for us?"

"You are my children," he replied. "I will not desert you. Your mother trusted me. Why can you not trust me? I am your father."

"You sired us on our mam's body, Llywelyn ap Gruffydd," she returned coldly, "but when have you ever been a father? When you came here it was to see *her* and to pleasure yourself. Because of you I have never seen another living being in all my life but for you, my brother, our mam, and that old crone who helped birth Glynn."

"I saw you did not starve or go unclad," he defended himself. "What more is a father needed for, lass? A man must fight and strive to gain his position and keep it. There are enemies to be defeated. New lands to gain. That is a man's world. A woman's is her children. Everything was as it should be between your mother and me. Now, let us bury her and your wee sister. Then I will take you with me to a place of safety."

Vala and her infant were placed with care in the wet grave. Her shroud had been laid over her face. The earth was filled in as Glynn sobbed his little heart out, cradled in his sister's protective embrace. The setting sun, in a burst of red and gold glory, lit the skies to the west. Ap Gruffydd raised a small mound over the grave and then replaced the strips of greenery he had first removed from the site. This way the grave was not likely to draw attention of either wild beasts or anyone who might pass by this remote place.

"We must remain the night here," he told his children. "Rhonwyn, you will gather up what you wish to take for both you and your brother. We will depart tomorrow at first light. Go inside now while I see what I can hunt up for dinner for you. Keep the fire going."

When he returned, two skinned coneys in his possession, he found the cottage swept and neat again. The bed he had so often shared with Vala, however, was stripped of its straw mattress. He said nothing, broiling the rabbits over the open fire and dividing them among himself, his children, and the dogs. Rhonwyn had set the little table, adding some of his bread and cheese. The rest, he knew, she had saved for the morning. He watched as she carefully pulled the meat from the bones of the rabbit, feeding it along with bits of bread and cheese to her little brother. Only when he was satisfied did she, herself, eat. She had learned well from her mam, he thought sadly.

She'll be a good mother some day. I must make an advantageous marriage for her. She's a pretty lass.

The children slept together on their pallet, wrapped in their sheepskins. He made certain the fire did not die in the night. When the dawn came Llywelyn ap Gruffydd arose and stood in the doorway of the cottage. It would be the last time he would ever come here, he knew. He had not expected Vala to die before he did. She had been so strong and healthy. She had been just fourteen when he had first seen her in his uncle's house. He had taken her away with him, and his seed had planted itself in her womb the first time he breached her. She had been a virgin. Nine months later she had borne Rhonwyn as easily as a cat having her kittens. Then two years later, Glynn. That she should begin her travail two months before she should have, and die of it, surprised him. He would go to a priest and acknowledge these two offspring of his body.

The sun was now just about over the horizon. He turned back into the cottage and roused his children. They finished what was left of the rabbit, the bread, and the cheese. He gave them each a sip of wine from his flask. Glynn coughed as it slid down his throat, but Rhonwyn swallowed the liquid facilely.

"So you like wine," he chuckled.

"It is good," she replied.

"Do you have everything you wish to take?" he asked her.

"There isn't much," she answered, "but I've put it in our mam's shawl." She handed him the small bundle, its corners tied together, if not neatly, tightly.

"Go outside, and take the lad," he told her. "I will be there in a moment."

"What are you going to do?" she demanded of him.

He looked directly at her, his dark eyes meeting her green ones. "I'm going to burn the cot," he said, but she did not, to his surprise, object. Instead she nodded, and taking her brother in her charge, exited the dwelling. Ap Gruffydd emitted a small bark of laughter. Vala had been all softness and spicy sweet. This daughter of theirs was as hard as flint. Even as I am, he smiled to himself grimly. He took the reed torch he had made earlier and thrust it into the fireplace to catch the flame. When it was burning well he walked about the small cottage, setting it ablaze as he worked his way toward the open door.

Once outside he flung the torch back into the room and stood with his son and his daughter, watching as the cottage burned itself to the ground. When there was nothing left of the little building, he said, "We will go now. The ground is wet, and the embers left will not spread." He went to his horse tied to a nearby tree, undoing the reins. "Rhonwyn, you will ride behind me. Glynn before me." He lifted the little boy onto the saddle, noting the sudden fear in the child's eyes as he did so. It was the first time his son had ever been astride an animal. "Addien is a well-trained beast, lad. Someday I will see you have a horse every bit as good. Perhaps one of his offspring. Would you like that?" He pulled himself up onto his mount, putting a strong and comforting arm about Glynn.

"Aye, Tad" came the reply, a bit unsure, but the little voice was strong. He was no longer afraid.

Ap Gruffydd reached down to his daughter and drew Rhonwyn up behind him. "Put your arms about me, lass," he told her, and when she did he signaled Addien to move along.

"Where are we going?" Rhonwyn asked him.

Ap Gruffydd thought a moment. Where were they going? Then he replied, "Cythraul. It's a fortress that belongs to me, and not more than a half day's ride from here."

They rode the morning through, the dogs loping along beside them, ap Gruffydd asking once if his children desired to stop to rest, but they did not. He was pleased to see they were made of strong stuff. He would leave them at Cythraul, but after that, what? He needed time to consider their fates, for he had never expected to have their care. They were Vala's responsibility, but Vala was dead. He sighed aloud and unaware.

He loved her, Rhonwyn thought. At least I know that to be truth. Both Glynn and I came from that love, but he has no feelings for us, I think. What will happen to us. A fortress? Why would he leave us in a fortress? What is a fortress? she wondered. I will not be afraid. If I show any fear, then Glynn will be afraid. He is already frightened by losing Mam. I must be strong for my brother. Mam would want me to protect him and see him safe. *But I am afraid.*

Then before them arose a dark stone edifice that seemed to spring from the mountain.

"Cythraul," ap Gruffydd said, riding straight for the dark pile of rock.

They heard his name being called from its heights as they drew nearer. Then they rode through the open ironwork of the entrance. Rhonwyn would later learn the ironwork was called a portcullis. The courtyard was suddenly alive with men. One took Addien's reins, while another reached up to lift both her and her brother down. Ap Gruffydd dismounted, giving orders that the beast be fed and rested. Then he said, "Where is Morgan ap Owen?"

"Here, my lord!" a deep voice boomed, and a barrel-chested man came forth. He was tall and had a black beard, and his hair was tied behind him although the top of his head was bald.

"We must talk," ap Gruffydd said, and walked toward a tower, which seemed to be the only building in the fortress. It was built into the walls at one corner of the structure. Inside, he told his children, "Go, and warm yourselves by the fire pit." Then he accepted a wooden goblet of bitter beer, swallowing it down in several gulps, and seated himself in the lord's chair. "Vala is dead. These are our children. The girl is just five and called Rhonwyn. The lad is three and named Glynn. I want to leave them with you while I decide what is to be done for them," he told Morgan ap Owen, the captain of Cythraul.

"Your word, lord, is my command" came the reply, "but why here, and why me? This is a great honor you do me, entrusting me with the care and safety of your offspring."

"You were Vala's blood kin, Morgan, and besides, I didn't want to exhaust them by taking them farther. They have never, until today, been off the hillock where Vala had her cottage."

"What about your brothers' households?" the captain queried.

"Few knew of Vala. And no one knew until today that I had children by her. Now you know, Morgan ap Owen. You and I and a priest of my choosing. You know the danger. My enemies would kill the lad and use Rhonwyn as a pawn in some marriage. I am far past my youth, and if I do not marry, Glynn will one day be my heir. As for Rhonwyn, it will be her father who arranges her marriage, not strangers." He smiled at his longtime friend. "They are small, Morgan. Surely you can find a place for them here."

"There is a bedspace for important visitors near the fire pit. They can have that," Morgan ap Owen answered his overlord. "But what am I to do with them?"

"They are children. They will amuse themselves. Just keep them safe for me, warm, and well fed," ap Gruffydd said.

"What am I to tell my men?" the captain asked.

"Just say these children are of special importance to me" came the reply. "They will draw their own conclusions no matter, but admit nothing to anyone."

"Will the children speak?" ap Owen wanted to know.

"Rhonwyn, Glynn, to me!" their father commanded, and the children came to stand by him. "You are my offspring, my blood, and I am proud of it; but you must not admit our relationship to any. Rhonwyn, I know you understand, but you must make your brother comprehend the danger. Can you do it, lass?"

The green eyes met his, and she said briefly, "I can."

"Good girl," he praised, and gave her a quick kiss atop her head, chuckling at the surprised look that encompassed her features. Then he arose. "I must go now. I am expected elsewhere this day, and while I may be late, I must get there."

"Will you return?" Rhonwyn asked him.

He nodded.

"When?" she demanded.

"When the time is right, lass. You will be safe here at Cythraul. Morgan ap Owen is blood kin to your mam. He will guard you with his life. Promise me you will obey him, both of you."

"Aye," Rhonwyn said dispassionately.

"Aye, Tad!" little Glynn piped, eager to please his sire.

Ap Gruffydd lifted up the little boy and kissed him on both cheeks before setting him down again. Then he looked at his daughter. She met his gaze straight on, her look neither warm nor cold. "You haven't made up your mind about me yet, have you?" he gently teased.

Rhonwyn shrugged her narrow shoulders. "I don't

really know you, but I am grateful you came yesterday, and I am grateful you have brought us to a place of safety. More than that I do not know, nor can I say, Llywelyn ap Gruffydd."

He nodded. "You are my daughter and honest to a fault," he told her. "Take care of the lad, Rhonwyn. I will be back." Then ap Gruffydd turned and, in his captain's company, left the hall of the tower.

"*Tad!*" Glynn called after the retreating figure.

"He'll be back soon," Rhonwyn comforted her brother. "Let us explore this place that is to be our new home, Glynnie-lad," she coaxed him, turning his thoughts from ap Gruffydd. "It is a tall tower."

When the day had finally waned, and the hall filled with the men-at-arms, the two children felt almost lost for a time, but then Morgan ap Owen set them up upon the high board and told his men, "These wee ones are of great importance to our lord Llywelyn. They are to be kept safe and not mistreated. I am going to appoint eight of you to be their particular guardians: Lug, Adda, Mabon, Nudd, Barris, Dewi, Cadam, and Oth. I choose you. Just make certain these two younglings don't fall off the walls."

There was much good-natured grumbling among the eight, but they were all good men and secretly pleased to have been so honored. It didn't take an educated man to figure out that these were the lord's children, even if Morgan ap Owen hadn't quite said so. The lad had his stamp, and the girl, for all her fair hair, was obviously his.

"They're his, aren't they?" his lieutenant said to his captain.

"I have not said so" was the response; "Nor should you" came the veiled warning.

Rhonwyn listened to this exchange as she sat feeding her little brother. Their sire was obviously a very important man. After the meal the chosen men gathered about

them like a pack of kindly, grizzled watchdogs. Rhonwyn was mostly silent, letting her little brother capture
the men's hearts, for Glynn was, and always had been, a
very winning child. When he began to grow sleepy, one
of them, Oth, picked up the boy and tucked him in the
bedspace.

"You had best go, too," Oth told her.

"I am older," Rhonwyn replied. Then she looked
across the hall at several of the men who were kneeling
on the floor. "What are they doing?" she asked Oth.

"Dicing," he answered her. "It is a game."

"I want to learn," Rhonwyn said.

"Do you?" he answered with a chuckle. "I don't know
if the captain would approve, lass."

"Why not?" she demanded.

" 'Tis a game of chance," he explained.

"I don't understand, Oth," she told him. "I am very
ignorant of the world, you see, having lived all my life on
the hill with my mam."

He nodded. "I see," he said. "Well, then, perhaps I
shall teach you to dice myself, but not tonight. You have
had several hard days, and you need your rest. I will wager you have never before today ridden. There is a small
mare in the stables that no one uses. I can teach you to
ride, too. Would you like that?"

Rhonwyn nodded eagerly. "Aye, I would!"

"Then crawl into bed with your wee brother, who is already asleep. Tomorrow will be a very busy day for you."
Oth led her, unprotesting now, to the bedspace in the
stone walls of the tower. Lifting her up, he tucked Rhonwyn in beneath the furs next to Glynn. "Good night,
lass," he said, and then left her.

"Well done," Morgan ap Owen praised him quietly.

"What in Jesu's name does ap Gruffydd mean by leaving those two wee children here?" Oth said. "What kind

of a place is Cythraul for wee ones?" He picked up a wooden cup and drank down his beer.

"He'll be back soon enough for them," Gamon ap Llwyd replied. "They're his only offspring, unless, of course, he has a few others hidden about the countryside."

"He was faithful to my cousin Vala," Morgan ap Owen said quietly. "I will wager there are no others, and did I tell you not to speak of them thusly?"

"We all know they are his," Gamon ap Llwyd said.

"Poor lad and lass," Oth replied. "Their mam gone and them brought to a place like this. Still, if we are not to have them long, we must make their time here a good one. The peace is holding for now."

Aye, Morgan thought to himself, the peace is holding, but for how long? And if it broke, Cythraul would be in the thick of it, being located so close to the border, guarding a mountain pass between what was known as the "Welshry" and the "Englishry" sections of the Marches.

It had been blessed providence that the prince had arrived at Vala's cottage when he did. Had he not, the children would have died as well. Oh, Rhonwyn would have tried hard to survive and keep her baby brother safe, but she was only a wee girlie. Their tragic end would have been inevitable. But ap Gruffydd had come in time and saved his offspring. Yet Morgan ap Owen knew that the prince would not be returning soon. He had other, greater problems. God only knew how many years these two children would remain at Cythraul.

There were several things to consider. Clothing was the first. Dewi, one of the men he had appointed to look after the children, was the fortress's tailor. He must clothe both Rhonwyn and Glynn in boy's attire. That way anyone spying on them or sheltering with them would see the children, assume them to be the sons of one of the men at Cythraul, and think no more on it. Anyone seeing a little girl among them would assume there were women at Cythraul also. Such a notion could prove dangerous to the safety of the fortress.

And what was he to do with the children during the day? He could neither read nor write, nor could anyone here. If Rhonwyn was to make a good marriage one day, she should know something, but who was there to teach her? Well, that would be ap Gruffydd's problem. The men at Cythraul fortress could hardly be expected to raise two children as a gentle dame would. Why hadn't ap Gruffydd taken them to his sister, the Abbess Gwynllian? They would have had a far better opportunity at Mercy Abbey than at Cythraul; but ap Gruffydd took the easiest route where his son and daughter were concerned. His passion was for his country, which was why he had put off the matter of his marriage. Even now, approaching forty, he had no idea of finding a wife and siring a legitimate heir.

Morgan ap Owen shook his dark head despairingly. Two small children to care for. What had ap Gruffydd been thinking? He looked about the hall. Most of his men were now wrapped in their sheepskins as near to the fire pit as they could get. Rising, he went outside and checked the preparations for the night. The gates were barred and locked. The watch stood upon the walls. All was quiet and peaceful. Above him the skies had finally cleared, and the stars shone brightly. A crescent moon had already set. A cold wet nose pressed itself into his hand. Absently he reached out and stroked his favorite dog, a large Irish wolfhound.

"Well, Brenin, 'tis a fine responsibility we have been given. I'll be expecting you to watch over our young guests. The lad is small yet and less likely to mischief, but I fear for his sister. Headstrong like her tad, she is, and clever, I'm thinking."

The dog whined as if in agreement and pushed his master with his massive head.

Morgan chuckled. "You're getting old, Brenin, that you would go in on a fine night like this, but I'm ready for my bed, too." Together master and beast returned to the hall. Morgan ap Owen found his bedspace, but to his surprise the dog went and lay before the two children. The captain smiled. He always knew Brenin understood him no matter what anyone else said.

Chapter Two

Ap Gruffydd's children were no better than peasants, Morgan ap Owen thought as he watched them over the next few days. They had known nothing but their cottage and their hill. They hadn't even had a pet to keep them amused. They were at first wary of Brenin, but the great wolfhound quickly won over the bolder Rhonwyn and her shy little brother. Soon he was carrying Glynn about on his back as the child tried to emulate his sister, whom Oth was teaching to ride.

"We ought to get the laddie a pony," Oth remarked one evening in the hall. "He's wearing out poor old Brenin, and we all know how the captain will feel if the dog dies."

There was a nodding of heads in agreement.

"Hold still, you wee vixen," Dewi said as he measured Rhonwyn for her tunic. "You're worse than water running over rocks."

Rhonwyn giggled. "Lug says I have very little feet. He measured me for boots of my own yesterday. Will I like boots, Dewi? I've always gone barefoot, I have."

"You must learn to wear boots," Dewi told her. "I'll make you some nice hose to wear under them."

"What are hose?" she asked curiously.

"A cloth covering for your legs and feet," he told her. By the rood, these children knew so little! "Hose will help keep your feet warm in winter and the bugs from biting your legs in summertime, lass."

"You're making her hose?" Lug interrupted. "I'll have to wait then to make the boots, for I must measure her again when she is wearing the leg coverings, Dewi. You might have told me before I made the pattern."

"You've not cut the leather yet, have you?"

"Nay, you told me just in time," Lug said.

Morgan ap Owen restrained a chuckle. His men, all of them, were absolutely besotted with the two children. He needn't have appointed a guardianship, for they were all eager to look after ap Gruffydd's offspring. They carried the boy about when he tired, which he seemed to quite easily. They made certain the choicest bits of the meal were put in Rhonwyn and Glynn's bowls.

A bit subdued at first, the children began to grow more comfortable with their new home. At one point later, Morgan did not ask how, a dappled gray pony was found along with a small saddle. Glynn joined his sister in her riding lessons. On his feet Glynn was sensitive and timid, but astride the pony he quickly became an excellent, even daring horseman, frequently besting Rhonwyn, who had absolutely no fear of anything at all.

Both youngsters roamed the fortress at will. After they had been seen several times playing with sticks as they would swords, small weapons were forged for them, and the lessons began, as well.

Glynn was easily wearied with the rough games that Rhonwyn so liked. He preferred the company of the fortress cook, Gwilym, who kept him amused with wonderful and fanciful tales of fairie folk, warriors, and beautiful maidens—some pure, and some devilishly wicked. Gwilym often told his tales to the men in the hall on winter evenings. He had a deep rich voice that could call forth magical and mysterious stories. Sometimes he would sing the history of the ancient Cymri, accompanying himself on a small lute. Glynn attached himself to the cook like a winkle to a rock. No one seemed to mind, as Glynn was a gentle child. While the men liked him, they were not quite certain what to do with him. His attachment to Gwilym solved the problem for all quite nicely.

Rhonwyn, on the other hand, was far easier to understand, even if she was a little girl. Morgan, himself, taught her swordplay, which she very much enjoyed. He taught her how to use a main gauche, a dagger held in the left hand while one used one's sword in the right. Barris, the blacksmith, made Rhonwyn her own small kite-shaped shield. Oth devised a padded body armor, called an arming doublet, for her practices. She learned to use a javelin and a mace. Next to the sword, however, Rhonwyn's favorite weapon was an alborium, a bow made of hazelwood. She became extremely quick and very proficient with it, particularly astride her horse. Guiding her mount with her knees, the reins wrapped about the saddle's pommel, she used the bow with deadly intent while coming at a full gallop. By the time she was ten there wasn't a man in the fort who wouldn't have fought at her side and felt safe.

For the next few years a series of truces ensured the peace between England and Wales. The English king, Henry III, was involved in a serious power struggle with one of his greatest lords, Simon de Montfort, the Earl of Leicester, who also happened to be his brother-in-law. The rebellion of de Montfort and the barons was a popular one, for Henry was a weak king. Meeting the opposition at Oxford, he reluctantly signed a treaty limiting his royal power. Three years later the king repudiated the Treaty of Oxford, saying his word had been forced. While he walked cautiously for a time, eventually the Baron's

War broke out, and the king was defeated by de Montfort. The very first Parliament was summoned, consisting of lords, bishops, knights, and burgesses, who were the representatives of the towns.

De Montfort's next move to ensure peace to the west was to formally, in the name of the crown, recognize Llywelyn ap Gruffydd as prince of Wales and overlord of *Magnates Wallie*, or all the great men of Wales. Llywelyn was now a vassal of England, and his power was at its absolute height. Shortly thereafter, however, Prince Edward, the king's eldest son, defeated de Montfort at Evesham, killing him. Wales, nonetheless, was left in peace. It suited England to permit the Welsh autonomy for the time being. After all, there was Scotland to the north to contend with and the French across the channel, who had now in their possession almost all of England's French territories. A treaty was proposed to be signed between Henry III and Prince Llywelyn.

Isolated at Cythraul, the news of all these goings-on still managed to filter through, brought by travelers seeking shelter. Rhonwyn, while interested in the news brought to Cythraul, pretended indifference. She had no love for her father, knowing his rescue of his children those few years back had been nothing more than chance. Bringing them to the fortress was merely a duty done, for the men of Cythraul had drummed one lesson into Rhonwyn uerch Llywelyn: duty to family and country first. If her father ever asked a duty of her, Rhonwyn knew she would grant it despite her dislike of ap Gruffydd. He had sired her. He was her overlord. She owed him duty. She thought it unlikely, however, that she would ever be called upon to perform a duty for ap Gruffydd.

He had yet to marry, although he was in his late forties. There were rumors of a possible alliance with a daughter of Simon de Montfort, but a lady of such distinguished lineage—she had a king of England, a king of France, and a Holy Roman Emperor for uncles—could not possibly accept a mere prince of the Welsh for a husband. Or could she? The lady in question, however, was in France, so she could not be asked.

Rhonwyn had turned fifteen now, and Morgan ap Owen began to worry. She dressed like a boy, but while her breasts were small they were still visible beneath her tunic. There wasn't anything feminine about her other than her chest. She strode boldly about like any young man at Cythraul. Her fair hair was cropped short. She could outride anyone at Cythraul, even her brother.

It had been easier when she had been a little girl, but now, Morgan fretted, some of the younger men were beginning to look at her with lust in their eyes. He had twice in the last months seen her cornered. While she had attacked her foolish admirers so that one of them sustained several broken ribs and the other had his nose broken in two places, Morgan ap Owen knew it was just a matter of time before Rhonwyn would be forced to face the reality that she wasn't one of the lads, but rather a pretty lass.

Before he might consider what to do about the situation, Llywelyn ap Gruffydd rode suddenly into Cythraul one day. He had not been to the border fortress since that day ten years ago when he had brought his children to Morgan ap Owen. This time he did not come alone, but rather with a troop of about twenty men in his train. The watch on the walls had called out the sighting of an armed party and then called again to say it was the prince himself. The portcullis was raised and the gates to Cythraul thrown open to welcome the lord of them all.

"My lord prince, we are most happy to see you," Morgan said, coming forward. "What news?"

"I have signed a treaty with King Henry. We will keep the peace a while longer, Morgan ap Owen." Ap Gruffydd looked about. "Where are my children?" he asked.

Before the captain might answer, Oth came forward with Glynn, and Morgan said, "Here is your son, my prince."

Ap Gruffydd looked at the lad and was pleased. The boy looked relatively healthy. He was almost as tall as his father, with dark blue eyes and black hair, but he was a bit thin. Ap Gruffydd remarked on it to his captain.

"Lads are gangling at his age, my prince," Morgan answered. "He is growing, and we cannot keep him filled up with food." He smiled at Glynn, who grinned back mischievously.

"How old are you now, lad?" the prince asked his son.

"Thirteen, Tad," the boy replied.

"Have you been happy here at Cythraul?"

"Aye, Tad!" was the enthusiastic reply.

"Good! Good!" ap Gruffydd said. He looked about. "Where is my daughter, Morgan?"

"She is out hunting, my prince."

"So she has been taught to ride," ap Gruffydd said, sounding satisfied with the news. "Excellent!"

"Rhonwyn is the best rider and soldier at Cythraul!" came Glynn's endorsement. "All the men say so, Tad!"

Ap Gruffydd chuckled. "A soldier, is she?" He was amused by his son's innocence, but then all the boy had ever known in his thirteen years were places of isolation. Perhaps that should change, but first he had his daughter to deal with, and her future was assured.

"Aye, Tad," the boy continued, and Morgan ap Owen could only silently stand by. "Rhonwyn is very skilled with sword, main gauche, javelin, and mace, too. With the alborium, she never misses her target. She's our best hunter, Tad!" It was obvious the boy was extremely proud of his sister.

Ap Gruffydd's attention had been quite engaged by his son's recitation. He looked to his captain. "You taught my daughter how to use weapons, Morgan?"

"It was either teach her or have someone get injured, my lord prince" came the reply. "She wore padding and even has her own armor. We thought it best."

"My daughter is the best soldier at Cythraul, I am told. Did you teach her nothing but warfare?"

"It is all we could teach her, my lord prince," Morgan replied.

"And my son? Have you taught him warfare, too? Why is he not considered as skilled as his sister?" came the query.

"I do not like weapons, Tad," Glynn spoke up for himself. "Oh, I can use a sword if I must, and I ride well, but I do not like warfare. I cannot bear to see anything killed, even an animal."

"Jesu! Mary!" ap Gruffydd swore, startling the boy, who shrank beneath his father's fierce gaze. Seeing it, the prince asked, "What do you like, Glynn ap Llywelyn?"

"I . . . I l-like poetry, and tales of daring and magic," he half whispered. His father was not pleased. Did he not like stories?

"The lad has the makings of a fine bard," Morgan said. "Gwilym our cook has taught him to play the harp and all the stories and poetry he knows. You'll see tonight in the hall what an excellent young bard you have sired, my lord prince."

"A lass who's a warrior, and a lad who is a poet. Jesu!" ap Gruffydd said. Then he laughed at the absurdity of it.

At that moment there was a clatter of horses behind them at the fortress's entrance, and a party of hunters came through.

"Ho! Cousin Morgan," their leader called out to the captain. "I've brought you a fine young deer for our dinner!" The speaker rode directly up to Morgan ap Owen and pushed the deer from the saddle to fall at the captain's feet.

"*Rhonwyn?*" Llywelyn ap Gruffydd didn't know whether to be pleased or horrified at the young ruffian who suddenly stared down at him at the mention of her name.

Recognition dawned in the green eyes. "By the rood, lads! 'Tis my sire, the prince, come to pay us a call." She slid easily from her saddle and bowed mockingly. "My lord prince, I am at your service."

He glared at her intently. Aye, she was female. Her bosoms betrayed her, but other than that her sex was indistinguishable from any of the other men in the fortress. Her hair was cropped like a man's and dirty. *She was dirty.* Why had he thought she would be like her mother? Like his delicate and gentle Vala? "Jesu! Mary!" he swore. Then anger began to overwhelm him. He turned on Morgan ap Owen.

"This is how you have raised my daughter? To be the toughest soldier at Cythraul? What the hell were you thinking, Morgan?"

Morgan ap Owen wasn't in the least intimidated by his prince. "What did you expect us to do, Llywelyn? Ten years ago you brought me a five-year-old girl-child and a wee laddie of three. You left them here and have not returned once in all that time to see how they were. I did my best by them. They have been well fed and clothed and, aye, loved by the men of this fortress! We taught them what we could. Honor. Duty to you and to our people. What else was there?"

"You might have taught her that she was a lass!" roared the prince of Wales.

"How?" demanded his captain. "There are no women here, Llywelyn. We guard the Welshry for you. Oh, occasionally my men seek out a local whore, but they are not the kind of women we bring into the fort, nor are they the kind of women you would want your daughter associating with, *my lord prince*. Do not complain to me. Rhonwyn is a fine young lass even if she has not learned how to simper and preen like the highborn ladies you have undoubtedly been associating with, *my lord prince*. Do not blame me that your daughter has not the feminine traits you desire her to have. If you wanted her to have those virtues, you should have taken her to your sister, the abbess, instead of bringing her here! Come into the hall now. I need a drink if we are to continue this argument."

Ap Gruffydd burst out laughing again and followed his captain. Inside the hall they quaffed cups of apple beer that had been aging in barrels since the previous autumn. The beer was strong with just a hint of sweetness. Their immediate thirst satisfied, they sat by the fire pit, and the prince explained the reason for his visit.

"I have promised Rhonwyn in marriage," he said, "but the bridegroom will expect someone in a gown with a gentle manner, not this breeked and swearing huntress you have created out of my child. I thought she would be like her mother, but she isn't at all."

"How could she be?" Morgan answered. "She has had no example but ours to follow, and we are a fort of rough men."

"Jesu! Mary!" the prince swore softly again.

"Can't you find another of your female relations for this man?" the captain asked sensibly. "Did you ever even bother to acknowledge Rhonwyn and Glynn to the church?"

"Aye, that was done years ago. The prior in Cwm Hir at the Cistercian monastery was told. He has documents with my signature." Llywelyn ap Gruffydd sighed deeply and shook his head.

"The marriage is the unwritten portion of the treaty I signed with King Henry at Montgomery. As a show of good faith, I offered Rhonwyn in marriage with one of the king's chosen Marcher lords in the Englishry. His name is Edward de Beaulieu, Lord Thorley of Haven Castle. Having offered my daughter, I cannot substitute another without appearing to be deceitful with King Henry. It could jeopardize everything I have worked for, Morgan. Certainly you can understand why I will not do that."

The captain nodded. "Aye, I can, Llywelyn. You have worked hard for our people, but what are you to do now? Rhonwyn is hardly anyone's idea of a blushing bride." He chuckled and his gaze went across the hall to where the girl was dicing and drinking with her companions. It was not Rhonwyn's fault that she was so unsuitable. "She is a virgin," he said as if to cheer his overlord. "Of that I am certain. She has no interest in the young men, although of late several have approached her. She has physically injured them in her refusals."

"At least that is to the good," the prince remarked dryly. "I shall have to take her to my sister at Mercy Abbey. Gwynllian will be able to make her into a maiden fit to wed with a lord. I know now I should have done that in the first place, Morgan. And perhaps Glynn might have been better off there, too, until he was old enough to be fostered out, but I didn't want anyone to know of the children while they were so helpless. And I didn't want to separate them when they had just lost their mother so tragically. I should have come back for them." He sighed. "The years have gone too quickly, and there never seemed to be enough time for them. Still, at least my children have survived." He chuckled. "The English were mightily surprised when I announced I had a young daughter of marriageable age. How they would have loved to have Rhonwyn as their hostage these years past."

"It might have been better for her if she had been their hostage," his captain replied. "She would have been treated with honor and raised as she should have been raised, Llywelyn. Will you take the lad, too?"

The prince shook his head. "Nay. They are grown now and can be separated. Glynn can remain with you for the present."

Morgan ap Owen knew what that meant. Glynn ap Llywelyn was of no current use to his father, and so he could stay where he was. Perhaps it was better that his lord wasn't married. He was not the best of fathers. He knew Glynn would be devastated to lose the sister he loved so devotedly, but, Morgan thought, at least the prince wouldn't attempt to make the boy into a rough soldier. Glynn was better off with the people who understood him best, and they were here at Cythraul.

"When will you tell her, and when will you take her?" the captain asked his overlord.

"I must take her immediately, for the wedding is set for a month from now. We will have to get to Mercy Abbey as quickly as possible." He looked across the hall. "Rhonwyn uerch Llywelyn, to me!" he called out.

She arose to her feet almost reluctantly, tossed the dice to one of her companions, spit into the rushes, and then sauntered across the floor to where Morgan and her father sat by the fire pit. She bowed, but the courtesy was almost insulting. "What do you wish, my lord prince?" she asked him. Despite her demeanor, her voice, he found, was musical.

Morgan arose from his seat. "Sit, Rhonwyn," he said.

She looked at him with startled eyes, but sat. Then she saw the captain leave them. She was alone with her sire. What did he want of her?

"How much do you know of my accomplishments?" he asked her.

"Enough to realize you are a great lord," she replied.

"I ratified a treaty several days ago at Montgomery with the English king. Part of the treaty agreement was a marriage between my blood kin and an English lord. It is a show of good faith between us. You are to be wed in a month's time to Edward de Beaulieu of Haven Castle. He is not an important man, but his family descends from one of the first of King Henry's sons, born on the body of the heiress of Thorley. Haven Castle is small, but the lands it possesses are prosperous. You are most fortunate to have gained such a fine husband," Llywelyn ap Gruffydd told his daughter, watching closely to gauge her reaction to his words, but for a long minute Rhonwyn said nothing, and he could not help but wonder what she was thinking. "Well?" he finally demanded.

"What is a marriage?" she said at last.

The four words stunned him. His mouth snapped open, and then closed again. His first thought was that she was simpleminded, but then he knew that not to be the truth. Why would she know of marriage here in this place? "A marriage," he said slowly and carefully, "is the formal and legal union between two people. It is an honorable estate, Rhonwyn. The treaty I have signed at Montgomery with King Henry must offer an outward show of trust between us besides our signatures and seals on the parchment. In a case like this it has always been the custom to make a marriage between the two sides. Do you understand at all what I have said to you, my daughter?"

"What does this marriage involve?" she finally asked of him. "What am I expected to do? I have been taught I have a duty to you, my lord, and I would not be derelict in that duty or bring shame upon your good name."

"You will become Edward de Beaulieu's wife, his mate. You will be expected to manage his home and give him children of your body."

Her green eyes had widened slightly at his words, but she yet remained calm. "I have absolutely no idea of how to do any of the things you have told me I must, my lord prince. Have you not another female relation of your blood who would be better suited for this marriage?"

"Nay, I do not, Rhonwyn, but more important, I have given my word that it is my daughter who will marry Edward de Beaulieu. Having given my word, I must keep it."

"Aye," she said, understanding his pledge was a matter of honor. "You are my lord, and I have been taught I owe you a duty," Rhonwyn began. "This marriage is my obligation to you, is it not?"

"It is," he said. How amazing. She was incredibly ignorant in almost every way, but she understood duty and honor. He must thank Morgan. He had expected tears and refusal, not this calm acceptance.

"My lack of knowledge and unfamiliarity with the world outside of Cythraul may prove an embarrassment to you, my lord prince. I do not wish to be a liability. I would not have people say Llywelyn ap Gruffydd has gulled the English by sending an unsuitable and uncivilized bride. What will you do to help me?" It was a reasonable request, and it pleased him that she was aware of her deficiencies.

"We will leave on the morrow for Mercy Abbey, where my sister, your aunt, is the abbess. She will help you to become the lass you must be, Rhonwyn."

"And my brother? What of him?"

"He remains here," the prince said. "I have no use for him at the moment, and he is still but half grown." He saw the look of anger in her eyes, but she strangely remained silent. "You do not like me, Rhonwyn, do you?" he probed.

"Nay, I do not, my lord prince. You gave me life, and you saved my brother and me from death once, but I do not like you. Why should I? You have done nought but a scant duty for us, but both Glynn and I will repay that duty with duty of our own."

"Do you have any clean clothing?" he asked her, suddenly weary of their conversation.

"I have what I wear, my lord. You sent no coin or fabric. Cythraul has little to spare. My cousin and his men have done their best by us. If it would please you, I will wash my garments. There is a warm wind to dry them in the night, and if they are a bit damp on the morrow, what matter."

"And wash yourself," he ordered her. "What have you done with your beautiful hair, lass?"

"Long hair does not fit under a helmet, my lord prince," she answered him sharply.

"Leave the helmet here," he said. "You will not need it, nor the weapons with which I am told you are so proficient. I am to bring the English a sweet virgin to wed, not a warrior maid whose skills will terrify them and lead them to believe I meant the bridegroom harm."

To his surprise Rhonwyn laughed aloud. "I am not like others my age, my lord prince, am I?"

"Nay, lass, you are not," he admitted. "Go now."

Dismissed, she hurried to find her brother in the kitchen with Gwilym. She told him everything that had passed between her and their father. Then she turned to the cook. "I need your help," she said.

"Whatever I can do, Rhonwyn," he replied.

"Hot water is the best for cleaning. Will you boil it up for me? I have been told to wash both my clothing and my person before we leave in the morning. Glynn, go and beg Morgan for the use of his extra sherte. I must have something to wear while I wash my own garments and to sleep in tonight while my clothing dries."

Glynn ran off to do his sister's bidding.

"After I've fed the hall, we'll set up a rack by the fire to dry your things," Gwilym said. "The wind will be too damp, and you shouldn't ride wet on the morrow. After the meal, while I entertain the hall, you come down and do what you must. I will warn the captain and the prince of your intentions, and they will see you are not disturbed."

She was not as she scrubbed her chemise, her sherte, and hose. Her tunic she brushed thoroughly of dirt and dust. Then after she had hung her garments on the drying rack, she polished her well-worn boots. The kitchen of the fortress's main building was located beneath the hall. Rhonwyn barred the doors leading to the kitchen garden and the hall. Satisfied she was secure, she removed Morgan's sherte and climbed into the small oak washtub to bathe herself. The water was still warm and very pleasant. On the rare occasions that she bathed, she did it like her companions, in a nearby stream. Cold water, however, was not conducive to a long stay. The thin sliver of soap she had used to wash her clothing easily removed the dirt from her person and hair.

Rhonwyn climbed from the tub and rubbed herself dry with a rough cloth. She couldn't ever remember having been totally naked. Morgan had always insisted she bathe in her chemise when she went to the stream to wash herself. Curiously she began to examine her body. Her breasts seemed to be growing larger each year. She had a thick tangle of curls on the mound between her thighs. It was just slightly darker than her pale hair. Since she had caught a glimpse of Glynn once with the same thatch, it didn't bother her as much as her burgeoning breasts. She pulled the sherte back on, then sat by the kitchen fire to comb out her short, wet hair.

She could hear Gwilym and Glynn in the hall, their voices rising in a duet. She climbed the stairs and slipped back into the hall, going to her bedspace. She and Glynn now had separate sleeping areas, for Morgan had decided several years ago that they were both too big in form to make sleeping together comfortable any longer. Now her brother was singing a tale of love lost and found again. Rhonwyn felt her eyes growing heavy with the sweet sound of his voice.

Glynn came to wake her just before dawn, climbing into the sleeping space with his sister to ask, "What will happen to me now, Rhonwyn? Why is Tad leaving me here alone?" He pressed his thin frame next to her, seeking reassurance and comfort.

"He says you are but half grown, and so he has no use for you yet," she answered her brother, putting a protective arm about him.

"I am afraid," the boy admitted.

"Nay, you need not be," she tried to reassure him. "You will be in the place you know best with Morgan, who is our mother's kin, and with Gwilym. Both care for you as they would a son, little brother."

"Some of the others do not like me. They say you are more our father's son than I am," Glynn told her.

"Do not listen to such things," Rhonwyn replied, thinking angrily she would like to get her hands on those who would hurt her brother.

"We have never been parted, Rhonwyn." His face was woebegone. "Where is Tad taking you? Why can I not come?"

"I must learn to be a wife. You cannot come with me

to Mercy Abbey. It is a place for women only. But when I am married to this lord, I will ask him to let you come and live with us, Glynn. There is more, I am beginning to realize, to the world in which we live than just Cythraul. You are not meant to be a soldier like the prince. There is something that you can be, but you cannot learn that here at Cythraul. Tell no one of what I have said to you, except perhaps Morgan and Gwilym. I have never lied to you, Glynn. I promise you I will send for you when I can." She kissed his cheek, and then shoved him from the bedspace. "Go to the kitchen and bring me my clothing from the drying rack."

He ran off, and Rhonwyn lay quietly for the next few minutes. She was wide awake now and a little nervous. Today she would leave her home forever. Soon she would leave the prince's realm as well for England. What was it like? Would it have the green hills and deep valleys of Wales? Would she like this lord she was to marry? Would he like her? Did it even matter? She had a duty, and she would perform it to the best of her ability so as not to bring shame upon her lord father.

Glynn had returned with her garments, and Rhonwyn dressed herself carefully beneath the furs. Then climbing from her bedspace, she ran her fingers through her cropped hair to neaten it. She pulled on the boots Glynn had left by her bedside, stamping her feet. The boots were just a bit short now. Her feet were obviously still growing. She pulled her tunic down and buckled her belt about her narrow waist, sliding her dagger with its horn handle into its sheath.

In the hall the men were stirring now and hurrying out into the courtyard to pee. Gwilym brought a kettle of porridge from the kitchen and began ladling it into the round trenchers of bread upon the table. Rhonwyn sat in her usual place with Glynn and ate silently. Higher up the board Morgan sat with Llywelyn ap Gruffydd, eating and talking. Occasionally they would glance at her, and Rhonwyn wondered what they were saying about her. Around her the men ate silently or spoke in low morning tones.

Finally the prince arose. "It is time for us to leave. Rhonwyn, are you ready? Where is your pack, lass?"

"I have nothing to carry but what I wear, my lord," she answered him. "You have instructed that I leave my weapons behind." Rhonwyn stood.

Llywelyn ap Gruffydd looked at his daughter. She seemed very young and vulnerable in the light of the morning. She was well scrubbed, he could see, but her garments were practically threadbare and as simple as any soldier's. The brown tunic, unornamented and plain, made her look so pale, yet the girl was in good health. For a moment he felt guilty that he had not, until he needed her, thought of her. "Say your good-byes, lass," he instructed her gruffly, and then he left the hall.

They crowded about her, these men who had raised her since she was just a wee girl. Rough soldiers, with tears in their eyes. Their voices broke when they instructed her to be a good lass, remember what they had taught her, and not forget them. They turned away, one by one, each wishing her good luck. But Morgan ap Owen, who loved her best, said, "This is your home. I am your blood kin. If you need me, I will come." Then he kissed her cheek and led her out into the courtyard where the prince and her brother awaited her.

Glynn had been crying, she could see. Rhonwyn put her arms about him. "Don't," she pleaded, "or I could weep, too. Be patient, and I will send for you, brother. We will not be parted for long."

"You never cry," he said softly. "You are the strong one."

"And you the clever one," she replied, kissing his damp cheek. "I love you, Glynn. You are safe here at Cythraul."

Glynn gave her a half grin. "Tad sees what I am and is too wise to make me change. I shall make up a poem about you, Rhonwyn, and sing it in the hall tonight. They shall all weep for you, sister."

The siblings hugged, and only ap Gruffydd's voice broke their tender embrace.

"When you come to me," Rhonwyn instructed her brother, "bring my weapons with you, Glynn, but tell no one. Do you understand?" She looked directly into his eyes, and then smiled once more.

Rhonwyn mounted her horse, a gray gelding with a black mane and tail that Morgan had obtained for her two years ago when she had outgrown the dainty old mare. The gelding was a big beast with large hooves. Ap Gruffydd was a little surprised to see his daughter mounted so, and remarked on it.

"The animal is steady," Morgan ap Owen replied. "I wanted her to have a safe horse."

The prince turned his mount and led them through the gates of Cythraul and down the hill upon which it sat. Rhonwyn rode by his side. They did not speak. Behind them the troop of men accompanying ap Gruffydd also rode silently. Rhonwyn realized that even the hooves of the horses were relatively quiet as they moved along. It was unlikely an enemy would hear them until the soldiers were upon them. When the sun was at the midpoint in the sky, they stopped.

"If you want to pee," ap Gruffydd said, "go into the bushes."

She took his advice, going deep into the greenery. When she returned she was handed a chunk of bread and a wedge of cheese. She ate swiftly, cramming the food into her mouth. The prince passed her his flask, and she swallowed the liquid within without thinking. The taste of apple on her tongue told her it was cider. They remounted and continued on their way.

As they crossed an open meadow Rhonwyn said low, "How long will it take to reach our destination, my lord?"

"Until tomorrow, late," he told her.

She was about to offer to hunt for their dinner when she realized she didn't have her bow. She swore softly beneath her breath, and the prince chuckled.

"You cannot say words like that any longer, Rhonwyn," he told her. "Ladies do not swear, and I fear your aunt would beat you black and blue if she heard such language."

"She had best not raise her hand to me," Rhonwyn responded darkly. "I am not an animal, and I have never allowed anyone to beat me."

"Morgan did not punish you when you were naughty?" Ap Gruffydd was surprised by the revelation.

"He did not feel he had the right to lay his hand on your children. He had other ways of punishing us. He would forbid me from my horse or take my alborium from me so I could not hunt. Glynn was rarely bad. A harsh look could set him crying," Rhonwyn told ap Gruffydd. "My brother is a gentle lad. He is not meant to be a soldier, but there are so many things he is good at that there is surely a place for him in this world."

The prince said nothing more. He was no fool and understood what she was telling him, and he had seen his son was not fit for a military life. He had spawned either a bard or a priest, he was not yet certain. Once they could determine if the boy liked women, then he would know. He could not be sure if he wanted a priest in the family. His sister the abbess was more than enough.

He smiled to himself. Gwynllian would certainly be surprised to learn he had two children. She was always railing at him for not getting married, and he was always telling her he did not have time for a wife and family if Wales was to be independent. Well, it was true. Vala had been content to wait in her cottage for him to come. She had never whined or complained at him for not being more attentive. Vala had understood what he was doing. How many wives would have? Soon enough he would need a highborn mate whose family and connections could help him keep what he had gained. *But not yet.*

He glanced sideways at his daughter. While she had her mother's coloring, she was his spit, although her features were more softened and feminine. He smiled to himself again. His timing was always just right where his children were concerned. He had come just in time to save them from death. Now he was just in time to keep Rhonwyn from becoming a soldier. Gwynllian was going to have her work cut out for her. His daughter was ignorant and crude. It was going to cost him a large gift to Mercy Abbey to turn her into a refined and blushing bride for Edward de Beaulieu, but if anyone could do it, it was Gwynllian.

As the sun was setting behind the western mountains, they stopped once again. A camp was set up with a fire over which roasted the rabbits his men had caught along the way that day. The horses were led to a nearby stream to drink, and then allowed to browse about the trees where they were tied. The company ate and then settled down for the night. Rhonwyn had never slept outdoors before. She found it both exciting and a little frightening. The night noises seemed louder and more mysterious than the noises she heard during the day. Still, she managed to get some sleep before the prince was shaking her awake.

As they rode in the cold and dark dawn hour, ap Gruffydd handed his daughter an oatcake to eat. It was hard and virtually tasteless. She chewed it slowly nonetheless, quieting the rumbling in her stomach. She already missed Gwilym's hot morning porridge. They rode again until the noon hour, stopped to rest and water the horses, then continued on once more. The countryside was beautiful and lonely. They passed no fortresses or cottages.

In the very late afternoon as the sun was sinking, they crested a ridge, and there in a lovely valley below stood a cluster of stone buildings. It looked a bit grim and forbidding in the late autumn light.

She heard a noise and turned to the prince. "What is that sound, my lord?" she asked.

" 'Tis the pealing of a bell, Rhonwyn. Have you never heard a church bell, lass?" He was surprised by her ignorance as always.

"I don't even know what a church is, my lord," she replied.

He chuckled richly. Oh, Gwynllian was going to have her hands full. His elder sister had always lorded over him and his brothers when they were growing up. Now he would have his revenge for all of them. He would wager that Gwynllian had never had a lass like Rhonwyn in her custody. He almost wished he could be there to see the inevitable confrontation that was sure to ensue between his daughter and his sister. Then it dawned upon him how much alike the two were. He laughed aloud.

"What amuses you, my lord?" Rhonwyn inquired of him.

"Nothing, lass, really nothing," he told her. "That—" He pointed with a gloved finger. "—is your destination. That is Mercy Abbey."

"Will I like it there?" she wondered.

"Probably not," he replied honestly. "You have a great deal to learn, Rhonwyn, in a very short time. It is important that you learn else I be made to appear a liar. I have enemies."

"I am not surprised," she said dryly.

He laughed again. There was an honesty about his daughter that he very much liked. "You have a duty to me, Rhonwyn uerch Llywelyn. What you have to do will not be easy, but I know you can do it for you are not, I have been told, someone who shirks a duty, and you are loyal."

"My kinsman, Morgan ap Owen, speaks kindly of me," Rhonwyn said with a small smile, "but he does not lie. I will do what I must to meet my obligations to you, prince of Wales, *and I do not lie.*"

Chapter Three

Gwynllian, the lady abbess of Mercy Abbey, looked down her long thin nose at her brother. They could have been twins, so similar were they in face and form. "And what, O prince of Wales, brings you to my house this day?" she demanded of him. She was a tall, thin woman whose long black robes and startling white wimple made her appear even taller and more spare. An ebony crucifix, banded in silver and adorned with a silver lily in its center, lay on her almost flat bosom.

"Can I not come to visit my only sister without reason?" he replied jovially. Jesu! He hated having to beg.

"You came six, or was it seven, years ago, Llywelyn. You were seeking funding for your never-ending disputes with the English or your fellow Cymri. I cannot remember which. We gave you what we could, and you were as quickly gone. Now what do you want, brother, and do not waste my time in prevarications and half-truths," she said sternly.

Ap Gruffydd reached behind him and drew Rhonwyn forward. "This is my daughter," he said to his sister.

Her mouth fell open, and then closed with an audible snap. "Well, Llywelyn, you have surprised me for the first time in years. You are certain, of course?" The abbess peered at her niece and immediately recognized her as kin.

"Her mother was my mistress," he began. "She gave me two children, first a daughter, then a son. She died attempting to birth a third child. I came by chance and found my children yet alive. I brought them to Cythraul. The lad, his name is Glynn, is still there."

Gwynllian's brown eyes swept over the girl at her brother's side. She hardly looked like an orphan of the storm. She looked hard and quite capable of taking care of herself. "How long ago did you leave your children at Cythraul?" she asked her brother, fearing the answer.

He flushed guiltily. "Ten years ago," he said.

"Ten years and seven moon cycles," the girl spoke up for the first time. The look she gave the prince was scathing.

"Why bring her to me now, Llywelyn?" the abbess said.

"I spent the summer in Shrewsbury, hammering out an agreement with the English king, Henry. My ally, de Montfort, is dead, and Henry's cub, Edward, is a fierce man. I thought to make a treaty with Henry so that his heir will leave us in peace. The pact was signed at Montgomery at the end of October. You know the customs, Gwyn. I offered the English my daughter in marriage with one of their lordlings."

"But when you went to fetch her she wasn't quite what you had expected, was she, Llywelyn?" The abbess chuckled. Then she looked to her niece. "What is your name, child, and what have you done to your hair? And do you know your age?"

"My name is Rhonwyn uerch Llywelyn, and I like my hair kept short."

"She was fifteen April first last," ap Gruffydd said.

"Who raised her?" the abbess inquired.

"Morgan ap Owen, my captain at Cythraul" was the reply.

"Were there no women at this fortress?" the abbess exclaimed, shocked.

" 'Tis a fort in the Welshry. Women don't belong there," ap Gruffydd told his sister.

"No, they don't, yet you left your daughter there! Llywelyn, you are truly the most thoughtless and foolish man I have ever known, for all you have managed to become prince of Wales," the abbess said angrily. "Why did you not bring Rhonwyn to me in the first place? What do you expect me to do with her now?"

"Cythraul was nearer to her mother's cottage, less than a day's ride. To bring my children to you would have taken me almost three days of traveling. I had not the time."

"Could you not have instructed Morgan ap Owen to bring them to me, you dolt?" She swatted at him indignantly.

"She isn't fit to be wed," he said, his voice desperate.

"Has she become a whore then?" the abbess demanded.

"I am no man's whore!" Rhonwyn said angrily.

"Nay, nay, that is not it, sister!" ap Gruffydd replied. "She is ignorant. Totally ignorant. Morgan and his men loved my children and protected them, but they could teach them only what they knew. My daughter has a knack for war and weapons. She is, it seems, a worthy successor to me. My son prefers to compose songs and poetry, and has no talent for a warrior's pursuits at all. He's only fit to be a bard or a priest. You must teach Rhonwyn how to be what she is meant to be. A lass, not a lad. How can I give her in marriage when she doesn't even know what marriage is? She must be taught the Norman tongue, for as you see she speaks only our language. She needs to learn how to wear skirts, not chausses and braies. She must be a Christian, sister, yet she has no idea of religion or faith. She says moon cycles, not months. I don't even know if she has her woman's flow yet. You must gentle her, Gwynllian, so that in a month's time I may take her to Edward de Beaulieu, at Haven's Castle, to be wed."

The abbess laughed aloud. "*A month's time?* You are mad, Llywelyn! It will take more than a month to tame this bedraggled, fierce-eyed wildcat you have brought me. If indeed I can do it at all. If she does not cooperate, then you are out of luck, brother. How could you promise a daughter you had not seen in ten years to an English treaty marriage? What in the name of all that is holy were you thinking? *Were you thinking at all?*"

"Then what the hell am I to do, Gwyn?" he asked her, running a big hand through his dark hair.

The abbess turned to Rhonwyn. "Do you understand any of this, my child?"

"Aye, I do," Rhonwyn said. "My lord has explained to me that a marriage is a formal and respectable union between a man and a woman. It is honorable. It is my obligation to my lord to take part in this marriage. I know how to do my duty."

"Well," the abbess remarked to her brother, "she may have little learning, but she is, I believe, intelligent." She turned to her niece. "You are willing to be married to Edward de Beaulieu?"

"Is there a choice in the matter?" Rhonwyn said.

"Nay, there is not," the abbess told her.

"Then I am willing, and will do my duty" came the cool reply.

"You have much to learn, my child," the abbess said.

"Then teach me," Rhonwyn answered.

The abbess turned to her brother. "Tell Edward de Beaulieu that his bride is finishing her education at Mercy Abbey and will leave here in early April for Haven Castle. A messenger will arrive before her to announce her coming, but she will be there before midmonth. He may prepare for the marriage ceremony then, *and you will bring your daughter to him yourself.* It is unlikely your future son-in-law will object to this arrangement. He may have some small pursuits and matters to clear up before a bride can come to him." She smiled suddenly at him. "This favor will cost you dearly, Llywelyn."

"I know," he responded wearily.

She chuckled. "I shall make a list of my demands, none of which are negotiable, brother."

He nodded. "Whatever you want, Gwyn," he said.

The abbess turned again to her niece. "Your first lesson, my child, is in how to address me. When I speak to you, you will conclude your answer with the words *my lady abbess*. Do you understand, Rhonwyn?"

"Aye, my lady abbess" came the reply.

The nun smiled. "Excellent!"

I like her, Rhonwyn thought to herself. She understands me as no one ever has understood me.

The abbess reached out, picked up a small bell on the table and rang it. Almost immediately another woman, dressed in the same fashion, entered the room.

"Yes, my lady abbess?"

"This is my niece, Sister Catrin. She will be staying with us for the next few months, preparing for her marriage to the lord of Haven Castle. She is a true innocent, raised in an isolated place by a group of pagans. Give her a chamber in the guest house. Rhonwyn, you will stay there until I send for you. Bid your father farewell now, my child."

Rhonwyn turned to the prince and bowed politely. "My lord."

"I shall return for you in the spring," he said.

Rhonwyn laughed wickedly. "*Will you, my lord?* I certainly hope so."

The abbess's lips twitched with amusement as she saw the color flood her brother's face.

"This is different, Rhonwyn," he told her through gritted teeth. "This is a matter of my honor."

Rhonwyn nodded her head slightly in acknowledgment, and then followed Sister Catrin from the abbess's receiving chamber.

"She has your temper," Gwynllian remarked, amused.

"I hope you will find it as humorous when you must deal with her," he shot back. "Now write your damned list of demands, sister."

"On reflection I realize it is not necessary to write a list. I can tell you exactly what I want. First, you will pay the expenses for your daughter's schooling. We are not a rich house. You will go to Hereford and purchase a generous supply of fine materials so we may garb her properly for her marriage and subsequent life. You will take a pattern of her feet and have proper shoes made for her. You will purchase veils, gloves, a good jeweled girdle, as well as some small but fine pieces of jewelry. She is your daughter, Llywelyn, and if you are the prince of Wales, then the lady Rhonwyn is a noblewoman of the first ranking.

"And while you are in Hereford, you will go to the Convent of Saint Mary, on the east side of the town. They are a very small house and always in great financial distress, I am informed. They possess a saint's relic that I want, brother, for this abbey. It is a fingernail paring from St. Cuthbert himself and is kept in a bejeweled golden box on the altar in their church. Pay what you must, *but bring me that relic, Llywelyn.*"

"You want me to go into England and negotiate for a saint's relic with a nun? Before or after I purchase lovely fabrics, fine pieces of jewelry, and the other geegaws you desire for my daughter?" he snapped. "Name your price, Gwynllian, and I will pay it, but I will not go myself! I have much work to do keeping the peace."

"You will have no peace, brother, if you do not deliver your daughter to be wed to the Englishman; and you cannot bring her to them as she is. They would refuse her, and say you had insulted them and compromised the treaty. We are not so isolated here that I do not know Prince Edward will prove a dangerous enemy to you once he is king. I told you there would be no negotiation between us in this matter. Rhonwyn may remain here while you go and bargain for my relic, O prince of Wales. When you return with it, I will begin her tutelage, but not a moment before then." She drew herself up to her full height and stared directly at him. "The longer you delay, Llywelyn, the less time I have to turn this mutton you have brought me into a sweet little lambkin."

"You are the damnedest woman," he complained to her. "You always were impossible, Gwyn, and I suspect that Rhonwyn is just like you." He laughed. "Very well, I will go myself and dicker for your saint's discarded fingernail. If necessary," he told her darkly, "I will steal it, but you shall have it, sister, and then you must keep your part of our bargain."

"Do not steal it, Llywelyn," she warned him sternly. "If you do, I cannot display it. I am not capricious in my desire for this relic. I would draw pilgrims to Mercy Abbey to ask the saint's blessing. Such a relic will prove profitable to us."

"It did not to St. Mary's in Hereford," he remarked.

"That is because they could claim no great miracles of it," the abbess replied with a small smile. "I am certain the saint's fingernail paring will be more content with us and work to the glory of God and Mercy Abbey, brother. In fact, I sense it in my heart."

He laughed roughly. "You are a devious woman, Gwyn-llian, and I thank God you were not born a man. Owain,

Daffydd, and Rhodri, our brothers, were easy opponents, but you, sister, would have been stronger than all
three of them. I am not surprised you are abbess here."

She smiled archly at him. "Always remember, Llywelyn, that I am your equal. Our brothers were not."

"Are these all your demands?" he asked.

"I will also want a virile young ram, twenty ewe sheep,
and a bag with a donation of ten gold coins. I will take either bezants, ducats, or florins, but their weight must be
true. Make certain none of the coins has been clipped.
These are all my requirements," she finished. Her dark
eyes were dancing with pleasure at his look.

"You will beggar me, sister! The sheep I can obtain,
but where the hell am I going to get so much gold for
you? It is too much!"

"No negotiation, Llywelyn," she reminded him.

He swore a particularly vile oath, and the abbess
laughed as he glared at her.

"I haven't heard those words in many years, brother,"
she mocked him. "I had almost forgotten they existed."

"My daughter had better be able to compete with any
princess alive when this is over and done with, sister," he
warned her.

"She will," the abbess promised. Then she softened a
bit. "It is already dark, brother. May I offer you and your
men shelter for the night?"

"Nay," he snapped. "If I stay a moment longer with
you I may be tempted to kill you, Gwynllian. There is a
moon. We'll ride on. I said my farewell to Rhonwyn, and
now I bid you adieu." He bowed briefly, and then
stamped from the receiving chamber.

The abbess smiled softly as the door closed behind her
brother. His brief visit had proved highly fortuitous for
the abbey. He would do all she had asked him because he
needed Rhonwyn for a treaty bride. Then Gwynllian grew

more thoughtful. It was an enormous task she had been set, and she had to complete it successfully. Then suddenly she realized her brother had not taken Rhonwyn's foot pattern. Ringing for a nun, she sent the woman quickly after her brother so he could complete the task and get her niece decent shoes in Hereford.

She glided from her receiving room and across the abbey quadrangle to the guest house. There she found Sister Catrin seated with Rhonwyn. She dismissed the nun and joined the girl by the brazier.

"Well, he's gone. I've exacted a very high price from him for my help. You are going to have to work very hard, my child." She chuckled. "I could always get the better of your father and our other brothers. You know none of them, do you?"

"Nay, my lady abbess. At Cythraul, Morgan told me that the prince had overthrown and imprisoned his elder brother, Owain, and his younger brother, Daffydd. The youngest brother, Rhodri, is not an ambitious man, it was said. He sounds like my brother, Glynn."

"If Wales is to be united, there can be but one ruler," the abbess answered her niece. "Your father finds it hard bowing his knee to any, even almighty God. He only knelt to the English because by doing so he obtained what he wanted."

"There is no shame in that," Rhonwyn considered.

The abbess chuckled. "You are a practical lass, I see. That is to the good. I told your father I would do nothing to help you until he fulfilled his word to me, but that is not true, although he will believe it, having never caught me in a lie. You have so much to learn that we must begin tomorrow if we are to have any chance of passing you off as a noblewoman in six months' time. Llywelyn will do what he must for me. Now tell me, child, you have never had any women companions?"

"Not since Mam died," Rhonwyn answered her aunt. She looked about the little hall of the guest house. "Am I to stay here alone, my lady abbess? I have never been alone before."

Gwynllian shook her head. "I have two young postulants with us right now who are near your age. They will come and make their beds with you, Rhonwyn, so you will not be by yourself. They must, of course, attend to their own duties during the day, but you will be busy with your studies. They will share your chamber; you will eat together in the refectory with the community; and you may take walks in the gardens. We do not have a school like some other convents, so you will be unique as a student, my child."

"What of my horse?" Rhonwyn asked.

"It is safely in the stables. Do well at your studies, and I will permit you to ride it," the abbess said.

"But Hardd needs his exercise, my lady abbess!" Rhonwyn protested.

"You may walk him daily before your lessons, my child, but there will be no riding unless you progress in your duties," the abbess said. Then she held up her hand to prevent the further protest she saw on Rhonwyn's lips. "One of your first lessons is obedience, which means doing what you are told by your superiors. You obeyed Morgan ap Owen because he was your captain or superior. You must obey me for the same reason, my child. Obedience and good manners can cover a multitude of other sins, Rhonwyn. You have been raised in a community of rough men. I know they had good hearts, for I can see you miss them, and you would not had they been unkind; but soldiers are not the best example for a young girl to follow. Come with me now, and we will go to the refectory to have something to eat. Tonight I will excuse you and the companions I have chosen for you from

Compline, but beginning tomorrow you will attend mass daily." Then she patted Rhonwyn's hand. "You know nothing of God and our dear Lord Jesus, do you, my child? This is all very confusing, I can see. Do not be afraid of your innocence and your ignorance, Rhonwyn. You will quickly learn, I promise you. You are an intelligent girl, and your mind, I already see, is facile."

For the first time in her life Rhonwyn found herself uncertain and retiring. She followed her aunt from the guest house to the refectory, which she quickly learned was a place where the nuns dined. The women who lived in this abbey were called *nuns*. They were also called *Sister*, except her aunt who was *Reverend Mother* or *my lady abbess*. And the nuns were ranked according to the position they held within the community.

Her companions, Elen and Arlais, were called postulants and were the lowest on the abbey's social scale, being considered candidates for the religious order. The novices, and there were five of them currently, had completed their year's training as postulants and now were spending the next two years preparing to take their final vows. The vows were those of poverty, chastity, and obedience. Rhonwyn knew what poverty and obedience meant. Chastity, she learned, was a promise to remain pure, which meant no going beneath a hedge with a man or doing what her father used to do with her mother.

The nuns devoted their lives to God, the supreme being. She hadn't heard enough of God at Cythraul to make any sense of him. Now her new companions, Elen and Arlais, spent their evenings teaching Rhonwyn as they would have taught their children had they wed instead of entering the abbey. They found Rhonwyn rather fascinating, never having known anyone like her before, but they also treated her with respect, for she was the abbess's niece and the prince's daughter. Elen and Arlais were the daughters of freedmen who farmed their own land. The three girls got on rather well despite their dissimilar backgrounds.

Rhonwyn went with her companions to the early church services of the day, Prime, at six o'clock in the morning, and Tierce, the high mass, at nine o'clock in the morning. She attended Vespers before nightfall, but was excused from the other five canonical hours. After Prime she broke her fast in the refectory with oat porridge in a small bread trencher and apple cider. She then sat with Sister Mair until Tierce, practicing how to write both letters and numbers. Sister Mair did the lettering on the illuminations the abbey sold to noble households.

After Tierce, Rhonwyn studied with her aunt, learning Latin and the Norman tongue. To the abbess's delight her niece had a facility for languages other than the Welsh tongue and learned far more quickly than she had hoped. Within a month Rhonwyn was reciting the Latin prayers in the church services she attended as if she had been doing it all her life. And she was beginning to read as well. Her ability with the Norman tongue was equally swift, and Rhonwyn was soon conversing in that language on a daily basis with her aunt both in and out of the classroom.

Gwynllian uerch Gruffydd gave thanks before the altar of the church daily for her niece's progress. It was truly miraculous. After the midday meal Rhonwyn joined Sister Una in the kitchens so she might see how meals were planned and prepared. Here her progress was not as quick, and Sister Una complained to the abbess that her niece could burn water. The infirmarian, Sister Dicra, was kinder, for her new pupil seemed to have a knack for healing and concocting the potions, salves, lotions, syrups, and teas needed to cure a cough or make a wound heal easier.

"The lass has a healing touch, Reverend Mother," Sister Dicra said enthusiastically.

"She'll need it to cure the bellyaches she's going to give with her cooking," Sister Una remarked dryly.

"She doesn't need to know *how* to cook," the abbess said, "just how it should be done. The castle will have its own cook. Have you taught her how to make soap for both clothing and skin yet?"

"We begin tomorrow," Sister Una replied. "I hope she has more of a knack for that."

The abbess turned to Sister Braith. "How is she coming with her weaving, embroidery, and sewing skills, my sister?"

"Slowly," answered the nun. "Rhonwyn has little patience, as you know. She finds sewing and embroidery foolish. Weaving, however, seems to calm her. She says there is a logic to it," chuckled Sister Braith. "I have shown her how to spin, and she seems to like that quite well."

They were progressing. Slowly in some areas, faster in others, the abbess thought silently. "The fabrics have arrived from Hereford," she told her companions. "We shall have to fill Rhonwyn's bridal chest ourselves if it is to get done."

"And the relic?" Sister Winifred inquired.

"My brother sends word he has obtained it at great cost. He is bringing it to us himself."

The prince arrived several days later, accompanied only by two of his men. He handed the bejeweled gold box to his sister. "Twenty gold florins, this cost me," he growled at her. "The mother superior at St. Mary's-in-the-Gate ought to be hawking maidenheads, she haggled so closely with me. It had better be worth it, Gwynllian."

"Would you like to see your daughter?" the abbess asked him as she stroked her prize.

"You have begun, then?" he said eagerly, visibly relieved.

"Of course," she told him. "There was no choice if we are to be ready by spring, Llywelyn." She reached for the bell on the table and rang it, instructing the nun who answered her call to fetch the lady Rhonwyn at once.

Llywelyn ap Gruffydd gaped in surprise for a moment as his daughter entered the room. She was garbed in a graceful deep blue gown with long, tight sleeves and girded at the waist with a simple twisted gold rope. Her pale gilt hair was beginning to grow out. It was clean and almost to her shoulders now. On her head she wore a simple chaplet with fresh flowers. She bowed to her aunt first and then to her father.

"You sent for me, my lady abbess?" she asked.

"Your father wished to see you before he departed, my child," Gwynllian answered quietly.

"She's speaking in the Norman tongue!" ap Gruffydd said excitedly.

"I am learning, my lord. I am told this is the language the English use, although there is another," Rhonwyn replied.

"Aye, but what you're learning is what you'll need." The prince turned to his sister. "The transformation is amazing! Are you certain she isn't ready to go yet?"

"Nay, Llywelyn, she most certainly is not!" the abbess said. "Do not be in such a hurry. This is small progress, and we have much more to do, not to mention a wardrobe to sew. You cannot take her until the spring. Come on her birthday. Unless, of course, in the meantime, she decides to become one of us," the abbess teased her brother.

"God forbid!" the prince cried.

Rhonwyn laughed. "Have no fear, my lord, this life your sister, my aunt, leads is not for me. I will be ready to do my duty when you return for me in April."

"Bid your farewell, Rhonwyn, and then you are dismissed," Gwynllian said.

"Adieu, my lord," Rhonwyn told him, bowing again, then she departed the room.

"She never calls you *Tad*," Gwynllian remarked softly.

"The lad does," he returned. "Rhonwyn holds me responsible for her mam's death. She has never liked me, sister. With the logic of a child she wanted her mam all to herself, and she resented it each time I came to visit my fair Vala. She has never gotten over it, I fear, but it matters not as long as she respects and obeys me."

"I do not know how much she respects you, Llywelyn, but she will do her duty by you. Rhonwyn will do you proud, and if she proves to be a good breeder, her English lord will have a large family. She will need her husband's loyalty when you and the English eventually come to a parting of the ways, which I have not a doubt you will."

"That is her fate. Mine is greater," he replied. "Now, sister, I must go. You have your relic and everything else you have asked of me." He handed her two small leather bags. "My daughter's fees," he said, dropping the first one in her hand, "and your gold bezants," he concluded, handing her the second little bag. "I am pleased by the progress I see in Rhonwyn. When I return for her in the spring, I expect a complete transformation."

"You will have it, brother," Gwynllian said.

"I know I will. Your word has always been good, sister, and I thank you for what you are doing, even if it has cost me dearly."

She laughed at him. "Do not complain, Llywelyn. That for which you pay nothing is worth nothing. Godspeed to you now."

The winter came, and snow covered the hills. The sheep were brought in from the far pastures and kept within the walls at night to protect them from the wolves. It was

a festive season, Rhonwyn discovered. The feast of St.
Catherine was celebrated in late November, and there
were a host of other saints' days leading up to Christ's
Mass, which celebrated the birth of Jesus, whom Rhonwyn had now been taught was God's son come to earth
to expiate man's sins. For all her rough upbringing,
Rhonwyn found Christianity comforting. The notion of
a god's son dying for mere mortals was both generous
and honorable in her eyes. The abbess smiled when
Rhonwyn told her that. She was grateful her niece approved of the concept of religion at all. While she found
the thought of delivering a full-blown pagan to the English amusing, she did not think her brother would
agree. She giggled in spite of herself at the picture it presented. Then she saw to it that her niece was baptized on
Christmas Day.

With Twelfth Night came the end of the festive season.
Rhonwyn settled down and worked harder than ever.
She was learning that the brain was as difficult and as
skilled a weapon as her alborium. She was now put in the
care of Sister Rhan, a nun whose plump and cheerful
countenance belied an incredible intellect. Sister Rhan,
somewhere in middle age, had once, according to the
gossip Elen and Arlais offered, been a powerful lord's
mistress. If the rumors were to be believed, she had also
dressed as a boy and studied with the greatest minds in
England.

"You have intelligence, Rhonwyn," Sister Rhan said
the first time they came to study together. "Your intellect
and reason will serve you far better in the long run than
your body. That is how I held my lord's interest for so
many years until he died."

"Then the gossip is true?" Rhonwyn was surprised to
hear the nun admitting to what she had now been taught
was a sin.

Sister Rhan laughed. "Aye, 'tis true, and I have never made a secret of it, my child. Once I loved and was loved. I was faithful to him as he was to me."

"But he had a wife," Rhonwyn said.

"Indeed he did, and a very good woman the lady Arlette was, too. She brought him excellent lands to add to his own and gave him healthy children whom she raised to be regardful and devout. He treated her with devotion and great respect, even as he did me. We each served a purpose in his life. When he died, his lady wife and I washed his body and sewed him into his shroud together. She is a benefactress of Mercy Abbey now."

"A man can love more than one woman, then," Rhonwyn said thoughtfully. "I did not know that. I thought once the choice was made and the vows spoken, a husband and wife cleaved to each other only."

"Ideally, but not always," Sister Rhan answered her. "But we are not here, my child, to discuss my past sins. You have mastered both Norman and Latin. You can read and write it as well, although sometimes you are impatient with your letters. Your housewifely skills are, at best, passable, but you do not shine in that venue. The abbess believes your mind can absorb more serious learning, and so she has sent you to me. We shall study together grammar, rhetoric, logic, music, arithmetic, and astronomy. I will help you to become a support to your husband, so even when he becomes bored with your young body, he will find your mind invaluable to him. You will find much satisfaction in aiding your lord for the betterment of your lives and the lives of the children you will have together, Rhonwyn."

"Then marital love doesn't last," the young girl observed.

"If there is love at all, and do not mistake lust for love," Sister Rhan warned her.

"What is the difference?" Rhonwyn demanded to know. "How shall I make the distinction?"

"Excellent! Excellent!" the nun approved. "You are thinking. The abbess was right to send you to me. Lust is when your bodies crave each other for no reason. The urge will be strong and fierce. Love, however, is an entirely different thing. Love is a powerful yearning not just for the body of the object of your affection, but for everything about him. You will be unhappy out of his sight. The mere sound of his voice will set your heart to racing. You will put his interests ahead of your own because you want him to be happy. Ideally he will feel the same about you. Just being held in his arms will bring you a warm contentment. Ah, my child, love is very difficult to explain. You will know it when it strikes you, and you will find that when you make love then, it is entirely different than just pure and unbridled lust."

"I know nothing of either marital love or lust," Rhonwyn said. "At Cythraul my brother and I were the fortress's children. Lately, however, young men newly come into our midst had tried to feel my breasts and kiss me. I beat them with my fists, and the others beat them afterward with rods for their temerity. Was what they attempted lust?"

The nun nodded. "It was. And you felt nothing toward them?"

"Nay," Rhonwyn replied vehemently. "They were pockmarked lads and nowhere near as skilled as I am with weapons. I think I must respect the man who uses my body and loves me."

"A wise decision, my child. Now, let me turn the subject to the matter of arithmetic. It is best you have some familiarity with computation and calculation. That way if your husband goes off to war, you will be able to be certain the steward doesn't cheat you. You know your numbers, I am told, so let us now begin." She held up two fingers on her right hand. "How many?" she asked.

"Two," Rhonwyn said.

"And now how many?" The nun revealed two fingers on her left hand.

"Two there as well," Rhonwyn said.

"But how many altogether?" Sister Rhan asked.

Rhonwyn quickly scanned the digits, counting mentally. "Four."

"That is correct, and that, my child, is called adding." She reached into a basket by the table where they sat and brought up a device with several rows of beads, which she set on the table. "This is called an abacus, Rhonwyn. Now watch." She slid two beads from one side of the instrument to the other. "Two and two more equal how many?"

"Four!"

"Take away one bead. How many?"

"Three!"

"Excellent. That second calculation is called subtraction," Sister Rhan explained.

They quickly discovered that Rhonwyn had a talent for arithmetic. Each day she increased her knowledge until Sister Rhan assured the abbess that her niece would never be cheated by anyone. At least not where arithmetic was concerned. Grammar and logic appealed to the young girl, but while her handwriting improved markedly, Rhonwyn seemed to have no real talent for rhetoric, and she knew it.

"My brother would do well with it," she told her teacher. "He makes up stories and poems, and puts them to music that he sings in the hall of Cythraul. I think he will be a great bard one day."

Her time was growing shorter at Mercy Abbey, and her days, it seemed, were busy from dawn to dusk. Her two

companions, Elen and Arlais, ended their trial as postulants and became novices. The three girls had never really
become close, having different interests, but Rhonwyn
was pleased that they were halfway to attaining their
heart's desire. Rhonwyn, on the other hand, was suddenly
beginning to consider her forthcoming marriage. She
would not meet her husband-to-be until just before they
married. Such a thing was not unusual, her aunt said.

Now, as well as increasing her education, Rhonwyn
was being fitted for her wardrobe. Her father had brought
fine materials indeed for his daughter, and Gwynllian
could not complain at him for being niggardly in either his
choices or the quantity. There were silks and velvets and
brocades as well as linen and fine cottons. The fabrics
were rich and colorful. Rhonwyn was shocked, however,
to learn women did not wear braies beneath their gowns.

"I've worn mine all along since you put me in a
gown," she told her aunt. "What is substituted to cover
the bottom?"

"Ladies wear nought beneath their chemises," Gwynllian replied.

"*Nothing?*" The girl's eyes were wide.

"Your skirts will cover all, I assure you, Rhonwyn,"
the abbess said. "It is quite acceptable."

"I don't think it respectable" was the answer.

Gwynllian's lips twitched, but she managed to keep
from chuckling. Her niece was more prudish than she
would have expected of a girl raised in a fortress of men.
Were it not for the child's continuing warlike tendencies,
the abbess would have believed her a candidate for the
nunnery, and not marriage. But Rhonwyn still rode daily
outside the gates of the abbey, galloping along at a
breakneck speed that had the porteress almost swooning
at Rhonwyn's maneuvers.

On March the twentieth the abbey celebrated the feast

of St. Cuthbert, who had been a bishop of Lindisfarne and whose fingernail paring now resided in its bejeweled gold box on the abbey's church altar. It was bruited about that the relic could cure a variety of minor illnesses, but as it was not a large memorial great miracles could not be expected of it. But the pilgrims came nonetheless to touch the gold box and pray to the saint. The abbey coffers grew at a modest but steady pace that day.

April first, the day marking Rhonwyn's sixteenth birthday, came, and Llywelyn ap Gruffydd appeared to reclaim his daughter. Her cool, elegant demeanor was slightly intimidating, but her manners were flawless. He was rather astounded to learn of all her accomplishments since her arrival at the abbey almost six months ago. He was equally appalled by the amount of baggage she would be leaving with, but accepted his sister's explanation on the matter and her dictate that he could not leave until the morrow.

Rhonwyn had been turned from a rough-speaking half-lad into a beautiful young woman. Her cropped hair had grown out. It was parted in the center and hung down her back, contained by a simple silver ribbon. Her bosom seemed larger, which was to his mind all to the good. Men liked a woman with plump breasts. She no longer walked with determined strides, but rather glided gracefully. The hands that had held a sword were now perfumed and soft, and the long fingers that had so skillfully drawn her bow now plucked at the strings of the mandora in her lap while she sang softly. The English could have no complaints about his daughter.

"You have worked a miracle, Gwynllian," he told the abbess.

"Yes," she agreed with a small, arch smile. "She is more than well worth the price you have paid for her transformation. However, brother, I must be honest with you. Were Rhonwyn not an intelligent girl, none of this would have been possible. And you should show the men of Cythraul some appreciation, for they are the ones who taught her honor and duty."

"While turning her into a rough, foul-mouthed soldier," he grumbled at his sister. "And that cost me a fortune to reverse. I am tempted to burn Cythraul down about their ears!"

"This is not someone else's fault, Llywelyn," the abbess said sternly to her brother. "This mishap was your failing. You know it, and you know why. Put it behind you, and tomorrow take your daughter to England to her husband. Remember, however, this time you travel with a *lady*, and not a laddie." Then the abbess chuckled at her own small play on words.

The morning of April second came, and Rhonwyn's baggage was loaded into a sturdy cart. She bid the sisters farewell, taking special time to thank those nuns who had given her all the knowledge she now possessed, particularly Sister Rhan and the abbess.

"Remember, my child, that you will always have a home and a refuge here at Mercy Abbey," Gwynllian told her. "May God bless you with happiness and many children."

"Not too many," Rhonwyn teased her aunt. "But I do promise to save at least one girl for you, my lady abbess."

With a chuckle, the abbess hugged her niece, kissing her on the cheek. "Godspeed, Rhonwyn uerch Llywelyn," she said.

Mounted upon Hardd, Rhonwyn rode through the abbey gates by her father's side. She heard the portals close behind her, but she was not sad. She was free from the constrictions of the nuns at last and off on a new adventure. They had turned her into a mannerly lady, but they had not tamed her spirit nor dimmed her enthusiasm for life. She had spent these past months in earnest study so she could be worthy of her father's name and her new position. Now she must turn her mind to Edward de Beaulieu, the man who was to be her husband. She couldn't even begin to imagine what he would be like, but over the next few days of their journey she tried.

Chapter Four

"The messenger has arrived from Prince Llywelyn, my lord," the servant said, bowing to his master.

"Bring him into the hall" came the reply.

"Yes, my lord." The servant bowed again, and backed away some feet before turning about. He returned only moments later. "The messenger from Prince Llywelyn, my lord."

Edward de Beaulieu glanced briefly at the rugged Welshman.

"My master and the lady Rhonwyn will be here by nightfall, my lord," he said. Then he fell silent.

"I await them" was the brief answer.

Cold bastard, the messenger thought as he bowed to the lord of Haven Castle and departed the place to ride back to ap Gruffydd with the reply.

Edward de Beaulieu watched him go, and then absently took the silver goblet of wine his servant offered him, staring into the dancing red gold flames in the fireplace. He wasn't ready to marry, yet he would shortly have a wife. A wild Welsh girl half his age. But having no betrothal agreement with another and being located so conveniently near the border, the king had chosen him to be his sacrificial lamb in this treaty marriage. He had considered refusing, but Prince Edward had stared hard at him when the king announced his decision, and Edward de Beaulieu had known he dared not refuse. The prince was an enemy he was not interested in having.

When the Welsh prince had asked the marriage be delayed until this spring because his daughter was completing her education at Mercy Abbey, Edward de Beaulieu had been pleased to acquiesce. He had an attractive mistress and was in no hurry to wed. When he thought of it, though, a convent-bred wife did have her advantages. She would be meek and obedient, keeping his home in excellent condition and bearing his children. Haven had known no lady since his mother had died seven years ago. While he had enjoyed the company of his mistress, Renée de Faubourg, these past months, he had pensioned her off several weeks ago, with her own house in Shrewsbury and an annual allowance he placed with a reputable goldsmith. A wife was to be respected, and if the truth be known, he was beginning to tire of Renée.

He wondered what the Welsh girl would be like. She would probably be small, for so many of the Welsh were. And she would have dark hair and eyes and a fair skin. He wondered if she spoke the Norman tongue or if she was conversant only in Welsh. It probably didn't matter a great deal as no words were really needed when a man took a woman to his bed. She would eventually learn, of course, if she was to control the servants.

Still, he couldn't help but feel annoyed at having been forced to this marriage. But the girl had had no choice either, and was not to be blamed. Hopefully they would like one another and could come to an arrangement that would guarantee peace between them. He was uncomfortable, however, having Llywelyn ap Gruffydd as a father-in-law. The prince was a dangerous man and extremely ambitious. Haven would be caught between him and Prince Edward, who liked not the Welshman one bit, for ap

Gruffydd had supported the prince's uncle, Simon de Mont-fort, quite openly against the king. Prince Edward might not have a great deal of respect for his sire's style of governance, but he did love his father.

De Beaulieu arose and left the great hall, going to the south tower where his bride's apartments would be located. The young serving girl his steward had chosen to serve the bride turned startled eyes on him as he entered the dayroom. She curtsied quickly, keeping her frightened eyes lowered. He looked about the room. The furnishings of oak were polished, and the stone floor well swept. The lamps burned without smoking. There was a bowl of daffodils on a table. He smiled.

"You have done well, Enit," he told her. "Your new mistress will arrive by nightfall, I have been informed. She may want to bathe after her journey. Make certain a tub is ready."

"Yes, my lord," Enit said, bobbing another curtsey. Her uncle was steward at Haven, and this was a great opportunity she had been given, particularly considering her mother was Welsh and not English. Enit was sixteen and had been in service at the castle for five years. She was a plain rather than pretty girl, with brown hair and eyes.

Edward de Beaulieu left the apartment and went in search of his priest, Father John. All the legalities had been signed and sealed at Montgomery with regard to his marriage. All that was left was for the priest to perform the sacrament. He decided upon the morrow so his bride might have a proper night's rest. The king had personally instructed him that the marriage was to be consummated on his wedding night.

"I do not trust ap Gruffydd," Henry had said. "Breach the girl, and make certain the bloody sheet flies from the castle top on the following morning for all to see."

"Use her well," Prince Edward had continued. "You

want her with child as quickly as possible, my lord, else her sly sire attempt to annul your marriage and take her back to use to better advantage elsewhere. The Welsh are not honorable peoples, but with ap Gruffydd's daughter in our power, we may keep him under control. He must love the wench that he has kept her so secretly all these years."

Edward de Beaulieu now reached the priest's quarters. "Father, my bride approaches and will arrive at Haven before night. We will celebrate the formalities on the morrow."

"My lord, the girl is young and gently reared," the priest said. "Will you not give her some time to know you?"

"We must wed no matter," Edward de Beaulieu said. "Let it be sooner than later. Ap Gruffydd will remain to see the deed done, and I would have him gone from Haven as quickly as possible. Though this match be the king and prince's decision, I do not want the Welshman here any longer than necessary lest I later be accused of some misdeed. These are dangerous times, good father."

The priest shook his head. "I cannot disagree with you, my lord," he said sadly. "I will marry you tomorrow afternoon. That will give the lady Rhonwyn time to recover from her long trek."

"Agreed," Edward de Beaulieu said, and left the priest. As he crossed the courtyard of his castle, he called to the watch upon its heights, "What do you see?"

"Nought yet, my lord" came the reply.

Edward de Beaulieu decided suddenly to go to his stables. "Saddle my horse," he told the groom who hurried forth to meet him.

"How many men will you be taking with you, my lord?" the groom asked him.

"No escort," he said. "I am riding out to meet my bride, and I am safe on my own lands."

The black stallion was brought out, and the lord of Haven Castle mounted him and rode forth from his home. He was pleased to see the fields were already being plowed for planting. Soon those fields would be golden with wheat and barley. In his meadows the black-faced white sheep browsed, followed by their gamboling and enthusiastic lambs, which were in plentiful supply this year. He possessed a large herd of cows who gave a rich milk that was made into butter and cheese and sold in Shrewsbury on market days. Beyond his fields were great stands of woods where he might hunt. And below the hill on which his castle stood, the river Severn flowed.

He stopped in his passage and turned about to look at his home. It was a fine castle, small and elegant in structure, not at all great or impressive like others he had seen. The grayish-brown stone of which it was built was mellowed with age and in some places covered in ivy. There were four towers, one facing each compass point. Despite the castle's battlements, its interior was more that of a comfortable manor house. Edward de Beaulieu loved his home. The one good thing, he thought, about his marriage was that he would have children with whom to share his love of Haven Castle. For her sake, he hoped his bride would like it, too.

He turned his horse again to the road the Welsh prince and his train would be traveling. He rode for several miles before coming upon Llywelyn ap Gruffydd and his party. He stopped, allowing them to approach. The prince rode forward and greeted his son-in-law.

"Are you eager then, Edward de Beaulieu, to meet your bride?"

The Englishman smiled sardonically, but before he

could answer the girl rode forward, stopping at her father's side.

"I think him curious," she said in a sweetly musical voice. "Is that not so, my lord?" Her look challenged him.

He answered as quickly, "And you, lady, are you not curious as well?"

Rhonwyn laughed aloud, but did not speak. Suddenly her eyes were lowered, and she appeared every bit the meek convent-bred wife he had been told would be delivered to him. He was confused.

"May I welcome you to Haven Castle, my lord prince. And the lady Rhonwyn as well. I know your journey has been arduous. My home is but a few miles onward. There is warmth and wine. I know you will want to rest, lady. Our marriage will be celebrated tomorrow afternoon."

Well, she thought, he wasn't giving her a great deal of time, was he? And since she had not ever imagined what he would be like, Edward de Beaulieu came as a pleasant surprise to Rhonwyn. He was tall and lean, a man obviously used to physical pursuits. The shape of his face was oval, as were his silvery gray eyes. His nose, longer rather than shorter, had a bump in it and had obviously been broken at one time. He had high cheekbones, and his mouth was long, the lips narrow. His hair, which was cut short, had a bang. It was the warm brown color of oak leaves on the forest floor in autumn. The big hands guiding the black stallion so skillfully were square, the nails pared and short. He would not be unpleasant to look at across the hall.

If she had examined him in their brief encounter, so had Edward de Beaulieu scrutinized her as well. He was astonished by the lady Rhonwyn's beauty. He had not expected it at all. A small, dark Welsh girl was what he had anticipated, not this slender creature of medium height with delicate features and even more delicate coloring. The silk gauze veil she wore did little to hide the glorious pale gilt of her hair. *And her eyes!* They were every bit as green as the emeralds in his sword's hilt. Her cheeks were brushed with rose, her brows and lashes startling ebony against her snowy complexion. Her nose was in perfect proportion with her heart-shaped face, narrow and flaring only in the nostrils. Her mouth was small, but the lips were full.

Llywelyn ap Gruffydd watched the man at his side with amusement. He knew precisely what he was thinking. "Her mother descended from the Fair Folk, a fair race in ancient Cymri. She is beautiful, isn't she, despite the fact she favors me in her features?"

"I had not noticed," his companion said, still slightly dazed.

"She'll give you beautiful children. Her mother did before she died. And she is accomplished, my lord. You have noted she speaks the Norman tongue as well as our own Welsh and Latin."

Flushing, Edward realized he hadn't noticed at all, but then he gained mastery over himself and said, "I am pleased we shall be able to communicate easily. Tell me of her other achievements, my lord."

"The nuns tell me she has great skill in weaving and spinning as well as in making medicines, poltices, and salves," ap Gruffydd replied.

"I am knowledgeable in calculating and logic," Rhonwyn told her bridegroom, moving her mount to his other side.

"These things are not important for women," her father quickly said, as if she had told Edward de Beaulieu something unseemly.

"I beg to differ with you, my lord, but they are most important. What if my husband should go to war, and I be left in charge of the castle? Do you think I want the servants cheating him in his absence? This knowledge is important for me to know. And, my lord—" She turned to Edward. "—you had best know the worst of me. I can both read and write."

He nodded solemnly, but said nothing. This was not at all what he had expected. Not at all. Everything he had imagined was now blown away with the wind in the reality of this beautiful girl he was to marry on the morrow.

"She is musical," ap Gruffydd said, eager to cover her deficiencies.

"All the Welsh are musical to some extent," Rhonwyn replied dryly, and Edward de Beaulieu laughed aloud.

Haven Castle suddenly came into view. He reached out and took her gloved hand. "Welcome home, my lady Rhonwyn."

She was silent for a moment, and then said softly, "How lovely!"

They rode up the hill, across the drawbridge, and into the courtyard. De Beaulieu noted his father-in-law taking in every aspect of the castle's defenses, and hid a smile. The wily Welsh prince would never enter Haven by force, and after his daughter's marriage it was unlikely he would ever enter it again. Once they were wed, Edward would allow no divided loyalties in his house.

Dismounting, he lifted Rhonwyn from her horse. She did not look at him but rather kept her glance modest and averted. He was already confused by her manner. Quiet one moment and outspoken the next. When they reached the door of the castle residence, de Beaulieu surprised Rhonwyn by picking her up in his arms and carrying her over the threshold. " 'Tis an old custom to carry the bride over the sill into her new home," he said, setting her back on her feet.

"We are not wed yet, my lord," she replied.

"All the legalities are signed and sealed, my lady. It is only for the priest to say the words over us. Licitly, you have been my wife since the treaty was ratified at Montgomery last autumn."

"I was not aware of it," Rhonwyn assured him. "I am not conversant with the law."

"I would not expect you to be," he told her as he led her into the great hall. "Are you thirsty? Or perhaps you would prefer to rest in your chamber? I have had my steward choose a young maidservant for you. Her name is Enit, and she will care for you."

"You are kind, my lord. I have never had a servant," Rhonwyn said. "I am quite capable of looking after myself."

"My daughter has been raised simply," ap Gruffydd said, quickly interjecting himself into the conversation before Rhonwyn said something she should not. "Mercy Abbey is not grand in material comforts." He shot his daughter a quelling look that obviously did not intimidate her at all.

She shrugged, her return glance almost mocking.

Now what was that all about, de Beaulieu wondered, and how was he to get to the bottom of it?

"I should enjoy some wine," Rhonwyn said quietly.

The lord of the castle signaled to his servants, and the requested wine was immediately sent for.

"Come and sit by the fire," he invited her. "April can be a cold month despite the fact it is spring." He seated her on a bench facing the blaze.

Rhonwyn leaned forward, pulling her gloves from her hands and holding them toward the warmth. Even in profile she was beautiful, he thought. He took a goblet of wine from the serving man and handed it to her. She smiled up at him gratefully, taking it and admiring the beauty of the silver, its base studded in green stones.

Slowly she sipped the wine and felt its warmth coursing through her veins.

"Will your guests arrive in time for the wedding?" ap Gruffydd asked his son-in-law jovially.

"There will be no guests," de Beaulieu replied. "I have no nearby family. My closest kin are my cousins, Rafe de Beaulieu and his sister, Katherine. I have not yet told him of this marriage, for Rafe has always hoped I would wed Katherine. I suppose I might have, but there was no formal, or even informal, agreement between us. Besides, I could not be certain when you would arrive. You, your men, and my servants will witness the ceremony, but the formalities were settled months ago, my lord prince. I could bed your daughter tonight and be within my rights, but I prefer to wait until we have celebrated the sacrament in my church."

Rhonwyn blanched at his words. The bedding was something that no one at Mercy Abbey had explained, and she was damned if she would ask her father. She remembered him with her mother and assumed it would be the same, although she had never quite known what they were doing, for their bodies had always been pressed so closely together. A small flame of rebellion burned deep within her. She wasn't certain that she wanted this bedding. If she was de Beaulieu's wife, wasn't the treaty marriage agreement satisfied? She arose suddenly.

"I am weary, my lords. I would retire until the morrow."

"I will show you to your chamber, my lady," de Beaulieu said, then turned to ap Gruffydd. "I will return shortly, my lord, and we will have food." He took Rhonwyn by her arm and led her from his hall. "Your rooms face southwest, lady. It is the warmest tower."

"My possessions . . ." she began hesitantly.

"Will have been brought to your apartment by now. Your young maidservant, Enit, will be unpacking for you."

Suddenly Rhonwyn burst out, "I have never been in such a fine place, my lord. Am I truly to be mistress here?"

He smiled at her ingenuousness. "You are mistress here now, lady. This is your home, Rhonwyn uerch Llywelyn." How charming she was, his convent-bred bride. He had to wed sometime, and now having seen this tender beauty, he thought that perhaps the king had done him a great favor, although that had not, of course, been Henry's intent when he had arranged this match with the Welsh prince. Rhonwyn was to all intents and purposes a hostage for her father's behavior; and he, Edward de Beaulieu, Lord Thorley of Haven, was her keeper. The marriage was a practical matter, but if they were content with one another, so much the better.

He led her up the stone staircase and down a short passageway, and then opened the door to her apartment. Enit, hearing them, turned and curtsied, looking anxious. "Here, lady, are your chambers. There is a dayroom for your pleasure, a bedroom, and a garderobe for your clothing, which also has a sleeping space for Enit." He led her from the dayroom, into her bedchamber. "That door connects with my apartment, lady." He pointed.

Rhonwyn scarcely knew where to look. To have all these rooms for herself alone! At Cythraul she had slept in her sleeping space in the hall. At Mercy Abbey she had been assigned a tiny cell in the guest house. But *this* was all hers. There were tapestries on the walls. Sheepskins on the stone floors. Fine oak furniture the like of which she had certainly never seen. The bed appeared to her eyes to be huge and was hung with gold-and-green brocaded velvet curtains. There was a red fox coverlet atop it.

"I have two fireplaces?" She was astounded.

"Then you are pleased?" he asked her.

She turned, eyes shining. "Aye, my lord, I am pleased!"

"Would you like Enit to fetch you something to eat before you retire?" he asked her. Her eyes were so green. How could someone as hard as ap Gruffydd produce such a delicate creature for a daughter?

"Thank you, my lord. I should like something to eat, but I could not sit in the hall with my father another minute. I am weary," she quickly explained, "for we rode several days from sunup to sunset."

"I am glad for your coming," he replied, "but your father should not have exhausted you so, Rhonwyn. I shall speak to him."

"Do not bother, my lord. He will soon be gone from here, will he not?" She turned to look out the window to where the sun was setting. "How beautiful it is! I shall never grow tired of this view." Then she turned back to him. "You are kind. I thank you for it."

He flushed at her words, saying, "I suspect it will be easy to be kind to you, Rhonwyn. Now I bid you good night. Enit will see to your needs. We will meet tomorrow at the altar." He bowed and was gone.

"With your permission, my lady, I will fetch you some food," Enit said, looking anxiously toward her new mistress.

"Yes, thank you," Rhonwyn replied absently, and when she heard the door to her chambers close behind the girl, she began a closer examination of her quarters. In a chamber—what had he called it? A garderobe!—she found her clothing neatly stored. There was a small door at the end of the garderobe. She opened it and was astonished to find a stone seat built into the wall. The seat had a hole in it. Next to the stone seat was a large bucket of water. She had never seen anything like it. What could it be? Enit would know. She closed the door on the dark stone seat and moved back out into the dayroom. The small fireplace was flanked by winged creatures on either side. In the center of the room was a rectangular oak table with tall high-backed chairs at either end of it. There was an oak settle adorned with a tapestried cushion to one side of the fire. There were two tall, narrow windows overlooking the hills and through which the setting sun now spilled into the room, turning the gray stone floors and the snowy sheepskins rosy. Rhonwyn stood in the alcove of one of the windows, looking out at the dark hills. Just a few days ago she had been on the other side of those hills, in Wales.

With a soft sigh she sat down on the settle before her fire. Could she really be the lady of Haven Castle? The abbess had assured her that she could, but it was all so strange and not just a little frightening. She didn't know if she really wanted this, and yet it was a duty, an obligation owed to Llywelyn ap Gruffydd, who had given her in marriage so easily and expected her to be everything a lady should be. But I am not a lady to the manor born, Rhonwyn thought rebelliously. Six months ago I was but one of the soldiers at Cythraul fortress. I would have as soon killed an Englishman as marry him.

She arose and began to pace restlessly. I am not certain I want to direct my servants and order provisions that we do not grow or make ourselves, she thought. I want to ride and hunt with my alborium, not sit meekly by the fire, weaving and spinning. Damn ap Gruffydd for condemning me to this life! I cannot be penned up any longer! How I bore those months at the abbey are beyond me, but I cannot be held captive like some wild thing they wish to tame. Oh, God! And what of the intimacy I must have with this man who is my husband? I know not what is expected of me, and I am not certain at all that I want to know!

The door to her dayroom opened, and Enit came in

bearing a tray that she set down on the table. "I thought you might be hungry, but as you are tired, I chose delicate foods, my lady," she said. "Come now and eat while it is still hot."

Rhonwyn got up and came to the table, where Enit seated her. Then the young serving woman set before her new mistress a silver server upon which was roasted capon breast, small new peas, and a large crusty slice of hot bread, the cheese atop it browned and melting. There was also a silver goblet of fruity golden wine.

Rhonwyn fell upon the food, eating with gusto. When she had cleared half her plate she grinned up at Enit. "I have never been known for having a dainty belly. My kinsman, Morgan ap Owen, says I eat like a barbarian."

Enit looked momentarily distressed. "Have I brought enough, then, my lady?"

Rhonwyn nodded. "Convent fare was not half as tasty," she chuckled. "What about you, Enit? Have you eaten?"

"I will in the kitchens afterward, my lady," the girl told her mistress. "We have kitchens beneath the hall, which is considered very modern. Most castles have a cookhouse, separate in the courtyard, but often the food is cold when it arrives. The master does not like cold food. He even created a device to bring the food quickly into the hall. It is a shaft in the walls that runs from below. The food is put upon a platform and by means of ropes drawn up into the hall."

"That reminds me," Rhonwyn cried, jumping up and signaling Enit to follow her into the garderobe. "What is this?" she demanded, opening the small wooden door that concealed the stone seat.

"You sit upon it and perform your necessary bodily functions, my lady," Enit said. "When you are through, I flush the shaft clean with the water in the bucket. Is it not wonderful?"

"By the rood!" Rhonwyn swore, the words slipping out most unexpectedly, and then she blushed.

But Enit giggled. "I know," she said, understanding. "My uncle, who is the steward here, says all the best castles have them. It is nice not to have to go outside and pee on a cold morning, my lady."

Now it was Rhonwyn who giggled. "I have so much to learn, Enit. I have been raised in virtual isolation my whole life, and in Wales we have not these wonderful modern conveniences. Tomorrow I would speak with your uncle so he may inform me of all these wonders."

"Tomorrow is your wedding day, my lady," Enit reminded her.

"Then the day after tomorrow," Rhonwyn said. "Is there a priest in residence here who says the mass?"

"Yes, my lady. It is Father John, and he says the mass at the hour of Prime each day."

"You will see I am awakened in time to be there," Rhonwyn told her servant. If there was one thing the abbess had impressed upon her niece, it was that daily attendance at mass was essential if one was to set a good example to one's servants. "Now, let me finish my meal. The hole in my belly is not quite filled." She sat down again at her table and ate the food remaining upon her plate.

When she had finished, Enit offered her lady a bath, but Rhonwyn refused, wanting to sleep. Instead, Enit brought a silver ewer of warm water for her mistress to wash her face and hands in so that she would not get grease upon the sheets. "Among my possessions you will find a small stiff brush, Enit. Bring it to me," Rhonwyn instructed the girl after she had washed. And when the brush was in her hand she showed Enit how she kept the yellow from her teeth, brushing them vigorously, then rinsing with her remaining wine and spitting it into the basin. "In future I will want mint leaves to chew to sweeten my breath. Sister Dicra taught me that," she explained to Enit.

Enit helped her mistress disrobe, carefully brushing the gown and putting it away. She drew the shoes from Rhonwyn's feet, promising to clean them before the morrow. "Will you wear your chemise to bed, my lady?" Enit asked.

"Not this one, for the sleeves are tight," Rhonwyn said. "You will find a white chemise with long wide sleeves among my possessions. That is what I prefer to sleep in, Enit."

Enit rummaged through her lady's chest and found the required garment. She helped Rhonwyn out of the one and into the other. "If you will seat yourself, my lady," she told her mistress as she placed the gown chemise in the garderobe, "I will brush your hair." Then as she did she sighed admiringly, "Ah, to have such a crowning glory, my lady Rhonwyn. I have never seen hair like this. Surely it is spun from thistledown and touched by the sun itself."

"I am said to be descended from the fairy folk of ancient Cymri," Rhonwyn told the girl as she braided her hair for the night. "They were fair like I am, like my mam was, not dark like ap Gruffydd and his ilk."

The servant helped her mistress into her bed, saying, "The fire should go the night, my lady, and keep you warm. If you need me you have but to call and I will come, for I am not a heavy sleeper." She blew out the small taper by the bedside and entered the garderobe where her own sleeping space was located.

Rhonwyn lay quietly. So, here she was. In the castle that was to be her home for the rest of her life. Tomorrow she would be a wife. Ap Gruffydd would depart. Good riddance to him! She would be alone with Edward de Beaulieu, who seemed pleasant enough. Would he allow her to have her brother here? It had been six months since she had been separated from her younger sibling. She had promised Glynn, and she had to keep that promise. While she had been at the abbey there was no hope of their being together, *but now* . . . Surely one small boy could not matter to this lord, and God only knew ap Gruffydd had no use for his son. He would remain at Cythraul the rest of his days if she could not rescue him. What if the fortress were attacked by the English or by another faction in opposition to ap Gruffydd? Glynn could be killed or worse if ap Gruffydd's enemies learned who he was. She had to gain his custody as quickly as possible. *She had to!*

Enit awakened her just as the darkling skies were showing signs of growing lighter. She dressed quickly in a simple dark brown gown with a girdle of delicate copper links. Enit put a matching fur-lined cloak over her shoulders, and together the two young women hurried to the small church that was located within the castle's walls. There they attended the mass, and afterward the priest came forward to greet the girl who would be the castle's new mistress.

"You are rested now, my child?" Father John asked her. "I was sorry we did not meet at table last night."

"I was very wearied from my journey," Rhonwyn explained. "The prince was most anxious to deliver me lest the English think he had reneged on his promise to marry his daughter to King Henry's man."

The priest heard the faint tone of mockery in her voice. "You are content with this arrangement, my child?" he gently inquired.

"I am told I must marry, good father, if I have no calling to God's service, which I most assuredly do not." She laughed. "It is my duty and my obligation to my prince to accept his decision in this matter. The lord of this place seems kind and has been most considerate of me. I have never had a suitor, nor is there anyone who has captured my fancy. This match is acceptable to me."

"Good," the priest replied. "I am happy to see what an obedient and dutiful daughter you are, Rhonwyn uerch Llywelyn. You will undoubtedly be an obedient and dutiful wife as well. The lord has asked that the ceremony be performed after the hour of None. Will that be acceptable to you, my child?"

Rhonwyn's eyes twinkled at the priest. "I have only but to be there, good father, do I not?" she told him. Then she and Enit hurried off.

The priest watched her go, and he could not keep a small smile from turning up the corners of his mouth. The new lady of Haven Castle was a touch independent and headstrong, he could see. Well, she would need her strength. She was very much like her aunt, the abbess of Mercy Abbey. He had once served in the church there some ten years back. He sensed a disdain in his new lady for her father, and wondered why. Still, she seemed quite reconciled to her fate, so he had to assume that all would be well.

Because it was considered ill fortune for the bridegroom to see the bride prior to the marriage ceremony, Rhonwyn kept to her chambers until it was time for her to go to the church again. Enit dressed her in the gown her aunt had made for the occasion. It was cream-colored silk, the neckline high and rounded, the sleeves long and tight. Over it she wore a sleeveless gown of gold and silver brocade with a matching fabric girdle studded with tiny pearls. Her stockings were plain and gartered at the knee. Her shoes had a pretty painted toe. Enit brushed her hair, leaving it loose to signify her virginity. The servant set a small fillet of twisted gold-and-silver threads on Rhonwyn's head.

There was a knock at the door, and Enit opened it to reveal Llywelyn ap Gruffydd. She curtsied.

"Run along, lass," he told her. "I would speak with my daughter before I bring her to the church." He gently pushed the girl from the chamber and closed the door behind her.

"What do you want?" Rhonwyn demanded of him irritably.

"To remind you that whatever you may feel toward me, you are still the daughter of the prince of all Wales and Welsh by your birth. Remember it, Rhonwyn uerch Llywelyn. I will expect you to write to me regularly, my daughter."

"Can you actually read?" she mocked him. Then her look hardened. "I have worked hard to overcome your neglect of me, my lord, and I have accepted your choice of a husband for me. I have done my duty by you; but once the priest says that I am Edward de Beaulieu's wife, my loyalty will lie with him. Do you understand me, my lord? *I will not spy on my husband or on the English for you!*"

"Your duty . . ." he began to bluster, but Rhonwyn cut him short.

"I am doing my duty, my lord, but shortly you will no longer have charge over me. My English husband will, and I will not betray him. What more do you want than you already have, Llywelyn ap Gruffydd? You have Wales and a strong England is your overlord. If you do not deceive them and keep faith with your sworn word, what future difficulties can you have, my lord? And how dare you ask me to break faith with the man who will be my husband? My mother never broke faith with you. Do you expect me to be any less than Vala uerch Huw? Ah, I despise you, ap Gruffydd! Now take me to the church so I may be quit of you!"

"Your mother loved me and would have done whatever she had to to ensure my safety and well-being," the prince said.

"But I do not love you, my lord," Rhonwyn told him.

"I gave you life, wench!" he snarled at her.

"And until today, that is all you have ever given me," she snapped back at her. "I thank you for today, though, ap Gruffydd, for now I shall be free of you for all times!"

"There is no arguing with you, is there?" he said, suddenly amused. She was so like Gwynllian. And how had that happened?

"No," Rhonwyn said quietly. "There is no arguing with me, my lord, prince of all the Welsh. Now," she repeated, "take me to the church."

Chapter Five

Edward de Beaulieu, dressed in a tunic of olive green and gold, awaited his bride in the church. He smiled with encouragement as Llywelyn ap Gruffydd led his daughter forward, placing her small hand in his. The bridegroom noted with pleasure how perfectly his wife spoke Latin as she made her responses and recited the prayers. When they were finally officially pronounced man and wife, he turned her face to him and gently kissed her lips. The startled look in Rhonwyn's green eyes surprised him greatly.

" 'Tis the kiss of peace between us," he told her softly.

"I have never been kissed before," she responded.

Then the reality of all the other things his convent-bred wife had never done rose up to assail him. The king wanted the marriage consummated immediately lest Llywelyn take his daughter back on some pretext or another to use her in a more advantageous marriage. Yet it was painfully obvious that his bride was a true innocent. Still, he owed the king his allegiance and would do what had to be done, although he would do his best to be gentle with the girl.

The day had been mild and sometimes sunny, but now as the evening approached, it was beginning to grow cloudy, and the spring rain was threatening. The little wedding party returned to the hall where a fine meal was served. There was lamb and venison and a lovely fat duck that had been roasted and garnished with a sweet sauce of raisins and figs. There was a blankmanger—chicken cut into pieces and mixed with rice boiled in almond milk, salt, and seasoned with sugar, then sprinkled with fried almonds and anise. Rhonwyn had never eaten it before, and she knew almost immediately that it would be a favorite of hers.

There was fresh bread, sweet butter, and a fine sharp cheese. A bowl of new peas was offered. The cook had made a small subtlety of colored almond paste and sugar, a couple in a cockle being drawn by a swan. It sat upon a silver dish surrounded by green leaves. It was admired and praised by both the bride and the groom, who drank a toast to each other afterward with rich red wine.

The day had waned, and the rain was beginning to beat against the shutters of the hall windows. Rhonwyn called for her mandora, and settling it in her lap, played and sang for her husband and the prince. She sang in both her own Welsh tongue—rich, mournful tunes her father translated for his son-in-law—and spritely, amusing songs in the Norman language that brought a chuckle to Edward de Beaulieu. He was beginning to believe that his bride was the most perfect creature on God's earth, and looked forward to being alone with her.

Finally when she had ceased her entertainment, he said, "Perhaps my lady, you will want to retire now."

She blushed, and ap Gruffydd chortled, saying, "You could not have a purer maid in your bed tonight, my son, had God himself chosen you a wife, and not King Henry. Remember she is a virgin when you satisfy your lust."

"My lord," Rhonwyn chided him sharply, "your words are unseemly and very indelicate."

"And your caution unnecessary, for I see what my wife is," Edward de Beaulieu told his father-in-law. Then he took Rhonwyn's hand, and raising it to his lips, kissed it tenderly. "I will join you eventually, my lady wife," he said quietly.

She glided from the hall with as much dignity as she could muster, thinking her father crude and her husband gallant. In her chambers she found Enit awaiting her. Her servant had arranged for Rhonwyn to have a bath. The tall oaken tub had been brought from its storage space in the garderobe and filled while they had eaten the wedding feast in the hall below. Enit helped her mistress to disrobe and then step into the tub. The warm water felt wonderful. Rhonwyn pinned her long hair atop her head with a tortoiseshell pin.

"Put my garments away," she told Enit. "I am quite capable of washing myself. What is that delicious scent? It is so delicate."

"Heather," Enit replied. "My mother makes an oil from the flowers she gathers on the hill each year. I put some of it in the water, my lady. I hope you like it." She bustled about, brushing Rhonwyn's overgown and undertunic, storing them away in the garderobe.

"It's lovely," Rhonwyn answered. "I've never had a scented bath before. It's quite wonderful, and I thank you." She took the washing cloth and some of the soft cleansing soap from a stone crock, and set about washing herself. The tub had been set before the fireplace in her dayroom. Rhonwyn splashed happily.

Then the door to her chambers opened, and she heard her husband say, "Enit, you will sleep in your mother's cottage tonight."

"Yes, my lord" came the dutiful reply, and Rhonwyn heard the door close again.

"Are you enjoying your bath, lady?" Edward de Beaulieu asked.

Rhonwyn turned slowly so as not to spill water onto the floor. He wore only a sherte that came to his knees. "My lord," she said, "am I allowed no privacy in my bath?"

"I have always enjoyed watching my women bathe," he said quietly.

"*Your women?*" Her eyes had widened at his words.

"Surely, lady, you do not think me a virgin," he responded. "I am a healthy man with healthy appetites. I have kept my share of mistresses. I shall no longer, however, now that I have a wife."

She nodded. It was reasonable, and his promise to remain faithful to her was comforting.

"You are flushed with the heat of your bath, Rhonwyn. It is very becoming to you," he told her.

She did not answer him, for she was not certain what to say. How she hated being made to feel a fool, but this was a situation she had never imagined.

"Are you coming out of your tub soon, Rhonwyn?" he asked her.

"How can I when you are standing here, my lord?" she replied.

"It is my right to see you as God fashioned you, wife," he told her, and his silvery gray eyes were twinkling.

"But I have never stood as God fashioned me before any man," she responded quickly. "I am not certain I can."

Reaching over the edge of the high wood tub, he put his hands beneath her arms and quickly lifted her out of the water, setting her down upon the floor. He drew a deep breath of pleasure. She had sweet little round breasts that begged to be loved.

With a gasp of both surprise and shock Rhonwyn snatched at the drying cloth and covered her nakedness. "That was unfairly done, my lord!" she scolded him.

"Has no one ever told you that all is fair in both love and war, my lady wife?" His eyes were burning a hole in the cloth.

"There is no love here, my lord, so we must be at war," she declared, "and you will find I am no easy enemy."

Reaching out, he plucked the pin holding her hair atop her head. Then wrapping a hank of the gilt mass about his hand, he pulled her against him, looking down into her beautiful but determined face. "You belong to me, Rhonwyn, as my warhorse belongs to me, as my weapons and my castle belong to me. I am your husband, and I have certain rights that I am privileged to take of you. Certainly you know that." He brushed his lips across her forehead. "You are young and innocent and shy. I understand your fears, but our marriage must be consummated."

"I barely understand what you are asking of me, my lord, but must this consummation take place tonight? Can we not have time to know one another better? We have only just met."

"What difference does it make, tonight or another night, eh, lady? Were you any other man's daughter but ap Gruffydd's, I should gladly honor your request, but you are not. My king fears your father will seek to take you back if the marriage is not immediately consummated. That he would seek an annulment and use you in a more advantageous marriage with an enemy of King Henry."

"Aye," Rhonwyn agreed, "he is that wily, my lord."

"I will be as gentle with you as I can," he promised her, caressing her cheek.

Without realizing, she drew back from his touch. "My mother died when I was five," she said. "I know nothing of what is expected of me. The nuns did not speak on it. I saw the prince atop my mother, but I never knew what transpired between them. I am sorry for my ignorance, but there it is, my lord, and I should rather be honest with you even if you think me a fool for my stupidity."

"You are a convent-bred virgin, Rhonwyn. You are not expected to know what transpires between a man and his wife until your husband teaches you," he said gently.

"My lord, I am not convent bred. I spent the last months with my aunt, the Abbess Gwynllian, but before that I lived at Cythraul," Rhonwyn told him.

"Let us get into bed, wife, and then you can tell me," he suggested, releasing his hold on her. Taking the toweling from her, he dried her as best he could and then led her into her bedchamber. Rhonwyn quickly climbed into the bed, and her husband, pulling his sherte off so that he, also, was naked, joined her. It was done so swiftly that she had no time to really examine him as he had examined her. "Now, tell me, Rhonwyn, what is Cythraul?"

"A fortress in the Welshry, my lord. It was only chance that ap Gruffydd discovered my brother and me the day after our mam died from birthing too soon our new sister. When he had buried them, he took Glynn and me to Cythraul and left us in the charge of our kinsman, Morgan ap Owen. That is where we remained until ap Gruffydd came to fetch me several months ago."

"And you were raised by your kinsman's wife?" de Beaulieu asked his bride.

Rhonwyn shook her head. "Cythraul, my lord, is a fortress of men. There were no women there at all. It would have been too dangerous if the English came over the border, you see," she attempted to explain.

"*There were no women at Cythraul?*" He looked down into her face to see if she was making mock of him.

"None, my lord," Rhonwyn responded softly.

"And would it not have been as dangerous for you and your brother if your enemies attacked this fortress?" he said.

"Perhaps when we were little, before I learned how to be a good soldier, my lord," she told him frankly.

"A soldier?" he said weakly. Surely she was mocking him, but he could see that she was quite serious.

"I ride, they say, as if I were part of my horse," Rhonwyn said. "I can use a sword and main gauche extremely well. I am passably proficient with a mace and a javelin, but it is with an alborium that I excel. I did most of the hunting for Cythraul from the time that I was ten. We ate very well."

"And your brother is equally soldierly?" She had to be playing a game with him. Women were not soldiers, good or otherwise.

"Glynn has no interests in weapons or war. He is a poet, a singer of songs. Ap Gruffydd has no use for him," Rhonywn explained.

"Rhonwyn, tell me that you are jesting with me," he begged her.

"Why would I do such a thing, my lord? Nay, I do not jest."

"But you are so . . . so beautiful! You are educated," he said.

"When ap Gruffydd came to Cythraul six months ago and found he had two sons," she chuckled, "he took me at once to my aunt. All I have learned I learned in the last few months, for I swear to you I could speak no language but my own before then. I knew not our dear Lord Jesus, or anything else, for that matter, but war and weapons. The prince of Wales needed a daughter for this treaty marriage. My aunt saw he got a perfect daughter back, and believe me, it cost him dearly."

Edward de Beaulieu was astounded by her story. "That is why he put the marriage off until now," he said thoughtfully.

"Aye," she agreed. "You call me beautiful, my lord. Six months ago I don't think you would have thought so. My father should have put his children with my aunt when he found us nine years ago, but Cythraul was closer, and it was easier to leave us there. Fortunately for my brother and me, our kinsman, Morgan ap Owen, has a large and good heart. I had no woman to model myself after until I went to my aunt the abbess. I am certain that lasses raised in a normal way know enough about consummation not to be considered fools. My aunt is a holy virgin. If she knew of such things, she did not discuss them."

De Beaulieu suddenly laughed. The entire situation was absurd, and yet the upshot was he now had a beautiful wife.

"You find this situation amusing, my lord?" She was puzzled.

"I can but imagine ap Gruffydd's chagrin when he came to fetch you and discovered you as you were. He must have been terrified, at least momentarily," Edward de Beaulieu chuckled.

"You do not like him," Rhonwyn said.

"I do not dislike him," her husband quickly replied.

"Nay, my lord, you do not like him," she insisted.

"Neither do I. I doubt I have seen him more than a dozen times in my life. While he was never unkind to us, his passion was for our mother, not his children."

"But none of what you have told me, Rhonwyn, changes our situation. This marriage between us must be consummated tonight," he said. Reaching out, he caressed her small breasts tenderly.

Rhonwyn squirmed nervously. "Please, don't," she told him.

"Why not?" he demanded half angrily.

"I am not used to being touched in so intimate a manner. It unsettles me, my lord."

"You will grow to like it," he assured her, brushing his fingertips across her right nipple teasingly.

"*Never!* It is all too possessing, my lord. It is as if you owned me, body and soul," Rhonwyn cried out softly, moving away from his bedeviling fingers.

"I have already told you, Rhonwyn, that I do own you. You are mine to do with as I please. Our marriage will be consummated tonight. If you let me, I will make the experience as pleasing as possible for you. I am not a man who takes his pleasure heedless of his woman's enjoyment. But whether you will or nay, I will have you, my fair wife." Then swiftly he was atop her—and as swiftly gasping with surprise at the dagger pressing against his throat. "What, will you kill me then to preserve your virtue, or do you fear I will learn you have no virtue?" he said in a hard voice.

"You will be the only man to have my virtue of me, my lord," Rhonwyn said, "but I will have something of you in return."

"What?" He contemplated taking the dagger from her.

"Ap Gruffydd will leave Haven once our marriage is consummated, will he not?" she asked.

"Aye. That is why he waits this night to see if he may snatch you back. He will go, however, on the morrow when I show him the bloody bedsheet with the proof of your defloration upon it. Why?"

"You must ask him before he leaves to send my brother, Glynn, to Haven," Rhonwyn said. "My brother is still a lad. We have never been parted until these past few months. I have seen how much there is in the world since I left Cythraul. I have learned and gained such knowledge as I never knew existed. I want those same advantages for my little brother. He is a gentle soul and does not belong in a fortress of rough men. Only that I was there and as great a roughneck as the others, was I able to protect him. Please, my lord, do this for me, and I will yield myself without further ado to your wishes and desires," she pleaded softly. "*Please!*"

Unexpectedly he grasped her wrist, disarmed her, and threw the dagger across the chamber. He slapped her lightly on the cheek. "In future when you seek a favor from me, Rhonwyn, do not threaten me with a weapon." Then he pinioned her hard and laughed at the anger in her eyes. "Such a fierce little virgin, it is," he said crooningly. "I will grant your request, Rhonwyn. Now, what have you for me in return?" His mouth came down hard on hers, forcing her lips to part, and he thrust his tongue into her mouth to ravage hers with wildfire.

Rhonwyn lay still, not knowing what else to do. He was almost gagging her with his tongue, and it was all she could do not to become sick. His lips began to kiss her face and her throat. She shivered. His kisses covered her breasts, her belly. She almost screamed as his fingers began to forage in her nest, pushing through her nether lips. She bit her lips until they bled as his fingers went deeper, slipping into a place she had not even known existed, probing her gently.

"This is the place where our two bodies will be conjoined," he told her thickly. "It is called your love sheath, and like a sword, my manhood will fill it, Rhonwyn, *now!*" He plunged himself inside her, and Rhonwyn screamed aloud as his manhood made contact with her maidenhead and thrust hard through it.

Oh, God, *she hated this*! It was impossible not to resist him now, and she fought him with all her strength, biting and scratching at him. "No more! No more!" she sobbed, but he only groaned a sound of distinct pleasure and thrust again and again into her body. Finally he stiffened a moment, and then she felt him relax and collapse atop her.

By the rood, the girl had aroused him, much to his surprise. And when she had stopped lying silent and had fought him, his lust had grown so hot he was surprised his head had not exploded. He knew it had not been a good experience for her, and he regretted it. Gently he kissed the tears from her pale cheeks and said, "There, Rhonwyn, it is over and done with now. We have both done our duty, and I shall leave you to recover yourself, wife." Catching his breath, he climbed from her bed.

Rhonwyn swallowed hard. "Glynn?" she said.

"Your father shall not leave Haven without giving me his promise to send the lad to us, Rhonwyn," he assured her. "Whatever you may think of me, I want you content."

"Do we have to? . . ." The question was unfinished, but he understood.

"Not until we are ready, Rhonwyn. We have done what was expected of us by king and prince. Now we will wait until you are happier. Good night, wife." He moved through the small arched door separating their bedchambers, and she heard the lock click shut.

For the first time in her life Rhonwyn wept.

Edward heard her on his side of the door and felt sadness that she was so unhappy. Hopefully these feelings would soon pass, especially when her brother arrived. He had never forced a woman in his life. It had never been necessary for him to do so. He felt guilt sweeping over him. Worse was the fact that he had enjoyed her despite everything. *Why?* He shook off the question. She was intelligent, and he had explained the situation to her. Her fears he understood, but her stubborn determination and her sudden threat to his person followed by a demand in exchange for her cooperation had truly infuriated him. She was his wife and therefore belonged to him! She must obey him, and that was all there was to it. Still, he had promised her a respite from his attentions, and he would keep his word. Common sense told him that it could not hurt for them to know one another better. He listened by the connecting door again. Her weeping had died away now, and he felt better for it.

Enit gently shook her mistress awake the following day. "You must wake, my lady. It is time to dress for the mass." The servant felt shy, for she knew Rhonwyn had lost her maidenhead the previous evening. She had been fearful that the master would be in her lady's bed yet, and was relieved to find it not so. She bustled about the apartment, laying out her mistress's clothing and skirting about the oak tub that still stood before the fire in the dayroom.

As she arose, Rhonwyn realized that she ached. She saw her dagger across the floor and hurried to pick it up. She always kept it beneath her pillow at night, for she had been taught an enemy can come upon you at any time. And an enemy had, but she had not killed him when she had the chance. Had it been necessary for him to be so rough with her? He had enjoyed it, the fiend! Well, at least she would not be bothered with his attentions any longer. He had promised her that, and she sensed that Edward de Beaulieu was a man of his word in spite of everything that had happened between them the night before.

Enit helped her lady dress. The two young women were silent. Together they walked to the church. Rhonwyn spoke the words of the mass quite automatically, startled to suddenly realize that her husband was by her side. Ap Gruffydd was nowhere to be seen, for he only went to church when it was absolutely necessary. When the service had been concluded de Beaulieu took his wife's hand, and they walked back to the great hall where the morning meal was being laid out. Rhonwyn saw the prince standing by the fire, a large goblet in his hand.

"You have not forgotten?" she asked de Beaulieu anxiously.

"Nay," he reassured her softly, "but in exchange, Rhonwyn, I would have you call me by my name from now on, wife. Will you do that?"

"Aye, Edward, I will," she responded low.

Llywelyn ap Gruffydd saw de Beaulieu smile down at his daughter, and the prince thought to himself, Perhaps it will be a happy union. For her sake, I hope so. In the end I did my best for her, Vala. "Good morrow," his voice boomed.

"My lord," de Beaulieu replied. "You will be leaving us this morning, Prince Llywelyn, will you not?" It wasn't really a question.

"Perhaps, if I am satisfied you are well and truly wed to my daughter, Edward de Beaulieu. Show me the proof of this marriage's consummation. I would see my daughter's innocence bespattered across the sheet of your nuptial bed."

Rhonwyn felt her cheeks burning at his words.

Her husband, however, turned to Enit and said, "Fetch the bedding, lass."

"Nay!" ap Gruffydd said. "I will go with the girl and see for myself, my lord. You cannot object to it, I am certain."

"Go then," de Beaulieu answered him calmly, but was angered that Rhonwyn should be so openly embarrassed by her own father.

When ap Gruffydd returned to the hall he said, "You did not spare her. That I could see. Very well, my daughter is now your wife. Other than paternal affection, I no longer have any claim upon her."

"*Paternal affection?*" Rhonwyn burst out. "You never had any affection for me, ap Gruffydd! How can you mouth such words with such piety? You ought to be ashamed of yourself!"

"*Rhonwyn.*" Her husband's voice warned her.

She was about to turn her scorn on him, but then she remembered. She was suddenly silent.

"Come, my lord, and let us eat," Edward de Beaulieu said. "I have a boon to ask of you."

They sat at the high board, Rhonwyn between her father and her husband. The servants bustled about. Small round trenchers of bread, baked fresh earlier that morning, were set before them. Into them the servants spooned an oat stirabout with bits of dried apple. A square board with a small cheese upon it was placed in front of them along with a platter of cold, roasted rabbit. Their goblets were filled with watered wine. They ate for a time in silence, de Beaulieu amazed and amused to see his wife's prodigious appetite. He wondered if she always ate like that, but he doubted it, considering her slender form.

Finally, when they were finished and the servants were clearing away the remnants of the meal, the prince spoke.

"What is it you would have of me, son-in-law?"

"Rhonwyn wants her brother here at Haven. She misses him," Edward de Beaulieu said. "If it would make her happy, then I am willing."

"So the English, having had my daughter, would now take my only son," ap Gruffydd said.

"Not the *English*, prince, but your daughter, his sister," de Beaulieu explained. "There is no trick in this, my lord. Surely you can understand that never having been separated until a few months ago, she misses him."

"Rhonwyn and her brother are my only offspring," ap Gruffydd said. "As she has had her value, so my son one day might prove useful to me. But if he is in English hands already, then his value is lost to me, son-in-law."

"You will marry eventually, Prince," de Beaulieu said. "You must for your heredity's sake. The children of your legal marriage will be of far greater value to you than the two children who were born to you on the wrong side of the blanket. Let Rhonwyn have her brother's company again, my lord. I swear to you that I will protect the boy from any political chicanery and send him directly back to Cythraul should I find I am unable to do so."

"I must think on it," ap Gruffydd said slowly.

Now Rhonwyn was unable to contain herself any longer. "Glynn means nothing to you!" she cried. "I will be here, and you will go your way without another thought or care for my brother. I know you well, O prince of the Welsh. Glynn is your son, but he is not you or your brothers. He has no ambitions other than to create beauty. Let me have him, my lord. You know in your heart that you do not want him."

"If I let you bring him into England, he could be a dagger turned against me one day, Rhonwyn," ap Gruffydd said.

"And if you do not let me have him, what will happen to him? Would you destroy him because of some imagined fear, my lord?" she said. There were tears in her green eyes, and Edward de Beaulieu vowed then and there if ap Gruffydd would not willingly let his son go, he, himself, would ride into the Welshry and bring the lad back to his wife. "Please, my lord prince," Rhonwyn pleaded. "Let me have my brother's company. You have said yourself that he is good for nothing more than the priesthood or poetry. Surely there is no threat to you in that."

"It is not Glynn who worries me, Rhonwyn. It is the English," ap Gruffydd said.

"I have said I would protect him," de Beaulieu replied.

"You are the king's man, son-in-law, which is why he chose you to be my daughter's husband," the prince said. "You are reliable and can be trusted. This is why I have waited so long to marry. I never wanted to be torn between my duty and the woman I loved. That is where you will find yourself, Edward de Beaulieu, if I put my son into your keeping. As for your wife, you do not love Rhonwyn. You barely know her. Perhaps one day you will have an affection for her, perhaps not. Therefore I believe your stronger loyalty would be to your king, and not to your wife and her brother."

"*Please, Tad,*" Rhonwyn said, slipping into the Welsh tongue.

"You have never before called me *father*," he answered her in the same dialect.

Rhonwyn smiled wryly. "It is unlikely I ever will again," she said honestly. "Let me have Glynn. I swear to you on my mother's honor that if I think the English mean to use him against you or Wales, I will either aid him to escape or kill him myself. You know I am worthy of your trust, Llywelyn ap Gruffydd. You know that as much as I love Glynn, that I will do my duty, whatever it may be. *Please!*"

"Say *it* again," he replied.

She hesitated a moment, and then said, "Please, Tad."

"You have my pride, daughter, but you know when to yield even as your mam did. Had you been my son the English would have truly had something to fear, Rhonwyn uerch Llywelyn." The prince turned now to his son-in-law and spoke Norman words to him. "My daughter has convinced me that my son's interests are better served here at Haven Castle rather than at Cythraul. Since you have given me your word to protect him, I will send Glynn to you."

"I know you have made Rhonwyn happy," de Beaulieu said quietly. "Thank you, my lord prince. You will find I keep my word, should it be necessary to protect your son from the crown. Since I do not intend to inform the king that the boy is with us, it is unlikely we should face any difficulties."

"Henry is indecisive, but his cub is far fiercer than most I have known," ap Gruffydd warned his son-in-law. "He will be king sooner than later, and you must remain on his good side. He is the best and the worst of all his ancestors, son-in-law. How long the peace will hold after he becomes king, I do not know. If we should meet in battle, Edward de Beaulieu, look away. I should not like to slay my daughter's husband, the father of my grandchildren." He arose from the high board. "I have remained here long enough. It is time for me to depart lest you one day be accused of conspiracy," he chuckled.

De Beaulieu arose, as did Rhonwyn. Together they walked the prince of all the Welsh to the courtyard where his men awaited him. Taking his daughter by her shoulders, Llywelyn ap Gruffydd kissed her first on the forehead and then on each of her cheeks.

"Farewell, my daughter. May God be with you always," he said.

"Farewell, my lord prince," she responded. "I thank you."

"For what?" he teased her.

"For my husband and for my brother," she replied, giving him a small and rare smile.

He chuckled. "A son. You should have been a son," he

said in his own tongue. Then he looked to de Beaulieu. "Farewell, son-in-law. God grant my daughter gives you many healthy sons and daughters."

"Thank you, my lord prince," de Beaulieu answered. "Godspeed!"

Ap Gruffydd mounted his charger and led his men from Haven Castle. His daughter and her husband stood for a short time watching them go, and then they turned back into the castle.

"How did you manage to convince him to send your brother to us?" de Beaulieu asked his wife.

"I called him *father*," she said. "I have never before called him that. The prince is a strong man, but he is also sentimental. My calling him father touched him. It was also a victory in his eyes. He felt I was forced to do something he had always wanted. He knows, however, that we are both victorious in this matter, for we have both attained what we sought," she finished.

"What did you promise him?" he wondered aloud.

"Nothing," she replied. "Why should I have to promise him anything, my lord?"

"Perhaps you agreed to send him certain information," her husband suggested softly.

"If you doubt or fear for my loyalty, then make certain that I am not privy to your delicate English matters," she told him. "I promised ap Gruffydd naught. I merely called him father, a word he has longed to hear from my lips. I had never done so before. There is nothing more to it, Edward."

"You will have to earn my trust, Rhonwyn," he told her.

"Whether you trust me or not makes no difference to me, Edward," she said coolly. "I must live with my own conscience."

"By the rood, you are the most aggravating woman I have ever known!" he said.

"Have you known many women?" she asked him sweetly.

"A wife should be meek and obedient to her lord's will," he said.

"My mother was meek and obedient. She gained no wedding band by her position and lost her life, I believe, because of it," Rhonwyn replied. "Hers is hardly an example I wish to emulate."

"You have a wedding band," he said softly.

"We have already satisfied the treaty between our two nations, Edward," she reminded him as softly.

He flushed, but then said, "Would you like to ride out with me and see the lands I possess, my lady wife?"

"Aye," she agreed, "I should, my lord husband."

So the truce was now set between them. They slept each in their own beds, but met at meals and rode together each day. His time was spent in overseeing the management of his lands, meeting with his bailiff and those freedmen who farmed portions of his lands and paid him in kind for the privilege. His flocks of sheep were large, his herds of cows ample. Fields needed to be plowed in rotation. Crops had to be planted and harvested and stored for winter. The days were busy and full.

Rhonwyn, with the help of Enit's uncle Alfred, the castle's steward, was learning the proper management of her home, putting into practice those lessons she had learned at the abbey. She was astounded by all the things she had to oversee and grateful now to the nuns who had given her some of the knowledge she would need. The year, Alfred told her, was a never-ending round of duties and chores. There was a time for slaughtering meat and salting it away for winter. The kitchen gardens had to be planted, the root crops stored in a cold place for use in the winter. The winters at Haven, Alfred said, were among the worst in all of England. Fruit had to be harvested at the proper time and turned into conserves and jellies. Apples, pears, and quinces could be dried as well as cold-stored. There was a time of year in which soaps, candles, and beer were made. The hives had to be well kept if the castle was to have honey. Sugar, sold in loaves at the Shrewsbury market fair each month, was expensive.

The weeks went by swiftly. April was followed by May, and then on one bright June day the castle watch called out that riders were approaching from the hills to the west. Three riders and a single pack horse. Rhonwyn could scarcely contain her excitement. She hurried to find Edward.

"The watch has spied a small party of three riders coming from Wales. It is my brother! It has to be Glynn!" she said. "Let me ride out to meet him, my lord! *Please!*"

"We will go together," he told her, and ordered their horses saddled at once.

They rode out with several men-at-arms in attendance, and with each pace the horses took, she grew more elated. Finally Rhonwyn could no longer contain herself and to Edward's surprise spurred her gelding forward into a gallop. A rider broke away from the incoming party, rushing forward to meet her. Edward de Beaulieu held his hand up to halt himself and his men even as the other riders ceased their movements as well. He watched, a small smile on his face, as Rhonwyn pulled Hardd to a stop and leapt off her mount, as did her brother off his. The two siblings flung their arms about one another, crying joyfully.

"Sister! Oh, sister, how beautiful you have become!" Glynn ap Llywelyn said admiringly.

"*And you!* You have grown so! You are taller than I am now, little brother! Oh, Glynn, I have so much to tell you, and you have so much to learn. I actually called him *Tad*, and he softened and let you come to me. Did I not promise you, Glynn?"

"I have your weapons," he said softly. "But you have become such a fine lady, Rhonwyn, will you want them now?"

"I will want them," she assured him. "Come now and meet my husband, Glynn."

"No greeting for us, lady?" a familiar voice called to her.

Rhonwyn turned. "Oth! Dewi! I greet you both." She swept them a curtsey, laughing as she did so.

"We scarcely recognized you, Rhonwyn uerch Llywelyn, such a great lady you have become," Oth, the more talkative of the two, said.

"I am no great lady," she replied. "Just a simple lord's wife. You aren't used to seeing me dressed so prettily, Oth."

"Good thing you didn't look like that at Cythraul, Rhonwyn, else we should not have been able to keep you chaste," he chuckled. "Go on now and take the lad to your husband. We'll follow behind."

Together the siblings walked their horses to where Edward de Beaulieu awaited them. When they reached him, Rhonwyn introduced her younger brother to her husband. Edward greeted the boy graciously, and Glynn responded in kind, Rhonwyn translating for both of them.

"That is your first task," she told Glynn. "You must learn the Norman tongue. It isn't hard. I learned very quickly."

"Far easier than the Welsh," Edward said in that same tongue.

Rhonwyn gasped with surprise. *"You speak Welsh?"*

"My nursemaid was of the Cymri," he said to her.

"Why didn't you tell me?" she demanded, suddenly

both angry and worried. If he spoke Welsh, then he knew exactly what she had said to ap Gruffydd to convince him to let her have Glynn—that she would free Glynn or kill him if the English tried to take him.

He grinned wickedly. "I wanted to surprise you one day." He turned to Glynn. "I shall not often speak Welsh to you, lad, for you must learn the Norman language if you are to succeed in this world. Do you understand me, Glynn ap Llywelyn?"

"Aye, my lord, I do," Glynn agreed, not comprehending the deviltry in his brother-in-law's eyes.

"How could you do that to me?" Rhonwyn said as she remounted her horse and they turned to ride back to the castle, Glynn between them. "How could you speak my native tongue and not tell me so?"

"Why do you think I was the one chosen to wed you, Rhonwyn?" He cocked an eyebrow at her. "King Henry asked who among the bachelor lords in the Englishry could speak Welsh well enough to take a Welsh wife. I was the only one to admit such a talent. It was thought you would not speak the Norman tongue. When you did, I saw no reason to bring up my own abilities, for I was pleased you cared enough about your impending marriage to learn my language."

"But you know then what I promised the prince," she said.

"And you should know I will never let it come to that," he told her fiercely. "Do you not think I realize that if you had to kill Glynn, you would then kill yourself, Rhonwyn? Do you think me so great a fool not to understand that? I can protect Glynn without compromising my loyalties. This I swear to you, my lady wife. Do you believe me, Rhonwyn?" His gray eyes turned to look directly at her.

She met his look searchingly, and then seeing the truth of this man's word, replied, "Aye, Edward, I believe you." "Good!" he replied. "We will not speak on it again."

Chapter Six

Glynn ap Llywelyn had never known a world such as that he entered into at Haven Castle. He had a chamber all his own. He was treated with deference as the son of the prince of Wales. At Cythraul he had just been Glynn, the lad. And more often than not he was known as Rhonwyn's little brother, not that he minded. He had new experiences, the first of which was his baptism into the Christian faith, his brother-in-law standing as his godfather. When his two companions, Oth and Dewi, admitted to not being certain if they had ever been baptized, they, too, were christened.

"There can be no heathens in my home," the lord said with a small smile. "Surely you have not been Christians before now else you would have taught Prince Llywelyn's children their faith."

"Have you been baptized, sister?" Glynn asked Rhonwyn.

"At the abbey with our Aunt Gwynllian, my godmother," she told him.

It was ap Gruffydd's wish that Oth and Dewi remain at Haven with his son. Edward de Beaulieu did not object. "A prince's son should have his own retinue, however small," he said graciously, but in truth he understood the real reason for ap Gruffydd's wish. Should the English ever threaten Glynn, his two watchdogs could get him safely over the border into Wales with neither Edward nor Rhonwyn being held accountable.

"You must learn the Norman tongue," Edward told the two Welshmen in their own language. "You will be of more use to me if you do. However, it is not necessary that strangers be aware of your skills." He winked at them meaningfully.

"Our loyalty is to our prince first, my lord," Oth told him honestly. "We are Welsh, not English."

"If the day comes when there is war between our peoples again," Edward said, "I will expect you gone without my saying it. I understand your loyalty, so I know you understand mine. Until that day, however, your loyalties must be with me, at least in part. Are we agreed?"

"The lady . . ." Oth began.

"Is my wife, and her loyalty, as you may ask her, lies with me now. As for the lad, that will be his choice to make. Be certain he does not forget his own tongue should he ever need it one day."

"You are more than fair, my lord," Oth replied, and he bowed.

Glynn's life now had more structure, and like his sister when she had first left Cythraul, he chafed at it. He was required to be at early mass with Rhonwyn. After he broke his fast he was schooled for several hours in a variety of subjects by Father John. Only in midafternoon was he free to ride or follow his own pursuits. Learning to read and write was for him a joy. Now he could copy the words to the songs he created onto parchment for all to see. With his brother-in-law's aid his manners became polished and elegant. Regular meals and plenty of food caused him to fill out and grow a bit taller.

One afternoon as he and Rhonwyn sat their horses

atop a hill in view of Haven, she said to him, "I believe you are truly happy, Glynn, for the first time in your life."

The boy thought a moment, and then he said, "Aye, sister, I am; and I am not afraid any longer. I was always afraid at Cythraul, especially after you left. Are you happy, Rhonwyn? Edward seems a kind man, but there appears to be little between you."

"We are only getting to know one another," Rhonwyn said to him. "I am told that marriages are always arranged affairs. There is an advantage to each side. Ours was a marriage devised as a matter of good faith between two warring parties. England wed to Wales. My husband and I are yet strangers. Now enough; I just have time for sword practice with Oth before the evening meal. Come on, little brother! I'll race you home," she cried, and spurred Hardd into a gallop.

From the castle heights Edward observed them as they sped down the hill and across meadows, scattering the sheep as they came. Unable to help himself, he chuckled. His wife was a changed person since the arrival of her younger brother. The love between the two had made him jealous until he realized that her love for Glynn was almost maternal. She had watched over the boy her whole life and felt responsible for his well-being. And the lad was certainly no trouble. He sopped up knowledge eagerly, being a very quick study. Rhonwyn had been correct when she said he was a gentle soul not fit for a soldier's life. He was now writing poems in the Norman tongue that he put to music.

Edward watched as Glynn and Rhonwyn entered the courtyard, dismounting their animals. Oth came forward with a padded garment, helping Rhonwyn to don it. Fascinated, Edward observed his wife as she was handed her sword, one that had obviously been made just for her hand. She began to practice her moves beneath the eye of the Welshman. Edward could hear him directing her sternly.

"You're out of shape, lady. Think! Think! And follow your instincts else you find yourself dead of your own carelessness." Oth picked up his own sword and began to block her blows. "That's it, lady!" He leapt aside, dodging her thrust. "You didn't anticipate that, lady! Ow!" He jumped back, swearing softly.

"And you didn't anticipate *that*!" She grinned at him, lowering her weapon. "I didn't hurt you, did I? It was just a tap, Oth."

"You're beginning to remember," he said with a rueful smile. "All right now, back to our practice, my fine lady."

The lord of Haven watched for a time as his beautiful wife turned into a warrior before his eyes. This was another side of Rhonwyn he had not anticipated. He found himself excited by this new knowledge, but he wasn't certain he approved. Surely such mannish activities could harm her abilities to bear him children. For now, however, he held his peace.

Rhonwyn was such a complex creature, and he really did want to know her better, but he was finding that it was not easy. They seemed to coexist, but nothing more. With Alfred's help she was learning how to manage the household. With Father John's aid she was becoming charitable to the less fortunate. His servants and his people liked her well. It was only he who seemed to be shut out of her life, although she was certainly polite and thoughtful of his well-being. But he had not entered her bed since their wedding night five months ago.

He wanted children, and it was certainly her duty to give him heirs; but each time he attempted to touch her, Rhonwyn shied away from him, distress all over her beautiful face. They could not go on like this, and if she

would not make the first move, he would have to do so.
But he needed to choose his moment carefully lest he re-
pel her even more. He needed to be alone with her, without her brother and his two Welsh watchdogs. Then fate
intervened in the person of Father John.

"I should like to take Glynn to Shrewsbury," the priest
told his lord one evening as they sat at the high board.
"He has never seen a town, and as you know, my lord, it
is a fine one." He turned to Rhonwyn, knowing her approval was paramount. "There is an abbey of monks,
lady, and many churches and shops. Trading vessels come
up the Severn from Bristol, for the river is very navigable.
Oth and Dewi would, of course, come with us. There are
many Welsh who visit the town regularly, and so they
would not stand out at all."

"What think you, Rhonwyn?" Edward asked her.
"And you, Glynn? Would you enjoy such an educational
journey?"

"Oh, I very much want to go, Edward!" the boy said
enthusiastically. He looked to his sister. "Rhonwyn,
please say I may."

"Perhaps I shall go with you," Rhonwyn said thoughtfully. "I have never seen a town either, little brother."

Glynn's face fell. "Oh, do you want to go?" he said,
his dismay very evident. This was obviously a trip he and
the priest had previously planned.

Edward leaned over to murmur in his wife's little ear,
"He is growing up, Rhonwyn. This is the first time in his
life he has been treated as he should be. As a prince's son
should be. His tutor wants to take him on a brief journey.
I don't think he wants his big sister with him, as much as
he may love you."

She had never before considered that Glynn would
grow up. He was her baby brother whom she had always
watched over and protected. She had brought him to

Haven and expanded his world. Now, like a little bird, he wanted to leave the nest to fly on his own. It came as somewhat of a shock. Surely he wasn't ready yet! Then she realized that Edward's large hand was covering hers in a comforting gesture. She turned her gaze to him, and he smiled at her encouragingly.

"I will take you to Shrewsbury myself one day," he promised her in a soft voice only she could hear.

Rhonwyn sighed deeply, and then she turned to her brother. "How long would you be gone?" she asked him.

"Just a week, no longer," Glynn replied.

"You must be certain no one knows you are the prince's son," she warned him.

"He can be known as Glynn of Thorley, a young relation of mine," Edward said. "It will be assumed he is my son by one of my former mistresses. In the care of the castle priest, it will be presumed that his mother is dead, which is, of course, a truth."

" 'Tis a grand idea!" the boy said enthusiastically. "When can we leave, Father John?"

"Would tomorrow be too soon, my son?" came the answer, and Glynn cheered. His sister, unable to help herself, smiled.

"You must have Oth and Dewi with you at all times," she said firmly, "and you will obey Father John without question, Glynn. If I learn you have been a wicked rascal, there shall be no more trips, my lad, I promise you," Rhonwyn sternly warned her brother.

He grinned at her happily, and the following morning he rode off with his little party with nought but a scant wave for his sister. To her surprise, Rhonwyn began to weep, and Edward, who was with her, put an arm about her shoulders. For once she did not shrug him off.

"There, wife, he will be back soon," he reassured her.

"He is growing up," she admitted. "Oh, Edward, what

shall I do when he goes off for good one day? I am so used to looking after him. What will I do?" she repeated.

"You will raise our children to be every bit the fine young man your brother is becoming, Rhonwyn," he told her.

"Our children?" She swallowed. "We have no children, my lord."

"Nor the hope of any unless we can together overcome your fears, Rhonwyn," he said quietly. "Our wedding night was a cruel time for you, but it was necessary for all the reasons that you well know. By the rood, wife, would you have your father still living with us?" he teased her as they walked back into the hall.

"Mary's blood, no!" she exclaimed.

He chuckled. "Do you think you know me well enough, my wild Welsh wife, that you will let me into your bed again? With your brother away it is the perfect time for us to attempt our reunion."

"Let me think on it," she said in a low voice.

"You have had almost six months to think on it, Rhonwyn," he told her, a slight edge to his voice. What the hell was the matter with her?

"Will you force me again, my lord?" she said angrily. "I know I cannot hope to overcome your strength, but I will hate you for it! I do not know if I can bear to be so *possessed* again."

"When passion is felt by both lovers, Rhonwyn, both are possessed, and the pleasure is sublime, I promise you," he responded patiently, yet he was impatient. Whenever the matter of conjugal relations came up, she behaved as if he were a monster.

"I felt pain and fear and loathing on our wedding night, my lord," she told him frankly. "I hated it when you covered my body with yours. I was helpless to your lusts, and there was no escaping it. I do not know if I can feel any other way."

"We do not have to mate at first, Rhonwyn," he said. "We will begin slowly, by touching. You are as free to touch me as I am to touch you, wife. We need not be in our bed or even unclothed at first. I do not think you would be fearful then."

"Does it always hurt?" she asked him pointedly.

"Nay. The first time when a maiden's virtue is taken from her, aye. But once she is used to her husband's lance sheathing itself on a regular basis, nay. There is no pain," he promised her.

Rhonwyn was thoughtful for a time. She didn't know if she could ever overcome her distaste for this *passion* of his, but for his sake she must try. Edward was a good man, and he had been very patient. "Can you bear to go slowly, my lord?" she asked him.

"I must for your sake," he replied honestly.

"Then I will try," she said.

"Why are you so fearful?"

Rhonwyn shrugged. "I cannot say," she told him. "I know what you want is a natural thing, particularly between a man and his wife, but I felt so powerless on our wedding night. Never before did I feel so impotent, and I never again want to feel that way, Edward. I will never forget seeing my mother helpless to ap Gruffydd's passions, not that she seemed to mind. Her whole existence was for him, so I was left to take care of myself and Glynn. It is true my kinsman and the men of Cythraul had charge over us, *but I was my own mistress*. I wanted to ride, and they taught me. I wanted to learn how to use a sword; they taught me. They even taught me how to dice, although they were reluctant to do so, especially afterward when I beat them. I was always in charge of my own being. Yet when we consummated our marriage, I was not in control of myself. You were in control, and I could not bear it." She bit her lower lip in vexation. "I am sorry, Edward. I truly am."

"But it is a man's place to lead," he said slowly, trying to understand her point of view, but he really didn't. Why could she not be obedient? He was half in love with her yet he did not know if he could be happy with a woman who constantly questioned him, and would not do her duty by him.

"*Why?*" she asked.

"Why? Because that is the way it has always been, Rhonwyn. Is that not what the church teaches? And did not God create Adam, the man, first?" he said somewhat tersely.

"And realizing his error," Rhonwyn replied quickly, "he created Eve, the woman, or so my aunt the abbess says."

"You are too independent for a wife," he said, shaking his head in mock despair, unable to be angry with her.

"I was raised to be so, my lord," she responded softly.

"Be independent, wife, except when you come to our bed. Then I would have you rely on me, Rhonwyn. I find that I am beginning to care for you in ways that have nothing to do with lust or desire, although I do desire you. I believe they call what I am feeling *love.*" He took her hand in his, and raising it to his lips, kissed it softly, first the back, and then turning it over, the palm.

The moist warmth of his mouth on her flesh sent a small shudder through her, but it was not, she decided, entirely unpleasant. She did not pull her hand away from his.

He drew her close and said softly, "Put your head upon my chest, Rhonwyn, and let me hold you for a moment." His arms came about her, but his grip was an easy one she might have broken away from if she chose to do so. "You are so beautiful, Rhonwyn uerch Llywelyn," he told her.

"Your hair is like moonbeams that have been spun with the sunlight by spiders. And it is as soft as thistledown, wife."

Her cheek rested against his doublet just below his shoulder. She could smell the scent of him, and it was not unpleasant.

Reaching out, he captured her chin between his thumb and his forefinger, tilting her head up to him. "You have eyes like emeralds."

"What are emeralds?" she asked ingenuously.

"The green jewels in my sword's hilt," he told her.

"You think my eyes are like green stones? For that is what those pieces of glass are. Green stones," Rhonwyn told him, not certain that what he had obviously meant as a compliment was truly a compliment.

Edward laughed. "Don't be so damned practical," he scolded her, and then he brushed her lips lightly with his before releasing his grip on her. "Emeralds are, in their unset form, exquisite jewels, and your eyes are exquisite, wife."

Her mouth was tingling as it had when he had kissed her at the altar. It was rather nice, she thought. "Your eyes are like a rainy sky," she told him, "and your hair is like an oak leaf in November."

He grinned at her. " 'Tis as pretty a compliment as I have ever received, wife."

Rhonwyn giggled. "I think you mad, my lord," she said. "Now I must go about my chores, for just because Glynn has departed and you are of a mind to play the gallant does not mean I have been relieved of tasks." She curtsied to him, and turning, hurried off.

Edward watched her go. He felt they had made a good beginning this morning. In the months she had been his wife he had grown to genuinely like Rhonwyn. He had told her the truth when he had said he had deeper feelings burgeoning within him. And it had all happened without kisses or copulation, much to his surprise. He had done what he must on their wedding night, but now that he knew her, he honestly desired her. He had heard of women for whom passion had no meaning. He hoped that his wife was not one of them. He prayed silently that she simply needed to be awakened. There was no pleasure in just satisfying an itch. He could do that with any female. He wanted to really love her and have her love him in return. Until now it had been easy to be patient. He sensed it would not be any longer.

That evening he invited her to play at dice with him, laughing when she won a silver penny. "You have been well taught, lady," he complimented her. "Next time I shall challenge you to a game of chess instead," he finished with a wry grin, rising from the game table and moving to his chair by the fire.

"I am skilled at that as well, my lord Edward," she told him.

The hall was empty, the servants gone. A fire burned in the fireplace flanked by their great stone lions. Edward de Beaulieu now sat in the master's chair with its leather seat and back.

"Will you sit in my lap, Rhonwyn?" he asked her.

What harm could there be in it? she thought. Rising from the game table, she sat herself within the curve of his arms. They remained quietly for a time, and then Rhonwyn said, "The harvest has proved to be excellent, my lord. The granaries are full. The orchards are ready to be picked, and if the rain holds off, we shall be able to start tomorrow."

"Why does your hair smell like heather?" he asked her, sniffing.

"Enit's mother makes the oil we put in my soap," she replied. "The apple crop would appear to be bounteous.

We should begin pressing the cider in another week or two."

"It's delicious, wife. The scent is delicate and suits you well." He sniffed again, and then kissed the top of her gilt head.

"My lord! Do you not wish to know how we fare here at Haven?"

"Tell me after the mass when we break our fast on the morrow," he said. "The evening hours should be for gentler pursuits." Then he tilted her back in his arms and kissed her, a lingering soft kiss that to Rhonwyn's surprise set her pulses racing. But as quickly as his mouth had made such delicious contact, he tipped her gently from his lap. "Go to your bed now, wife. I bid you pleasant dreams. I know that I shall have them this night."

Slightly dazed, she walked from the hall and climbed the winding staircase to her chambers. Enit was awaiting her and helped her prepare for bed. Finally alone, Rhonwyn lay in her bed, eyes wide open, considering what had happened this day. Would she be able to overcome her aversion to her husband's passion? She was beginning to hope she could.

The following day they had surprise visitors. Edward was in the orchards overseeing the apple picking. Alfred rushed into the hall where his mistress was seated, weaving a tapestry that would be placed over the fireplace. The steward was flushed and pale by turns.

"My lady! My lady! The lord Edward and his wife are but a mile from Haven! The messenger has just now come. What are we to do?"

"*The lord Edward?*" Rhonwyn was slightly confused.

"*The prince,* my lady! King Henry's son with his lady wife. What shall I do?"

Rhonwyn stood up. "We do not know if they will remain the night, but have the best guest chamber prepared just in case they do. Did the messenger say how many are in their party? The cook must be able to feed them all and well, no matter. Send John to the orchards to fetch my lord immediately! I must go and change my gown. I cannot greet the king's son looking like this. Hurry, Alfred! *Hurry!*" She ran from the hall, calling as she went, "Enit! To me, lass!"

But Enit, by some magic known only to servants, was already in her mistress's garderobe, pulling out a more elegant gown for her lady to wear. It was apple green silk with a sleeveless overgown of deeper green and silver brocade. She lay it with a silver brocaded girdle upon the bed even as Rhonwyn hurried into the chamber, pulling her everyday kirtle over her head as she came. After dressing Rhonwyn, Enit quickly redid her hair, parting it in the center and plaiting it, and then fixing the braids about Rhonwyn's head. A gauze veil with a small silver circlet completed the attire.

"Thank you," Rhonwyn said, jumping up and hurrying from her chamber. It simply would not do to have the prince and his wife arrive and have neither she nor Edward be there to greet them. She ran down the stairs, hearing Enit coming behind her.

In the hall the servants were running back and forth with wine and plates of fruit and cheese for the high board. The fire was built higher. Edward dashed in, his handsome face streaked with dirt. Seeing his wife, he gave her a wave and bolted out again, heading to his own chamber to change his clothing.

"They're at the foot of the hill, lady," Alfred said as a young lad ran in to whisper to him.

Rhonwyn swallowed hard. There was nothing for it. She would have to greet the prince and his wife alone. She walked from the great hall, down the corridor a short distance, and out the door of the castle to stand a moment on the stairway landing, even as the lord Edward and his wife rode into the courtyard. Then she glided down the staircase, reaching them as the prince dismounted and lifted his lady from her horse.

Rhonwyn curtsied gracefully and low. "My lord Edward, my lady Eleanor, I bid you welcome to Haven Castle."

The prince raised her up and looked directly into her face. "So you are ap Gruffydd's wench," he said.

"I am, my lord," Rhonwyn replied.

"You are not at all what I expected. The Welsh are dark, are they not, lady?"

"Most are, my lord, but my mother descended from a race who were known as the Fair Folk. While I resemble ap Gruffydd in features, I have my mother's coloring."

"You are far prettier than ap Gruffydd," Prince Edward said with a small chuckle. He turned away from her a moment. "*Mon coeur,* this is the prince of the Welsh's daughter and the wife of Edward de Beaulieu, the lady Rhonwyn." He turned back to his hostess. "My wife, the lady Eleanor."

Rhonwyn curtsied again, then rising, said, "Will you not come into the hall and be refreshed? There is both food and wine awaiting you and water with which to wash the dust of your travels away." She led them into the castle.

In the hall Edward de Beaulieu came forward and bowed to the royal couple. "Forgive me, my lord, for not being here to welcome you, but I was in the orchards when I was informed of your arrival. As I would not greet you in the clothing I have worked the day in, and as there was little time to change, I had to leave my wife to see to you both." He bowed to the prince again and kissed the lady Eleanor's gloved hand.

"Your wife did you proud, de Beaulieu. And I was

happy to be greeted by so fair a lady," Prince Edward said graciously.

Rhonwyn nodded to Alfred, who hurried forward with a tray holding four of the silver goblets with the green stones. He offered one to the prince first, and then to his wife, his master, and his lady.

"To the king," de Beaulieu said.

"To the king," his companions repeated, and they drank their wine as the prince's retainers filed into the hall.

"You will stay the night," Edward de Beaulieu said.

"We will," Prince Edward said. "Can you feed this lot of mine? There are twenty of them, and they carry oatcakes if you cannot."

"There is more than enough food at Haven for your men, my lord Edward," Rhonwyn said quickly. "I usually have the cook prepare too much, to be honest with you, but then the poor who come to our door are more easily fed. We had at least a half an hour's warning of your arrival," she said with a twinkle in her eye.

The prince burst out laughing. "You are nothing like your father, lady," he said jovially.

"You could not have given me a greater compliment, my lord Edward," she replied. "Ap Gruffydd is not a man whom I would emulate."

"You speak harshly of him, lady," the prince remarked.

"I mean him no disrespect, my lord Edward," Rhonwyn said. "He is a difficult man, but he did me a service when he arranged my marriage with my own Edward."

The prince nodded, and then his wife said to Rhonwyn, "Have you children yet, Lady Rhonwyn? We have had four, although we lost our daughter Joan shortly after her birth. Still, Eleanor, John, and Henry are fair children, and I am grateful to God for them."

"We were only wed in April," Rhonwyn answered the prince's wife.

"And you are not yet with child? You must pray to Saint Anne, lady, for she will not fail you." The princess smiled warmly at Rhonwyn. "I can see you care for your husband. The children will come. They always come from love."

The castle cook had worked a miracle, and when the dinner hour came, the food began to appear upon the tables above and below the salt with great rapidity. Bread and fruit had already been set upon them earlier along with small wheels of cheese. Now came roasted venison, enough for all. There were platters with capons in lemon sauce, and trout broiled in wine upon beds of cress, lampreys in Galytyne, a large dish of mortrews—a meat dish made with eggs and bread crumbs—and Rhonwyn's favorite, blankmanger. There was lettuce braised in wine and boiled peas; loaves of freshly baked bread and sweet butter. Apple beer was served, but at the high board where the prince and princess sat with Edward de Beaulieu and his wife, there was wine.

"You have no priest?" the prince asked.

"He has gone to Shrewsbury to visit friends at the abbey," his host said smoothly.

"I wished him to be here when I spoke with you on a certain matter," the prince said. "King Louis of France is preparing another crusade for next year. My wife and I intend to go. I have spent the summer traveling about, visiting various lords to ask who would go with me. Will you, Edward de Beaulieu?"

"Is it safe for you to leave England, my lord Edward?" his host asked, concerned.

"With my uncle de Montfort dead and buried, there is none who would oppose my father, *or me*. Once I become king, may it be many years hence, I cannot indulge myself. I am not my great-uncle, Richard Coeur de Lion. To rule England, I must be in England. Now is my chance to help retake the Holy Land and drive the infidel to hell and beyond. Will you come with me, Edward de Beaulieu?"

"I will go with you, my lord Edward" came the reply.

"And I, too!" Rhonwyn said enthusiastically.

The lord of Haven laughed softly. "My wife has a warrior's heart," he explained.

"But I would go with the prince!" Rhonwyn said earnestly, and before her husband might speak further, the princess spoke.

"I am going with my husband, my lord. If your lady wishes to go, I see no reason why she cannot come, *unless,* my lord, you do not wish her to come."

"Oh, Edward, please!" Rhonwyn begged him. "I do not wish to be separated from you now."

The emerald eyes were shining with excitement, and he suddenly realized that he did not wish to be separated from her either. "It will be a hard life, wife," he said.

"I have lived a hard life, my lord," she replied.

He sighed. "You must swear to me that you will obey me implicitly if I let you come with me," he warned her.

"I promise," she swore.

"I will be happy to have the lady Rhonwyn and her servant as part of my train," the princess said graciously, "*if,* of course, you let her come with us," she quickly amended.

"She may come, my lady Eleanor, and I thank you for your most gracious invitation to include my wife among your women."

"Thank you both!" Rhonwyn said excitedly.

How the hell did ap Gruffydd sire such a daughter? the prince wondered to himself. Fair of face and obviously good of heart. There would appear to be no guile in her. She seems content with de Beaulieu, and I am glad, now having met her.

He was pleased his host had agreed to come with him. It proved that Edward de Beaulieu was loyal to Edward Plantagenet. While he spoke as if his father would live a great deal longer, the prince knew it wasn't so. His father was over sixty now, and there were things his mother had told him that others did not know. But if the worst happened and his father died while he was on crusade, his mother, Queen Eleanor, was strong enough to hold the country together until his return. And if he died on crusade, he had two young sons in England whom his mother would protect with her own life. The dynasty would continue. He was content knowing that.

The prince and his wife departed the following morning, their business at Haven completed successfully. The two Edwards had discussed when and where they would meet. The lord of Haven had promised to bring with him one hundred soldiers whom he would feed, equip, and house at his own expense. He would also attempt to raise a group of ten mounted knights, but he quite honestly told the prince he could not guarantee it.

"Do your best," the prince said. "Every man who comes will be guaranteed forgiveness of all his sins by the church when we return to England. I have this on the authority of the archbishop of Canterbury himself, de Beaulieu. Those who die on this crusade will be guaranteed entry directly into heaven and will not have to go to purgatory. The pope has promised it."

The royal couple then rode from Haven Castle, taking the Shrewsbury Road.

When they had gone, Rhonwyn said enthusiastically, "I must begin more serious practice with my weapons if I am to be ready when we go on crusade."

The prince and his wife were scarcely gone when another visitor arrived at Haven. Rafe de Beaulieu had not been happy to learn of his cousin's marriage. Now as he entered the great hall he was greeted by the sight of Edward kissing the hand of a beautiful young girl. Surely this couldn't be the bride.

"Cousin," he said loudly, grinning as the couple broke apart. "And who is this pretty wench? Are you already bored with your wee Welsh wife, Edward? And where did you find this glorious creature?"

"Greetings, cousin, and as always you jump to wrong conclusions," Edward said. "This is my wife, Rhonwyn uerch Llywelyn. Sweeting, my nearest kin, Rafe de Beaulieu."

Rafe was stunned, but quickly recovering, he bowed to Rhonwyn, and taking up her small hand, kissed it. "Lady, my cousin's good fortune overwhelms me. All the Welsh I have ever known are dark." Jesu! She was absolutely magnificent. Poor sweet Kate was but a faint star to this girl's brilliant sun. For a moment he was angry that his sister should have been so cheated, but then the lady Rhonwyn wasn't responsible. She was only a woman and must do the bidding of her menfolk.

"You are welcome to Haven, my lord Rafe," Rhonwyn told him, thinking that he was arrogant. How dare he enter her home and assume ap Gruffydd's daughter was some tiny dark creature, and she was a woman of loose morals who was Edward's leman?

He could see the anger in her eyes at his assumptions, and he knew he couldn't blame her if she hated him. "I have come to pay my respects and bring you Katherine's good wishes, cousin," he said.

"Your sister is well?" Edward asked, and then he suddenly thought that Katherine de Beaulieu must surely be hurt by his apparent rejection of her. Kate had always been such a gentle and soft-spoken girl.

"She is well. She would have come but it is cider season, and Kate's cider is known throughout the region.

She will allow no one else to oversee its making," he chuckled. "She is a good chatelaine. I shall be hard-pressed to find a wife who can oversee Ardley as our Kate does."

Rafe de Beaulieu was a tall, slender man with Edward's light brown hair and light blue eyes. He and his sister were Edward's only living relations. They were the children of his father's younger brother. They lived on a small manor near the town of Shrewsbury, two days' ride from Haven.

"You will stay," Edward said, knowing full well the answer.

"Aye, just for the night. I must leave tomorrow," Rafe answered.

"Then you came out of curiosity?" Rhonwyn said sharply.

"Aye, lady, I did," he admitted with a grin, wondering silently how it was his cousin, Edward, was so damned fortunate.

"I shall see a chamber is prepared for you," Rhonwyn said, and with a smile at her husband and a cursory nod at Rafe, she hurried from the great hall of the castle. Their visitor, she decided, was an irritating fellow, and she was glad he lived two days' ride from Haven. She was not unhappy to see her husband's cousin depart the next morning.

Edward had said nothing to Rafe about the crusade. While he intended to ask him to steward Haven in his absence, he wasn't certain yet whether they would really go. He doubted King Henry would be happy to have his heir gone so far from England, and it was the king who held the purse strings the prince needed loosened to finance this great adventure. Rhonwyn, however, had no doubts that they were going, and no sooner had Rafe gone his way home she began to worry about her brother. "Oh, Edward! What are we to do with Glynn?

Ap Gruffydd will never allow us to take him with us, and you cannot leave him alone here at Haven. For some reason that I have never fathomed, Glynn adores the prince of the Welsh. He would not mean to betray us, but he could very well be persuaded by that wily man who sired us both. We cannot send him back to Cythraul. It would be too cruel, although Morgan ap Owen would care for him." Rhonwyn's face was concerned.

We. Us. His heart soared. She was beginning to think of them as one, even if she still held his passion at bay. "Perhaps we might send Glynn to the abbey school in Shrewsbury," he suggested. "They could teach him far more than Father John can. I will pay his fees myself, and he will be safe there from your father."

"But what of his identity?" she fretted.

"Glynn of Thorley," he reminded her. "He will be thought to be my get. I shall tell the father abbott that he is my relative, that his mother is deceased, and that his pater is not to be discussed. That is enough to give truth to the idea that I sired him. But Glynn must remain silent, Rhonwyn, regarding his true parentage. Can he do it?"

She nodded. "He can. He will be disappointed not to go with us on crusade, but he will be equally excited about going to the abbey school. Now that he has been exposed to learning, it would seem he has a great capacity for it. I think he might be a priest or a scholar."

That evening she curled herself in his lap again, and he stroked her silken head in a leisurely fashion. This time she had come to him. "We shall have little time once we begin the crusade to cohabit as man and wife," he told her meaningfully.

"We do not go for many months," she said softly, thinking that she must ask Enit's mother what could be done to prevent conception. If she was to yield herself to her husband's passions once again, she did not intend to conceive a child and thus be prevented from going with him on crusade. "Oh!"

His hand was gently fondling her breasts. "They are like the perfect round apples in our orchards," he told her.

Rhonwyn could feel her breath tight in her chest. His hand was very exciting, teasing tenderly at her bosom. She neither forbade him nor stopped him from his love play.

"I know it is too soon," he said, "but I cannot wait for the night when we lie naked, side by side, and I may cover those precious little orbs with kisses, wife."

"I am less afraid and repelled than I have been in the past," she admitted shyly.

"We are getting to know one another," he said. His hand removed itself from her breasts and tilted her face to his. He touched her lips softly at first, and then as her budding passion began to overcome them both, his lips took possession of hers with a deeper fierceness. She didn't resist, indeed her lips moved beneath his with a girlish innocence that enchanted him. Before she might grow fearful, before he might allow his desire for her to gain a mastery over them, he broke off the kiss, and looking down at her, said, "You are so lovely, Rhonwyn. I am in love with you, and I would have you be in love with me, wife."

"Give me time, Edward," she said to him. "I am only beginning to understand this thing you call passion, and I do thank you for your gentle patience with me."

"You are a prize very worth having, Rhonwyn uerch Llywelyn. How much sweeter our coming together again will be for the waiting we must endure." His gray eyes smiled down at her.

Reaching up, she touched his cheek. "I will try very hard not to keep you waiting too much longer," she promised him. Her slender fingers caressed his face.

Catching her hand in his, he kissed each of those fingers with fervor. "It shall be in your time, my love, for I want more than anything else for you to be happy."

"I am happy now, safe in your strong arms," she replied.

"On the night you tell me our waiting is over, Rhonwyn, I shall make you happier than you have ever known!" he vowed passionately.

Part Two

Rhonwyn 1270–1273

Chapter Seven

Glynn returned from Shrewsbury eager to recount his travels and small adventures. Rhonwyn had never known her brother to be so very talkative. "I saw ships that came upriver from Cardiff," he said excitedly. "And the abbey and the churches, sister! And the markets with all their goods and the shops! Never have I seen their like. I ate a pomegranate, Rhonwyn! It's a fruit from the south. There is so much more to the world than I could have believed possible. I want to travel some more when I am older. I shall earn my way singing my ballads in inns and festivals and noble courts."

"First you must finish your education," Rhonwyn told him. "And as much as I dislike mentioning it, our sire may have something to say about what you make of your life, Glynn ap Llywelyn. He may even plan a marriage for you as he did for me."

"Not until I have traveled the world," Glynn said firmly, and for the first time she saw ap Gruffydd in her brother.

As they sat at the high board that evening, Edward said to his young brother-in-law, "Would you enjoy going to the abbey school in Shrewsbury, Glynn?"

"Could I?" the boy asked, his eyes wide with hope.

"Perhaps next spring it could be arranged. While you

were gone Prince Edward and his wife came unexpectedly to Haven. King Louis of France is planning another crusade to the Holy Land next year. Your sister and I are to accompany the prince. While we are gone you must continue your education. What better place than in Shrewsbury?"

"My lord," Father John spoke up, "why would the prince come here? We are but a small Marcher holding and not important to him."

"Edward Plantagenet will sooner than later be England's king, good father. It is for the very reason I am a Marcher lord that he came to Haven-at-Thorley. *And the fact that I am wed to ap Gruffydd's daughter.* He seeks to divine my loyalties without asking. There was no way I could refuse him without arousing his suspicions. That my lady wife enthusiastically volunteered to go along has quite raised Prince Edward's esteem of me," Edward de Beaulieu finished with a chuckle.

"Why can I not go, too?" Glynn asked.

"Because, brother-in-law, I am certain your father would not allow it. There will be time for you to go on crusade when you are older. For now I think it best, and I believe your father will agree, that you continue your education in Shrewsbury," Edward replied.

"If you retake the Holy Land, there will be no more crusades," Glynn said gloomily.

"The Saracens and the Christians have battled back and forth over the holy ground for centuries now, Glynn. There will always be crusades, I fear. Do not despair. You will have your chance one day."

Martinmas, the feast of St. Martin, was celebrated on November eleventh. A fat goose was slaughtered and roasted to be served in the hall. On November twenty-fifth St. Catherine's day was celebrated with Cathern cakes and a beverage called Lambs' Wool, named for the roasted apple that floated in it, which was served in a special Cathern bowl. Edward presented his wife with a special brooch in the shape of a wheel made from silver and onyx. The twelve days of Christmas came and went, and it was January.

Edward de Beaulieu was already recruiting men to accompany them on crusade. He had been informed by royal messenger that while he was away, his taxes would be forgiven. He so informed his tenants and serfs that whoever accompanied him would also be excused from their taxes and rents. There was no shortage of volunteers under those conditions. The lord of the castle was able to pick and choose whom he would take with him. By mid-January the one hundred chosen men were hard at work training with bow and pike and stave. They learned how to use a battering ram and a siege weapon called a tarques. They learned how to dig beneath a wall so as to collapse it.

Three young men, from less important families than Edward de Beaulieu's and who had already been knighted but sought adventure, came to Haven-at-Thorley to join the lord's party. Such an opportunity was not to be missed, for if they performed well on the field of battle and drew favorable attention to themselves, their fortunes could be made. Sir Fulk, Sir Robert, and Sir Hugo all came with squire, horses, and weapons. They were welcomed and given places in the hall and at the lord's board. They were at first amused by the lady's desire to fight alongside them, but when they learned firsthand of Rhonwyn's skill with weapons, their laughter turned to respect.

Edward bristled silently at his wife's unorthodox behavior. As her passion for the crusade deepened, it seemed she became less interested in a shared passion between them. Yet his desire for her was growing daily, and he was forced on several occasions to restrain his jealousy at the open admiration for Rhonwyn of the three young knights. It was, he well knew, nothing more than esteem on the part of Sir Fulk, Sir Robert, and Sir Hugo. As for Rhonwyn, the company of the knights meant nothing more to her than that of Oth and Dewi. With warriors about her, she simply seemed back in her element once again. Edward de Beaulieu was beginning to wish that Edward Plantagenet had never come to Haven with his talk of crusades and with a wife who was both willing and able to follow him. At least the prince had legitimate heirs.

Rhonwyn had never been counted a fool. She sensed her husband's unhappiness and knew there was but one way to placate him. She must allow him possession of her body once more. She wondered if she could do it without showing distaste. She no longer worried about becoming enceinte, for Enit's mother had indeed known just what to use to prevent such an event. Each morning her maidservant brought her a draught to drink, but of course Rhonwyn knew she could never be certain of its effects unless there was the chance of her having a child.

She had to admit she found kissing and caressing less unpleasant than at first. Edward might become passionate with her, but he had never been cruel or rough but for that first night. Rhonwyn counted herself a brave woman. She did not fear battle or even death, but she did fear the marital act. It was simply too all-possessing, but she would have to learn to endure it as she endured the pain of a wound. Edward was a good man, and she owed him not just her loyalty but his rights as a husband. If he repudiated her, her father would be shamed, and she could not allow that to happen.

She gathered all her courage, and that evening before she departed the hall she whispered to him, "Perhaps tonight I am brave enough, my lord, to share my bed with you." Then she hurried to her chamber in the south tower. As was her custom since being civilized, she bathed and put on a clean chemise. Then she dismissed Enit. She waited, sitting on the edge of her bed as she brushed her long hair.

Coming through the door connecting their bedchambers, he silently took the pearwood brush and skimmed it down the silken length. He did not understand this change of heart that had suddenly affected her, but he sensed he must be tender with her. His arm slipped about her narrow waist to draw her back against him. He nuzzled at her ear, and all the while he brushed and brushed and brushed the swath of hair. Then to her surprise he ceased and efficiently plaited her tresses into a single thick braid, fastening it with the ribbon he pulled from her chemise.

He drew the garment off her shoulders, and it slid to her waist. Kneeling before her, Edward reached up and began to caress her small breasts. She shivered, but did not stop him. His fingers teased playfully at her nipples, arousing her slowly and carefully. Standing now, he drew her up with him and kissed her, his mouth working tenderly over hers. Here, at least, he knew she was not afraid, for his wife enjoyed kissing, it seemed.

Rhonwyn slipped her arms about his neck, and as her bare flesh pressed against his chest, she realized that he wore no clothes. She had been so intensely focused on her own situation that she hadn't even looked at him. Now she felt him against her. His thighs were hairy as was his chest, its fur tickling her. His lips were intoxicating, and for the briefest moment she allowed herself to become lost in his kisses. Then she felt *it*. His manhood burgeoning against her thigh, and she tensed once more. She knew what was to come next. He would cover her body with his big frame and possess her in a way that terrified her. And this time she could not cry out or struggle against him.

"*Trust me,*" he begged her, feeling her slender body becoming tight once more. He kissed her closed eyelids, the tip of her nose, the corners of her mouth. Pressing her back onto their bed, he murmured into her ear, "There is pleasure in a man and woman's coming together, my lambkin. Let me share that pleasure with you, Rhonwyn. *Please!*"

"I cannot help how I feel," she half sobbed. "Please, Edward, my lord, just do what you will with me."

He rolled away from her, and then propping himself upon his elbow, said angrily, "You are behaving like a whore, damnit! You spread yourself for me, and yet you feel nothing at all. *Why?*"

She was weeping now. "I do not know!" she said.

"Surely ap Gruffydd loved your mam and treated her well," Edward said, struggling to keep his lust under control.

"He did!" Rhonwyn cried. "Their passion for one another is the stuff legends are made of, I know now. They shut everyone and everything out of their lives, even Glynn and me. Their thoughts were only for each other."

"Do you fear to love me, Rhonwyn?" he asked her.

"Aye, I do!" she admitted fiercely. "I don't want to lose myself, Edward. Can you understand that?"

"I love you, yet am I any less the man I was when you met me?" he demanded of her.

"You seem kinder," she whispered. His hand was caressing her quivering belly.

"You make me want to be kinder, Rhonwyn, but that does not mean I have lost control over myself, nor will you if you love me. Ap Gruffydd's passion for Vala was a unique occurrence, an obsession they both felt in the powerful attraction they had for one another. Most marriage unions are not like that, my lambkin."

"What are they like?" she said low. His fingers were tangling themselves in her thick silvery bush. She was fearful, yet found it very exciting, and did not stop him.

"My parents despised one another. They were wed because their lands adjoined each other and my mother was an only child. My father's brother, however, fell in love with his own wife. They were happy together, and they respected one another. They were faithful till death, unlike my parents. My father kept a series of lemans. My mother grew more bitter over it as each day passed, but she would not let him in her bed after she had given him his heir. He died in the bed of one of his other women, and my mother would not wash his body for burial. My aunt came and did it. She was a gentle woman with a forgiving heart. My mother finally died several years ago, of her own bile, I am certain. Only the poor may have the luxury of marrying for love, Rhonwyn, but often those of our class grow to love our mates. I have fallen in love with you, and I feel a fury within me when other men admire you; especially because I know that I cannot have you any more than they can."

"*Oh.*"

"It cannot go on between us like this," he said.

"I know," she replied.

"Certainly you cannot fear what is familiar to you, wife. From this night on we will share a bed. You know I mean you no harm, but I want you, and by the rood, I shall have you!" His fingers caressed the pink slit that hid all her treasures. He pushed past it and began to tease at the tiny nub of flesh within. Soon she was moist, and he slid a finger deep inside her.

Rhonwyn gasped softly at this unexpected onslaught,

but she managed not to cry out. It wasn't really that awful. The digit within her moved slowly. Edward leaned over and began kissing her again, but then without warning his finger was withdrawn and his body was covering hers. Rhonwyn fought with herself not to scream as his weight pressed her down into the feather bed and mattress. His rock-hard manhood slid easily into her this time.

"There, lambkin, is it not better this time?" he murmured into her ear. His breath was hot and moist.

She couldn't speak. She could barely breathe, but she forced herself to embrace him so he should not know her terror, so that he might gain his pleasure from her and leave her be. He moved with increasing rapidity upon her, his manhood driving deep inside her until he collapsed. Finally he rolled away, allowing her to draw a deep breath of relief.

After a time he said sadly, "You had no joy of it, did you, wife?" Taking her hand up, he kissed the fingers individually. "I want you to love me, Rhonwyn, and by God there will come a day when you will!"

"I think I may," she told him, "and I shall never again deny you your rights, my lord Edward. In time I may come to gain happiness from our bodies joining. I am no longer fearful of your kisses or your touching. The rest will come in time, I know it!" I pray it, she thought silently as he gathered her into his arms and fell asleep. What was it, she wondered, that made her resist so natural a happening? If he had been a cruel man, she might have understood herself better. Still, something niggled at the back of her brain and fretted her over this passion between a man and a woman.

He continued to join her each night, and Rhonwyn grew quite used to having him beside her. She was actually beginning to find his bulk comforting. But for the nights when her woman's show of blood was upon her, he used her body regularly. While her fear of him had subsided, she could not seem to gain the same pleasure from their coupling that he did. It saddened them both, but Rhonwyn learned by caressing and kissing Edward, she offered them both some measure of enjoyment. For now it was all she could do but pray for some change that would one day allow her to delight in their coming together.

The winter subsided, and spring came. They had been wed for a year, and in that time had heard nothing from ap Gruffydd. Having received a message from Prince Edward, Edward finally sent for his cousin Rafe de Beaulieu. The crusade was to proceed. At Edward's call both Rafe and his younger sister, Katherine, came to Haven.

Katherine de Beaulieu was much like her brother in features, but in manner she was a quiet and deferential girl. She was eighteen to Rhonwyn's seventeen, and neither married nor betrothed. She did not, according to Rafe, have enough of a dowry.

"Our parents were of modest means. We always thought she would wed Edward," he said boldly.

"I told you I should give Kate a generous dower," Edward said through gritted teeth. "She is worthy of it, and my blood kin besides."

"I am content to remain at Ardley and care for your house, brother," Katherine said, openly embarrassed by her sibling's rudeness. Her fair skin was flushed.

"Will you remain at Haven with your brother while he is here, mistress?" Rhonwyn asked. "Or will you return to your home?" She ignored Rafe.

"My brother feels I should not be left alone at Ardley, cousin Rhonwyn," the girl said. "He has a trusted bailiff who will care for the manor in our absence. With your permission, in your absence I shall take your place over-seeing this household."

"You have my permission, cousin," Rhonwyn replied. "I should appreciate it if you would have young Glynn of Thorley home on his school holidays should he wish it."

"So, your wife is thoughtful of your bastard, Ned," Rafe de Beaulieu said, clapping his cousin on the back heartily. "Which of your wenches did you get the lad on, you sly dog!"

"Why do you put up with his rudeness?" Rhonwyn grumbled later when they had a moment of privacy.

Edward smiled. "Rafe is a good man, wife, but he loves his sister dearly and is jealous seeing you in what he believed would be her place. I know his tongue is sharp ofttimes, but his serfs and his few tenants worship him, for his heart is kind. He will not permit children beneath the age of ten to work in his fields more than three hours a day."

"I do not like him," Rhonwyn said, "although I think his sister a sweet girl with no jealousy or ambition in her heart. Rafe is arrogant and, I believe, sees himself in *your* place."

Edward laughed. "Nay, he does not, but I will agree his way is sometimes rough. But if you fear such a thing, give me a son, and Rafe will be forced to melt away, Rhonwyn, my wild Welsh wife."

She blushed, but she also smiled.

It had been decided between them that Rafe and his sister not know Glynn's true identity. Ap Gruffydd's son was far safer that way, and Edward was not really cer-tain how far he might trust his cousin. Rafe was his heir in the event he died without issue, but now that Edward had a wife and it appeared he had fathered a son on a former leman, perhaps his cousin would be less propri-etary of Haven. He had been very angry and greatly disappointed when Edward told him of the marriage that was to be arranged between him and the Welsh prince's daughter.

But Rafe de Beaulieu had not bothered to look for a husband for his sister now that there was a chance that Edward and his wife might not even return from the crusade they were embarking upon. Such a venture was a dangerous thing, and many who went never lived to see England again. If Rafe became Lord Thorley of Haven, he could make Kate a far better match than Rafe de Beaulieu of Ardley Manor could. By waiting, he increased both their chances. And what if the Welsh wench perished on crusade, but Ned came home? He could wed Kate to their cousin as his parents had always hoped. And if Ned perished and the lady Rhonwyn returned, he would marry himself to the Welsh girl in a trice and thereby gain Haven by both inheritance and marriage to ap Gruffydd's daughter, whose very presence would keep those marauders from his gates. He could sense that his fortune was already made.

Preparations for the departure were well underway as the spring deepened, and the fields grew green with new growth. Provisions had to be gathered and packed for the troop of men Edward had promised the prince. Horses were shod; wagons repaired, made solid, and packed. The women at Thorley had sewn all winter, making waterproof tents for the expedition: a large one for the lord and his wife, smaller ones for the knights and the foot soldiers. Was the grindstone packed? And the bedding and small furniture for the lord's tent? A separate wagon was loaded for the kitchen and its basic utensils.

Glynn was taken by his sister and brother-in-law to Shrewsbury to the abbey school where he had been enrolled. The abbott received them in his private chambers, and fixing Edward de Beaulieu with a stern look, said, "I want the truth of this boy's heritage, my lord, or I will not have him. It has been implied that he is your get, but I see nothing of you in this lad. You may speak to me as you would were we in the confessional, but for the safety of my abbey, I will know the truth."

"He is Glynn ap Llywelyn, my wife's younger brother, Father Abbott" was the immediate reply. "The prince left the boy in my charge months ago, as my wife had never been separated from her sibling, and from his character it is obvious to all that he is not meant to be a soldier. He loves learning and creating music, poetry, and songs. His true identity we have kept carefully to ourselves, for I would not have this boy used as a weapon against any. Even my cousin Rafe does not know who he is. We thought it better that it was believed he was mine."

The abbott nodded, understanding. "Does his father know where he is, my lord?"

"Aye, he does. When he brought the boy to us he left two of his men with the lad. I have sent them back into Wales to tell ap Gruffydd where his son is. He will not object. You have sworn this conversation between us is private, my lord abbott. Now I beg you to keep the secret of my brother-in-law's true identity hidden and to yourself alone. Should there be war between Wales and England while my wife and I are gone on crusade, the lad will disappear from your abbey, and no harm will come to you or your people, I swear it. Though Glynn's father thinks little of his inclinations for learning and his penchant for poetry, he loves the boy. Few if any know of his existence, although it is rumored that the prince of the Welsh has a son."

The abbott was silent a moment, and then he turned to Glynn. "Tell me, my son, are you content to be known as a bastard within these walls? As a nobleman's get, you will, of course, be treated well, but there will be some who may bully you for your supposed birth."

"I am a bastard," Glynn replied quietly, "for our father was not wed to our mother except in their hearts, my lord abbott. Still, I have been treated well my whole life. If there are those who seek to dignify their own paltry existences by denigrating mine, I can but pray for them. I have not a warrior's heart, I fear."

"You are most welcome to the abbey school, Glynn of Thorley," Abbott Boniface said with a small smile. The lad was indeed intelligent, and his quiet reply led the cleric to wonder if the boy might not be a fit candidate for the religious life. Only time would tell. "Bid your sister and brother-in-law farewell, my son," he said.

Glynn shook Edward's hand. "Thank you," he said simply. "I will pray for your success and speedy return, my lord."

"You may visit Haven whenever there is a holiday and you wish to go home. Rafe and Katherine will be your family until we return," Edward replied, giving the lad a quick hug and ruffling his dark hair.

Glynn turned to his sister. There were tears in Rhonwyn's eyes, and her lip was trembling with emotion. "Do not dare weep, sister," he scolded her gently, for the first time in their lives taking the lead. "This is what I want, and to be with your husband in the service of God is what you want." Glynn put his arms about Rhonwyn and hugged her.

She drew away from him, taking his face in her hands. When had he gotten so tall, so big? Was that a bit of beard starting to grow on his chin? She kissed him on both of his cheeks. "When I return you will be a man," she lamented.

"I should be a man eventually in any case," he told her

with a small smile, gently touching her cheek with his knuckles.

"You will study hard and obey the brothers," she said, suddenly stern with him. Then she lowered her voice. "If there is trouble, Oth and Dewi will come for you. Go with them without hesitation, Glynn. Promise me that, little brother."

"I promise," he answered her. He kissed her quickly on the lips and the forehead. "Go with God, Rhonwyn uerch Llywelyn, and return safely to us when you can." Then he turned and followed the brother who had come to escort him from the lord abbott's chambers.

Rhonwyn immediately burst into tears, flinging herself into Edward's arms and sobbing piteously.

"They have hardly been separated in all their lifetime," Edward explained to the abbott.

"It is good to see such devotion between a brother and sister," the abbott noted. Then he said to Rhonwyn, whose sobs were now sniffles, "We will take good care of your brother, my lady. I swear it."

"Th-thank you, m-my lord abbott," Rhonwyn managed to say.

They left the abbey and returned almost immediately to Haven where their party was ready to depart for the coast.

Katherine and her brother bid them adieu. "I shall pray every day for your safety and your success," she said softly. "Godspeed, cousins!" There were tears in her soft blue eyes, and Rhonwyn swallowed her jealousy when she thought Kate's gaze lingered a fraction of a second too long upon Edward.

"My husband and I thank you, dear Kate. We shall be grateful for your prayers," she returned.

Their train moved off down the castle hill onto the local road that would lead them to a wider and larger main road.

"What a woman she is," Rafe said softly. "The fates have played us both a nasty jest, little sister. You with your gentle ways would be a far better mate for Edward; and Rhonwyn with her fiery ways would find herself happier with me for a husband."

"Rafe!" Kate was shocked to hear him voice such sentiments. "Their union is the king's will," she said chidingly.

He laughed softly. "Do not scold me, Kate, for wanting what I shall never have. I firmly believe that they will both return one day."

The English army was to gather at Dover, and from there go on to Bordeaux. Their journey would be by both land and water. Barges took them from Haven down the Severn to Gloucester. They moved overland from there, skirting about the city of London and heading for their first destination at Dover. Arriving there in mid-May, they discovered that Prince Edward was not ready to go. Those already in Dover would leave England on one of the advance vessels for France and travel onward across the countryside for Aigues-Mortes on the Mediterranean Sea, meeting up with the French there. Prince Edward and his train would follow as quickly as possible.

"My wife was to be a part of the princess Eleanor's train," Edward told the port official in charge.

"She'll join the princess when Prince Edward reaches Aigues-Mortes" was the reply. "If she's going, she'll have to travel with you for now, my lord," the port official said. Then his manner softened. "There's another lady traveling on the ship I'm assigning to you, my lady. You'll share a tiny cabin and be company for each other. Her husband, too, is among the king's knights."

"My husband and I cannot be together?" Rhonwyn was distressed.

"The men will have to find places to sleep on the deck, my lady. You are going to war against the infidel, not on a honeymoon voyage," the port official said sharply.

"You will address me courteously, sir," Rhonwyn said, an equally sharp edge to her voice. "I am the daughter of the Welsh prince, not some country squire's wife."

"Your pardon, my lady," the official quickly replied. "With the prince being delayed, I am at my wit's end trying to make everything come out correctly."

Rhonwyn nodded regally at him, and her husband managed to suppress his amusement.

The vessel aboard which they sailed from Dover was a large one. All their men-at-arms and the three knights, their horses, and their equipment was upon it, as was a smaller party from Oxford. They sailed in a season of good weather, but were at sea for ten days before reaching Bordeaux. The boredom that had enveloped them aboard ship evaporated as they now headed south overland for France's single Mediterranean port of Aigues-Mortes. As they traveled, the road grew more and more crowded with noblemen, knights, and men-at-arms all bound for the same destination—and the crusade.

It was almost the end of June when they reached Aigues-Mortes. There they learned that Prince Edward had not left England yet. The English were not certain what they should do. The French king, frail, his eyes aglow with the fire of a zealot, came to speak with them all.

"We are assured," he said, "that your prince will join us, if not here, then in the Holy Land. He has sent word that those of you already here should follow me, and he will meet us as soon as he can. There are ships aplenty for you all. We are happy to have been chosen for so worthy a crusade on behalf of our dear lord Jesus Christ."

When King Louis had left them, the English began to talk among themselves. Some of them were angry, and others were reticent about following in the French king's wake without their own prince.

" 'Tis typical of Edward Longshanks to leave us here at the mercy of the French," one knight grumbled. "He was so damned insistent that we be ready on time, and then 'tis he who is still in England."

"He will come," another man said. "I have heard it was difficult getting money out of the king for this venture. King Henry did not want his son to go, but the queen finally prevailed upon him, saying that enough good men were joining with the prince that it would be churlish if he did not come now, having already promised."

"And just where did you obtain your information?" the first knight asked, disbelieving.

"The messenger from our king who came to King Louis" was the reply. "A friendly mug or two of ale always loosens a good man's tongue, and this fellow had ridden hard to bring his message to the French from our Henry."

"What of the women with us?" came the question.

Now Edward de Beaulieu spoke up. "They must come as they had planned," he said. "We can hardly leave them here in France at the mercy of strangers. Besides, if the prince comes straight through from England, as I believe he will, he will not stop at Aigues-Mortes, and then our ladies would be stranded. We must see the French make accommodation for them."

"Aye."

"Aye."

"Aye" came the agreement of the men gathered together.

The French were approached. There were only six English noblewomen and their maidservants in the group. The

French queen graciously invited them to travel to Carthage upon her vessel where they would be comfortable.

"After all," she reasoned to her husband, "these ladies were to travel in the train of my nephew's wife. We cannot simply cast them away. They are very brave, Louis, to have come with their husbands for Christ's sake. Until Edward and his wife arrive we must have a care for them."

The Eighth Crusade departed Aigues-Mortes on the first of July in the year twelve-seventy. The voyage to Carthage took them seventeen days and was uneventful but for their departure. Aigues-Mortes was France's only toehold on the Mediterranean, and it was a poor harbor. Separated from direct access to the sea by enormous sand dunes and girded about by large lagoons, the ships had to navigate through continuous and unceasing channels before reaching the open sea. It took a full day.

As they moved across the Mediterranean it grew increasingly warmer. Neither the English nor the French were used to such heat. The crusaders' encampment in Carthage was set up with its rows of tents, the great tent in the center of the camp belonging to the French king. There were cook tents for the soldiers and a hospital tent. Water was available but not in great supply, as some of the wells outside of the city of Carthage had obviously been deliberately poisoned. Sickness began to break out within the encampment despite the best efforts of the physicians to prevent it. Cesspits were dug for the epidemic of loose bowels that affected the men. They were quickly filled and covered even as new pits were being opened.

King Louis grew ill. He was not a young man, and the heat was taking its toll on him. Many around him were ill, including several of the English knights. When Edward de Beaulieu grew sick, Rhonwyn was at first overcome with fear, but then she rallied. The sickness, she suspected, came from the filth in the camp. She insisted on having their tent moved to the very edge of the encampment. The dysentery that affected him made his bowels run black and left him weak. Rhonwyn insisted the water her husband drank be boiled with three quinces, then strained through a clean cloth. Quinces were excellent for stopping dysentery, Rhonwyn knew. She then mashed the pulp of the stewed fruit with very sweet dates and fed it to him. The tent she kept scrupulously clean, emptying the night jar and cleaning it with vinegar and boiling water each time he used it. She recommended this manner of care to the French queen, but the king's physician laughed and said that Rhonwyn was old-fashioned. When the evil humors drained from the king, he would be well, and the crusade would continue as God had planned it.

Edward de Beaulieu had truly thought he was going to die, but then his wife's treatment began to work. His bowels stopped running, and his belly calmed. "Are you a witch?" he teased her.

"'Tis but practical medicine I was taught at Mercy Abbey," she said with a smile, coming to sit on the edge of the camp bed where he now lay. Leaning down, she took a sea sponge from the basin of warm water at her feet and began to bathe him gently. The infirmarian at the abbey had always said that dirt was nasty and attracted evil humors no matter what the priests said about cleanliness being a vanity.

"The water smells like you," he told her.

"I put a drop of my oil in it," she replied, sweeping the sponge over his broad chest. She worked swiftly for she did not want him to get a chill, if such a thing was possible in this heat. When she had bathed every bit of him and tucked him back beneath the coverlet, she emptied the basin and then came to sit by him again.

"Lay with me," he said, pulling her into his arms. He stroked her fair hair with his big hand. He was truly feeling better and was grateful for her kindness. In his illness he had thought often of his cousin Katherine and wished that Rhonwyn would be more like her. He felt no guilt for the secret reflection. Women should be like Katherine—who was nurturing and kind. It was true that the two young women had lived different lives, but still, Rhonwyn's sojourn at Mercy Abbey should have taught her that women must subject themselves to their husbands. Her recent behavior and nursing skills had given him reason to hope that perhaps Rhonwyn was becoming more the woman he desired and needed. He smiled down gently on her.

She could feel his heart beating beneath her ear as her head lay upon his chest. *I love him,* she thought suddenly. The mere idea of losing him makes me feel as if my heart would crack open. She had to tell him!

Looking up at him, she said, "Edward, I love you. I know I am not the most affectionate of women, but *I do love you.* If I should lose you, I would die, my lord. *I would!*" And suddenly tears were rolling down her pale cheeks, and she could not stifle them.

His arms closed back about her, and he replied, "Oh, Rhonwyn, my wild and sweet Welsh wife, do you not know how long I have waited and yearned to hear you say those words? Nay, lambkin, you cannot imagine. When I am well, we will consider the rest, but for now just knowing you love me renews my hope, and I already feel new strength pouring through my veins. I will get well all the quicker for knowing you care." He kissed the tears from her cheeks. "What a lass you are." And he smiled tenderly at her. She was indeed changing. He would get her with child as soon as his full strength returned, and then send her home with his heir in her belly. She would leave him without protest for by then she would fully understand her wifely duty to him. He smiled, well pleased, and kissed her lips softly.

King Louis grew worse with his illness. Dysentery and plague were rife among the crusaders. Worse, the infidels were sending out raiding parties to harass the invaders. The king's brother, Charles of Anjou, who was the king of Naples and Sicily, had been the one to convince his sibling that coming to Carthage and converting the emir would gain him favor with the pope. As the king grew weaker, Charles of Anjou began to talk of a truce. Finally, on the twenty-fifth day of August, King Louis IX died of his illness.

Several days later Prince Edward finally arrived from England to find his uncle already prepared for burial and the long trip home to France. Charles of Anjou was in the midst of negotiating a truce with the infidel, much to Prince Edward's fury.

"You are a traitor to all of Christendom!" he roared at the Frenchman. "I will not be party to such treachery! Jerusalem must be freed from the infidel, and instead, you cowardly dog, you seek to make a truce with our enemy! Faugh! You sicken me, my lord! I cannot be in your presence without wanting to puke!"

"You are free to pursue your crusade, my lord," Charles of Anjou said silkily. "With my brother dead, I must think of my own kingdom of Sicily. It is not as distant from the infidel as is your England."

Prince Edward left the royal tent and called for the English knights to meet with him. He told them what had happened and of his disgust with the French. "I am going on to Acre, and from there I will mount an expedition to take Jerusalem back from the infidel. Are you with me, my lords?" He raised his sword. "To the glory of God and of England!" he cried.

"For God and for England!" the English replied with one voice.

Prince Edward came to the tent of Edward de Beaulieu, smiling at Rhonwyn as he entered. "I am told, lady, that your lord improved each day, thanks to your tender care. Would that my aunt had heeded your simple advice, my uncle, King Louis, would be alive today." He waved his hand at Edward, who was struggling to arise. "Nay, my lord, lie back. I can see you are yet in a weakened condition." He sat on the single chair in the tent that Rhonwyn had fetched for him, and explained the situation. "If you feel you cannot continue on, my lord, you are free to return home with our blessing and our thanks."

"I will go on with you, my lord," Edward said. "Why did we come this far, if not to free Jerusalem? When do you leave?"

"It will take ten days or more to remount the expedition," the prince said. "Do you think you can travel by then?"

"Aye, my lord, I will be ready!" Edward said enthusiastically.

Rhonwyn bit her lip in vexation, but remained silent.

The prince arose. "I thank you, my lord, for your loyalty. I do not, as you well know, forget my friends, even as I remember my enemies." He turned to Rhonwyn. "My wife will be happy to receive you when you are able to leave your lord, lady," he told her, and then Prince Edward turned and departed the tent.

"You are not well enough to continue on," Rhonwyn said.

"I will be," he vowed.

"In ten days' time?" she scoffed.

"I have to be," he insisted. "Besides, the prince is overly

optimistic. It will take at least a fortnight before he is ready to depart, and he will not be traveling at a great pace, as he has his wife and her ladies with him. You must go and see the lady Eleanor. Enit will look after me while you are gone, lambkin."

"If I do not believe you well enough to travel, my lord, I shall say so, and let none stop me," Rhonwyn told her husband.

He chuckled. "Such a fierce little Welsh wife, she is," he teased her. "I promise to behave, lady, if you will make me well in time to go. How can we not follow in the prince's wake? Now go and pay your respects to his wife, Rhonwyn." He waved her off.

"I will see to him, lady," Enit promised.

Rhonwyn quickly bathed her face and hands. She smoothed her hair beneath its sheer veil, brushed an imaginary wrinkle from her gown, and hurried from their quarters to the royal English tent across the encampment. Having given her name and business to the guard, she was shortly admitted. She curtsied to Princess Eleanor.

"How nice to see you, Rhonwyn de Beaulieu," the prince's wife said. "Come, sit by my side and tell me of your good lord, whom I am told is ill. He recovers?"

"Aye, lady," Rhonwyn replied, and then she told the princess of their adventures to date. "I fear," she concluded, "that my lord will not be well enough to travel, but he insists otherwise."

"Men!" the lady Eleanor sympathized. "They all think they are indestructible." Then she laughed. "Go back to your good lord and make him well so he may have his wish. Then you will come and serve me as we make our way to the kingdom and city of Acre." She smiled warmly at Rhonwyn. "What stories we shall have to tell our grandchildren, lady."

"First I must have a child," Rhonwyn replied.

"You are not yet a mother?" The lady Eleanor's voice was filled with compassion. "We must make a special devotion to Our Lady's mother, Saint Anne. I have told you that she will not fail you. When you come to serve me we shall pray together."

Rhonwyn returned to her tent. She was suddenly filled with energy. "Find Sir Fulk," she told Enit. "I need to practice my sword-play." She turned to her husband. "Nursing you is hard work, my lord, but I feel the sudden need of exercise. Will you let me go for a little more time?"

He nodded, feeling generous, although her request was not pleasing to him. Still, he knew he couldn't expect her to change entirely overnight. A little bit of horseplay with Fulk could do no harm, and her new attitude was welcome to him. He then asked her, "What did the lady Eleanor say?"

"That men thought they were indestructible," she replied with a chuckle. "She bade me make you well enough to travel, and so I have no other choice, but first I will work off some of this surfeit of energy that I suddenly seem to have." She turned her back to him so he might fasten her padded vest.

"Wear your mail shirt," he instructed.

" 'Tis too hot," she complained.

"Nonetheless wear it, lady. Even in practice you fight fiercely and rouse the blood of your opponent. I do not want you harmed, lambkin." Nor did he want her ability to bear him children impaired by injury.

Her arming doublet secure, Rhonwyn pulled on her chausses over her legs, then her hauberk with its articulated shoulder plates and her mail coif. "I will be boiled alive in these things," she grumbled.

" 'Tis the price we warriors pay," he teased her. "Practice

out of the direct sun and not for too long. If you get sick, who will I have to so tenderly nurse me, my lambkin?"

"Fool," she mocked him. "You are only jealous that I get to play with my sword, and you cannot."

"I should prefer it if you played with *my sword*," he said with a wicked smile.

Rhonwyn blushed to the roots of her pale hair. *"Edward!"*

He grinned mischievously. "Come and give us a kiss, lambkin."

"You don't deserve one, saying such naughty things. I shall leave you to think on your sins, my lord, and perhaps when I return, I shall give you a kiss if you are truly penitent and deserve it." Then she picked up her weapon and ran from their tent.

He watched her go, a smile upon his handsome face. He would certainly not have believed that going on crusade with his wife would have brought them closer, but it had. Perhaps this was God's blessing upon them both for their faithfulness. For the first time in the months they had been wed, he was beginning to have hope.

Chapter Eight

Rhonwyn practiced her swordplay with Sir Fulk beneath an open awning on the shady side of the camp. Those who passed by and saw her assumed that the two knights were both men, for Rhonwyn's long hair was hidden beneath her mail coif. The high summer's heat made it difficult to drill for long periods of time without cessations for rest and water in between the exercises. It was during one of those short respites that the alarm rang out in the camp.

"Quick, lady, I must take you back to your tent," Sir Fulk said nervously.

"Nay," Rhonwyn responded, "this is our chance to meet the infidel in battle, Fulk! With the French negotiating a truce, when will we have another chance?"

"But when we reach Acre, we will battle for Jerusalem, lady. There will be time then," Fulk responded hopefully.

"Faugh! We cannot be certain of that," Rhonwyn said. "Neither of us has bloodied our swords yet, and you know had not my lord been ill, we would have by now! Come on! To horse, Fulk! To horse!" Then she ran off toward the pen where the animals were tethered.

For a moment Fulk hesitated. He knew that he ought to go to the tent and tell Edward de Beaulieu, but if he did, the skirmish would likely be over and done with before he even had time to find his own mount. The infidels harassed the crusaders several times daily, but they never remained long enough to engage them in serious battle. His decision made, Sir Fulk ran after Rhonwyn. It was not fair that she have all the fun.

At the horse pens, his squire had already saddled both her horse and his. Mounted, they charged through the maze of tents to where they could hear the sounds of action. Sir Fulk had to admit that his lady was absolutely fearless. She charged eagerly into the fray with a fierce war cry, her sword slashing right and left as she attacked her opponents.

It was so exhilarating, Rhonwyn thought as she fought the enemy. She had never before known such incredible excitement. There was a faint red mist before her eyes, and while she knew she felt fear, she was not afraid. Her skills would see her through, for she knew she was a more than competent warrior. She could almost hear Oth in her ear, directing her every move as if he had been right by her side. Her foes gave way before her, and she almost laughed aloud with her elation. Around her the English and the French seemed energized by her ferocity, and the infidels were suddenly aware of a new attitude in the enemy. This was no mere skirmish. For the first time this was a real battle. Rhonwyn could hear Fulk beside her, for he had a tendency to hum beneath his breath when he fought. Her sword plunged into softness, and she focused to see the shocked look on her victim's face as he fell from his horse to die on the sand beneath Hardd's hooves. A howl went up from the infidels. The casualty had obviously been someone of import.

She was overwhelmed with sudden surprise. *She had killed a man!* This was no mock battle. This was bloody reality, and the cries of the wounded and dying assailed her ears now as they had not before. Her sword arm fell, and in that moment Rhonwyn found herself surrounded by black-bearded infidels. Her instinct for survival rose up, and she attempted to fight her way out. Sir Fulk howled a battle cry as he came to her aid.

Rhonwyn was not certain how it happened, but she and her companion were completely cut off from the other crusaders. The infidels seemed intent on moving them away from any and all aid. One reached out and yanked the reins from her gauntleted hand. Then the troop galloped off, Rhonwyn in their midst, Sir Fulk in wild pursuit. Even in possession of her sword there was no chance to defend herself. She considered slashing the reins free from her captor, but she was so tightly wedged in the middle of them there was no room to fight her way out. She had no choice but to go along.

It had been late afternoon when the battle had begun. But now it was dark. The terrain was rough, and Rhonwyn noted their direction was toward a range of mountains in the near distance. When they finally came to a halt, the infidels pulled her from her horse and took her weapon. Sir Fulk was hauled from his mount and disarmed as well. Pushed to the ground, they were told by one of the infidels, "Sit," in hard, rough tones as he pointed to a spot near some rocks.

"Say nothing," Sir Fulk whispered to her.

Rhonwyn nodded. She knew as well as her companion that their captors had no idea she was a woman. They were given a small round flat bread and a cup of brackish water to share between them. When they had eaten and sipped the water, reserving a bit for later, Fulk spoke once again.

"Sleep. I will take the first watch, lady."

Rhonwyn nodded and closed her eyes, but sleep was not easy. They had to escape before much longer. As it was they were going to be hard-pressed to find their way back to the crusaders' encampment. *And Edward.* He was going to be absolutely furious with her. She would be fortunate if he didn't send her back to England immediately. She knew now that Fulk's had been the wiser path. She should have let him escort her back to her tent when the sounds of action had come to their ears.

What would happen if the infidels discovered she was a woman? She shuddered to even contemplate. Rhonwyn felt tears welling up behind her closed eyelids, and she struggled to force them back. If she allowed herself to give in to her fears, she could not think, and she had to think if she were to come up with a plan of escape. Sir Fulk was a good fighter, but he had no skill for tactics. Then to her surprise she actually dozed, but for how long she didn't know. Fulk was shaking her awake.

" We are moving on, lady," he said softly.

"It is night," she whispered back.

"There is a moon, and it is cooler to travel at night," he replied. "One of them speaks the Norman tongue. Get on your horse before any of them gets too close to you."

"We must escape," she said desperately.

"How?" His tone was bleak.

Rhonwyn mounted her horse, sitting despairingly as her wrists, still covered by her gauntlets, were lashed together to her saddle's pommel. She glanced over to Sir Fulk to find he had also been bound in the same manner. They rode on through the night, stopping only when the sun was high in the heavens. Again they were fed flat bread and a cup of water between them and told to sit beneath a rock overhang that sheltered them from the burning sun. Below them Rhonwyn could see the plain and the sea, but nowhere did she glimpse the city of Carthage or the crusaders' encampment.

"What will happen to us?" Rhonwyn murmured low to Sir Fulk.

"The one who speaks our tongue says knights are frequently ransomed, lady," he replied. "They are impressed with your fighting skills and say they are taking you to their leader in hopes he may convert you to Islam and to their side. They say you are too great a warrior, and none could pay the price of your ransom."

"Jesu!" Rhonwyn swore softly. She didn't dare ask what would happen if, or when, they learned she was a woman.

Sir Fulk knew what she was thinking, but there was nothing he could say that would be of comfort to her. If he had known this was going to happen, he would have killed her himself rather than let her end up in some infidel's harem, which was where she was certain to be taken. He had heard enough talk around the camp to know that fair-haired women were considered a great prize among the infidels. "We had best rest, lady," he said low. "We are sure to ride again once night falls and the moon rises."

Rhonwyn nodded. If she could retain the secret of her identity, there was just the slightest chance she might be returned to where she belonged, and Sir Fulk, too. She glanced a moment at her companion. He was just twenty, a stocky man of medium height with sandy hair and warm brown eyes. His family lived across the Severn from Haven. Edward had known Sir Fulk his whole life. He had been very brave to follow after her, but perhaps it might have been better if he had returned to the camp to raise the alarm that she had been captured. Sir Fulk had followed his instincts and not his head, but then so, too, had she, Rhonwyn thought ruefully.

They rode the nights through, resting in the daytime. The infidels gave her and Fulk water only once during their travel. At the end of their day she got more water, but even so she did not get enough to satisfy her thirst. Her thoughts were constantly of Edward. Was he all right? Would he ever forgive her this folly?

At the completion of their fourth night of travel they came through a narrow pass with sheer rock-lined walls to a green and verdant valley. Before them was a blue lake, and at the far end of the lake lay a small and gleaming white city. The infidel who spoke their tongue was riding next to them.

"Cinnebar," he said, and nothing more.

They rode onward, conscious now of other paths all leading to a single wide paved road. They passed a heavily ladened camel caravan as they went. A farmer and his son drove a large herd of goats ahead of them. A smaller caravan came behind them, the sweet-smelling spices it carried perfuming the air. It was all so fascinating that for a brief time Rhonwyn's fears left her, and she looked about her with interest. She would have quite a tale to tell Edward and the children they would have one day.

The traffic into Cinnebar now waited patiently at the city's gates for the portals to be opened this morning. As the sun rose over the eastern hills a great creaking and groaning was heard as the ironbound double doors were slowly pulled open to admit the travelers and commerce that stood outside. Identities were carefully checked, but their armed and mounted party was quickly waved through. The city's streets were narrow and twisting. They appeared to be riding upward, and at last they came out into a wide square before a great marble palace. Again their identities were perused at the entry, and then they were motioned inside. They rode into a small courtyard. The ground beneath their horses' hooves were of perfectly matched squares of black-and-white marble. The captives were aided in dismounting, their bonds slashed free.

The Norman-speaking infidel came to their side. "This is the palace of Rashid al Ahmet, the mighty caliph of Cinnebar, may Allah bless the names of his antecedents and his descendants in equal measure. Your fate is in his hands, but he will be eager to learn of the great Christian warrior, the slayer of his brother, who was considered the finest man-at-arms in all of Cinnebar. Come! Follow me!"

Rhonwyn had blanched at the infidel's words, and Sir Fulk's mouth fell open in surprise. They looked at each other in desperation, and then followed their guide into the palace. Once inside, they were brought into a small, attractive chamber. Water was brought so they might wash the dust of the road from their face and their hands. Plates of newly baked flat bread, sliced fruits, and a hot clear beverage smelling of mint were carried in to them, and then they were left alone for the first time since their capture.

"Do not eat," Sir Fulk advised her. "It could be poisoned."

Rhonwyn picked up a curved slice of melon and began to chew it eagerly. "If it is, I will die a quicker death than the one I face for having slain the brother of this caliph. We might as well eat, Fulk. Besides, I don't believe the food is tainted. They have not kept us alive this long to poison us now." She picked up a piece of flat bread and began to chew it. It was warm from the oven and delicious. The beverage, too, was excellent, sweet and aromatic. She had never had anything like it before.

Her companion considered her words, and then began to eat as well. When they had finished, they washed their hands and face in the silver basin again, and then seated themselves to wait. The chamber was very quiet. Fulk considered how he was going to protect Rhonwyn. When it was discovered that she was a female, and she most certainly would be exposed very soon, he truly feared what was going to happen to her. And without a weapon he was utterly helpless to aid her. Had he a weapon, he should slay her so that she would not have to suffer the indignity of being ravaged by her captors. Perhaps, however, they would be so outraged at a woman having killed the caliph's brother, they would simply and quickly behead her. He prayed silently for such a merciful outcome.

The door to their chamber opened without warning, and the Norman-speaking infidel was there. "Come," he said. "The caliph is giving his weekly morning audience."

They arose and followed after him through the cool marble corridors of the palace. Two ebony-faced guards stood on either side of a pair of tall, wide bronze doors. They wore cloth of gold balloon pants, gold medallions shaped like hunting leopards hung from gold chains around their necks and onto their chests, and silver tipped spears carved from pure onyx were clasped in their hands. Without a word they swung open the doors, and the trio walked through into the caliph's audience chamber.

The room was square. The pillars that rimmed it were of green-and-white marble decorated at the bottom and top with carved gold bands. The floors were white marble covered in thick blue carpets. Tall censers shaped like lilies burned aloes, and polished wood torches burned fragrant oil. At the far end of the room Rhonwyn saw a low carpeted dais upon which a man sat cross-legged. She could tell he was tall and slender with a long face and nose. He wore a short, well-barbered black beard about his mouth and chin. His beringed hands, which he seemed to use to punctuate his speech, were elegant and slim. He was dressed in a simple white robe, and upon his head was a small turban.

The room was filled with men. The caliph was obviously hearing grievances and mediating disputes of one kind or another. The captives remained at the rear of the audience chamber for some time and then finally were beckoned forward. The Norman-speaking infidel brought them to stand before the caliph's throne.

"Kneel, dogs," he hissed at them, shoving at Fulk.

"We kneel only to God and our king," Rhonwyn said defiantly.

The Norman-speaking infidel merely glanced to the side, and at once there were guards forcing them to their knees before the caliph.

Their captor began speaking, but almost at once the caliph held up his hand. "Speak in their Frankish tongue so they may understand what it is you say, Farouk, and defend themselves, if indeed they can."

"Yes, my lord" came the reply.

"Which one of them killed Prince Abdallah?" the caliph demanded.

"That one," Farouk said, pointing to Rhonwyn, who knelt, her head bowed, as she strove to conceal her identity.

The caliph arose quickly and descended the dais. He stood before the kneeling knights. Suddenly his nostrils twitched quite visibly. He looked hard at the two kneeling figures. He sniffed softly once, twice. Then with a swift motion he reached out and pulled Rhonwyn's mail coif from her head. Yanking her to her feet, he stared in surprise a moment before he burst out laughing, even as her long gilt hair tumbled from the top of her head and spilled down her back. *"A woman!"* He roared with laughter. "A woman has killed that arrogant braggart who was my half brother? *This is the fiercest knight in all of Christendom, Farouk?* You make a jest, do you not?" His admiring gaze took in her fair beauty.

"My lord! Surely this is sorcery! It was a mounted and fierce knight who killed your brother and whom we took captive. I swear it to you, my lord caliph! *I swear it!*" Farouk's face was filled with fear.

"Take your hands off me, infidel!" Rhonwyn snapped, pulling away from the caliph. "Your cowering dog does not lie. I killed your brother. He was a careless swordsman and deserved to die for being so reckless in the heat of battle."

"Ah," the caliph breathed slowly, "you are right, woman. Abdallah was a feckless warrior. So much so that he could be killed by a mere female. Are you as ferocious in your lord's arms as you are on the battlefield? We shall see, you and I." He prowled about her, reaching out to take a handful of her hair in his fist, raising it to his nostrils. "This is what I smelled. Your hair is perfumed, woman. The fragrance suits you. I have never smelled anything like it before." Releasing his hold on her hair, he caught her face with his thumb and his forefinger, holding it in an iron grip. "You have skin the unsullied white of the moon, and your hair is like pure golden gilt. You are beautiful, but then you must know it. The emeralds you have for eyes are fiery with your anger, I can see. I shall call you Noor, which means *light*. I am Rashid al Ahmet, the caliph of Cinnebar, and you shall be the jewel of my harem, Noor." He turned from her and spoke to a tall, distinguished black man. "Take her to the women's quarters, Baba Haroun. See she is properly bathed and well rested. Then bring her to me at moonrise. Find someone within the harem to act as her translator until she can learn our language."

"Wait, my lord," Rhonwyn said. "What is to happen to my companion?"

"Is he your lover?" the caliph asked her.

"Of course not!" she replied indignantly. "He is one of my husband's knights. His name is Sir Fulk Anthony."

"Since he is not your lover I will be merciful and not kill him. I shall ransom him, or if I cannot, then I shall sell him into slavery," the caliph responded. He was disappointed she was not a virgin, but then he hadn't really expected someone as beautiful as Noor would be. Still, these Frankish women were usually backward in the arts of love. He would enjoy teaching her, and there would be no difficulty with virginal fears, only her Christian virtue, which he would eventually overcome.

The tall black man, Baba Haroun, came to fetch her. "Fulk, go with God," she cried out to him.

"And you also, my lady Rhonwyn!" he called as he was taken away in the opposite direction by two guards.

Rhonwyn shook the man's hand off her arm and glared at him indignantly. "I will follow you," she said. "You do not have to drag me like some shivering creature."

Baba Haroun stared at her angrily, but then the caliph spoke to him, and he chortled, nodding.

"He does not speak your Frankish tongue, Noor. I have told him you are to be respected and treated gently," Rashid al Ahmet explained. "He is not used to women disobeying him." The caliph smiled, then turned away to conduct the next business on his daily calendar.

She was dismissed, and so having no other choice, she turned and followed the tall man from the audience chamber. He led her across an open courtyard into another section of the palace. The guards at the entry stiffened to attention as they passed. Down a dimly lit and scented corridor she followed until finally they came through a gilded archway into a large room with a bubbling fountain. The room was filled with chattering women of all hues. Seeing Baba Haroun, they grew quickly silent. He smiled a superior smile at Rhonwyn as if to say, You see, I am a person of some importance.

"Where is the woman Nilak?" he demanded loudly in Arabic.

A small dignified female came from a corner where she

had been seated. "Yes, my lord Haroun? How may I serve you?"

"Do you still have command of your Frankish tongue?" he demanded roughly of her.

"I do," Nilak said politely.

"Then this woman is now in your charge by order of our most worthy master, the caliph Rashid al Ahmet, may his name be blessed. She is to be bathed and well rested, for he desires her presence at moonrise. Tell her, and also inform her that bad behavior and disobedience will be punished by a beating on the soles of her feet until she cannot walk, but must crawl." He then shoved Rhonwyn toward Nilak.

The older woman caught the girl and said quickly in Norman, "Do not retaliate, child. The caliph's chief eunuch is a man who holds grudges. If you shame him before the other women, he will never forgive you, and no one, not even the caliph, will be able to protect you from his vengeance."

Rhonwyn swallowed down her anger and nodded at Nilak.

"Good," Nilak said softly. "Now, come with me and we will talk. You will tell me who you are, and I will answer all the questions I see bubbling upon your lips." She took the younger woman by the hand and led her off into a quiet corner, speaking a few quick words to a passing slave girl as they went. "I have told her to bring us mint tea and gazelle-horn pastries," she explained to Rhonwyn. "Sit, child."

"Who are you," Rhonwyn asked her, "and how do you know the tongue of the Normans?"

"I am called Nilak. It means *Lilac flower* in the Arabic tongue. My history is a simple one. My father was a merchant in Provence. The Moors raided the town in which I lived, and I was captured and sold into slavery. I was

twelve then. I have now seen forty-two springs. I was
brought to Cinnebar with a princess who was given to
this caliph's father as a gift. She died giving birth to a
daughter, the caliph's half sister. I raised the child until
she was given in marriage. I am too old now to sell off,
and so I am allowed to remain, being useful where I can
be. Baba Haroun is glad to have me as a translator when
girls speaking the Frankish tongue are brought here, as
they occasionally are. Now tell me, child, who are you,
and how came you here?"

Rhonwyn explained her adventures to the open-
mouthed woman.

"*You* killed Prince Abdallah?" Nilak said, awed.

"I did not know who he was," Rhonwyn replied. "He
was just an enemy in battle." She shrugged, then asked,
"Tell me about this Baba Haroun? Who is he?"

"The chief eunuch of the caliph's harem, child," Nilak
responded.

"I don't know what a eunuch is, nor a harem," Rhonwyn said.

"A harem is where the caliph's women—his wives, his
concubines, his sisters, and other assorted female relations—live. No real man but the caliph is allowed in the
women's quarters. A eunuch is a male who has been cas-
trated so he may not function as a real man would," Nilak explained. "Castration is usually done when young.
All men within these quarters—the servants, the slaves,
the guards—are eunuchs."

"And this Baba Haroun is in charge of the caliph's
harem?"

"Yes, my child, he is," Nilak answered her. "Obey
him, give him public respect and esteem, and you can
make him your friend. If you are to succeed here, you
will need his good will. Without it you are doomed to
obscurity, and obscurity is a lonely place."

"I do not intend to remain here," Rhonwyn said. "I shall escape and return to the coast where the crusaders are preparing to move on to Acre. My husband must be very worried and very angry by now."

Nilak's face became sympathetic. It was frequently this way with captives. They always wanted to flee, and that, of course, was not possible. "You cannot escape, my child," she began patiently. "It is very unlikely that you will ever again see the world outside this place except when you are taken for your burial. Besides, would your husband now receive you back into his heart, his house, and his good graces after you have been captured by the infidels? You are so fortunate, my child. You might have been raped and killed, but instead you have been brought into paradise on earth, for that is what Cinnebar is. The caliph is a strong ruler and a good man. If you can win his favor, if you bear him a son, your fortune is made. What better fate is there for a woman in this world?"

"But I have a husband," Rhonwyn repeated. For the first time in her life she was beginning to be frightened. Why had Fulk prevented her from escaping when they had the chance? All they had had to do was get back to the coastline and follow it to Carthage. She had seen the walls surrounding this palace. They were high and thick, and now she was trapped behind them. Forever, according to Nilak. It was a terrifying thought, and Rhonwyn began to shake with sudden fear.

Seeing it, Nilak put her arms about the girl. "There, child, it is all right. You will not be harmed, I promise you. Here, drink this," she said, offering Rhonwyn a small cup of the steaming fragrant beverage she had earlier imbibed. "Mint tea is very good for the nerves." She held the cup to Rhonwyn's lips, coaxing her gently. Then she turned to the slave girl who had brought the tea. "Go to Baba Haroun and tell him the girl is succumbing to shock. I will need a sleeping draught immediately if she is to be prevented from hysterics. And ask him if they have named her yet." Nilak turned back to Rhonwyn, who was now even paler. "Try one of these little gazelle-horn pastries," she said, offering it. "They are made with honey, raisins, and chopped almonds. I love them!" She picked up another and began to eat it. "Ummm, delicious!"

Struggling to gain control of herself, Rhonwyn took the pastry Nilak had offered her, took a bite, and began to chew it. It had no taste in her mouth. She swallowed, but put the rest of the pastry back down upon the plate.

Nilak reached out and took the girl's cold hand in hers. "It will be all right, my child, I promise you. This is a good life."

"I am Rhonwyn uerch Llywelyn, wife of Edward de Beaulieu, lord of Haven Castle. I do not belong here. *They must let me go!*"

Nilak gathered Rhonwyn into her arms and held her tightly.

It was at that moment Baba Haroun hurried over to the two women. "What is happening to her?" he demanded. "She must be ready to go to the caliph tonight."

"She is in shock, my lord Haroun. It is to be expected, after all. She may have come here as a warrior, but she is in reality only a young woman," Nilak murmured softly. "If the caliph is already taken by her beauty, we must treat her gently so our lord and master is not disappointed in either you or me."

"Your years have given you wisdom, Nilak," he grudgingly agreed, reaching into his voluminous red, black, and yellow–striped robe. "Here is a gentle sleeping potion that will calm the girl." He uncorked the little silver vial and poured it into Rhonwyn's cup.

Nilak put the cup to Rhonwyn's lips. "Drink, my child. We have put a mild dose of herbs into your tea to relax you. You need to sleep so you may face life as bravely now as you have always faced it in the past. Drink."

Rhonwyn didn't argue, gulping down the fragrant brew as if she couldn't escape fast enough. She hated this loss of control over her own life. Within minutes her eyes grew heavy. She didn't protest as Nilak led her to a couch where she lay down and promptly fell into a dreamless sleep.

"What is she to be called?" Nilak asked the chief eunuch.

"Noor," he answered her.

"How suitable," Nilak remarked. "Will you help me get her out of these odd garments, Baba Haroun? I do not want to entrust her to the other women of the harem quite yet. Has the lady Alia been informed of this girl's arrival and the caliph's interest?"

He nodded, thinking as he did that Nilak was perhaps a more valuable slave woman than he had previously considered. The lady Alia was the caliph's favorite wife. She had been wed to him when she was thirteen, and while he had two other wives and several favored concubines, it was the lady Alia who was his friend and his confidante now that the first flush of passion had passed them both. It was her son who would follow his father as the next caliph. She was well liked, feared, and respected by all in the harem.

"I have warned my lady of this new threat," Baba Haroun said. "She will come and see the girl as soon as we have gotten these clothes off of her."

They worked together, removing Rhonwyn's leather boots, her mail leg coverings, the chausses; her hauberk with its metal shoulder pads. Beneath the knight's garb they unlaced her padded arming doublet, and took off her braies, her hose, her chemise. Rhonwyn lay naked before them, her slender frame sweating and dirty but lovely.

"Allah! She is absolutely beautiful," Nilak said. "There has never been a woman here as fair, Baba Haroun."

The chief eunuch stood silent for a long moment, studying Rhonwyn. Her body was utterly flawless but for that ugly bush of hair at the junction where her two thighs met. That would be removed immediately. The limbs, however, were shapely and firm. The breasts small but nicely rounded with pert nipples. Bathed and properly garbed, she would be truly worthy of his master's bed.

"She is lovely," a new voice interjected, and they turned to find the lady Alia had joined them. "What kind of a girl do you think she is?"

"Warlike and difficult," Baba Haroun said immediately.

Alia laughed and patted his hand. "You are too protective of me, Haroun, and most prejudiced where any other woman is concerned. What think you, lady Nilak?"

"I am not certain yet, my lady, but this girl is, I believe, intelligent. I do not sense any wickedness about her, but she has been in my company only an hour or more. However, a woman who could convince her husband to allow her warlike pursuits is both clever and headstrong. She has been very brave these past few days, as you will come to see when I tell you her tale. Now she has only just realized her fate, and it has put her into shock. We will ascertain more of her character when she awakens in a few hours."

"Baba Haroun," the lady Alia said, "see that Noor is carefully guarded until I send the lady Nilak back to watch over her." She turned to the older woman. "Come, and you will tell me this girl's story."

Nilak followed the caliph's wife to her apartments, and they sat together as Nilak repeated what Rhonwyn had told her.

Alia was thoughtful for a few moments when Nilak had finished, and then she said, "Noor has done me a great favor in slaying Prince Abdallah, although she can hardly know it. Unless she sets herself up against me, she will have my friendship for that alone. If anything had happened to my lord Rashid, Abdallah would have killed my son to gain the caliphate for himself. Praise Allah he is now in Paradise, and not Cinnebar." Then her usually serene face grew concerned. "*He* is eager to possess her, they say. Will she be ready to go to his bed tonight, Nilak? He does not like to be disappointed, as you know."

Nilak sighed. "I cannot say, gracious lady," she answered honestly. "I do not know what the girl will be like once she awakens from her slumbers. Rest may restore her urge to resist."

"When she is bathed, bring her to me," the caliph's wife said.

Nilak arose and bowed to the lady Alia. Then she withdrew, hurrying back to where her new charge lay in a restless sleep, watched over by two armed eunuchs. "You may go now," she told the two guards, and sat down next to Rhonwyn. She beckoned to a slave girl and sent her for the embroidery she had been working on earlier. Receiving it, she bent over her needle once again.

Rhonwyn awoke, confused as to where she was, her mouth dry. Then Nilak's face came into her view, and the girl fell back against her pillows. "I am thirsty," she said weakly.

Nilak poured her a goblet of liquid and held it to her lips. "It is fruit juice," she said as Rhonwyn greedily gulped down the contents of the goblet. "How do you feel now, my child?"

"Still tired" came the wary reply. Then Rhonwyn looked down, and seeing she was naked, gave a small cry. "What have you done with my garments, lady?" She was blushing furiously, and there was nothing nearby with which she might cover herself.

"You could not sleep in those rough garments, my child. Your lovely limbs were prickled with the mail of your leg and arm coverings. Only that padding about your breasts saved them from being so evilly marked. Can you stand up? You must go to the baths and be washed. You have slept almost the entire day away."

"Could you not have put another garment on me?" Rhonwyn demanded.

"A clean garment on a filthy body?" Nilak sounded shocked.

"I am going nowhere without something to cover me," Rhonwyn insisted stonily.

"I realize you are not used to being naked, my child, but we are all females here," Nilak replied quietly. "Come now, do not be foolish. The baths will restore you." Nilak arose and held out her hand.

"No!" Rhonwyn said.

Nilak did not bother to argue further. Noor was going to have to learn obedience sooner than later. She signaled to two eunuchs. "The lady Noor is to be escorted to the baths and is having a moment of obstinacy. See that she overcomes it. I will meet you there." Then she moved off, crossing the main room of the harem, a small smile upon her pretty face as she heard the shriek of outrage behind her. She did not bother to turn about. The eunuchs had been given their orders and would carry them out. Nilak entered the baths and called for the bath mistress.

"Good day, Sarai," she said as the bath mistress came.

"Good day to you, Nilak. You are bringing me the warrior woman? Where is she? I hear he wants her tonight and there will be a great deal to do with this one."

"She is coming," Nilak said with a small laugh. "She objected to being naked, and two eunuchs had to escort her, I fear."

"Foolish creature," Sarai muttered. "These Frankish women are so ridiculous in their fear of nudity. Ah, here she is."

Rhonwyn was pink with her outrage. The two eunuchs had grasped her arms and hustled her through the harem, practically lifting her off her feet when she resisted them. When they put her down before the bath mistress and Nilak, she whirled and struck them both with her fists. "Barbarians!" she shouted angrily.

The eunuchs were surprised by her ferocity, but neither was hurt by the blows. They laughed and then departed.

Rhonwyn turned again and said to Nilak, "How could you let them do that to me, lady?"

"I do not argue with foolish girls," Nilak said sternly. "The rule in this world is obedience, Noor. When you do not or will not obey, you will be made to, my child. Now, you are not a stupid girl, so this should be the only lesson you will need."

"I will escape this place, return to my old world," Rhonwyn said defiantly.

"No, you will not," Nilak said implacably. "Even if by some miracle you managed to leave the palace, you would not know where to go, and you would be caught and brought back. You would be whipped upon the soles of your feet until you could not walk for three days. That is the punishment for disobedient slave girls. We do not mar the beauty of harem women, but unruly behavior must be punished. Cease your foolishness, Noor! We have much to do before moonrise. This is Sarai, the bath mistress. You will obey her, and I will be by your side to see that you do."

"You remind me of my aunt," Rhonwyn said. "She is an abbess."

Nilak laughed. "And did she have to speak so directly to you, my child?"

"Aye," Rhonwyn said, and then followed the two older women into the baths.

She had never thought herself a dirty woman, but she had also never known what clean truly was. She was rinsed and soaped. A silver instrument was used to scrape the dirt from her body. She was rinsed again. A thick peach-colored paste with a heavy fragrance was smoothed over her arms, her legs, beneath her arms, and atop her Venus mons. She was brought a cup of hot, sweet mint tea. When she had finished it, she watched in utter amazement as the paste was rinsed from her body, and her body hair with it.

Rhonwyn looked down at her mons and blushed. She had never noticed before how plump it was, nor the deep rosy slash that bisected its twin halves. There was an intense sensuality to her body now that made her very uncomfortable. Neither her nudity, nor their own nudity, seemed to disturb her two companions. What an odd world, she thought as she sat quietly while her fingernails and her toenails were pared almost to the quick and then smoothed and shaped neatly.

Her gilt-colored hair with its gold-and-silver lights was most thoroughly washed several times until she thought her scalp was going to be scrubbed raw. Then her hair was carefully dried by hands that toweled and brushed until her tresses almost floated like thistledown in a west wind. They lay her upon a raised and padded bench, and an old crone carrying a basket came from the shadows.

"This will be the hardest thing for you to bear," Nilak said. "Rafi will cleanse your love channel for you. There is no prurience in her actions, my child. Remain quiet, and she will not hurt you."

Rhonwyn's eyes were wide and startled at Nilak's words, but by now she realized that resistance was indeed futile. She tried not to tense as Rafi pulled her nether lips apart, bathing her gently in places Rhonwyn never knew could be bathed. The old lady's fingers pushed a soft cloth into her body, cleansing and purifying the path the caliph would take this night. Rhonwyn was amazed that she could be stretched quite that wide.

"He will enjoy this one, for while she is not a virgin, she is barely used," Rafi remarked to Nilak and Sarai. "Her pleasure jewel has not yet grown greatly." She cackled and looked down at Rhonwyn. "I am done now, my chick. May you know only joy in your master's bed."

"What did she say?" Rhonwyn asked Nilak.

"She says you are beautiful and wishes you joy" came the reply. "She is finished now, and you are ready for your creaming. Remain where you are. You will like this part," she said with a small smile.

A young eunuch, naked but for a loincloth, came with a tray of lotions and creams. Looking Rhonwyn over critically, he selected a lotion from his tray, poured it into his pink palm, and began to massage her body. Rhonwyn was shocked, but the young brown eunuch worked efficiently, her naked body apparently quite boring to him. His fingers dug into her shoulders and neck. He massaged her chest and breasts; her arms, hands, and fingers; legs, feet, and toes. Then he turned her over as easily as if he were turning a flat bread over a fire and began to work her shoulders again, her back, her buttocks, the backs of her legs and feet. Tense at first, Rhonwyn found herself relaxing in spite of herself and felt newly energized. These baths were the most deliciously decadent experience she had had in all of her life. She somehow thought that Edward would have enjoyed them, and the remembrance of her husband sobered her.

She was being prepared like a lamb for the slaughter for the caliph's bed. *Another man*. She had not been able to make happy the one she was wed to in the matter of passion. When she displeased this man, would he order her killed? Perhaps if he were unhappy with her, he would return her to the crusaders' encampment, and poor Sir Fulk as well. It was a slim hope, but one to which she would cling. She would tell the caliph honestly that she was unable to give or receive pleasure, and then he would send her back to Edward. There was nothing to be afraid of any longer, and she had certainly enjoyed these baths in the meantime. She would have to tell Edward all about them when she returned to him. Haven could certainly benefit by such civility.

Chapter Nine

The caliph's wife was a beautiful woman whose intelligence, kindness, and common sense had kept her close to her husband's heart for over fifteen years. She was Egyptian by birth, a slender lady with pale golden-colored skin, beautiful almond-shaped brown eyes, and long, thick dark hair that she wore loose and dressed with strands of tiny pearls. She wore a peach-colored silk kaftan trimmed with gold at the keyhole neck opening and the wide sleeves.

"Kneel to the caliph's wife, Noor," Nilak instructed her charge.

Rhonwyn knelt, but she did not bow her head.

A barely discernible smile touched the lips of the caliph's wife. The girl had pride, and properly channeled that was a good trait. It was just possible that this beautiful creature might make her husband a fourth and final wife. An ally against the two silly featherbrains who held the positions of second and third wives and who spent much time attempting ways to supplant her or cause trouble for her son, Mohammed. And if her son had not been there to follow his father, they would have fought with each other over whose son would, and then Cinnebar would have suffered the tortures of a civil war.

"She is ready?" the caliph's wife asked Nilak.

"She seems to have come to an acceptance with herself, my lady. She has been bathed and purified properly, and it is hoped that the reality of the possession will more than satisfy the caliph's anticipation," Nilak replied with a small smile. "She is lovely, isn't she?"

The lady Alia nodded in agreement. "Tell her I am pleased with both her beauty and her gentle manners."

Nilak repeated the words spoken by Alia to Rhonwyn.

The girl looked to Nilak and asked, "Am I permitted to address this lady directly, or must I speak to you?"

"You may address her and I will translate," Nilak responded.

"I thank you, my lady, for your kindness. I hope the caliph will see fit to release me back to my husband so I may cause you no distress by my presence," Rhonwyn said politely. Certainly the caliph's wife could not enjoy having all these women waiting for her husband's attentions. She would undoubtedly be delighted to get rid of at least one, and Rhonwyn would surely be delighted to go.

Nilak repeated Rhonwyn's words, adding, "She does not yet understand our ways, my lady, and like most captives dreams of freedom."

"*He* will certainly dissuade her of such notions," Alia said. "By morning she will be his devoted slave as so many others are. I do not quite know what it is about Rashid, but he has great charm to go along with his insatiable appetites for passion. Tell Noor I thank her for her kind wishes and that she pleases me. If her gentle behavior continues, she will have my favor."

"Fortunate girl!" Nilak exclaimed to Rhonwyn. "You have pleased her with your good manners. If you continue to do so, she says, you will gain her favor. The caliph's second and third wives have never, even on their first nights with him, had her favor."

"The caliph has three wives?" Rhonwyn was both surprised and shocked.

"He is allowed four under the law of Islam," Nilak answered her. "And as many concubines as please him. The only stipulation is that under Islamic law all his wives must be treated equally. If you delight him, you could easily become his wife, Noor. And with *her* favor, who knows what heights you might attain within this house? Your future at this moment is most golden, my child. Do not forget me in your greatness."

"I have no stature here," Rhonwyn said in practical tones, "nor do I wish any, as you well know. I do not go to the caliph to delight him, but rather to plead for my release, Nilak."

"Do not be foolish, my child. I have told you there is no way back to your world from Cinnebar. Make the most of the opportunity offered you in this time and this place," Nilak said.

"What does Noor say?" the caliph's wife asked.

"She frets she will not be able to please him," Nilak lied with facile grace. What else could she say? she thought. "I am attempting to reassure her that she is a delight to the eye and will indeed please our lord and master, the caliph."

The lady Alia smiled warmly. "How can she not?" she said with generous spirit. "Have her go and rest now, Nilak."

"We are dismissed," Nilak told Rhonwyn. "Arise, Noor, and bow again to the mistress of the harem who has favored you."

Obedient to her mentor, Rhonwyn stood and bowed to the lady Alia. How pretty she is, she thought. How can she bear sharing her husband with all these women? I should not want to share Edward with another. *Edward*. He had wanted a kiss from her before she went off to her sword practice with Sir Fulk, and she had refused him. How she wished now she had not.

They brought Rhonwyn a tray upon which was a warm flat bread, several slices of chicken breast, an apricot, and a dish of something creamy and white that Nilak said was called yogurt and made from milk. Rhonwyn was hungry and ate it all. An old woman came, and following Nilak's instructions, Rhonwyn opened her mouth for the servant who vigorously cleaned her teeth and mouth in a way she had never experienced, using a minted ground pumice, a rough cloth, a small brush, and minted water.

"Your breath should be fragrant," Nilak said.

Rhonwyn slept. When she awakened she was made to pee and was then bathed swiftly with rose water. Her mouth was once again rinsed, and she was dressed in a loose cream-colored silk kaftan beneath which a narrow filigreed gold chain with a single jewel had been affixed low on her hips. Her feet were bare. Her golden gilt hair was loose and flowing.

"Baba Haroun will bring you to the caliph," Nilak said.

"Will I see you again?" Rhonwyn asked.

"If you do not destroy your chances with your foolishness," Nilak responded, "you will see me come the morrow. I know what you secretly think, Noor. A final time I warn you to put all thoughts of escape from your mind. This is your life now. Better to be at the top of the harem than at the bottom. I know. I never had your chance, but if I had, my child, if I had . . ." She put her arms about Rhonwyn and gave her a quick hug. "I think your aunt the abbess would advise you even as I do, Noor. Ah, here is Baba Haroun to escort you. Go with him now, and remember to bow to the caliph as I have told you. I wish you joy, my child. He is said to be a magnificent lover."

It would make no difference, Rhonwyn thought, as

she followed the chief eunuch through the women's quarters and down a softly lit and scented corridor. If I could feel nothing with my beloved Edward, what can I feel with this stranger who says that I am his slave now and subject to his whims? If I cannot convince him to send me back to the crusaders' encampment outside of Carthage, then I am doomed.

The eunuch stopped before a set of double doors overlaid with gold leaf. He nodded to the two guards on either side of the entry, and they flung open the doors. Rhonwyn and Baba Haroun passed through, and the doors closed behind them.

The caliph stood awaiting them. Following Nilak's instructions, Rhonwyn fell to her knees and then flattened herself to the floor before the caliph, her forehead touching his bare foot. She found such a position degrading, but if she was to gain his cooperation, she must not antagonize Rashid al Ahmet.

"Prettily done, Noor," he said mockingly, "and not without a great cost to your pride, I am certain. Arise."

Baba Haroun helped her to her feet, and then to her surprise he quickly drew the kaftan off of her and as quickly withdrew from the chamber, leaving them alone.

It was useless to attempt to cover herself, Rhonwyn realized. She stood quietly, her eyes unfocused, struggling to conceal her shame.

"Put your hands behind your head," he said to her, surprised when she obeyed him. Had they drugged her into obedience? No. Her milky skin was faintly flushed, and she was deliberately avoiding his gaze. He smiled slightly and allowed himself a leisurely examination of his new possession. She was the most perfect woman he had ever seen in all his life. Her breasts were like little ripe peaches. Her limbs were nicely rounded but slender. He particularly liked her feet. They were small and slim with a high arch. Her narrow waistline flowed into shapely hips. He walked slowly about her, admiring her graceful long back and buttocks a bit plumper than he anticipated.

Standing behind her, he was unable to resist reaching around her to cup those sweet little breasts in the palms of his hands. They were surprisingly weighty for such dainty fruits. He buried his face in her hair, sniffing, then said, "What has happened to that delightful fragrance that earlier perfumed your locks, my exquisite Noor?"

"The scent is taken from the oil of a flower you do not have here in Cinnebar, my lord caliph," Rhonwyn answered. His hands were warm on her flesh and very disturbing, but if that was the worst of it, she would bear it for the sake of her ultimate goal.

His thumbs stroked idly across her nipples. "What is the flower? You shall have it, my beauty."

"It is called heather, my lord caliph. It will not thrive here in your climate," she replied. She wanted to pull away, but if she did, she would offend him, and then what would become of her?

"The plant may not grow here, my beauty, but we can import the oil for you. I shall give orders tomorrow that it be done." He released her breasts from his gentle grip and walked back around to face her once again. His eyes went to the chain that hung low on her rounded hips. From it hung a fat pear-shaped pearl that just touched the tip of the rose slash dividing her nether lips atop her plump mons. It was like a marker showing him the way to paradise. He wondered who had thought of such a clever touch.

"You may lower your arms now, Noor," he said.

"Thank you, my lord caliph," she replied.

"How mannerly you are, my beauty. From our first meeting this morning I would have suspected a tiny bit more resistance from you, and yet here you are, as meek as a lamb in one of my flocks. Now why is that, I wonder? Surely you have not so quickly reconciled yourself to your fate, Noor?" He cocked a dark eyebrow quizzically.

She was finally forced to focus her eyes upon him, for she could hardly plead her case without doing so. She swallowed hard, realizing he was clothed only in a bit of white silk cloth wrapped about his loins. He was almost as fair as she was, but for his hands and face, which were bronze with the sun. His body was devoid of hair, smooth and muscled yet slender, as she had earlier noted. He was by far the handsomest man she had ever seen. Nothing at all like her Edward, who, while attractive, could not match the perfect beauty of this man.

"*Well?*" he demanded.

"I cannot give you pleasure, my lord caliph!" Rhonwyn burst out.

"You mean you will resist my passion," he said.

Nervously she shook her head in the negative. "Nay, I mean, yes, I will, but it does not matter if I do or I don't. I cannot give you pleasure. I loved my husband, and he loved me, yet I was incapable of giving him anything more than my body. It was a terrible burden for us both. I am sorry, my lord, but now that you know, will you not send me back, and poor Sir Fulk with me?"

"No," he said. "I will not. There is not a woman in this world incapable of giving and receiving pleasure, Noor. With some it just takes longer or a different overture. I am sorry that you and your former lord could not find that happiness together, but I promise you that you will find it with me. Tonight perhaps, or tomorrow, but eventually, I promise you, my beautiful Noor."

"*No!*" she cried. What was he saying to her? The man was mad, surely! He could not possibly want her now.

Not after she had told him the truth of how she was incapable of passion.

Seeing the panic beginning to rise in her eyes, Rashid al Ahmet reached out and pulled Rhonwyn against him. "Do not be afraid, my beauty," he crooned at her, his hand stroking her head gently.

"You do not understand!" she half sobbed.

"But I do, my exquisite beauty, I do," he said softly. "You have never been drowned in a surfeit of bodily pleasure, nor have you ever been overcome with the delights of burning lust. I will open these worlds to you, Noor. I will not allow someone as beautiful as you to live in ignorance of pure hot passion and the delights that satisfying it can bring you. You are mine now, Noor, and I will never let you go." He tipped her face up and kissed her hard.

His words confused her, and worse, they frightened her. Why would he not believe her? Then his lips covered hers, demanding what she could not give him, and Rhonwyn, to her horror, began to weep.

Rashid al Ahmet picked up the sobbing girl and brought her to his bed, gently laying her down. Then he held her in his arms as she gave vent to her sorrow. He said nothing, for he knew that nothing he said would comfort her. She was slowly and reluctantly coming to the realization that he, and not some Christian knight, was her fate. If she had indeed loved this man despite their inability to pleasure each other, then it would be a hard acceptance, but the caliph believed this girl was strong and would sooner than later succumb to her fate.

Edward! she cried within her mind. *Edward!* She could not believe that he was gone. That that life was over and done with forever. She could accept what the caliph was offering her or she could die. Dying, however, would not return her to Edward except perhaps in spirit.

And what of him? Would he accept her loss easily? Their marriage, after all, had begun in political expediency. She did not doubt that he had grown fond of her as she had of him, but she was now gone from him. When he returned to England, to Haven, he would eventually have to remarry if he was to have heirs. He would probably choose his cousin Katherine this time. Katherine de Beaulieu was the kind of girl Edward should have had as a wife in the first place. She knew how to be a good chatelaine, and she was probably not frightened of passion and would quickly give Edward the heirs he needed. Yes. Perhaps it was better this way. She sighed deeply, her tears ceasing.

"It has been a long time since a woman felt free enough with me to weep against my chest," Rashid al Ahmet said quietly.

"Being a foreigner, I probably do not have their fear and respect of you, my lord caliph," Rhonwyn replied low. She hid her face from him. "I always look awful on the rare occasions I weep. I do not weep often. I think I have cried three times in all my life."

"I think you beautiful," he said, kissing her wet face. Rhonwyn smiled in spite of herself.

"Ah," he said, "you are recovering from your anguish."

"My heart aches, my lord caliph," she admitted. Why was it she could talk to this man as she never had talked to any other?

"Of course it does. You have lost much, my beautiful Noor. It is almost like a death, isn't it?"

She nodded. "Aye, it is."

"Why are you afraid of passion?" he asked her gently.

"I am afraid of nothing!" she insisted.

"You are afraid of passion," he said. "Why? Tell me who you are and what land creates such beautiful women." He sat up now and drew her to his side.

"I am Rhonwyn uerch Llywelyn—Rhonwyn, daughter of Llywelyn. My father is the prince of all the Welsh. My mother was his lover. I have a younger brother. When our mother died in childbirth my father took us to one of his castles to be raised. Unfortunately, he did not think to put us where there were women. I was raised among men, and thus copied their behavior."

"They taught you to fight," the caliph said.

"Aye, but only because I begged them to teach me. I loved them and wanted to be like them. Then one day my father appeared after many years and said I was to be wed as part of a treaty between him and the English king. He was horrified to find his daughter was more a lad than a lass. I was sent to my aunt, the abbess of a small abbey. For six months I was instructed in women's things, and then I was taken to England to be wed to Edward de Beaulieu, the lord of Haven Castle. When my lord decided to come on crusade, I said I would accompany him."

"And could not resist the call to arms, so you thus ended up my captive," the caliph said. "But where was your husband, Noor, that he allowed you into such danger?"

"He was ill with fever and a running of the bowels," she replied. "He was getting better and knew I suffered from a lack of exercise. When I said I would practice my swordplay with Sir Fulk, he agreed. During the battle I was captured and poor Sir Fulk followed after me. Had he not, he might be free."

"I shall not sell your knight off, for it would be a poor reward for his dutiful and faithful behavior toward his master's wife. I will set him the task of teaching my son Mohammed how your crusaders fight. It could prove useful to the lad one day. Does my decision please you, Noor?"

"Yes, my lord, and thank you," Rhonwyn said, daring to look up into his handsome face.

"I am said to be kind to those who please me," he murmured, and he bent to kiss her small ear. Then he let the tip of his tongue explore the delicate whorl of flesh.

What is he doing? Rhonwyn thought, feeling the hot wetness in her ear. She shivered. Edward had never done that. "*Oh!*"

His teeth gently worried the fleshy lobe. He pushed the mass of her hair aside and began to kiss the soft nape of her neck, intrigued by the tiny golden curls that sprang from it. They had perfumed her body with a mixture of rose and lily. It was an intoxicating fragrance that set his pulses racing. He nipped tenderly at the back of her neck.

"*Oh!*" She started nervously.

"Did your husband ever taste you, Noor?" he asked her. He took one of her hands and licked the palm slowly. Then he began to suck each of her fingers in turn, finally taking three of the digits into his mouth at once, murmuring his approval as he did so.

She was astounded by his behavior. It was surely depraved. Why did he not simply use her and be done with it? Then he surprised her further by laying her flat, his tongue licking at her body in long, leisurely sweeps. "*Please!*" she said.

He raised his dark head a moment. "Please, *what*?"

"Don't do that, my lord! Oh, please, don't do *that*!"

His tongue was laving over her breasts now. She could actually feel the flesh swelling. Her nipples puckered as if they had been touched with ice. Rhonwyn knew the panic was rising up in her, and to her surprise he seemed to sense it, too.

He said, "Why are you afraid, Noor? I am not hurting you. I am merely tasting your flesh, and I find it utterly delicious. I intend to bath your entire body with my tongue. There is nothing wrong in what I do."

"It is strange to me," she said weakly.

"Do you find no pleasure in it?"

"Nay!"

"You will eventually, my beauty, when you stop fearing the unknown and start to enjoy the pleasure I can give you this way," he told her. Then he continued onward.

Rhonwyn closed her eyes and attempted to ease her fears. He was right. She was being foolish. He wasn't hurting her at all. The fleshy tongue was warm, and she began to feel a tiny tingle when it swept over her skin, leaving it wet and then cool. He moved over her belly and then across her Venus mons, which caused her to cry out, startled and not just a little nervous to be touched so intimately.

He raised his head and laughed softly. "You are not ready yet, my exquisite Noor," he told her.

"R-ready for what?" she quavered.

"In time, my precious," he said mysteriously, and then began to lick her right thigh. His tongue moved down her leg to her feet, which he kissed most passionately. Then he sucked each of her toes in turn before beginning on her left leg.

"You are mad," she managed to gasp.

"Your flesh is an opiate of which I cannot get enough," he responded. Then he turned her over onto her belly and licked the soles of her feet until she giggled. He bathed her legs and her buttocks, running his tongue up the split between the twin moons of her bottom and raising another surprised cry from her. He only laughed again and continued onward until her back and her shoulders were damp with his excesses. He finished by giving her neck a final nip, then turned her over again.

"You're shivering," he said low, and brushed her lips

with his lightly. "Have I begun to melt the ice that surrounds your cold northern heart, Noor?" He ran his tongue along her lips tauntingly. "Now, my beauty, it is time for you to begin your lessons in pleasing your lord and master." He leapt from the bed, pulling her up with him.

"Undo the wrapping about my loins," he commanded her.

"You will be naked," she said foolishly.

He chuckled. "I will." He reached out and undid the delicate chain about her hips, laying it aside. "Come now, my beauty. Why do you demur? You know what a man's body looks like. There should be no surprises in store for you."

"You are constantly surprising me, my lord caliph," she admitted to him, blushing as she spoke.

"The wrap," he firmly pressed her.

With hesitant fingers Rhonwyn loosened the cloth and then pulled it away from him, laying it aside. Her eyes were carefully averted.

"It pleases me to see how modest you are, my Noor, but you may look upon the object of your defeat without fear. Come, my beauty, and touch it. I want to feel your hands upon me."

She shrank back from his words, her hands instinctively going behind her back.

"What? You have never touched a manhood? Allah! Allah! You are practically a virgin, Noor. Come now." Reaching out, the caliph drew the resisting hand forward and placed it upon his smooth groin. He could feel her desperate to pull away, and so he kept his own hand firmly on hers. "There, now, my beauty, let your fingers explore and caress me."

She knew she should not, but the temptation was simply too great. She had always been curious about Edward's manhood, but had never been brave enough to touch him. Now here was this man inviting her to do so, and she couldn't resist, particularly when he lifted his hand off hers. She brushed her fingertips across his mound. Her hand closed gently about his manhood. It pulsed within her palm, and she could feel it swelling with each passing moment. Unable to stop herself, she caressed its great length, her breath coming a bit more quickly now. He was warm and hard in her hand.

"That's it, my beauty," he encouraged her. "Now cup my twin jewels in your palm. They are cool to your touch, are they not?"

She nodded slowly.

"They are filled with the seeds of life, Noor. When you are ready I will plant those seeds within you, my beauty. Cease your sweet torture now. In a moment or two I shall not be able to restrain my desire for you, and you are far from ready to meet my passion."

Her hand dropped away, and she hid her head in his shoulder. Those last moments had been very exciting, and she could feel her heart beating faster than it had previously.

"Your Christian men put women into four categories, Noor. Wives, mothers, whores, or saints. They do not share the secrets of pleasure with their mates. We men of Islam do, and we do not confine ourselves to only one woman. Such a thing is unnatural for a man. No one woman can satisfy all a man's passions."

"They tell me you have three wives, my lord caliph."

"I do, although the two younger I may dismiss, for they are quarrelsome creatures ever at odds with the lady Alia and the other women of my harem. Indeed, they may have been responsible for the death of a particularly lovely girl I had decided to favor. Baba Haroun is still investigating, and he will get to the bottom of the matter, I promise you. He is very protective of the lady Alia."

"Lady Alia is a gracious lady and was kind to me," Rhonwyn told him.

"She has already spoken in your favor, my Noor, which is why I will be patient with you." He tilted her face to his again and began to kiss her with far more passion than he had previously. Her instinct was to fight him, but something else overcame Rhonwyn, and she instead melted into his embrace, her mouth softening beneath his.

Why am I doing this? she silently asked herself. But she had no answer. All she knew was that this man was strong and gentle, and her will to resist was growing weaker. What if all they told her was true? That she could not escape Cinnebar. And what if Edward would not have her back? She had surely disobeyed him by involving herself in battle, as he had forbade her. Oh, God! I do not know what I am to do! What was the matter with her?

"I cannot give you pleasure," she whispered as she pulled away from his mouth.

"You already have," he told her softly.

"I do not know how to receive pleasure," she said desperately.

"I will teach you," he promised her. Then his mouth was hungrily seeking hers again, his tongue pushing past her lips to do battle with her senses.

Rhonwyn half sobbed, her resistance dissolving as her curiosity aroused itself. Perhaps her inability to know pleasure was Edward's fault. Their first mating had not been pleasant. But this man was different. Mayhap he could teach her to relish passion. She could not know if she would not yield herself to him. And if she was not to return to Edward de Beaulieu, then what else was there for her but this life? As Nilak had told her, life at the top of the harem was better than at the bottom. She pulled away from him again. *"Teach me, my lord caliph,"* she told him. *"Teach me of passion!"*

He took her face between his two hands and gazed directly into her emerald green eyes. His eyes, she noted for the first time, were a deep, deep blue, almost black. "My passion is a fierce thing, Noor," he warned her, "and you are easily fearful and shy. I want you with every fiber of my being, but I want you to know great pleasure as well. I can see you know little of the delights between a man and a woman. I will show you all those sweet enjoyments, but you must know that I will not harm you or hurt you or give you pain in any of these pursuits. If you are afraid, you will not be abashed and unable to tell me. Our pleasure can be approached in a variety of ways, and all are equally delicious. Will you trust me, my beauty?"

She nodded, her heart hammering with anticipation. Why had not her husband ever said these things to her? For a moment she was angry at Edward, but then she realized that he probably knew as little as she did about passion, although as a man, he would assume he knew all.

The caliph began to kiss her face gently. Her lips. Each of her cheeks. The tip of her nose. Her closed eyelids. Her forehead. Then releasing her face from their soft grip, his hands began to caress her body, smoothing down her neck over her shoulders, sweeping along her long back to cup her buttocks in his hands. He fondled the twin moons, and some deep instinct made her arch her body. With a soft cry he covered her straining throat, her chest, and her small swollen breasts with kisses. He buried his lips in the hollow of her throat, growling low. "How you intoxicate me, my beautiful warrior woman," he said in his deep voice. Then he gathered her up into his arms again and deposited her upon his bed.

Rhonwyn felt her heart thudding rapidly as he stood looking down at her. She did not love this man. Indeed he almost frightened her with his dark intensity, but something deep within her wanted him to continue onward. It would end in the terrifying act of coupling, she knew, but she still wanted to know everything he had to teach her, wanted his lips on her, wanted his hands that roused such feelings of utter roiling confusion inside of her.

He stared down on her for a moment before coming to lay by her side. She could have no idea of how beautiful she was with her perfumed breath coming in little gasps from between her sweet ripe lips. She did not know how exquisite her body was, silently inviting, almost wanton in her unrealized need to be loved by him. He lay his dark head upon her breasts. "Your heart beats so swiftly," he said to her.

"I am afraid, yet not afraid," she told him.

"Remember, I will not harm you, my lovely Noor. I will only love you and give you joy."

"I trust you, my lord caliph," she said in a low voice.

He raised his head and leaned over to kiss her breast. Then his mouth closed over its nipple, and he suckled upon her.

She started nervously, but then she let herself enjoy the exciting sensation of his mouth and tongue upon her tender flesh. Her hand reached out to caress his dark hair. It was surprisingly soft to her touch and slightly curly. Her slender fingers entwined themselves in and out of the curls even as he began to worship her other breast in the same manner as the first. Edward had loved her breasts in this manner, too, but it had not seemed quite so exciting, more of a perfunctory thing. *Or was it that this was so forbidden?*

His hands and mouth began to roam over her quivering body as his tongue had earlier. His hunger was building, even if his instincts warned him to move slowly. Her belly was taut beneath his mouth; the insides of her thighs were as soft as the finest Cathay silk. Her own fragrance filled his nostrils. Unable to prevent himself from doing so, he kissed her mons, then slowly ran his tongue down the pouting slash that hid the gates to paradise and all of her most precious treasures.

Rhonwyn shuddered at the touch of his tongue that now began to probe at her innermost secrets. His fingers gently drew her nether lips apart, holding them in a firm grip as his tongue caressed the flesh within. She felt his tongue acutely, particularly when it touched a most sensitive part of her. The tongue worried and worried at her. She felt a building of sensation within. Edward had touched her there, but always with his finger. The caliph's tongue was far more exciting. Rhonwyn gasped as the first distinct feeling of pleasure swept over her. "*Oh!*" she cried, and shuddered hard. The tongue persisted, and she again was overwhelmed, crying out once more as she reveled in the sweetness that engulfed her.

"You see," his voice came to her through the mists, "you can feel pleasure, my beautiful Noor." He slowly pushed two fingers into her love channel, drawing them slowly back and forth, arousing her so that she would be ready to receive him. Carefully he began to cover her body with his, and then it happened.

Rhonwyn's eyes opened, yet they were sightless. "*No!*" she cried out, her voice filled with utter terror. "*No!*"

He ceased in his actions, quickly taking her back into his arms although his manhood felt as if it were going to burst. "What is it, Noor? What is frightening you so? Tell me, my beauty. *Tell me!*"

"He is hurting her! Oh, please, stop! Don't hurt my mam!"

Her words astounded him, but Rashid al Ahmet knew that the mind was a powerful weapon that could be used for good or evil; that could hide secrets and affect behavior in the most ordinary people. "Who is hurting your mother, Noor?" he asked her in kindly tones.

"I do not know him, but his garb is rich. He has come to our cottage. Mam is very afraid, yet he will not let her be! He calls her a whore and forces her to couple with him. He is hurting her! He is hurting her! Go away! Go away! Mam says our father must not know what has happened. She is bleeding. Don't weep, Mam. Don't weep!" There were tears on Rhonwyn's face now. "Mam says I mustn't let any man do to me what he has done to her. I must fight them! I'll be a good girl, Mam. I'll be strong for us both. The prince will never know. 'Tis our secret, Mam. *Our secret.*"

The caliph rocked her in his arms. No wonder she had not been able to feel any pleasure. His poor beautiful Noor, but now it would all change for her. "Who raped your mother, Noor?" he gently asked her. "You were very little, weren't you?"

Rhonwyn's eyes opened, and she shuddered hard. "I never knew who he was," she said. "Probably someone who knew my father and knew where our cottage was hidden. My mother never knew if the third child she carried was his or the prince's. My father loved her and would have killed any man who touched her. I think that is what frightened her. She always said there was greatness in ap Gruffydd, and it should not be denied. She would not have wanted to be the cause of his failure. I was just four when it happened, and my brother still at her breast."

"Do you understand now what she meant when she warned you not to allow any man to do to you what was done to her? She did not mean you should not enjoy mutual pleasures, Noor, only that you should not find yourself in her unfortunate position." He stroked her hair tenderly. "Poor lady. How she must have suffered, and what a terrible secret both you and she kept. Sleep now, my beautiful one. Later when you awaken, I shall make love to you as you should be loved."

She was puzzled. She could see his manhood was still stiff with his desire for her. Reaching out, she touched him, saying, "I will not be afraid now, my lord caliph."

"You will be less fearful when you have slept, my beauty," he advised her. "You have faced terrible demons just now. Sleep the residue of them away, and then I will take you to paradise as a reward for your bravery, sweet Noor." He kissed her forehead.

"I am no longer a child, my lord caliph," Rhonwyn told him. "I am a warrior woman, and now I have confronted that which has secretly terrified me all these years. I need no rest, but I do need your passion to prove to me that I have truly overcome my terrors." She held out her arms to him.

Rashid al Ahmet covered her body with his own. His manhood, rampant and hungry for her, slid easily into her love channel. He watched her face carefully, but there was no longer any fear in her eyes. It had been replaced by a budding wonder and eager anticipation of what was to come. She was wonderfully tight and hot. "You are indeed fearless, my beautiful warrior woman," he complimented her. Then he began to move upon her.

Rhonwyn closed her eyes, enjoying the incredible sensation of him as he pushed slowly within her. She could feel the throb of his manhood as it delved into her depths. She was acutely aware of every tiny sensation he elicited from her. When he began to thrust and withdraw, thrust and withdraw, Rhonwyn knew that her mother, who had loved ap Gruffydd so dearly, would have never denied her this marvelous sense of utter delight. She arched her body to match his rhythm, crying out as a tiny sharp pulse of pleasure began to envelop her, building until it crashed over her like a large wave, leaving her weak and satisfied, piercingly aware of his hot love juices that were discharged deep into her now well-plowed field.

When she was finally able to breathe normally again, she said shyly, "That was wonderful, my lord caliph!"

"Rashid," he said to her. "My name is Rashid, and I shall never let you go, my beautiful Noor. You are mine forever!"

She lay her golden head upon his smooth chest, strangely happy, and yet deep within her heart she whispered a single word: *Edward!* It was her husband, Edward de Beaulieu, she loved, and not this intense man. Yet it had been Rashid al Ahmet who had delved into her deepest secret and drawn it forth from the darkness in which she had kept it hidden all these years. Her husband, to whom she had been wed a year, had not been able to do that. Rashid al Ahmet, caliph of Cinnebar, into whose presence she had been brought as a prisoner only this morning and into whose bed she had been taken this night—it had been he who had touched her as no other man ever had. *Why?*

She had to admit that his passion was magical, and she had obviously pleased him greatly. If she continued in his favor, who knew to what heights she could reach in Cinnebar, but it was not what she wanted. She wanted to return to Edward and share herself with him as she had never been able to share herself before. She owed the caliph a great debt for that. Still, what her heart desired was impossible. *But was it?* Only time would tell, and in the meantime she would continue to share herself with the caliph. She sensed that she was just beginning to learn all that he had to teach her, and she realized that she was now a most eager pupil.

"What are you thinking?" he demanded, raising her up so he might look into her beautiful face.

"I am thinking that you have much to teach me, my lord Rashid," Rhonwyn answered him honestly.

The caliph laughed aloud. "Aye," he said. "We have only just begun, my beautiful Noor. We have only just begun!"

Chapter Ten

"Awaken, my child." Nilak's voice came to her through the mists.

Rhonwyn's eyes opened slowly, focusing upon her surroundings, at first confused as to where she was, but then remembering.

"Oh, Noor, how you have pleased the caliph! He left you to sleep and gave orders that you should not be disturbed until the sun was at the mid-heavens. The entire harem is talking. They cannot ever remember a time when he left a woman to sleep in *his* bed after he had taken his pleasure. Come, child, get up now. We must go to the baths and then to your new apartments, which are next to the lady Alia's! You are very much in favor, and 'tis said the second and third wives are quite angry. The gossip is that you will be made his fourth wife, for he is besotted by you, fortunate girl!"

Rhonwyn tried to absorb all of Nilak's words. She stretched her limbs gingerly and felt a slight soreness between her thighs. He had coupled with her a second time last night, and it had been even better than their first encounter. She was confounded by it all, although he had carefully explained to her that the memory of her mother's rape, buried deep within her mind, had been the cause of her inability to enjoy passion. Now released from that terrible pain, she was free to let her passions take her where she would. His words had disturbed her deeply, and she again wondered why Edward had not been able to find the answer to the riddle of her unresponsiveness.

Nilak gently tugged on her arm. "My lady Noor, you must come with me now," she insisted.

"Yes, yes," Rhonwyn answered her, arising at last, but her attention was only partly focused on the older woman who was slipping a silken garment over her.

"*They* say he returned from his morning meal to watch you in sleep for a short time," Nilak said. "What did you do, child, to entrance the caliph so?" She led Rhonwyn from Rashid al Ahmet's apartments and down the hall into the women's quarters.

Rhonwyn was startled to note that slaves and harem women alike bowed to her politely as they passed by. By the rood, she thought, Nilak does not just babble uselessly. Rhonwyn's wits were beginning to sharpen once again. She had already divined from Nilak's chatter that to survive in this place she needed power. Power came from several sources. The caliph. The lady Alia. And Baba Haroun. She already had the caliph's favor, and she could probably keep it if she were clever. It was his first wife and the chief eunuch she needed to win to her side.

She had no quarrel with the lady Alia. Indeed, the caliph's wife had treated her with great kindness. She wondered how that lady would feel now with all the gossip regarding the caliph's infatuation. No matter, Rhonwyn told herself, I will be polite and quiet spoken toward her. As for Baba Haroun, he is obviously devoted to the lady Alia. He will never really trust any other woman who might threaten his mistress's position, Rhonwyn realized. Still, I will be respectful toward him and consider any advice he may give me. If he will not be my friend, at least I shall not have him as an enemy.

They entered the baths, and as Sarai hurried forward to greet the new favorite, a silence fell among the other women there. Sarai greeted Rhonwyn, and then taking her single garment from her, she personally took charge again of the bathing procedure. The other women began to chatter softly once more, but two who were seated together having their toenails pared stared hard at Rhonwyn.

"The one with the dark blond hair is Fatinah, the second wife," Nilak said softly. "The chestnut-haired woman is the third wife, Hasna. How they glare at you," she chuckled low. "Their jealousy is plain."

"Can they harm me?" Rhonwyn asked.

"They might try," Nilak said honestly.

"Will Baba Haroun protect me from them?"

Nilak nodded. "He will, but you must still be cautious, my lady Noor. We will choose your servants carefully."

"I want no one but you serving me," Rhonwyn replied. "Your fate is now tied to mine, and so I believe I can trust you, Nilak; but should you ever betray me, I will kill you with my own hands."

Nilak looked startled, but then she laughed. "You will have no cause to, my lady Noor. Being your confidante is a better position in my old age than caring for the children of harem women. I will never betray you. I swear it!"

They bathed together, and then when they had finished they entered the chamber where the women liked to gather afterward, drinking mint tea and gossiping. Rhonwyn saw the lady Alia surrounded by her women and immediately went to her. Kneeling before her, Rhonwyn placed her hands in those of the caliph's first wife, her head bowed. "I greet you, great lady," she said quietly.

Alia smiled wryly, but then she said to Nilak, "Tell the lady Noor that her gesture of respect shows me her good breeding. I hope she will soon learn our tongue so we may converse together. She remains in my favor, for she has touched our lord's heart, yet even knowing it, does not flaunt herself as others have in the past." Her gray-brown glance flickered briefly to where the second and third wives sat. "The lady Noor may sit by me and join me in a cup of tea."

Nilak carefully repeated the first wife's words. Her trembling voice could scarcely mask her excitement. She settled herself at Rhonwyn's feet, translating for the two women as they spoke. A tiny blue-and-white porcelain cup was placed in Rhonwyn's hand.

"You have pleased my husband greatly," Alia said. "Rashid is a good man, although he has little tolerance for fools."

"I did not know there was a kingdom here in the mountains behind Carthage," Rhonwyn said.

"Cinnebar has been here since the beginnings of time," Alia responded. "It has never been conquered because it is so remote. The wealth of our gold mines, while comfortable, is not so great that we attract undue attention. We also mine alabaster and peridot."

"You are not so distant that you escaped the sword of Islam," Rhonwyn remarked.

Alia laughed. "In the beginning Cinnebar worshiped various gods, as did most peoples. Then came a physician named Luke who converted our people to Christianity. Are you shocked, Noor? Yes, I can see you are, but many who were once Christians in this region converted to Islam when it came. Here in Cinnebar it happened several hundred years ago, when a princess from Baghdad married the ruler of Cinnebar. It was she who converted the people of Cinnebar. There are still Christians and Jews among us, and they are welcome as long as they obey our laws. We have never had any difficulties, as we respect each other's manner of worship. After all, Noor, we all worship the same one God. We all honor the ancient augurs. Abraham. Isaac. Moses. You Christians accept Jesus of Nazareth as the messiah. We in Islam believe he is a great prophet, although we hold that Mohammed is the greater. Are these small differences a cause for warfare?" Alia asked Rhonwyn.

"Yet men war over them," Rhonwyn replied.

"They are foolish, aren't they?" Alia responded. She lowered her voice. "Men have not the inner strength of women, which is why God made women the bearers of new life." Her eyes twinkled.

Rhonwyn could not suppress a giggle. "How wise you are, my lady Alia," she said quietly. "I think I can learn much from you."

"We are going to be friends," Alia said. "I knew it when I first saw you, Noor. Ah, here is Baba Haroun."

"My lady Alia." He bowed. "I have come to escort the lady Noor to her apartments."

"I will come with you," Alia said, rising. "And she will need servants of her own."

"I want only Nilak," Rhonwyn said quickly as she stood.

"Lady," the chief eunuch protested, "you have become a favorite of the caliph. You cannot be served by just one woman."

"Why not?" Rhonwyn demanded.

"It is not proper," the eunuch said fussily. "You are the new favorite."

"I have been here but a day," Rhonwyn said. "Perhaps the caliph will decide he does not favor me."

Nilak was almost dizzy with all the translation involved.

"She is fearful of who to trust," Alia said to the chief eunuch. "I think she is very wise. Fatinah and Hasna have been glaring at her ever since she entered the baths, Baba Haroun. I want her well protected. Do you understand me? I like this girl. She will be no threat to me even if she falls in love with the caliph. This is the ally I have been seeking. I will give Noor two young slave girls from my own staff. They are well trained and trustworthy. Tell her, Nilak."

Nilak repeated Alia's offer to Rhonwyn, adding, "You cannot refuse her, my lady, else you say without words that you do not trust the caliph's first wife."

"I accept my lady Alia's most gracious offer and thank her for her understanding," Rhonwyn said sweetly.

Nilak repeated Rhonwyn's honeyed reply.

Again Alia smiled wryly. Then she laughed. "You must teach her our tongue as quickly as she can learn, Nilak. I really do want to be able to speak with her. How can we two plot and plan if we cannot understand one another?"

Nilak chuckled and repeated what the caliph's first wife had said.

Rhonwyn burst out laughing. "Tell my lady Alia I shall endeavor to learn her language as quickly as possible."

A small smile touched the lips of the chief eunuch. He had had his doubts about the foreign warrior woman, but it was obvious that she had a generous spirit and a good heart. And his mistress, who had always been a very intuitive woman, liked her. "Come," Baba Haroun said, and he led the women from the gathering room in the baths to the lady Noor's new apartments. Flinging open the doors, he said, "Enter, my ladies."

The apartment was charming with its pale pink marble walls and painted ceilings. There were two medium-sized rooms and a small room where the serving women could sleep. Both of the larger chambers opened onto a small garden with a spectacular view of sky and mountains. It gave Rhonwyn the illusion of freedom, which it had been designed to do. There was a small bubbling pool in the garden and a fountain in the dayroom. The furnishings were rich with ebony and marble, silks and diaphanous gauzes, gold and silver, thick carpets, and colored glass lamps that burned fragrant oils. The cushions in the seating area were velvet and brocade. The bed in the bedchamber sat upon a gilded dais and was hung with green silk.

Rhonwyn found herself at a loss for words. It was the most beautiful place she had ever seen. Even Haven had nothing like this within its stone walls. She turned this way and that, admiring something new that caught her eye each time she thought she had seen it all. "It is lovely," she finally managed to say. She turned to Alia. "Thank you."

"I am glad you are pleased," the caliph's first wife said. Then her eye lit upon a tray of plump apricot halves. "Baba Haroun, what a lovely touch. They look delicious sitting in their honey glaze." She reached for a fruit, but the chief eunuch slapped her hand away.

"No, *lady!*" he cried out. "I did not order that these fruits be placed in the lady Noor's apartments." His black eyes grew opaque. "Would you take the lady Noor to your apartments, please, my lady Alia?"

Alia nodded. Her golden skin was suddenly pale.

"What is it?" Rhonwyn asked Nilak, confused.

"We are to go with Lady Alia," Nilak answered.

"Why?" Rhonwyn persisted.

"Baba Haroun did not order the apricots be brought to you. I believe he thinks they are poisoned," Nilak said quietly.

"*Poisoned!*" Rhonwyn was now pale herself. "Who would want to poison me? I have not been here long enough to make enemies."

"You have found favor with the caliph," Nilak replied. "That is enough to give you enemies, my child. Come now."

They followed Lady Alia to her apartments just down the corridor. Nilak told the caliph's first wife that she had explained the confusing situation to the lady Noor, who was understandably shocked.

"Do not be afraid, Noor," Alia said, putting an arm about Rhonwyn. "No harm will come to you. I will see to it."

Rhonwyn nodded, smiling weakly at Alia as Nilak translated.

"I shall now seek among my younger maidservants for two slave girls to serve you," the caliph's wife said. "And Nilak will, of course, remain your companion." She left Rhonwyn and Nilak, who were now seated together in a quiet corner.

"Why is she so kind to me?" Rhonwyn asked.

"Because in you she sees an ally against Fatinah and Hasna," Nilak said frankly. "When the caliph took Fatinah as his second wife, Fatinah attempted to lord it over the lady Alia. It was a very foolish move, because the first wife always has precedence over the other wives and the concubines or any woman in the harem except possibly the lord's mother, but the caliph's mother died when he was a child. Fatinah bore the caliph a son, but by then he was tired of her vexatious behavior. Although it is not the lady Alia's way to complain, Baba Haroun had kept the caliph fully informed of Fatinah's behavior. While our master was grateful for his second son, Omar, the boy's mother was no longer of any importance to him."

"And then he fell in love with Hasna?" Rhonwyn was curious.

"Hasna was the daughter of one of the former caliph's most faithful counselors. She was the child of his old age. When he was on his deathbed he begged our caliph to take Hasna as a wife. He had no other children, and Hasna's mother had died giving birth to her. Rashid al

Ahmet agreed. At first Hasna was meek and respectful, but then Fatinah infected her with her venom and jealousy. Hasna gave birth to a daughter, and before she lost her husband's love, she had another daughter. These two creatures spend most of their time scheming to overthrow the lady Alia, for they are too stupid to see it cannot be done. Even if that good lady died a natural death, the caliph would not return them to his affections. Several months ago the caliph's eye lit upon a particularly lovely slave girl from the island of Sicily. His passions were engaged, but the girl died suddenly after nibbling on a dish of pistachio nuts that had been left in her chamber. No one knew from where the nuts had come, although one of Fatinah's servants had been seen by a harem woman near the dead girl's chamber during that fatal day. When questioned, however, the harem woman claimed she could not remember which servant or if, indeed, it had been one of Fatinah's women at all."

Rhonwyn laughed almost bitterly. "I am here against my will. I don't want to infatuate the caliph, but I have, and now these two women want to murder me for it. Would that I had never left England."

"It will be all right, my child," Nilak assured her.

"What will happen now?" Rhonwyn wanted to know.

"This time, I believe, Fatinah and Hasna have gone too far," Nilak said grimly.

And as if to give emphasis to her words, terrified shrieks were now heard coming from the main gathering room of the harem. Her expression grim, the Lady Alia rejoined Rhonwyn and Nilak. There was the sound of pounding footsteps, and the doors to the lady Alia's apartments burst open to admit a very young and frightened slave girl. Behind her came Baba Haroun, the look on his face merciless. The girl flung herself at Alia's feet, sobbing and babbling.

"She is begging the lady for mercy," Nilak said softly.

"She says she had to do what she was told by her mistress. That she herself would harm no one. She begs Lady Alia to spare her life."

The slave girl clutched at Alia's hem and pleaded as Nilak translated her words to Rhonwyn.

"Lady, gracious lady, spare me! I am the lowest of the low and could not refuse when my mistress commanded me!"

"Did you know the fruit was poisoned?" Alia asked.

The slave girl shook her head in the negative.

"She lies!" snapped Baba Haroun. He grabbed the slave girl by her arm and shook her roughly. "The truth, you spawn of a she-camel!"

"I did not know! I did not know!" the girl insisted.

The chief eunuch slapped the slave girl brutally several times. "I shall whip the truth out of you, girl!" he roared.

"*I did not know,*" the girl sobbed brokenly.

"But did you suspect your mistress and her friend might want to harm the lady Noor?" Alia gently probed.

The slave girl nodded, adding, "But I am only a slave, my lady, and I could not be certain what they were doing. They did not do it in my sight, so how could I accuse them of perfidy?"

"You could have come to me," Alia said quietly.

"They would have killed me if I did," the slave girl half whispered.

"Now I will kill you," Baba Haroun said fiercely, and the hapless slave shrieked, wrapping her arms about Alia's legs.

"No, Baba Haroun," the caliph's first wife said. "The girl is correct, and only sought to survive. It is Fatinah and Hasna who must be punished severely for this attempt on Noor's life. And, I am certain, the murder of poor Guzel. Tell me, girl," she said softly, caressing the slave's head comfortingly, "what do you know of Guzel's death. Did you bring her the pistachio nuts?"

"Nay, lady, 'twas another. The lady Hasna's servant," the slave said low.

"Were the nuts poisoned?"

"So it was rumored among the others" was the reply.

"Take the apricots to Fatinah and Hasna, Baba Haroun. See that they eat them all," Lady Alia said in a soft voice. "I grow weary of their misbehavior."

"What of their children?" he asked.

"Omar is but four, and the girls three and two. We will raise them properly. Under our tutelage Omar shall become his brother's right hand instead of his nemesis, eh?"

"You are merciful, my lady," the chief eunuch said.

"Remove the children before the others," she advised.

"It shall be done, my lady" was the obedient answer.

"She is going to kill them?" Rhonwyn was surprised.

"Fatinah and Hasna have crossed the line," Nilak said. "You are new here, and so you do not know what they have done in their never-ending attempts to harm the lady Alia and her son, Mohammed. There are none here who will mourn their passing."

"What will the caliph say?" Rhonwyn wondered.

"What happens here in the harem is the province of the lady Alia and Baba Haroun. It is he who will explain to the caliph what happened. It is unlikely that the caliph will have any objection."

Rhonwyn suddenly saw the caliph's first wife in an entirely new light. Beautiful, obviously intelligent, and certainly kind, Alia was completely capable of being ruthless when she had to be. Rhonwyn shuddered.

"Are you chilled, my child?" Nilak asked anxiously.

"Nay," Rhonwyn said quietly.

"You are surprised that the lady Alia can be so unflinching, aren't you?" Nilak said. "She is royalty, Noor.

Her father was a prince of Egypt. She knows how to rule and what must be done when necessary. She has never hesitated to do what she must and will protect the caliph and their son at whatever cost."

"What shall I do with this girl?" Baba Haroun asked his mistress.

"I shall take her into my own household," Alia said. "She is really a good girl who simply found herself with a bad mistress. Now go and do what must be done, Baba Haroun."

"As my lady commands," the chief eunuch said, bowing low and then backing from the chamber.

"Get up, girl, you are safe now," Alia said, pulling the slave girl to her feet. The slave kissed Alia's hands in gratitude. "What excitement! Let us have some mint tea and music to calm our nerves. Noor, come and sit by my side," the caliph's wife said.

Within minutes slave women appeared, bringing tiny cups of the sweetened mint tea and an engraved silver plate covered with stuffed dates and tiny crescent-shaped pastries filled with chopped nuts, raisins, and honey. A slave played upon a lute, singing softly. The air was suddenly fragrant with the scent of aloes. The tiled fountain in Alia's gathering chamber cooled the room in the afternoon heat. Rhonwyn ate the treats eagerly, as she had had nothing to eat since being awakened earlier.

"When it is safe you will go to your own apartment, Noor," Alia said. "I imagine you will want to rest before Rashid desires your presence tonight. He is a most passionate lover, isn't he?"

Rhonwyn blushed furiously at Alia's query.

The caliph's wife laughed and reached out to touch the younger woman's warm cheek gently. "How old are you?" she asked.

"Seventeen, I think," Rhonwyn answered.

"A married woman, and still so innocent until your night with Rashid," Alia teased. "When I was your age I had a three-year-old son. Do you want children, Noor?"

"I do not know," Rhonwyn said frankly.

"Our lord will give them to you, Noor, for his seed is potent," Alia replied. "I hope you will learn to love him. For all his manly strength he needs love to sustain him and make him stronger, as do all men, although certainly none of them will admit to it."

Suddenly from another part of the harem muffled screams were heard. Rhonwyn paled and looked to Nilak, but her translator was silent, her lips pressed together in a tight straight line. She glanced to the lady Alia, but the face of the caliph's wife was serene, as if she had not or could not hear the shrieks. Rhonwyn swallowed hard. Although she knew what was happening she had not imagined the executions of Fatinah and Hasna would be so public or so vocal. Neither of the two women could be very intuitive to have resisted the authority of the caliph's first wife. It was not a mistake Rhonwyn intended to make while she resided in Cinnebar. Alia's friendship was important to her survival, and Rhonwyn meant to keep it.

Suddenly Alia spoke and Nilak said, "It is over now, child. Do not look so stricken. They deserved their fate. The lady Alia is extraordinarily patient and has borne their unforgivable behavior for several years. Today's attempt upon your life was but the final straw to break the camel's back. The harem will be a better place now."

"I must accept your word for that," Rhonwyn said, and sipped her mint tea, which was now cool.

"You have been giving her the elixir?" Alia asked Nilak. "Until I can be certain of her character, I do not want her belly swelling with Rashid's offspring. Her exceptional beauty has captivated my husband. Will she use her power over him for good, or will she become like the others? I want to avoid another incident like today's."

"I have put the elixir in her tea each morning," Nilak answered. "As she does not speak our language there is no one to tell her of such things, my lady. I will do whatever you command me regarding this girl."

"I like her," Alia said. "I think I have read her correctly and that there is no malice in her. Right now, however, I know she longs for her husband and her homeland. Rashid's passion toward her will soon change that. With Fatinah and Hasna gone, he will take her for his wife, I am certain. Two wives for the caliph of Cinnebar are quite enough, don't you think? One seems rather paltry. Four is a bit ostentatious. Two is sensible, and just right. Noor is healthy and young. She will give our lord several children when the time is propitious. Begin tomorrow to teach her our language as I have previously commanded you. I long to speak with her directly, Nilak."

Baba Haroun reentered Alia's apartments. He went immediately to his mistress and bowed low. "It is done, lady. Shall I have their bodies set out for the wild dogs?"

"No," Alia said. "They were my lord's wives and the mothers of his children. Have them buried immediately in an unknown place. But first escort the lady Noor back to her apartments. She is sensitive and not quite used to our ways yet. She understands what happened had to happen, but her heart is gentle. She will need time to recover if she is to please our lord tonight, Baba Haroun. Unless she proves unworthy of my friendship, she has it. Do you understand me? This girl is not my enemy, nor do I expect her to be. Hasna and Fatinah were common creatures. Noor, like me, is the daughter of a prince."

"I understand, my lady Alia," the chief eunuch said, bowing again, and then he turned to Rhonwyn and bowed once more. "I will escort the lady Noor to her quarters," he said to Nilak.

Nilak gasped with her surprise. Never before had Baba Haroun bowed to any other woman in the harem but Alia. She imparted this information to her charge. Rhonwyn arose, and taking Alia's hands in hers, she kissed them. Then she followed the chief eunuch from the apartments of the caliph's wife without another word, Nilak scurrying in her wake.

When they were once again in Rhonwyn's chambers, Baba Haroun said to Nilak, "You will tell your mistress that I am her friend and mentor as long as she is true to the lady Alia. Should she ever betray my mistress, I will personally strangle her with my bare hands."

"You will tell the chief eunuch," Rhonwyn replied when Nilak had translated, "that I am a prince's daughter, and betrayal is not in my nature. I am grateful for Lady Alia's friendship and the wise counsel she has provided me with. I will be grateful for the counsel and friendship of Baba Haroun as well."

The chief eunuch smiled slightly, then asked, "Are you truly reconciled to this life that it has been fated you will now lead, Noor?"

Rhonwyn shook her head. "Not yet," she told him.

"Your honesty is to be commended," Baba Haroun said. Then he bowed to her again and departed the chamber.

"Oh, fortunate girl!" Nilak cried. "How can you fail to succeed now with the aid of both the lady Alia and Baba Haroun? You must rest, for the caliph will desire your presence tonight surely."

"I am hungry," Rhonwyn complained. "I have had nothing but sweets since I awoke. I want a meal else I faint in the caliph's arms from starvation, Nilak. How will you explain that?"

"If you faint in the caliph's arms, Noor, he will think you are overcome with passion for him, which is to the good," Nilak teased.

"Chicken," Rhonwyn said firmly.

"I will go to the kitchens myself," Nilak said, and hurried from the chamber.

She had been gone but a few moments when two young slave girls entered the apartments and bowed to Rhonwyn.

"Halah," said one, pointing to herself.

"Sadirah," said the other, making the same gesture.

They then set about preparing a small table for Rhonwyn's meal, chattering to each other as they did so. Rhonwyn realized these were the two serving girls Alia had promised her. They looked harmless enough, although she knew everything she did would be reported back to the caliph's wife even as Nilak reported her words. She smiled to herself and sat next to the fountain in her gathering room. To her surprise it had several water lilies and four small golden fish who swam busily about, darting amid the lily pads. She sighed. Everything about her was so peaceful and beautiful. It was probably the most idyllic place in which she had ever been.

Rising, she walked out into her garden. The mountains beyond and below the edge of the terrace were a hazy blue. She suspected that on a clear day she might even see the sea beyond. She needed to get to the sea. By the sea was Carthage—and the crusaders' encampment. How long now had she been gone from Edward. Six days? Seven? She had to find him again. She had to get back to him. What did he think happened to her? Would he have determined that the warrior who was captured was his wife? Had he looked for her? Would he indeed appear in Cinnebar, demanding her release? Oh, Edward, she thought sadly. What have I done? I love you! I love you! But will I ever see you again? She felt the tears coursing down her pale cheeks and struggled to regain control of herself. She looked up, startled at a touch on her shoulder.

Halah stood by her side, and the young slave girl pointed back inside. Then she made eating motions with her hands and mouth.

Rhonwyn nodded, giving the girl a weak smile. Brushing the evidence of tears from her cheeks, she arose and reentered her apartments where Nilak was busily setting out a meal with Sadirah's aid. Rhonwyn's nose twitched. There was indeed chicken, a small whole one stuffed with rice and raisins. There was a dish of cooked grain with bits of onion in it, flat bread, a honeycomb, and a bowl of fresh fruit. Rhonwyn sat down and began to eat eagerly, tearing the fowl in half and biting into it. "Delicious!" she pronounced, scooping up some of the stuffing with her fingers and popping it into her mouth.

"You eat like a ruffian," Nilak scolded. "Where are your manners, my child?"

"I'm hungry!" Rhonwyn protested. "I cannot even remember the last time I was fed. Do you mean to keep me half-starved all the time?"

"If you eat too quickly, you will get pains," Nilak advised.

"I am thirsty," Rhonwyn replied.

Shaking her head in despair, Nilak poured fruit juice from a silver decanter into a silver goblet. "Drink slowly," she said. "Do you approve of the two slave girls Lady Alia has given you?"

"They seem pleasant and efficient," Rhonwyn remarked.

"They are. Tomorrow we will begin your lessons in Arabic, my child. Lady Alia is most anxious that you learn."

"I hope I have the facility for it," Rhonwyn said, "but then I learned the Norman tongue readily enough. My own language, Welsh, is difficult for outsiders to learn." Rhonwyn turned her attention again to her meal, eating almost everything that had been brought to her, including a peach and a small bunch of grapes. When she had finished, her face and hands were bathed with scented water, and Halah cleaned her mouth and teeth.

"Now," Nilak said, "you must rest."

Rhonwyn did not argue. Her belly was comfortably full now, and it was hot. There was not even the slightest breeze stirring. Sadirah took her garments from her, and Nilak brushed her long gilt-colored hair. Rhonwyn was then content to lay naked upon the beautiful bed with its green silk gauze hangings, and was quickly asleep, her dark lashes brushing like small butterflies against her fair cheek.

"She is so beautiful," Halah said softly.

"They say the caliph fell in love with her at first sight," Sadirah murmured low.

"Do not be ridiculous," Nilak scolded them. "When the caliph first saw her she was garbed in men's clothing. I know, for I helped remove them. She was dirty and smelled like a stable."

"The gossip in Lady Alia's apartments is that he will make the lady Noor his wife now that Fatinah and Hasna are gone," Sadirah said. "That would mean our new mistress would be the second wife."

"If that is indeed so," Nilak replied, "then you have Lady Alia to thank for raising you up. You were merely two among many unimportant slave girls in her service. Now you are the serving women of the caliph's new favorite, who may possibly become his wife."

"She will be a wife. I am certain of it," Halah said.

"We are fortunate. She would appear to be a kind lady like Lady Alia."

"She is," Nilak assured them. "There is no meanness in her."

The three women went about the business of removing all evidence of Rhonwyn's meal and neatening up the apartment. The afternoon slipped into evening. Eventually Nilak sent the two younger servants to bed, but she remained watching by her mistress's bed. She was not surprised when the caliph entered the bedchamber, garbed only in a loose white robe. Arising from Rhonwyn's side, she bowed silently to him and departed the room, closing the door quietly behind her.

Rashid al Ahmet looked down upon the woman he called Noor, and his heart contracted in his chest. She had been in his possession two days, and while he certainly lusted after her, there was something more in his heart. He liked the contradictions of her. The fierceness and the vulnerability. He would never, he sensed, have all of her. There would always be a tiny something she would withhold from him, and therein lay the challenge. He removed his garment and lay down next to her. She was in a very deep sleep, and he was not surprised, considering all that had happened to her in the last week.

She had been on her side, but he gently drew her onto her back so he might look fully on her. His fingertips caressed her breasts, and she murmured contentedly. He smiled. Last night he had only begun to plumb the depths of her passions. He drew the back of his hand across her torso then, bending, began to kiss her lips with deep, hungry kisses.

Rhonwyn sighed and stretched lazily. The lips on hers were warm, and they grew more demanding with each passing moment. She faintly protested this intrusion into her sleep, but then she felt his fingers seeking between her nether lips. Two of the fingers pushed easily into her love channel while the ball of his thumb began to tease at the badge of her sex. His kisses were bruising her lips, but she didn't want him to stop. Her arms slipped up to embrace him. His thumb played with her until the tension was almost painful. She shuddered as it broke, but rather than stopping he began anew, arousing her again and this time to a greater height than before. Rhonwyn was now fully awake.

"Look at me, you adorable little bitch," he growled against her kiss-swollen mouth.

Rhonwyn's emerald green eyes opened and looked directly into those of Rashid al Ahmet. "As my lord wills," she said softly.

The two fingers thrust deep, and she cried out with undisguised pleasure. His white teeth flashed a smile against his sun-darkened skin. "Are you beginning to know passion?" he said provocatively. His thumb worried at her throbbing jewel.

"Yesss," she hissed, panting. *"Oh, please!"*

"Please what?" His tongue licked at her nipples.

"Please!" she repeated.

"Tell me what you want, my beauteous Noor," he replied.

"You!" she half sobbed.

He laughed low, and then rolling onto his back, he lifted her up, lowering her slowly on his raging manhood. When she was settled he reached up and began to fondle her breasts.

Rhonwyn was astounded. His manhood was deep inside her. She felt its length, hot and throbbing, yet it was she who would appear to be the dominant. Her eyes widened.

"Ride me, my adorable Noor. I am your stallion," Rashid al Ahmet told her. "Surely you are not afraid?"

She moved hesitantly at first, and then at his smile of open encouragement she began to move more surely upon him as he gently drew her forward, his hands slipping about to cup her buttocks.

"That's it, my beauty," he said. "Brace your hands, Noor. That's right, my precious. Ah! What pleasure you give me!"

Rhonwyn had found the proper rhythm now, and she rode the caliph enthusiastically for some minutes until he gently turned her onto her back, delving deeper into her softness, watching the change in expression on her lovely face, amazed when they attained nirvana together, crying out with utter satisfaction.

After some minutes Rashid al Ahmet laughed aloud. "What a woman you are becoming, my lovely Noor," he said.

Rhonwyn could feel that her cheeks were hot. She had been so wickedly bold, and she had liked it. "I never knew you could . . ."

"You are going to be astounded at what we can and will do together, my adorable one," he said, his deep laughter rumbling up again from his chest. "You are, I am pleased to note, an eager pupil." Leaning over, he kissed her again, running a finger along her bruised lips. "Do you like your apartments?"

"Aye, I do. Especially the garden with its sweeping views of the mountains, my lord."

"Good!" he said. "Are you hungry? I am. I have not eaten since morning."

"I shall have my servants bring you food, my lord Rashid," Rhonwyn said, arising from her bed. "And while we eat, will you tell me of your day?"

His dark blue eyes grew warm with approval. The whole palace was gossiping that he intended to make Noor his wife, but until this moment he had not decided the matter. It was a foolish man who thought only with his cock. Her newly unleashed passion was commendable, but it was her care for his welfare and her interest in his doings that brought about his final decision. He would indeed make Noor his wife. Like Alia, she was a nurturing creature, quite unlike the two who had been disposed of this day. And two wives, he thought, was more than enough for any man, even a caliph of Cinnebar. Tomorrow he would speak with the imam. "Aye, Noor," he said to her. "I will indeed share my day with you as we eat."

Chapter Eleven

"Well, Edward de Beaulieu," Prince Edward said, "do you think you are strong enough to continue on, or will you return to England? You have been very ill, and I will not count it against you, particularly under the circumstances."

"I will go on with you, my liege" came the answer, "but first I must seek my wife and Sir Fulk. They are surely being held captive nearby and can be ransomed."

"Perhaps," the prince responded, "but I wonder if that is so, for we have received no ransom demand, nor have we been attacked since that day when your wife so bravely led our men. What a woman! I should like to see her and her companion, Sir Fulk, safely returned."

"I will follow you in seven days' time, my lord, if I cannot find Rhonwyn. But I know that I will," de Beaulieu said tersely. The prince's remarks about his wife's courage were somehow irritating.

"I will pray God that you do, my friend, but if in seven days' time you have found no trace of her, then you must give up your search. She will have been either sold into slavery in some nameless place or ravaged and killed. I am very concerned that a week has gone by and we have had no word, but you must search, else you and your honor not be satisfied, I know. I surely would not be. You know the road to Acre." The prince patted Edward de Beaulieu's shoulder.

"I have one favor to ask of you, my liege. Will your good wife take Rhonwyn's maidservant into her train until I find Rhonwyn? I cannot keep Enit safe among all these men, and she is a good lass, betrothed to one of my own people."

"Of course," Prince Edward said. "Have her gather her possessions, and I will escort her to Eleanor myself."

Enit began to weep when she was told of her fate. "Please, my lord, let me stay with you and wait for my mistress to return."

"Nay, Enit, it is not safe," de Beaulieu told her. "You will be reunited with your mistress in Acre, but in the meanwhile I know you will be secure with the princess's train. My search may be dangerous, and I cannot have you about to worry over. Now fetch your things and go with Prince Edward."

"Yes, my lord." Enit sniffled, but she did his bidding, gathering up her few possessions and following forlornly after Prince Edward as he departed de Beaulieu's tent.

"There is one less worry," Edward muttered almost to himself. He was still feeling weak, but at least he was on his feet again. In the morning he would take his two knights, and they would seek Rhonwyn and Sir Fulk. *Rhonwyn*. His wild Welsh wife. He didn't know whether he would kill her or kiss her when he found her. *And Fulk!* Where was his common sense that he allowed his lord's wife to run off into battle and then get them captured? To his credit Fulk had at least followed after Rhonwyn.

De Beaulieu understood that Rhonwyn was different from other women by virtue of her upbringing, but he had never liked it. He could even understand her desire to bloody her sword for the first time in a real combat, although most women he had known would have fainted at the mere thought of such a thing. Her mistake had been in becoming overconfident. Her passion for the battle should not have outweighed her caution, but it had, allowing her to be surrounded and then captured. But why had they taken her off and not simply killed her? He needed to know more than he already did. He called Sir Hugo into his presence and asked him to seek out someone who had been in the heat of the battle. Sir Hugo returned with a rather grizzled and gruff knight, Sir Arthur Sackville.

"I had heard it was a woman," Sir Arthur said, shaking his head with disbelief. "But I could not quite fathom such a thing. Your wife, you say?"

"Aye," Edward answered. "She is the daughter of ap Gruffydd, the prince of the Welsh."

"Magnificent creature!" Sir Arthur enthused admiringly. "She raced into the very center of it all, rallying us furiously! For the first time I felt our crusade was a truly holy and blessed thing, my lord. It was as if the angels were on her side."

"Did you see her capture? Why did they take her instead of simply killing her?" de Beaulieu pressed.

"They didn't really. She had just killed the nobleman who led the infidels. I think it was in coming to his defense they found themselves surrounding your wife, although they certainly did not realize they had a woman. But they raced off with her in their midst. A single knight galloped after them, but I do not know his name."

"Sir Fulk," Edward said. "He was my man and should not have allowed Rhonwyn into battle, although even I know it would have been difficult to stop her once her mind was set on it. Who was the man she killed?"

"I have no idea, my lord de Beaulieu. One of their nobles by his garb. I am sorry I can help you no further," Sir Arthur said.

"Can you tell me in which direction they went?" Edward asked.

"Toward the mountains," the knight said. "Of that I am absolutely certain. They rode to the mountains, although why I do not understand. There is nothing out there, you know."

"There must be something, else why would they have gone that way?" Edward replied.

"Nomads and their flocks, perhaps, but nothing else." Sir Arthur paused as if considering his next words. Then he said, "My lord de Beaulieu, while the infidels could not have known at first that the knight who battled them so fiercely was a woman, they would have eventually found her out. They have surely ravaged her and killed her by now. Yours is a tragic loss, I realize, but you will have to accept it sooner or later, I fear. And if by some miracle your lady survived, would you want her back after other men had used her? Forgive me, de Beaulieu, for saying it, but she is lost to you. God help her, she is gone." He bowed to Edward. "I am sorry I could be of no real help to you." Then he exited the tent.

"Be ready to ride at moonrise," Edward said quietly to his two knights. "See to the horses and water now."

"He's mad," Sir Hugo later said as he and the other knight did their lord's bidding. "Sir Arthur is probably correct, and the lady is dead or worse."

"You knew her," Sir Robert responded. "If she were your wife, would you not at least attempt to find her? I know I would."

It was after midnight when the waning moon rose and they departed the crusaders' encampment. They rode toward the mountains, dark shadowed mounds upon the horizon. Above them in the clear black sky the stars twinkled in lonely splendor. Their journey ceased when the sun became too hot for travel. Then they would water the horses from the supply they carried and shelter in the gray shadow of the rocks. For four days they rode, but they saw nothing. No tents. No livestock. No people. Everything about them was wilderness. There was absolutely no sign of any civilization, even in the foothills of the mountains. Not a trace of human habitation was visible. It was as if the earth had opened up and swallowed Rhonwyn.

Edward's heart grew heavier with each passing day. He finally accepted what everyone had been telling him. Rhonwyn was gone. His beautiful wild Welsh wife was lost to him. He would never see her again. Giving the word to his two grateful knights, he turned their horses back to the sea, directing their steps toward the Acre road so they might join Prince Edward and his crusaders. On the first night of their return journey as his two knights slept, Edward hid himself among the rocks and wept for the woman he believed he loved. But in the days that followed, his heart hardened toward her. Everything that had happened was her fault. She had avoided her marital duties and given him no heir. Then she had insisted upon coming on crusade when a responsible woman would have remained at Haven, praying for his safe return and doing her duty as his chatelaine. It was one thing for a queen or a princess to come on crusade, but the wife of a simple lord had no business being in the midst of such an adventure.

His thoughts began to stray to his cousin Katherine. He would need a wife when he returned home to England. His cousin's family had always hoped he would marry Katherine, and now he would. She was fair enough and obedient to boot. There would be no nonsense over his possession of her body, and Katherine would gladly give him heirs as quickly as his seed took root. Aye, Katherine would be the perfect wife for him. Arriving in Acre, he hired a scribe and dictated a letter to his cousin Rafe.

Rafe de Beaulieu was surprised when in the spring of
the next year he received his cousin's missive from Acre.
"You are to be married!" he told his sister. "The Welsh
wife has died, although I should not have thought a
healthy girl like that would succumb easily, but she has!
Edward wants you for his wife. When he returns home
you will be wed, sister. This is just what the family has always wanted, Kate!" And yet while pleased for Kate, he
grieved secretly for the beautiful Rhonwyn. If she had
been his he would have kept her safe.

"We must pray for the lady Rhonwyn's soul," Katherine said quietly. "I liked her, for she was as good as she
was beautiful. All the servants have told me that."

"Pray for her then, sister," Rafe said, and seeing her
stricken look, continued, "I am rough spoken, Kate, and
well you know it. Forgive me. In my happiness over your
good fortune I did not consider the misfortune of the
lady Rhonwyn. She was beautiful, and we had no quarrel with her. I will pray for her also."

It was Father John who brought Glynn the news of his
sister's demise. The boy was, as was expected, devastated
by the news. "Do you want to go home to Wales?" the
priest asked him. "To your father?"

Glynn swallowed hard. "Nay," he said. "Rhonwyn
wanted me to be educated, and I will not disappoint her,
good father. I will remain in school. I thank you for coming to tell me, for had I learned of this at Haven on my
next visit, I should have given everything away in my
grief. How did my sister die?"

"Edward did not say. I expect it was too painful for
him," the priest replied. "We will learn the truth when he
returns home to Haven, but not until then I fear."

"I do not sense my sister dead," Glynn said thoughtfully. "I would have thought if she had died I should have
known, we were that close, good father."

"Do not allow your Celtic mysticism to overcome your Christian sense, my lad," the priest warned him as he turned to depart.

Glynn murmured as if in agreement, but in his heart he did not acquiesce to the priest's words. Until he learned from his brother-in-law exactly how his sister had died— that Edward had seen it himself—Glynn could not believe that Rhonwyn was gone from this earth into the next. *Not his sister.* She had too strong a will to die young.

Alone in his dormitory Glynn began to play upon his lute, composing as he did so another ballad about a warrior woman called Rhonwyn, and he suddenly felt a sense of great comfort sweeping over him. *She is not dead!* he thought. But what has happened to her? It was then the thought entered his mind. He would go to Acre himself and find Edward. Then having learned the truth, he would find Rhonwyn.

Glynn ap Llywelyn went into the town several days later to seek out Oth and Dewi. His two guardians had been sent back from Wales by his father when Glynn entered the abbey school. In order to maintain themselves they hired out as men-at-arms for local folk traveling the countryside, but their base was in Shrewsbury, to which they always returned. They boarded with an elderly widow who felt safer by their frequent presence. Glynn made his way through the town's narrow streets to the widow's house by the river.

"Good morrow, Mistress Ellen," he greeted her cheerfully. "Can you tell me if Oth and Dewi are in town today?"

"Just back yesterday, young master. They are working my garden for me," the old lady replied. "Go along through."

"Jesu, lad," Oth said, catching sight of Glynn, "you seem to grow bigger each day. What is it the good brothers feed you?"

The two Welshmen embraced Glynn.

"Father John has been to see me," Glynn said without any preamble. "He has had a letter from Edward saying that Rhonwyn has died."

"I don't believe it!" Oth burst out.

"Nor I," Dewi agreed.

Glynn smiled with relief. "Good, because I do not feel the loss of my sister's presence at all," he told the two. "Edward must believe such a thing or he would not say it, but until I learn for myself just what happened, I cannot accept that Rhonwyn is gone from us. I mean to go to Acre where the crusade is now settled. Will you two come with me?"

"Aye," they answered with one voice.

"Good," Glynn replied. "Now, I have considered this carefully. Neither Rafe de Beaulieu nor his sister know my true identity. They will wonder if I do not come to Haven, and they will worry, for I am believed to be Edward's bastard. I shall visit them shortly and tell them that because I am considering the priesthood, I am being sent to one of the order's other schools in France for a year. As for the father abbott, you two shall come to him in three days' time, for he knows my true identity, and you will tell him that my father, ap Gruffydd, desires me to join him for several months, and you have been sent to escort me to him. We will then go to Haven and from there to the Holy Land."

"What of Father John?" Oth asked. "Will he believe your little tale of school in France? He is no fool, lad."

"I will tell him the truth," Glynn said. "He cannot betray me lest he betray Edward's subterfuge to his kin. I do not believe he will do that."

Oth looked at the boy who was now sixteen and practically a man. He would not have expected such a daring plan from the gentle Glynn, but it was obvious that the lad meant to seek his sister out no matter what anyone else said. "What are we to do for traveling funds?" he asked in a pragmatic tone. "Dewi and I have some coins put aside, but we'll need more than what we have."

"I have my allowance," Glynn said. "I've never spent it but for strings for my musical instruments. I have almost everything Edward gave me last year, and I will ask Rafe de Beaulieu for more since I am going to France." He chuckled. "And if we run out of funds, I shall sing for our supper."

"Well, then," said Oth, "there is nought to keep us from our travels, Glynn ap Llywelyn. We shall come for you in three days' time."

And when they did the father was most sympathetic. "Of course Prince Llywelyn would want his son with him under the tragic circumstances," he said. Father John had told him of Rhonwyn's demise. "We have been praying for the lady's good soul ever since we learned the terrible news." He turned to Glynn. "We shall eagerly await your return, Glynn ap Llywelyn. Go now and comfort your father."

"You're a true Welshman," Oth said approvingly as they rode through the city gates. "You played your part well and never once looked guilty over the lies we told that good priest."

Glynn merely grinned at his companion.

At Haven Castle the boy appeared alone and told his tale to Rafe de Beaulieu and his sister. Father John lifted a questioning eyebrow but said nothing.

"So you are considering being a priest," Rafe said enthusiastically.

"Why should this make you happy?" Glynn said.

"Because you are my cousin Edward's get. He will wed my sister, Katherine, when he returns from crusade. While you are a bastard, if Edward should die, you might attempt to usurp my sister's children from their rightful inheritance. As a priest I can trust you and your intentions, Glynn of Thorley."

Glynn felt a terrible fury welling up within him. Rhonwyn was barely dead, according to Edward, and he was already planning a new marriage. I will kill him, Glynn vowed silently to himself, and then he caught Father John's eye. He swallowed his anger back down, but it still burned within him as he said, "Your devotion to your sister is commendable, Rafe."

"What is this all about?" the priest demanded of Glynn when they were finally alone.

"I do not believe my sister is dead," Glynn replied. "You scoff at my Celtic mysticism, but there has always been a bond between my sister and me. It is not that I am grieving or unable to accept the truth in this matter. If Rhonwyn were dead, I should feel it. I do not, and if I do not, she must be alive. I am going to the Holy Land to find her and to find out from my treacherous brother-in-law what has happened to her. How quickly he plans his remarriage."

The priest sighed. "I see I cannot dissuade you, Glynn," he said. "May I assume Oth and Dewi are nearby?"

"They are and will be my companions in this adventure." The boy's eyes twinkled. "You must see that Rafe de Beaulieu gives me a fat purse for my journey to France and my year's stay there."

"What did you tell the abbott?" the priest demanded.

"That my father had called me back to Wales," Glynn replied. "It seemed a plausible explanation."

"Aye," the priest said. "If you must lie, 'tis best to keep it simple." He sighed again, then advised, "Go to Dover, Glynn. There are still ships sailing for the Holy Land with men who wish to join Prince Edward. A young minstrel and two men-at-arms will easily find passage on one of these vessels. This is a good time of year to go, as the seas will be calmer than in winter."

"You will pray for us, father, will you not?"

"I will pray hard for you, Glynn ap Llywelyn. You go, I fear, on a fool's errand, but if it will satisfy your heart and soul to make this journey, then I cannot deny you. If Edward de Beaulieu says your sister is dead, God assoil her good soul, then surely she must be, for what reason would he have to lie? He cared for the lady Rhonwyn."

Glynn shook his head. "Like you, I am puzzled, but I also know in my heart that my sister lives. Why Edward believes her dead I cannot say, but I go to learn the truth of the matter."

"I will see you well funded," the priest promised.

The monies were handed over, and Glynn departed Haven Castle the following day, a fat purse well hidden on his person and Father John's blessing ringing in his ears. Joining Oth and Dewi down the road, he turned to look back and wondered if he would ever see Haven again. While startling, the feeling did not distress him. His goal was to find Rhonwyn, and in that he would not be deterred. He had grown not just physically but intellectually during his time at the abbey school. While he still preferred music and poetry to armaments and fighting, he had found he was capable of being tough and hard when he must be so.

They spent the next few days riding across England to Dover. There, as the priest had told them, were vessels preparing to depart for the Holy Land and Prince Edward's crusade. They took passage on a sturdy ship with a Welsh captain who, looking at Oth, claimed kinship with him through a female relation and welcomed them aboard. After three days at sea the captain and Oth had traced their family connection to the sister of Oth's grandsire, who had been the captain's grandmam. Oth explained to his kinsman that Glynn was also their kinsman and a minstrel going to the Holy Land to entertain the soldiers. During the seven weeks of their voyage Glynn entertained the captain and the crew with his ballads, his sweet voice rising above the roar of the sea.

Once into the Mediterranean the days and the nights grew warmer and then hot. Their vessel stopped at several ports to unload and take on cargo, food, and water. Finally they reached Acre, an ancient city reputed to have the finest port on the Mediterranean. Once Acre had belonged to the Syrians, but in the seventh century it had been captured by the Arabs. It had changed hands several times during the early crusades, but was now firmly in the hands of the Knights Hospitalers who had held it for almost a hundred years as part of the kingdom of Jerusalem.

Glynn, Oth, and Dewi disembarked their ship and quickly found themselves in the crowded, noisy, and dusty streets of the city. Their ship's captain had directed them to a small inn where they would not be cheated or robbed if they were careful. Reaching the inn, they were relieved to find the innkeeper, a large buxom woman of indeterminate age, spoke the Norman tongue.

"I am Glynn of Thorley, minstrel extraordinaire and sent to you by Captain Rhys, mistress. These two are my bodyguards, who are quite capable of keeping the peace within your inn on the best of nights or the worst," Glynn told her with an elegant bow.

"You are seeking employment?" she asked them, her hands upon her ample hips.

"We seek temporary shelter, mistress," Glynn said, "but we are willing to work for it and for our supper."

"Why temporary?" the innkeeper demanded of him, licking her lips provocatively as she looked at Oth.

Oth winked at her.

"I have come to Acre seeking my good overlord, Edward de Beaulieu, who is with Prince Edward," Glynn answered. "If he is in Acre, I will find him, and if he is not, I may at least learn where he is, mistress."

"I can accommodate you," the innkeeper said. "You may have your days free, but your nights you must give to me ... to entertaining my customers, I mean. And your men will be at my beck and call in the evenings as well. Is it agreed?" For the first time she looked directly at Glynn, surprised at his youth.

"It is agreed, mistress," he said with a smile. He thought her a pretty woman with skin as white as milk and black, black hair.

"My name is Nada," the innkeeper said. "It means *giving* in the language of the Arabs, and I am known to be a most generous woman." Her gaze was again on Oth. "Do your companions have names, young minstrel?"

"They are Oth and Dewi," Glynn responded with a gesture toward the two men.

"There is a nice room behind the kitchens," Mistress Nada said. "Come, and I will show you. Then, perhaps, you would like to have a decent meal, for from the look of you, you haven't had good food in over a month. I like my men with more meat on their bones."

"The better to eat you alive," Dewi murmured to his companions in their own tongue. "You're a lucky dog, Oth. She looks like she'll prove a right lusty fuck!"

"I'll see if she has a sister," Oth returned softly.

The inn, in a whitewashed dried mud building, had a hard-packed dirt floor. Inside it was cool and dim. The wooden tables were well scrubbed, their benches tucked neatly beneath them. They followed the innkeeper through the main room of her establishment into a bright kitchen at the rear of the building. From the rafters there hung sheaves of dried herbs and fruits. Pots boiled merrily over the fire. From the ovens came the delicious smell of baking. The three women servants glanced briefly at them, then returned to their chores. The men could see a courtyard beyond the kitchen through its narrow windows.

"Your room is through there." She pointed. "It has a door to the courtyard. It is clean and dry, I promise you."

Glynn stepped into the chamber, followed by Dewi. Oth, however, remained in the kitchen with the innkeeper. He backed the woman up into a wall alcove and fumbled her ample breasts. Nada smiled broadly, showing strong white teeth, and rubbed herself against him in a decidedly suggestive manner.

"There is no time now," she said, "and besides, you will need a good meal first so you may be filled with strength. What does Oth mean?" Her hand slipped into his breeches, and she fondled him, her black eyes widening as she felt him hard and large in her palm. "Leave us," she called to her three servants, who immediately obeyed.

"*Giant,*" he said meaningfully. "Dewi will keep the boy away." Then he turned her about, pushing her down over her kitchen table even as his hands were raising up her skirts so he might have access to her. His manhood found her love channel easily, and Oth thrust himself into the woman with a groan, working himself back and forth as she eagerly pushed her plump rump into his groin.

"Ah, that's good, you devil!" she moaned. *"Don't stop!"*

He pleasured her for several minutes, and then said, "Sorry, lass, but 'tis just a taster I can give you now. Yer right. I do need my dinner." Then he emptied his seed into her with a lusty sigh.

Nada let out a long hiss of breath, collapsing slightly upon her table. As Oth withdrew from her she slowly straightened herself up and turned about to face him. "My rooms are on the other side of the courtyard," she told him, pulling her skirts down and giving him a quick kiss. "I can use a lusty lover . . . temporarily." Then she left the kitchen.

"I thought a man rode atop the woman," Glynn said as he and Dewi came forth from the chamber.

"Not always," Oth replied. "Have you had a woman yet, lad?"

Glynn nodded. "In Shrewsbury there's a girl who spreads her legs for a ha'penny. My friends at the school took me. I've been twice."

"And you liked it?" Oth questioned Glynn.

"Aye, 'tis why I went again," the young man replied.

The two older men laughed. "Well, in that you are your father's son," they told him.

Then Oth said, "Since you've made a beginning of it, we'll teach you what you need to know, young Glynn. Acre is as good a place as any for a young fellow to sow his wild oats."

"But first I must find Edward," Glynn said, all business again.

"We'll find him," Oth promised.

And they did, although it took almost a full week. During the hot days they sought out de Beaulieu, while in the evenings Glynn's sweet voice filled Mistress Nada's inn and poured out into the streets. Word of the young minstrel spread quickly, and the inn was packed with men of all lands listening to Glynn as he sang ballads old and familiar and some that he had himself composed. The inn's guests quickly found a new favorite in "The Warrior Woman," which Glynn had composed about his sister. The serving maids had taken to practically tiptoeing when Glynn was entertaining. They had also taken to coming into his chamber at night to pleasure both him and Dewi while Oth was with Mistress Nada.

"The woman's insatiable," Oth complained to Glynn and Dewi the day they found Edward de Beaulieu.

Edward immediately recognized Oth and Dewi, but at first he did not recognize their companion. Glynn was no longer a young boy but a man. "What," he demanded, very surprised, "are you doing here?"

"Where is my sister?" Glynn demanded.

"She is dead of her own foolishness," Edward replied bitterly. "Come, sit down out of the sun, Glynn. How did you leave Haven?"

"Haven stands as it did the day you departed it with my sister. Your cousin Rafe and your bride-to-be, Katherine, eagerly await your return," Glynn said rancorously. "Tell me of my sister. How did she die? Were you not there?"

"We were at Carthage," Edward began, signaling his servants to bring cool wine for his guests. "I was ill with fever and a terrible flux of the belly and bowels. Rhonwyn nursed me devotedly, only allowing Enit to sit with me a few hours each night so she might sleep. All around us men were dying like flies, but Rhonwyn moved our tent away from the others and kept it and me scrupulously clean. I owed her a debt for saving my life. King Louis died, and Charles of Anjou made peace with the infidels. Prince Edward would not have it and made plans to move on to Acre.

"Rhonwyn had been penned up with me for weeks. I suggested she go with Sir Fulk to play at sword practice. I saw she was well garbed for it, though she argued with me because of the heat, but then, properly dressed, she and Fulk went off to the practice field. Shortly after, the infidels began one of their little attacks on the encampment. It was routine. They did it each day. It was never more than a skirmish, and nought ever came of it. There were rarely any injuries and certainly no casualties.

"Rhonwyn obviously decided to bloody her sword in real combat, and Fulk, it appears, went with her. Her headpiece ensured that no one knew she was a woman. They say she rallied the soldiers magnificently. It became a serious battle, and the infidel was beaten back. Unfortunately Rhonwyn got cut off from the main body of soldiers. She was captured, and Fulk, riding after her, was taken, too. I spent four days with Sir Hugo and Sir Robert seeking any trace of her. There was none. It is the opinion of those who know about such things that she was probably found out, then raped and murdered. She might have been sold into slavery somewhere, but that, it seems, is unlikely, for she was not a virgin," Edward de Beaulieu finished.

"My sister is not dead," Glynn ap Llywelyn said. "If she were, I should sense it in my heart."

"Glynn, I am sorry," Edward said, reaching out to the young man whom he genuinely liked.

"*She is not dead!*" Glynn shouted. "And I will find her, Edward."

"If you find any trace of her, it will be nought but her bones. I have prayed for her each day since she was lost to me," Edward said angrily.

"You have prayed for her while seeking another bride," Glynn replied furiously. "And Rafe de Beaulieu lords it over Haven, even as his sister waits meekly for your return!"

"Rhonwyn should have waited meekly for my return," Edward said.

"If you had wanted Rhonwyn to await your return, then you should have forbidden her to accompany you, Edward. I think it pleased your vanity to have her with you as the lady Eleanor was with Prince Edward. It was my sister, I know, who first expressed enthusiasm for the crusade, and not you. Rhonwyn, ap Gruffydd's daughter, made the king's son look favorably upon you, and Edward Plantagenet will be England's king far sooner than later, we all know," Glynn said with devastating veracity.

"Am I to be condemned then by *you*, a mere singer of ballads, a Welsh outlaw's bastard get, for considering the future of my family?" Edward de Beaulieu demanded. *He would not be made to feel guilty!*

Glynn smiled scornfully. "When I find my sister, I shall tell her the kind of man she is wed to, although I already suspect Rhonwyn knew, for even I could see you were not a well-matched pair. Had you been, perhaps you might have mourned my sister's loss instead of hurrying to make a match with your cousin Katherine."

"Your sister was a coldhearted bitch," Edward declared heatedly. "She would scarcely allow me my husbandly rights. Why do you think there were no children? My seed is strong. I have fathered my share of bastards, Glynn, but Rhonwyn would not let me near her. At least Katherine is eager for children and will give me legitimate heirs."

"How convenient that my sister should suddenly disappear then," Glynn said. "Or did you arrange her mysterious *disappearance*?"

"Do you think me so without honor, then?" Edward demanded.

"*Yes,*" Glynn ap Llywelyn said deprecatingly. Then he smiled a silent challenge at his brother-in-law.

Edward de Beaulieu's hand went to where his sword would have been in battle. His eyes flashed irately at the younger man.

"My lord," Oth's voice broke in amid the tension. "Glynn has not the skill to fight you. He is angry beyond reason, as you well may understand. You are the man in this matter."

"Get from my sight," Edward said to Glynn. "I do not want to see you ever again!"

"I am not afraid to fight you!" Glynn declared passionately.

"Come, lad," Oth said softly. "He will certainly kill you, and then who will there be to find our Rhonwyn?"

"I place a Welsh curse upon you, Edward de Beaulieu," the boy said. "May you have only daughters!" Then he turned and left the courtyard.

Edward laughed mockingly. "Would that his sister had shown me such passion," he said to Oth. "Take him home before he gets himself killed. Perhaps ap Gruffydd can do something with his son. He is no longer my responsibility, nor do I want him."

Oth nodded silently, and then followed after his young master. While he had managed to keep Glynn from getting himself killed, he was in total agreement with the lad. The Welshman had always thought de Beaulieu coldhearted, but now he was certain of it. Still, what could they do now? If the Englishman was telling the truth, and there really was no reason to think he wasn't, then where had Rhonwyn gotten to? Thinking about it hurt his brain, and when they reached their inn he gladly followed Nada to her chambers, as was her custom in the afternoon heat.

She rubbed his head, taking the ache away, and he pleasured her into temporary repletion, saying afterward, "I want to buy you a gift, Nada. What would you like, remembering I am a poor man?"

She laughed her husky laugh. "A gold bangle will not harm your finances, Oth, but you must remember I wear only gold ornaments that come from the caliphate of Cinnebar. Their goldsmiths are truly without equal. Later this afternoon when it is cooler, we shall shop together at the only merchant in all of Acre who carries jewelry from Cinnebar. He will charge you little, as it is for me."

"*Cinnebar?* I have never heard of such a place. Where is it?" Oth leaned over and kissed the fat nipple on her big breast.

"It is a tiny kingdom, fairly isolated, in the mountains to the west and south of Carthage," Nada told him. "They have famous gold mines and other wealth, but it is small and so difficult to reach that no conqueror will bother with it." She reached out to encourage his manhood to action again. "They were once a Christian state, but then converted to Islam. Their rulers were allowed to take the most rare of titles, *caliph,* which means defender of the faith. Oh, that's nice," she purred as her lover sheathed himself inside her once again. "I shall truly miss you, Oth," she told him.

He used her fiercely and roughly, as she liked, exhausting her into sleep at last. Oth then lay by his mistress's side, considering what she had told him. Was it possible, just possible, that the lady Rhonwyn had somehow ended up in Cinnebar? Edward de Beaulieu claimed to have sought for her for several days, but he had gone only into the foothills of the mountains. Oth knew from the talk he had heard in Acre that a fair woman, virgin or not, was most highly prized here in the slave markets by the Arab lords, whose own women were dark haired, dark eyed, and darker skinned. What if the men who had captured her had taken her to Cinnebar and sold her as a slave?

When Nada finally awoke and they dressed he asked her if such a thing was possible.

"Of course" was the firm answer. "Even if she was not the most beautiful girl in the world, her hair, her eyes, and her skin would make her most valuable. You say she is beautiful? Then her captors would have treated her gently in order to gain the highest price for her. Most likely Cinnebar is where they would have taken her. Any longer trip, and your mistress might very well have died, not being used to the climate. Her captors would have known that and would have wanted to turn their profit as quickly as possible lest she sicken on them."

"How can we get to Cinnebar?" Oth asked Nada.

She smiled broadly at him. "How fortunate you are that I took you for my lover," she said. "Gold jewelry from Cinnebar is for the wealthy, not a mere innkeeper. Fortunately the shopkeeper I am taking you to meet is my cousin. His sister is married to a merchant of Cinnebar. Melek is a resourceful woman, and she will help you. The first thing we must do is find a caravan going to Cinnebar. If not from here, then from Carthage, or Alexandria, or Damascus. You will probably not be able to travel directly, for caravans to Cinnebar are rare."

"We could travel by sea to Carthage, could we not?" Oth said.

"Yes," Nada said thoughtfully. "We will speak with my cousin the merchant about it. He will know, and perhaps you can act as his agent. He would pay your passage then, so your pretty young master would have only two passages to concern him." She looked at him longingly. "Oh, I am indeed going to miss you, Oth. It will be a long while, if ever, before I find another lover like you!" She patted his rump affectionately, and then said, "Let us go now. I want my gold bangle so I may always remember you, my little Welshman." Then with a chuckle she was off, and Oth dutifully followed behind her.

There would be time enough this evening to tell Glynn about this most interesting bit of news, and they might as well begin looking in Cinnebar as anywhere else. It seemed most logical. He would miss Nada, too, Oth thought. She had indeed proved a lusty fuck, but it was her good heart and easy laughter that had delighted him as well. Still, they would surely have a few more hot afternoons before he and his companions departed. *If God was kind*, Oth considered with a grin.

Chapter Twelve

"You came to me practically a virgin, and now you are probably the most wanton creature I have ever known," Rashid al Ahmet teased his beautiful second wife. "Ah, yes, you witch!"

She knelt before him, her hands and her mouth entertaining the various aspects of his manhood. One hand gripped him, keeping him steady within her mouth while her tongue encircled him, tantalizing him expertly, even as the fingers of her other hand bedeviled his pendulous jewels, stroking them, tickling them lightly as he grew harder and harder in the warm cave beyond her succulent lips.

He kneaded her gilt-colored head as she continued to arouse him, but finally he said in a thick voice, *"Enough, witch!"*

Rhonwyn looked up at him with a wicked smile. Then swinging her lithe body about, she knelt upon all fours, elevating her milky white bottom to him. "Does it please my lord to play the stallion with his willing mare?" she taunted him. Turning her head, she looked over her shoulder at him seductively. She was burning for his passion.

"*Yes!*" he growled, kneeling behind her and thrusting easily into her hot, wet love channel, pushing deep, withdrawing, and thrusting again. "I cannot get enough of you, my exquisite Noor. It pleases me that you now feel the same way."

She whimpered her open pleasure as his fingers dug into her hips, steadying her against his onslaught. His lance probed her deeply, sending ripples of shivers down her spine. Until the caliph she had never even dreamed of such pleasure, and the thought struck her as it always did when Rashid made such passionate love to her: that she wished she might have shared this loveliness with Edward de Beaulieu. Her head spun, and she half sobbed, "Oh, Allah, 'tis wonderful, my lord! Do not cease! *Do not cease!*" She reached the apex of her delight, shuddering violently as it shattered over her, receded, and left her weak. Her body collapsed onto the carpet. But withdrawing, he turned her onto her back and pushed his manhood into her again.

"*Not yet,*" he ordered her. "I am not ready, my fair Noor, and you are too quick to grasp your pleasure, just as a greedy child with a sweet. I must teach you more self-control." His dark eyes mocked her as he moved slowly, deliberately, upon her, arousing her once again to heights to which she did not think she could return so soon. And when he was satisfied at last, his love juices burst, flooding her channel, leaving them both but half-conscious as the pleasure drained slowly away. He rolled onto his back, drawing her onto his chest within his embrace. "Ah, Noor, my love, you are magnificent."

His words comforted her as she fell into an exhausted sleep, not even knowing when he arose and carried her to her own bed, drawing a light coverlet over her beautiful body. The caliph of Cinnebar smiled softly upon his beautiful second wife. His life, it seemed, had become so perfect since she had entered it over a year ago. At first she had been but a beautiful possession, but then he realized he had fallen in love with her.

He was a fortunate man, Rashid al Ahmet thought to himself. Two beautiful wives. Both loving and compatible with one another. Could Paradise be any better than this? Although he still occasionally took his pleasure with one of the concubines in his harem, it was but a momentary diversion. It was Noor whom he loved with a young man's passion, and now he wanted children by her.

He was more than well aware of the methods used within his household to prevent conception. He even approved. The two wives he had executed had given him three children between them. His younger son, Omar, and his two little daughters. Mohammed, his heir who was fourteen, was now allowed sterile harem damsels for his pleasure. Rashid al Ahmet knew the dangers of too many sons and but one kingdom to inherit. His younger brothers had always been difficult to control even before their father died. Kasim had, quite fortunately, died of a fever at age fifteen, and his own exquisite Noor had slain Abdallah in battle. Now he wanted a child from this wife he called his warrior woman. He would speak with Alia and with Baba Haroun, for it was just possible they would know how he might be certain of fathering only a daughter on Noor, not a son to perhaps one day challenge Mohammed and even Omar. He smiled down on Noor, and then left her sleeping peacefully in her own bed.

His first wife was sympathetic to his desires, but his chief eunuch was fiercely against it.

"Your life is peaceful and perfect right now, my lord. You have a son who is just about a man. You have a second son who should, Allah forfend anything happen to the first, be there to succeed. There is no certain way to guarantee the lady Noor would bear you a daughter. Think, my lord, think! Lady Noor is a fierce woman despite the passion you have for one another. She has killed without regret. She could kill again if the matter involved her own son. Do not put her in that position, or yourself, or Lady Alia, my lord," Baba Haroun said seriously.

"I must think on it," Rashid al Ahmet replied. "I do long for a daughter as beautiful as she is."

"Does she wish for a child, my lord?" the chief eunuch asked.

"She has not said so," the caliph answered.

"Then let well enough alone, my lord," Baba Haroun pleaded.

The caliph turned to Alia. "What are your thoughts on this, my honored first wife? You are remarkably silent in this matter."

"As always, Rashid, I want what will make you happy," Alia told him. "Mohammed is fourteen now, and little Omar almost six. If Noor gave you a son, I cannot see any danger to my son. By the time this child was grown Mohammed would have fathered his own sons, and Omar, too. Besides, I do not see that kind of ambition in Noor. And she might indeed give you a daughter, not a son. But if she has expressed no wish for a child, you would be wise not to force the issue for now."

"I must think on it," the caliph repeated, but both Alia and Baba Haroun knew that he had already made up his mind. He wanted a child from Noor and would not be satisfied until he had one.

"My lord, of interest to you, perhaps," Baba Haroun said, "there is a young poet in the city—the foreigners call him a minstrel. His songs are drawing many to the tavern of Akram Yasir. I have gone myself and heard him. He sings in both our language and the many languages of the world. Perhaps before he goes on his way we should have him to the palace to entertain. He is pleasant to look upon and nicely spoken. I believe the harem ladies and the children would enjoy him, as I am certain would you, my lord."

"Very well," the caliph said, "you may issue my invitation."

The chief eunuch bowed low and hurried off.

The caliph left his first wife, and Alia sent one of her women to ask the lady Noor if she would come and join her. Rhonwyn came willingly, for she liked Alia and enjoyed her company. When the first wife dismissed all of her women so that they were alone, Rhonwyn knew that something important was about to happen.

"What is it?" she asked Alia.

"Do you love Rashid?" Alia said softly.

"I respect him and I love his passion," Rhonwyn replied carefully.

"But do you love him?" Alia persisted.

Rhonwyn shook her head. "No," she said quietly. "My memories of Edward de Beaulieu are yet strong in my head. Perhaps one day they will not be, and I will love Rashid. Allah only knows he has been patient and kind. You arouse guilt within me by asking such a question, Alia. Why is it you do so? Surely you do not think I mean Rashid any harm?"

"No, no!" Alia replied. "I ask because of something he has said. He wants a child from you, Noor. Do you want a child?"

Rhonwyn looked astounded. "*A child?* I had not thought of having a child. A child would bind me to Rashid. With Edward . . ." She paused, and then said, "You know how it was with Edward, my friend. We were just beginning to explore our love when I was snatched away from him. Thinking on it, I know now that I should have liked to have borne Edward's children. Why does Rashid want a child of my body? He has children to follow him. I am his plaything, his latest passion. I am certainly nothing more to him than that, Alia."

"He loves you, Noor. Do you not realize it? Rashid is

in love with you. That is why he wants a child of your body." The caliph's first wife looked deeply into the eyes of her beautiful companion. "Oh, my poor Noor," she said. "You have been awakened to passion, but you know nought of love, do you?"

"I love Edward!" Rhonwyn cried.

"I wonder if you really did, my dear. I wonder if he truly loved you. You did not know each other long enough, and your relationship, from what you have told me, was quite adversarial most of the time you were together. You were yet a child, playing at your games of war with your weapons. You were careless and heedless of what would happen to you, else you would not have rushed off to join a battle and be captured. You would have withdrawn to your sick husband's side at the first alarm of trouble, Noor. But you did not. You thought only of yourself, not of Edward de Beaulieu, didn't you? I say these things not to distress you, my friend, but to waken you.

"You are loved by a good and powerful man. Open yourself to that love. Passion shared between two people who love one another is far more potent than passion merely shared between a man and a woman, my Noor. This I know from my own experience. A child born of such a love is a most fortunate child," Alia concluded.

Rhonwyn's hand had gone to her mouth in startled realization as Alia had spoken to her. She had been a child. Selfish and determined to have her own way in everything. What a disservice she had done Edward. And ap Gruffydd as well. But despite Alia's words, Rhonwyn knew she could not love Rashid al Ahmet as Alia did. More than ever now she wished she could return to Edward de Beaulieu and tell him of all she had learned. Not just of passion but of herself. She wanted them to begin again, but it was impossible. She would have to go through life bearing the guilt for thoughtlessly abandoning him for her own pleasure. And she had an added guilt in the caliph who loved her.

"You look so stricken," Alia said. "I did not mean to make you unhappy, Noor." She reached out and patted her friend's arm.

"Nay," Rhonwyn said. "You have but made me face myself for the first time in my life, Alia. I am not certain I like what I see. I wonder if I understand what love is at all."

"Let Rashid teach you!" Alia pleaded.

"How can you say that to me when it is obvious that you love him with all your heart? How can you so willingly share him, Alia?"

"*Because* I love him, and *because* it is our way," the older woman said. "It is not possible for one woman to satisfy a man. A man is like a honeybee and needs many flowers to keep him happy."

Rhonwyn shook her head in despair. "Four years ago," she said, "I lived in a border fortress with my brother and a garrison of rough men who had raised me. I knew nothing of being a woman. I didn't even know God, Alia. My brain aches with all I have learned in these last years." She sighed. "I will try to love Rashid, I promise you, but why would you encourage me to have a child? What if it is another son? My son could rival your son. Do you want that?"

"Mohammed will follow his father and will be years older than any son you bear our lord," Alia said assuredly.

"Is it custom that the eldest son follows his father here in Cinnebar?" Rhonwyn asked Alia.

"No," Alia answered, "but everyone knows Mohammed is to follow his father onto the throne of Cinnebar."

"What if I bear the caliph a son? What if the caliph does not go to his reward in Paradise until that son is twenty years of age? What if he loves my son better than yours because of the love he has for me? And loving my son better, he names him the next caliph? How would you feel about that, Alia?" Rhonwyn asked her friend.

Alia's face was a mask of her conflicting emotions, but then she answered honestly, "I should not like that, Noor."

"And therein lies the danger," Rhonwyn replied. "I would rather have your friendship, Alia, than bear a son to rival yours."

"But you might have a daughter," Alia said, "and he truly desires a daughter from you. He has already fathered two sons and two daughters. You could have a daughter, Noor."

"His passion is hot and potent for me, Alia. His seed is copious when he releases it into my hidden garden. *I could have a son.* I know what is done to prevent conception here in the harem, for Nilak has explained it to me. Please, give me a little more time before you withdraw that special brew from me. I need to think. So do you. He need never know. I care not if he thinks me barren, Alia. He will not stop loving me or gaining pleasure from my body. Perhaps I can even learn to love him a little bit to add to his delight," Rhonwyn said.

"She speaks more sense than I would have thought," Baba Haroun said, stepping from behind a wall hanging. "Do not scold me, lady, for listening. You know that my duty to you is paramount. Have I not been with you since you were but a child in your father's house? Lady Noor is wise to consider all the consequences of the caliph's desire. What, indeed, if the caliph loved a son of her body more than Prince Mohammed? She would not, I believe, encourage such a thing, for there is no malice in her, but we cannot control the caliph's feelings, as you and I know. A son of Noor's body could prove a catastrophe for Cinnebar. For us all, my lady Alia! Listen to the lady Noor."

"Fate, my dear Baba Haroun, will take its course no matter what we do. The Jews have a saying: *Man plans. God laughs,*" Alia said quietly. "If Rashid desires a child of Noor, then it is her duty to give him one. I am willing, however, as head of my lord's harem, to let her wait a little more before she must fulfill that duty."

"It will be as my lady wills," the chief eunuch said.

Rhonwyn bowed her head in obedience to the first wife, but afterward told Nilak of all that had happened.

"A child!" Nilak said excitedly. "That would be wonderful, my dear lady. I knew you were fortunate the day I first laid eyes upon you. The lady Alia is correct when she says the caliph loves you. Many in the harem are very jealous of you, although you would not notice it, having no acquaintance with the other women."

"The others bore me," Rhonwyn said. "They seem to do nothing but lay about beautifying themselves and hoping that the caliph will notice them. I far prefer Lady Alia's company."

"There is to be a special entertainment for the harem shortly," Nilak told her mistress. "A famous young musician who has been in the town entertaining at a tavern. He is to come to the palace in a few days and sing for us, it is said."

"How is that possible, since we are not allowed to be seen by others?" Rhonwyn asked.

"The harem, but for the lady Alia and you, will be seated behind screens. You two, however, are permitted to sit at the caliph's feet, suitably veiled, of course. There are but a few invited guests. The vizier, the caliph's treasurer, the imam. No others. It is an informal event, my lady Noor."

"I always enjoyed music," Rhonwyn said, "although our music is different than yours."

"These musicians are foreigners. They sing and play in many languages, I am told. Perhaps even yours," Nilak replied.

"I doubt it," Rhonwyn said with a smile. "Welsh is a difficult tongue. Almost as difficult as Arabic."

"Which you now speak flawlessly and without even an accent," Nilak praised the younger woman.

"When are we to hear these musicians?" Rhonwyn asked.

"Baba Haroun has not yet announced their coming" was the reply. "It should be soon, though."

The mere mention of an entertainment to which they were to be invited set the harem women abuzz with excitement. The mistress of the wardrobe was besieged with requests for clothing and jewelry. Gossip ran rife about what the lady Alia and the lady Noor would wear. The fact that they would be seated by the caliph and not behind the screens caused a great deal of jealousy.

"The wives always have more privileges, and why?" one girl whined as she braided pearls into her hair.

"Because they are wives and have children," another more sensible and practical woman said.

"The lady Noor has no children," the first replied.

"But she is easily the most beautiful woman in the world," the practical woman answered, "and besides, the caliph loves her."

The other women nodded in agreement. It was certainly no secret that Rashid al Ahmet was utterly besotted by the beautiful Frankish woman. The lady Noor, to give her credit, however, seemed modest despite their master's grand passion. Even the lady Alia was her friend.

The date for the entertainment was announced, and the excitement grew to a fever pitch. The evening the musicians came, the harem was shepherded by Baba Haroun and his minions into the great hall of the caliph's palace. The veiled ladies sat behind the sheer fabric screens, their view visible but faintly obscured. Rashid al Ahmet sat upon a low-cushioned golden and bejeweled throne set upon a black marble dais. On his right his eldest son, Mohammed, was seated upon a low stool, his head only reaching the height of his father's hand. On the caliph's left his other son, Omar, was similarly ensconced. The ruler of Cinnebar was garbed in a black-and-gold brocaded silk robe. There was a small gold turban upon his dark head with a large ruby in its center. His two sons were dressed in simple white robes, but their heads were bare.

The lady Alia sat upon a scarlet silk cushion to the right of her husband and just one step below the dais. She wore a scarlet kaftan decorated with gold, which complemented her coloring. The lady Noor sat upon a cushion of silver cloth to the left of the caliph and two steps below the dais. Her simple kaftan was turquoise blue in color, trimmed in silver. Both women wore sheer matching veils over their heads and drawn across their faces for modesty's sake, although anyone looking closely could have seen their features. Still, no man in the room among the few guests would have been so rude.

A hush descended upon the hall as the three musicians entered and bowed low to the caliph. They were swathed in the white robes and burnooses of the land. The tallest of them stepped forward as the other two sat upon the floor, their instruments at the ready.

"My lord caliph, I shall first begin with a song native to my own land and sung in my own tongue," he said.

Rhonwyn started. *That voice!*

The musicians began, and the tune was familiar to her.

"My sister, if you are among these women, you must contrive to sing back to me now so I may know it," sang

Glynn ap Llywelyn. "I have sought long for you. Sing to me, my sweet sister."

"You must not start at the sound of my voice, brother, but I am indeed here," Rhonwyn's voice rang out. Then she turned to look up to the caliph. "They sing a song native to my homeland in my own Welsh tongue. The singer invites all who understand him to join in, my lord. Please allow me to do so or at least explain if I may not."

"Sing, my beautiful golden bird," the caliph said generously. "I was not aware of what a lovely voice you had. You will sing for me alone in the future, Noor."

"Thank you, my lord," Rhonwyn replied. Then turning back to the musicians, she sang, "He says I may sing with you, for he does not know who you are, brother. Your song must be short else suspicions be aroused."

"I have come to take you home, sister," Glynn sang. "My musicians are Oth and Dewi. Tell us, how we may accomplish the impossible?"

"Remain in Cinnebar, brother. Use whatever excuse you must, but remain. I will find a way to contact you. It will not be easy, but I will succeed in time. Be patient and do not leave me now that you have found me. 'Tis best we end our song now, sweet brother. How I long to embrace you once again," Rhonwyn's voice soared sweetly.

"I shall do as you say, dearest sister. I shall not leave you. I shall not leave you. I shall not leave you," Glynn finished the song. Then he bowed to the caliph.

"Tell me the tale of your song, my minstrel friend," the caliph said.

"It is a story about a widowed mother whose only son goes off to war. She fears for him in the ensuing months as she hears nought of him. Finally, when she has just about given up hope, her son returns, my lord. He promises never to leave her again. It is a simple tale, you understand. Now, however, I shall sing to you a song that is currently quite popular in Damascus. But would you first tell me who the lady was who sang with me?" He bowed again.

"My second wife," the caliph answered. "She is a student of languages."

Rhonwyn could scarcely conceal her excitement, but she did. *Glynn!* Her little brother. How had he come to this place? It was a miracle, and now she needed another miracle.

For the next few days she considered her course of action, but finally had to admit to herself that only the chief eunuch, Baba Haroun, could help her. *But would he?* The tall black man held the power of life and death within the harem walls. Even Rashid al Ahmet did not have such total control as did his chief eunuch. Rhonwyn sent her serving woman Sadirah to request an audience with Baba Haroun. Sadirah returned, saying the eunuch would expect the lady Noor in his chambers within the hour.

"Why do you wish to speak to *him*?" Nilak probed none too subtly.

"The caliph wishes me to have his child, as you know, but I have been reluctant, as I would have no child of mine in competition with Prince Mohammed. I love his mother too well. Still, even the lady Alia wants me to become a mother. The three of us spoke on this several days ago. I promised Baba Haroun that I should talk with him on it further. After all, does he not have the best interests of the caliph at heart?"

"If you had a son, there is no guarantee that Prince Mohammed would be the next caliph of Cinnebar," Nilak said craftily.

"That is just the kind of thing I fear," Rhonwyn scolded the older woman. "Prince Mohammed is his father's heir. He must remain so for the safety and best interests of Cinnebar, Nilak. Now, I must go and see Baba Haroun." She hurried from her apartments.

The chief eunuch sat awaiting her, drawing upon his water pipe. He was alone. "Sit, Noor." He gestured to a pile of colorful cushions across the tiled table. "How may I be of service to you? It must be something very serious, for you have never before sought me out." His fine dark eyes viewed her curiously.

"Though I should never say this aloud to anyone else, Baba Haroun, I believe you always put your mistress's best interests above all—" She paused a moment, then continued. "—even the caliph."

He nodded silently, a small smile upon his lips. "Go on," he said, so low she could scarcely hear him.

"I do not want to give the caliph a child. I do not believe you want me to, yet how long may we continue to deceive my lord Rashid or the lady Alia? And if I am forced to have a child and it is a son, why, even my serving woman Nilak suggests that such a child could supplant Prince Mohammed in both his father's heart and the succession. It would seem I am about to become a great difficulty. But what if I could solve this conundrum before it becomes a problem?"

"How?" he asked her, rather intrigued by her astute grasp of the situation.

"If I were no longer here, the matter of another son would no longer be an issue, would it?" Rhonwyn said softly.

"You are suggesting that I allow you to escape from Cinnebar," the chief eunuch said. It was not a question.

"Yes," she replied quietly.

"And just how could such a thing be accomplished without the caliph's knowledge or my destruction, Noor?" Baba Haroun asked wryly.

"First you must swear to me that you will not kill

him," Rhonwyn said. "If I thought I was responsible for his death, I could not live myself."

"*Who?*" the chief eunuch demanded, suddenly very interested.

"My younger brother," Rhonwyn told him.

"But how . . ." Baba Haroun began.

"First your promise. You are a man of your word, I know, Baba Haroun. Give me your promise, and I will explain," Rhonwyn told him.

The chief eunuch considered a long moment, then he said, "You have my promise, Noor. I shall not kill your brother. Now please explain to me what it is you are talking about."

"The young minstrel who entertained in the great hall of the palace several evenings ago is my brother, Glynn ap Llywelyn. He has been seeking me. He began his entertainment by singing in our native tongue and asking if his sister were here. I answered, as you know. It was not a song he sang, but rather we communicated briefly using our native tongue and the music. He remains in Cinnebar awaiting my instructions."

"Astounding!" Baba Haroun said, amazed. He had never in all his years heard of such a coincidence.

"If Rashid is allowed to dwell too long on this child he desires of me," Rhonwyn said softly, "his heart will be broken doubly. That must not happen, Baba Haroun. The caliph is a good man. I do not want to harm him, but I do not love him as Alia does, and I want to go home. Surely my brother's finding me is a portent. He did not come on crusade with us. I left him at the abbey school in Shrewsbury, in England, near our home. He was but a child. Now suddenly he is a man. He has sought me out and found me. Is this not fate speaking?"

The chief eunuch nodded thoughtfully. He was a man

who believed in signs and marvels. "How would you proceed, Noor, *if* I were to agree to help you?" he asked.

"The caliph will not simply release me," Rhonwyn said, and her companion nodded again in agreement. "I must therefore appear to have died. He will mourn me, I know, but eventually he will forget me."

"Not easily," Baba Haroun admitted. "I know him well, and he does not give his heart lightly, but I believe I have a way to distract him from your loss. Prince Mohammed's two harem damsels are kept sterile, but that can be changed. If one of them should conceive and the caliph were to be able to look forward to being a grandfather, then he should have something to rejoice in rather than dwell upon his mourning. It could even be said Allah was replacing his love for you with another love. Now, because I can see you have been thinking on it, how will you die?"

"I shall accidentally fall from a cliff at the edge of my garden in the night," Rhonwyn said. "If bones and hanks of my hair were found there, it would be assumed I fell and that the wild dogs had devoured me. The hair will assure that the caliph believes in my death, for you know how he loves my hair and its unusual color."

"In reality, however, I shall smuggle you from the palace," Baba Haroun said, taking up the thread of her thought. "That I can do, Noor, and easily. It must all be done in a single night. And you, my clever beauty, will be disguised as a boy. Your party will join a caravan headed for the coast, and in just a few days you will be able to seek out a vessel bound for your native land."

"Then you will help me!" Rhonwyn said excitedly.

"I will help you," Baba Haroun replied, "but I do so only to safeguard the happiness of my beloved mistress. She does the noble thing in saying the caliph must have his way in order to be happy. She has been raised to think of her lord first. But you, Noor, were raised to think of yourself first. I contemplated the possibility of seeing you contract some disease, sicken, and die before you might give the caliph a child. If my mistress cannot or will not protect herself and her son, then I must. It is my duty. However, I hold no malice against you. You have been respectful and loving of my lady Alia. I will, therefore, aid you, Noor."

"Thank you, Baba Haroun," Rhonwyn said, her heart hammering against her ribs as she spoke. That he would have stooped to her murder truly frightened her.

"Return now to your quarters, Noor. I will contact your brother, and we will make all the necessary arrangements. You will be told when the time is come. You are pale, Noor, but you need have no fear of me. You, yourself, have solved the problem we had, and I will not betray you for the love we both bear the lady Alia." He smiled a quite kindly smile at Rhonwyn. "Go."

She got to her feet, remembering to bow to this powerful man. Then she hurried from his quarters, not quite certain whether she should rejoice or not. She could not know until the moment came if she would really be free or if he would betray her. Living in the harem had taught her one thing, and that was that you could trust no one completely. Still, she knew she had not made an enemy of Baba Haroun. Surely he would keep his word.

"What did he say?" Nilak demanded as Rhonwyn reentered her apartments. "I will wager he is in no hurry for you to bear the caliph a child. He is loyal first to Lady Alia." She made a disapproving face.

"Of course he is," Rhonwyn said, "and that is as it should be. He has been with her since her childhood in her father's house. I am not certain in my own mind that I am ready to become a mother yet."

"If you wait much longer, you shall see gray in that gilt

hair of yours," Nilak scolded, and two other serving women giggled. "You are past eighteen, my lady Noor, and not getting any younger. If our lord Rashid wants a child of you, then you must give him a child. It is your duty."

"Be silent!" Rhonwyn suddenly snapped. "You over-step your bounds, Nilak. My entire life I have done my duty and never once shirked. If it is Allah's will that I give the caliph a child, then I shall. Now, leave me, all of you. I would be alone with my thoughts."

The three serving women withdrew, and Rhonwyn walked out into her small garden. The little fountain with its splashing water was soothing to her, and she very much needed to calm herself after her meeting with Baba Haroun. The heady scent of the Damascus roses touched her nostrils, lulling her into a more placid frame of mind. She walked slowly down the crushed marble path to the carved stone bench that overlooked the mountains. Her vista faced west, she knew, for each evening she watched the sun set behind those forbidding dark peaks. Once, with Nilak and Halah holding on to her tightly, she had gone to the edge of her garden and peered down. There had been nothing below but rocks and a gray-green scrub growth. She had gotten dizzy, and her servants had hauled her back. Anyone falling from this height would surely be killed.

"Nilak tells me you have spoken to Baba Haroun about having a child." Rashid al Ahmet sat down beside his second wife.

"Nilak takes much upon herself," Rhonwyn replied, irritated.

"She but wants your happiness," he said, taking her hand in his and kissing her fingers one by one.

"I am happy," Rhonwyn said. "She does not under-stand that being with you is my happiness, Rashid. Why

do you want a child of me? You have children, so it cannot be your vanity, for you could satisfy that urge on any
of your women whenever it pleased you."

"I want a child of you because I love you," he said quietly, and drawing her into his arms, he began to kiss her
passionately. "*I love you, Noor!* I want our love to be
complete, and only a child can give us that completion.
Do you understand? Ah, yes, I believe that you do." He
kissed the tears slipping from behind her closed eyelids.

"You make me ashamed for being so selfish," Rhonwyn said honestly. And he did, she thought sadly. He did
love her, but she did not love him. Not while Edward de
Beaulieu still lingered in her memory.

He stroked her hair tenderly, and then his hand slipped
within the opening of her kaftan, and he cupped one of
her breasts in his palm. He fondled her, his thumb rubbing her nipple into a sharp point. She murmured softly,
and Rashid reached down, drawing her kaftan up and
off her body, rendering her naked for his pleasure. Pulling her into his lap, he bent her backward slightly, his
mouth closing over the sensitive peak. He suckled hungrily
on it. Rhonwyn whimpered as her deep arousal began.
He would not cease, she knew, until she had satisfied him,
and he, her. Her hands reached out to caress him.

He nursed upon both her breasts until they were actually sore. Then his mouth moved across her torso, and it
was as if his lips were fire upon her skin. When he kissed
her hard upon her smooth Venus mons, a bolt of lightning seemed to penetrate her body, and she shuddered.
His pointed tongue ran along the shadowed slash dividing her nether lips. It teased her, down and up and down
again. He lay her upon the stone bench and, kneeling before her, used his two thumbs to open her to his view.

"You are like a pink shell from the sea," he told her.

"Your little jewel is perfectly formed. It but waits for my touch, my beautiful, my exquisite wife."

The point of his tongue touched her, and Rhonwyn gasped as a sensation, more acute than any she had ever before felt, slammed into her. *"Rashid!"* She could say no more. The wonder of his passion was too intense for her. Each day it seemed to increase.

He laughed as her love juices pearled upon her coral flesh. "Can I not teach you patience, my love?" he gently scolded her. Then opening his robes, he revealed his engorged manhood and, straddling the bench, he lowered himself upon her. He thrust deep, smiling as she gasped aloud with his fierce entry. Then gathering her into his arms, he murmured as he raised them both up into a seated position. "Wrap your limbs about me, Noor, as I stand." Then he arose and walked, carrying her into her bedchamber where he pressed her up against a wall and began to move upon her.

Rhonwyn's eyes widened with surprise, and he laughed.

"Here is something new for you," he teased her as she clung to him, her arms tight about his neck.

"It is interesting," she managed to say, "but I want you atop me, my lord. I want to feel your weight upon me. *Please!*"

He laughed again. "How you have changed, my precious one," he told her, but he complied, moving to her bed and falling with her upon it.

"Yes!" she cried out. *"Yes!* Oh, that is good, my lord! Do not cease this pleasure, I beg you! *Do not cease!"* Her legs still wrapped about him, she tightened the muscles of her love channel around his plunging lance and smiled wickedly into his eyes when he groaned. "Do I please you, my Rashid?" she demanded. Her nails dug into his shoulders. "Alia swears you liked this." She tightened herself again.

"I do," he groaned. *"Oh, my love, I do!"*

Then she forced his passion from him, and his love juices filled her as Rhonwyn sighed her own deep pleasure. Once Edward had told her that a shared passion was a better passion, and it was. She wondered how much greater her pleasure would be if she loved this man called Rashid al Ahmet who now lay upon her breasts, gasping with his own exertions. Absently she stroked his dark head, wondering as she did how long it would be before she could escape Cinnebar and return to her husband, Edward de Beaulieu. To show him that her fears were gone and that she could love him completely and freely. For that they owed the caliph of Cinnebar a great debt, but she suspected that she could not dwell too greatly upon that fact.

She was eager to learn the plans for her escape, but Baba Haroun said nothing, and some weeks went by before he finally called her into his private chamber. Rhonwyn went, her heart hammering, not knowing if he meant to kill her or give her her freedom. Her beautiful face, however, showed no hint of her fears. "You sent for me?" she said, bowing politely to him.

"The plan is completed," he replied without any preamble.

She raised a questioning eyebrow.

"Tonight," he said low. "Your women will be given a bit of poppy in their mint tea to assure their deep slumber. I will come for you myself, Noor. The shattered bones are ready to place along with the kaftan in which your women see you last. It will be shredded and scattered along with your unique hair. It will be enough to convince all that you have fallen and perished."

"How will you place all of the debris?" she questioned him.

He smiled enigmatically. "You cannot see it from your

terrace, of course, but there is a small door just below it. Such entries are common in this palace. They were placed there as a means of escape when the palace was built. Few know where they are located, not even the caliph, but I do. I will personally place these items on the rocks below before I aid you in your flight, Noor. Now, no more questions. If Nilak queries you, tell her we have decided the time is propitious for you to have a child. The caliph wishes it, and the lady Alia wishes it. Then later I shall speak to her myself regarding the matter."

"What if the caliph wants to visit my bed tonight?" Rhonwyn said.

"He will not," Baba Haroun said with assurance.

"How can you be certain?" she demanded.

The chief eunuch chuckled. "Because he will be tasting the charms of a red-haired virgin from the Basque region I recently purchased for him in the marketplace for just this occasion. The caliph has a particular weakness for virgins. Her initiation into the amatory arts will keep him busy the entire night. Surely you understand his appetites for passion by now, Noor."

"Indeed," Rhonwyn said. He claimed love for her, yet he could be tempted by a virgin, she thought irritably.

"Go now," Baba Haroun said. "I will come for you when the time is at hand."

"My brother?"

"Will be waiting along with those two rather disreputable fellows he travels with. Oth and Dewi, I believe they are called," Baba Haroun said.

"They are not disreputable," she said softly. "They are the kindest and best of men, Baba Haroun. They helped to raise me."

"So they told me, and in the most execrable Arabic I have ever heard spoken aloud," Baba Haroun said dryly. "They love you even as I love my mistress, Noor. That more than anything else convinced me that I was doing the right thing in helping you to escape Cinnebar."

She caught up his two large brown hands and kissed them. "Thank you! Thank you, Baba Haroun!"

He was startled by her generous gratitude. He drew his hands from her light grip. "You know why I aid you, Noor, and yet in doing so I must betray my master. I do it gladly for the lady Alia, but I will bear the guilt all my days. Rashid al Ahmet truly loves you. Your *death* will pain him greatly. I do not know if I shall ever be able to compensate him for your loss, but I will try."

"Do you censure me then, Baba Haroun, for my desire to leave Cinnebar?" Rhonwyn asked him.

"You cannot help yourself, Noor. In your heart you hold a memory of love for Edward de Beaulieu. All my master's love cannot hope to overcome that other love. So, I will help you to go this night."

There was nothing left to say, Rhonwyn knew, and so she bowed again to the chief eunuch. His words made her feel sad, and yet she could not change how she felt. She hurried from Baba Haroun's private chamber, swallowing back her excitement as she did. She must not be stopped now. *Not when her freedom was so close!*

Part Three

Rhonwyn 1273–1274

Chapter Thirteen

Rhonwyn looked down upon Nilak. The older woman slept hard, snoring softly in her drugged slumber. Reaching out, Rhonwyn gently touched the woman's head in tender farewell. Nilak had been so good to her. "Don't put her to minding the children," she said softly to Baba Haroun. "She hated it."

"I shall place her in the household of Prince Mohammed's favorite. The girl is sweet natured but has no older woman to properly guide her. Nilak should do quite admirably," he concluded wryly. "Come now. We haven't much time, my lady Noor. The evidence of your demise has already been placed below your terrace. I am grieved you had to cut your hair, but it will grow back." He led her from her quarters through the dimly lit corridors of the palace.

To her surprise they passed no one, not even the guards. "I want Sir Fulk," Rhonwyn said suddenly.

"He will surely expose the life you have lived here," the chief eunuch said.

"Even so, I cannot in good conscience leave him behind," she replied. "Besides, I intend to tell my husband everything."

"He will either not believe you or spurn you, Noor,

but as your heart is good, I anticipated your request. The knight awaits you with your brother and his two men."

"How are we to leave Cinnebar?" she asked.

"You are joining a caravan headed for the coast," Baba Haroun told her. "You will be at Carthage in a week. From there you are on your own, but you will manage quite well, I suspect." He stopped suddenly and began counting the tiles upon the wall. Then he pressed against one and a door sprang open in the wall. "The passage is straight," Baba Haroun said. "It is just a few feet. Come, I must light your way." He disappeared into the dark passage, and she followed, starting as the door closed behind her. Within a minute or two, however, another door opened ahead of her. She could see several dark figures. She hesitated, and then she heard Glynn's voice.

"Rhonwyn, hurry!"

She turned to face the chief eunuch. "Thank you," she said simply, and then moved past him to join the others.

"Go with Allah," she heard him say, and then the door closed again behind her.

"Come on!" Glynn said. He took her hand, and they hurried off.

"Where are we?" she demanded of him.

"A back alley outside the palace walls," he said low. "Now be silent, sister, else the guards on the heights hear us."

"Where are we going?" she whispered.

"To our lodging to complete your disguise," he told her, and then she was quiet.

They finally reached a small house, entering it quickly so as not to be seen by any in the street. Rhonwyn flung off her cloak and hugged her brother first, then Oth and Dewi. She turned to Sir Fulk, who appeared to be in remarkably good health.

"You were not mistreated?" she queried him.

"Nay, my lady. I was set to instructing the young prince in the arts of war. I am treated very well. I have even learned enough of their tongue-twisting language to get by quite nicely. I am grateful for your help, but I don't want to come with you."

"*What?*" Rhonwyn was very surprised. "Why on earth not, Fulk?"

"In Cinnebar, my lady, I hold a position of importance as the heir's military instructor. I am a younger son and can never hope to attain such worth or influence in England as I have here. The caliph's son likes me, and I like him. We are not so far apart in age. I am his senior by only six years. I believe I shall have greater chance for advancement here in Cinnebar than if I go home to England. My parents are both dead, and I have but two elder brothers. There is no lass who waits for me. I came with you tonight because Baba Haroun said you would not believe him if he told you these things. He did try to dissuade you from taking me, didn't he? But you, he said, would insist. He likes your sense of duty and loyalty."

"But how will you get back into the palace, Fulk? You are a slave as I was," Rhonwyn said in a worried tone.

"The young prince freed me months ago," Fulk explained. "He said a slave should not be teaching him the things he needed to know. I can come and go in and out of the palace with impunity, my lady."

"What am I to tell your brothers?" Rhonwyn asked him.

"That I died bravely defending you, my lady," Fulk said with a small smile. "The truth, we both know, would but bring them shame. That a brother who went so nobly off on crusade to free the Holy Land from the infidel, but then joined the infidel, would be more than they could bear or understand. But I must do what is best for me. Here in Cinnebar I can practice my own faith without fear of reprisal, which is more than any Jew or man of Islam can do in England. I wish you Godspeed, my lady." The young knight bowed to her as he kissed her hand. Then he turned and departed the chamber.

"At least my conscience is clear," said Rhonwyn slowly. She turned to her brother. "Where is Edward?"

"I saw him last in Acre," Glynn responded, "but there is something I must tell you, Rhonwyn. Edward truly believes you are dead. He is preparing to marry his cousin Katherine de Beaulieu when he returns to England."

"Then we must get to Acre quickly," she replied.

"Nay," Glynn said. "We must return to England so that you will be at Haven awaiting your husband when he returns. The lady Katherine is a sweet woman, but her brother, Rafe, is a hard man. They must be dispossessed and returned to their own manor. You are perfectly capable of husbanding Haven until Edward returns to England."

"And just how am I to force Rafe to give up his hold on Haven?" she demanded of her brother.

"Our tad will aid you if you ask him, sister. This is no time to be over-proud, Rhonwyn," Glynn said bluntly.

"Better we go to Acre so Edward sees me and does not believe it is a hoax played upon him," Rhonwyn said.

"*Nay!* For once, sister, do what is asked of you and do not be willful. This is what has gotten you into difficulties all along, doing what you wanted instead of what was right and expected of you. Edward is angry that you dashed into a battle. He is angry that you were captured and lost him one of his knights. He will believe nothing of you but the absolute truth, but I fear his anger when he learns you have known another man. It will take every bit of your strength and knowledge to convince him that he should not disown you," Glynn told her earnestly.

"I love him," Rhonwyn said as if her love could solve the problem. "I know he loves me." But having heard what her brother reported, she was now not so certain of her husband's love. How could he have given her up for lost so easily and made plans to marry Katherine de Beaulieu? She was confused as to what to do, and then Oth spoke up.

"Better you be at home awaiting him like the wife he wants you to be than suddenly appearing before him in Acre, lady."

"Are you certain it would not be better for us to go to Acre, Glynn?"

Glynn nodded his dark head. "We must go to England as quickly as we can, sister," he told her firmly. "Now, you need to get ready to travel. Our caravan leaves at first light. There on the shelf is a bowl, a rag, and two pitchers. The large pitcher contains a dye for your skin. You must cover your entire body with it. Our host's daughter will do your back for you, but you will dye your hair black with the contents of the smaller pitcher. Your clothing is laid out on the chair. Pantaloons, a shirt, a vest, and boots. You already have your cloak. Be careful with it, and do not lose it. Baba Haroun has sewn a cache of gold coins into a secret pocket for you."

"Why must I be totally dyed?" she demanded, sniffing at the pitcher. "The stuff smells foul."

"It won't once it's on. You are too fair, Rhonwyn. You have not the look of a young man used to the outdoors, and you must. If your pant leg rode up and your white skin were seen, or if you squatted to pee and your bare white bottom were visible, it would give the game away. I know it must be difficult taking orders from your little brother, but please, for all our sakes, do it! Dye your hair first so the girl who helps you afterward does not know your hair's true color. It is for her safety," Glynn concluded.

They left her. Rhonwyn sighed. She had cut her hair so that it now bobbed at the level of her chin. Hopefully it would grow quickly, and by the time Edward returned home it would be a respectable length once again. Rhonwyn stripped naked, and finding the pitcher of black dye behind the larger pitcher, she poured it into the basin, mixing it with a tiny bit of water, and then dipped her head, her fingers moving rapidly through her scalp to completely cover her tresses. She then rinsed her hair with clear water and hoped the transformation was complete, for she had no glass or metal mirror in which to check her efforts. She quickly began rubbing the brownish dye from the larger pitcher into her skin. When only her shoulders and back remained white, she called out, and almost immediately a young girl entered the chamber.

"Here, lady, let me finish the task you have begun so well." She took the rag and began smoothing the dye down Rhonwyn's back and across her shoulders.

It took a moment to sink in, but Rhonwyn suddenly realized that the girl was speaking in the Norman tongue. It had been many months since she had heard it, and she wondered if she could still speak it herself. She and Fulk had spoken together in Arabic, and her brother and Oth had spoken in the language of the Welsh. The words, however, came easily when she tried. "You speak the tongue of the Franks," she said.

"My father—this is his house in which you are now standing—is a merchant. I am his only child and help him in his business. Sometimes I even travel to Carthage. I speak several languages."

"You speak well," Rhonwyn noted, and then said nothing more.

When the dye covered her skin completely and had dried, she dressed. The merchant's daughter had departed the chamber with all the evidence of Rhonwyn's disguise. She was pulling on her boots when her brother entered and looked her over with a critical eye.

"You've bound up your breasts?" he asked.

She nodded and stood up for his final inspection.

"Have you found the secret pocket in your cape?" he asked her.

"There are actually two," she told him, "and both are well hidden and well filled. I will keep my cape with me at all times."

"Good! Now, here is our story. I am the minstrel and entertainer. You are my brother and one of my musicians, along with Oth and Dewi."

"What instrument do I play?" she teased him.

"The tambourine," he said seriously. "That way if we must perform, you cannot make any error. Any fool can play the tambourine."

"Thank you," Rhonwyn said dryly.

"We are ready to go," he told her.

"You have become so serious, Glynn," she said to him.

"We are not yet out of Cinnebar, sister. I will not rest until our feet are once again on good Christian soil, nor should you," he explained. "I am angry that Edward de Beaulieu gave you up so easily. He looked for you for only several days before following Prince Edward to Acre. I told him you were alive! *I felt it!* But none of them would listen to me, Rhonwyn. Now it is my duty to return you to Haven Castle and to your husband. I will do what that fine knight of yours could not. I will bring you home!"

Her eyes filled with tears. "You are a man," she said softly.

"Aye," he agreed. "Now, sister, let us go. Do you know what today is? It is the eve of Christ's Mass. With luck I shall have us home by Midsummer's Eve, possibly before. Come now!"

They traveled by caravan to the coast, taking a ship from Tunis to the port of Cagliari on the island of Sardinia. After several weeks in Sardinia they found a vessel that was sailing for Aigues-Mortes, in the kingdom of Languedoc. As it was winter the seas farther north were not safe, and so they decided to travel overland to Calais, crossing over into England from there. They purchased horses in Aigues-Mortes. The beasts were serviceable, but not so fine that they would be stolen by any except the most desperate. Glynn also purchased a sword for his sister and a dagger as well.

Their Arabic garb was bartered for the more conventional clothing of the region. Rhonwyn exchanged her pantaloons and vest for chausses and a tunic that came to her calf. She retained her sherte, her cloak, and her boots. The roads were never really safe, and so they traveled with various trains, paying their way with their songs. It took many weeks to reach the French coast.

In the month of May, however, they finally arrived at Calais. There was no difficulty in obtaining passage aboard a vessel crossing the channel. Selling their horses, they paid their passage, reaching Dover on the following day. There they once again purchased mounts for their journey north and west across England to Haven Castle, traveling still in their guise as musicians. In Worcester Rhonwyn sent her brother into the market to see if he could find a fine gown. Even he understood that she could not arrive at Haven with her skin brown and in chausses. The dye had long since worn off her hair, and her tresses were growing, having reached her shoulders once again.

The walnut juice that had stained her skin had faded during their weeks on the road, but Rhonwyn's skin still

had a sallow look about it. The night before they reached
Haven they stopped to camp by a stream, and Rhonwyn
bathed for the first time in weeks, scrubbing her skin
with a rag and a small piece of soap she had had Glynn
purchase along with the gown. While she was aware hot
water would have done a better job, Rhonwyn was satisfied with the results. Besides, tomorrow at Haven she
would have her hot bath.

In the morning she dressed herself in her gown of deep
blue velvet and the overgown of a lighter blue silk with
open side lacing and a center split. There was a twisted
blue silk rope girdle about her waist, and she wore a
simple white veil with a small circlet that matched her
girdle. Before they even came in sight of Haven, Glynn
stopped their progress, saying, "I leave you here, sister.
Oth and Dewi will escort you home."

"Why will you not come?" she asked him.

"Because Rafe de Beaulieu does not know my true identity, Rhonwyn. I told him I was going to France to contemplate the priesthood when I left the abbey school in
Shrewsbury. I can hardly appear with you in tow and
easily explain it away. Oth and Dewi will go with you.
They will say your father sent them to see if they could
find you, and they did. Where you have been is not anyone's business but Edward's. Answer no questions from
any others."

"Where are you going?" Rhonwyn asked her brother.

"Nowhere. I will be here, and Oth and Dewi will keep
me informed as to what is going on at Haven. There is a
cave in the hillside in the woods that will shelter me.
They know the way. Go now and reclaim Haven for
yourself and your husband. If you need our tad's aid in
ousting Rafe de Beaulieu, sister, I will ask him myself."

The guards at the portcullis gaped with surprise as
Rhonwyn rode through and into the courtyard of the

castle with her escort. She dismounted, and the first person she saw was Father John.

He paled and crossed himself. "Be you a ghost, lady?" he quavered.

"Nay, it is I, Rhonwyn, and I have at last come home," she answered him.

"God have mercy on us all," the priest said. "Lady, you must come with me, for I have much to tell you."

"In time, good father, in time," Rhonwyn said. "I want to go into the hall." She hurried into the castle, the priest running after her in despair. As she entered the hall she saw Enit and called to her. Looking up and seeing the mistress she believed dead, Enit screamed and fainted as the other servants familiar to Rhonwyn gasped with shock. "What is the matter with them?" Rhonwyn said, turning to the priest.

"Surely you know they all thought you dead. The lord sent a message to me and to his cousin when you disappeared. When he returned home from the Holy Land alone we believed it a truth, my lady."

"*Edward is here? At Haven? When?* Is he in our apartments?" Rhonwyn ran from the hall and up the winding staircase, the priest running after her once again.

"Lady, lady! Wait! There is something you must know!" His tone was so desperate that Rhonwyn stopped and turned to him.

"What must I know?" she said.

"Lord Edward is married," Father John told her.

"I know. He is my husband," Rhonwyn said.

"Nay, lady. He is Lady Katherine's husband," the priest replied.

"How can he be wed to Katherine when he is wed to me?" she demanded angrily. Her heart was hammering furiously.

"You were believed dead, my lady Rhonwyn." The priest led her back into the hall.

"He hardly mourned me, did he?" she said bitterly.

"You could not be found. There was no trace of you at all. What else could he think? Everyone said you were dead. He finally joined the prince at Acre, but he had never really recovered from his illness. Prince Edward sent the lord home last summer. At the lord's request both the church and the courts declared you dead, leaving Edward de Beaulieu free to remarry, which he did last September. He is not a boy, my lady. He needed a wife to give him an heir."

"Father, I am told we have a visitor." Katherine de Beaulieu came into the hall.

"Indeed, lady," Rhonwyn said, turning to face her rival. Then she gasped with complete shock. Katherine's belly was so distended that it was more than obvious she was with child. A child that would be shortly born. Rhonwyn's hand went to her mouth to stifle her cry of pain.

"Oh, God!" Katherine whispered, her own hand going protectively to her belly. "They said you were dead."

"Perhaps it were better that I was," Rhonwyn replied harshly.

At that moment both Edward and Rafe de Beaulieu ran into the hall. Edward rushed to Katherine's side, his arm going about her protectively. His eyes blazed angrily.

"You bastard!" Rhonwyn shouted at him.

"So, vixen, you have returned, have you? Well, you are not welcome here, lady. Get you gone!" he said coldly.

"Hospitality was gentler here in my day," Rhonwyn said dryly. "It touches me, Edward, to see how deeply and truly you mourned my alleged death. Did you ever love me at all, or was it simply the treaty between my father and your king? I shall go to the king, Edward, for you have wronged me terribly by your actions. I disappeared, but there was no proof of my death."

"Was I to wait forever, lady? You were gone, and no trace of you or Fulk could be found. No ransom was asked. What could any of us think? Was I to mourn you for the rest of my days?" he demanded.

"You did not mourn me at all!" she cried. "You wrote to your cousin asking for Katherine's hand within a month of my disappearance. Then you hurried home afterward to undoubtedly have both church and state declare me dead. It is the only way you could take another wife. Oh, Edward, I loved you, and you betrayed me!"

"You do not know the meaning of love, you cold-hearted bitch," he declared. "And now that you have magically reappeared in our midst, just where were you all these months?"

"In the harem of the caliph of Cinnebar," Rhonwyn said with devastating effect. "Rashid al Ahmet made me his second wife, and he loved me, but I could not love him, for I kept a memory of our love within my heart. How tragic that that love was naught but a deception on your part. In our months of separation I hoped, I dreamed, I prayed that I might be able to return to you. The very thought of you is what kept me alive. Then my brother came, and I was able to escape. I have ached to return to Haven and to you, Edward de Beaulieu. 'Tis a fine homecoming you have given me."

"*Whore!*" he hissed furiously at her. "You shared another man's bed, and you dare to tell me?"

Rhonwyn shook her head sadly at him, but her sorrow was for him. She was not defeated by this turn of events. "Poor Edward," she said pityingly.

"Did this caliph find your cold heart and resistant

body a pleasure, or did he actually wring a cry of passion from you?" Edward said rancorously.

"He taught me the true meaning of passion," she said quietly. "And, aye, he wrung many a cry of pleasure from me, Edward. He sought to learn the reason I felt such fear of being in a man's arms, and finding it, he freed me from my fears. I came home to share with you all he taught me. Now, instead, I find myself homeless and husbandless. I must decide what I am to do. How dare you, who have lain with others, criticize me. Your actions have shamed us both, but more important, when my father learns of this turn of events, he will be greatly offended, Edward. Your poor king will have to make amends to ap Gruffydd for what you have done. I have learned in my travels since I arrived in England that the king is not well at all. They say he will die before Christ's Mass. But I shall have my justice of you before then, I promise you." Then Rhonwyn turned to Katherine. "You may have him, lady. I think you perhaps better suited to Edward de Beaulieu than I ever was. I would not harm you or the child you carry. Both my brother and I are more than well aware of the stigma of bastardy. It is there even for a prince's children."

"Where will you go?" Katherine asked.

Rhonwyn thought a moment, and then said, "I do not know."

"Then you will remain here at Haven until you do know," Katherine said generously, and turning to her outraged husband, she told him, "The house is mine to direct as I will. Whatever anger you may feel toward the lady Rhonwyn, you cannot throw her out into the cold after her long journey. She must shelter here for the time being. That is my wish."

"As you please, dearling," he answered her. Then looking at Rhonwyn, he said, "Where is Glynn?"

"Where you cannot harm him, my lord."

"Did I ever contemplate such a thing?" he demanded, outraged.

"You were my husband then, and I trusted you. You are no longer my husband, and I do not trust you," she said icily. Then she said to Katherine in a more kindly tone, "Lady, I thank you for your generous offer, but I think it best I leave this place." She bowed to them all, and with Oth and Dewi in her wake, she left the great hall.

Rafe de Beaulieu watched her go, his silvery blue eyes narrowed and contemplative. She had been a beautiful girl, but she was a far more beautiful woman, he thought. And clever to have realized that his sister was a better wife to Edward than she could have been. Her instincts intrigued him, as did her talk of passions unleashed. He wondered where she would go now and just what she meant when she said that she would have justice of his cousin. Strangely, he believed her when she said she meant Katherine and her unborn child no harm. But what was to happen to Rhonwyn uerch Llywelyn?

She departed Haven Castle, her head high, but her sight was blurred by the tears that filled her eyes. He had not really loved her. The shock of that knowledge burned into her heart and soul. How could she have been so damned naive? She would have been better off with the caliph, but that door was tightly closed to her now. She could not go back to Cinnebar no more than she could come back to Haven.

"Where are we going?" she finally asked her companions.

"To your brother, lady. Then we will decide upon how to kill Edward de Beaulieu," Oth said grimly.

"You cannot kill him," she said quietly.

"Surely you do not still love him?" Oth said angrily.

"Nay, I do not love him, but you cannot kill him. They would blame me. I have had enough shocks today to last my lifetime, Oth. I mean to go to King Henry to complain of Edward's treatment of me. Certainly the king will compensate me for what has happened. Then, too, I must be declared alive once more in the courts."

Glynn, as she had suspected, was outraged by what had happened at Haven. He was ready to storm the castle himself and slay Edward de Beaulieu, but Rhonwyn dissuaded him as she had Oth and Dewi.

"He must be made to pay somehow," Glynn said irately.

"Yes, but how?" Rhonwyn asked.

"I am taking you to Mercy Abbey," Glynn said suddenly.

"I am not of a mind to join a religious order," his sister replied. "Do you assume my life is over because my husband has disowned me, little brother? It is not, I assure you!"

"I'm taking you to Mercy because our aunt will certainly know how you may proceed. Our upbringing at Cythraul did not prepare us for such deceit, sister. You surely have an honest grievance against Edward de Beaulieu and must be compensated by him. I am a poet and a dreamer. I do not know how to advance your cause, but she will."

"How can you be certain of that? You never met her," Rhonwyn said to him.

"The abbess Gwynllian is well known in religious circles for her intellect and cleverness, sister. Her fame extends even as far as Shrewsbury. It will take us several days to reach her house, so we must begin now, Rhonwyn. Where else can you go to lick your wounds in safety and consider what you are to do next? Certainly not to our tad."

"Let us ride," his sister replied tersely.

They rode hard, resting the horses between dusk and dawn, eating oatcakes and wild berries, drinking from the streams of water that dotted the countryside. They came to Mercy Abbey in late afternoon. The cluster of stone buildings did not, this time, seem quite so forbidding as they had when she first saw it. Again the church bell was pealing for the office of None. Entering through the abbey gates, they waited for their aunt to emerge from the church.

Gwynllian had never met Glynn, but she recognized him immediately. Seeing Rhonwyn by his side, she said, "Praise God, you're alive! What has happened? Why are you here unannounced?" Her eyes mirrored her deep concern. "Come into the chapter house, and we will talk." Her glance flicked to Oth and Dewi. "You know where to put the horses," she told them. "Then go to the kitchens, and they will feed you. Come," she said, turning back to her niece and her nephew. She led them into her privy chamber and poured them each a small cup of wine. She motioned them to seats as she took her own. "Now," she said, "why have you come to me? Does your father know you are here and alive? And will it cause an incident with the English?" she demanded of them.

"It is a long story," Rhonwyn began. Then she told her aunt of what had happened in the several years since they had last seen one another. "I did not know where else to go," she finished. "I am too fine a lady now to live at Cythraul, aunt."

"Aye, you are," the abbess agreed.

"What am I to do?" Rhonwyn said. "Edward de Beaulieu has treated our family with great disdain. Surely he can be made to pay for that insult, but I have no idea where to begin."

"Do you want him dead?" her aunt queried.

Rhonwyn shook her head. "That would be too easy," she replied. "The lady Katherine I hold blameless in the matter. She is meek and was subject to her brother's will."

"Do you want *him* dead?" Gwynllian asked, half jesting.

Rhonwyn actually laughed aloud. "Nay. I do not like Rafe de Beaulieu particularly, for he is arrogant and obviously has a lofty opinion of himself. However, he loves his sister and did what he believed was best for her even as my own brother, Glynn, did when he sought me out in Cinnebar."

"Restoring you to life legally will not be difficult," the abbess said thoughtfully. "Your existence cannot be denied. It is plain fact." Her long elegant fingers drummed lightly upon the long table before her. "As to the rest I must speak to the bishop at Hereford. Edward de Beaulieu discarded you without any real proof of your demise and quite hastily contracted another marriage without a decent period of mourning. But your induction into an infidel's harem as his second wife will surely stand against you, Rhonwyn. You were a Christian knight's wife, and yet you yielded to the lustful blandishments of another man. There are many who will think you should have died rather than succumb."

"Then they are ignorant of the harem," Rhonwyn replied spiritedly. "I had not even a knife to cut my food. I was constantly watched. There was absolutely no way I might have ended my life even if I had wanted to do so. But all I wanted was to escape and return to my husband, not knowing that he had already betrayed me!"

"That attitude will assuredly gain you a certain amount of sympathy," the abbess noted, "but it will not completely exonerate you."

"I was faithful in my heart to Edward de Beaulieu. He was not so faithful to me," Rhonwyn replied stonily.

Her aunt smiled. "Stoke the fires of your outrage, my child, and we shall gain some justice for you. Are you sure you wish to pursue this path?"

"I must, else my honor and the honor of our family be compromised," she said. "Ap Gruffydd is a proud man, and this reflects upon him badly unless we can obtain some compensation for the slight upon our escutcheon, aunt."

"I am forced to agree with you, my child," the abbess said. She turned to Glynn. "Have you nothing to say in this matter, ap Gruffydd's son? By the rood, how much you look like your father in his youth!"

"At first," Glynn said, "I thought to slay de Beaulieu, but my sister dissuaded me. She does not wish me to have a stain such as that upon my conscience, especially as I intend to return to the abbey at Shrewsbury and eventually take holy orders."

"So you would become a monk, Glynn ap Llywelyn?" the abbess said quietly. How interesting that her brother's son leaned toward the church and not toward a kingdom of his own.

"I have seen the world, aunt, and while I find it interesting, I am not meant for such a life. Soon my music and my poetry shall be in praise of God alone. The peace of the contemplative life is what I seek. I prefer its discipline and order to the hurly-burly of the world at large."

"Does your father know of your decision, nephew?" Her fine brown eyes scanned his face.

"He will, although I know he considered this would be my path long ago when he came to fetch Rhonwyn. Tomorrow I will send Oth and Dewi to find him so he may be made aware of what has happened to my poor sister."

Rhonwyn hit him a blow upon the arm that staggered Glynn.

"Ouch!" he yelped.

"I am not to be pitied, brat!" she snapped at him. "It is my honor that has been besmirched. But make no mistake, Glynn, I need no man to make my life complete. I never did and I certainly don't need your pity!"

"There are but two paths for a respectable woman," Glynn said. "Either she enters into marriage or she enters a convent."

"I am no longer respectable, it would seem," Rhonwyn mocked him, laughing. "Therefore I may do what I please and plot my own course through life, brother. I am considering becoming a merchant and using the gold Baba Haroun so generously sewed into my cloak to set up a shop in Shrewsbury. I shall import silks and spices from the east and grow richer with each passing year. I shall take young men for lovers, and when I send them away because they have begun to bore me, they shall go grieving but wiser for their time with me."

The abbess burst out laughing, although her nephew looked shocked. "Thank God and His blessed Mother, Rhonwyn uerch Llywelyn, that you have not been broken by this experience," she said.

"My heart is broken, aunt, but only a little, and it will heal, I suspect. I returned because I believed in my heart that Edward loved me and would forgive my small sins. I wanted to share all that the caliph taught me about passion and make up to my husband for the early months of our marriage when passion frightened me so greatly I could scarcely bear for him to touch me. The loss is his, I fear, and he will never know the woman I truly am," Rhonwyn said softly. "I am very sorry for that."

The abbess nodded. "It would appear, my child, that you have more honor than Edward de Beaulieu. For that you may be proud."

Ap Gruffydd appeared at Mercy Abbey five days later, prepared to berate his daughter for leaving her marriage. When, however, he heard the truth, he erupted into a fit of rage. Rhonwyn, to her own surprise, calmed him at long last.

"I am no longer unhappy over this, but our family's honor must be assuaged, my lord," she told him.

"Are we back to *my lord* then?" he demanded.

"*Tad,*" she said with a small smile, mollifying him.

"I'll have another husband for you from King Henry else our treaty be broken for good and all," ap Gruffydd said.

"And have you kept so assiduously to that treaty, *Tad*?" she gently taunted him.

He laughed aloud. "I've had little part in your life, Rhonwyn, and yet you know me better than some of my closest associates. Why is that, I wonder?"

"Because I am like you, Tad. I am proud and have always followed my own path, and devil take the hindmost. It seems to have gotten me into almost as much trouble as it has gotten you." She smiled sweetly at him. "I think, however, that I may have learned my lesson."

Both Llywelyn ap Gruffydd and his sister, Gwynllian, burst into laughter. Rhonwyn's assessment of the situation was absolutely correct.

Finally the prince said, "There is much of your aunt in you, too, lass."

"Praise God and His blessed Mother!" the abbess responded fervently, and she crossed herself.

The prince grew serious once again. "King Henry has not been well these past few years. He will certainly be at his palace of Westminster in London. I will send him a letter, Rhonwyn, explaining that you are alive and returned home to discover yourself declared dead and your husband with a new wife. I will tell the English king that you do not desire to have Edward de Beaulieu back, as his new wife is with child. Besides, the betrayal and insult to you and your family make such a reunion impossible. I will ask for justice for my daughter, and tell him that you will come to Westminster by Lammastide to seek redress from the de Beaulieus. There is no viciousness in Henry Plantagenet, but beware his queen, Eleanor of Provence, who is called behind her back *the noble termagant*. She is and always has been ambitious for her family, and she will destroy without hesitation anyone that she believes a threat to them.

"Your dower portion, of course, must be returned to you. I cannot be expected to redower you for a new husband."

"I don't want a husband," Rhonwyn said.

"Nonetheless you must have one," her father said firmly. "We will not argue this point now, lass." He looked hard at her. "How is it possible that you have become more beautiful despite your adventures?"

Rhonwyn laughed. "You will not turn the subject that easily, Tad. I want no husband."

"Then it is the convent, daughter. How old are you now?"

"Nineteen, this April first past," she reminded him.

"We'll be lucky to find you a husband at your age. A widow with children is at least a proven breeder," the prince noted. "Do you want to enter your aunt's house, lass?"

"Nay," Rhonwyn said.

"Then another marriage is your only path," ap Gruffydd said.

Rhonwyn did not argue with him any further. She was a realist. The church would not accept her, for she would be considered a woman of ill repute—a disobedient wife who had run off to interfere in men's business and had been punished for it. And what man of good family would have for his wife such a woman? A woman who had given her body to an infidel? She wanted her dower back, and perhaps a bit of Haven's land for herself. That she would consider recompense for Edward de Beaulieu's behavior. Why argue with her father over something that would never be? There would be no more husbands for Rhonwyn uerch Llywelyn.

Chapter Fourteen

Eleanor of Provence, queen of England, had lived five and a half decades. She was still a beautiful woman, with silver-streaked auburn hair and amber eyes that missed little. In her youth she and her equally comely sisters had been considered the most beautiful women in Europe. Her eldest sister, Margaret, had married King Louis IX of France. Her younger sister, Sanchia, was married to her brother-in-law, Richard of Cornwall, king of the Romans. Her youngest sister, Beatrice, was the wife of Charles of Anjou, the king of Naples and Sicily. Eleanor's mother, Beatrice of Savoy, and her father, Raymond Berenger V, count of Provence, had reigned over a brilliant court renowned for its patronage of the troubadours. The count himself was one of the last of the great Provençal poets.

At the age of nineteen Eleanor had traveled to her sister's court in France, and from there across a winter sea to marry King Henry III of England. From the moment the couple laid eyes upon one another, it had been a love match. The queen had borne her husband six sons and three daughters. Two sons and two daughters had reached adulthood. While there were some who resented her Savoyard kinsmen—who, along with the king's French half brothers, had come to England to seek their fortunes—

the queen's chief care was for her family. Now her husband was slowly dying. She nursed him devotedly. Their kingdom was prosperous and secure. England was not involved in any wars. Their life was peaceful. And then there came from that rebellious Welsh prince a letter that the queen knew was going to cause difficulties.

She sat with the king in their dayroom. About them her ladies sat tending to various small tasks, their sewing and mending, the repair of a small tapestry. The queen's eyes scanned the letter, and she swore ever so softly beneath her breath. This caught the attention of her husband who lay upon his daybed, resting from the exertions of his morning bowel movement.

"What is it?" the king asked his wife weakly.

"Do you remember last year when Edward de Beaulieu returned home from Acre? His wife was alleged to have died, and he requested that she be declared dead so he might remarry?"

The king nodded.

"Well, she isn't dead. The prince of the Welsh's daughter appeared home this spring to find her husband no longer her husband, and his new wife full with a child. Ap Gruffydd is outraged that his daughter has been so insulted. The prince requests justice for his child, but says she will not have de Beaulieu back now, for she would not put the stain of bastardy upon his newborn son. Now isn't this a nice kettle of fish, Henry? Rhonwyn uerch Llywelyn will come to Westminster at Lammastide for your justice. What are we to do?"

"What does ap Gruffydd want?" the king asked cannily.

"His daughter's dower back from de Beaulieu. A new husband for the girl. And a penalty levied upon de Beaulieu for the affront. The Welsh prince suggests that some of Haven Castle's lands be given to his daughter to recompense her for the insult," the queen replied.

"It seems fair," the king said slowly.

"There is more to this than meets the eye, Henry," the queen told him astutely. "For one thing, what happened to the lady Rhonwyn that she became separated from her husband and our son's forces? We must send to Haven. Edward de Beaulieu should be allowed to speak for himself in this matter. Even if he believed his wife dead, he did remarry again in a rather hasty manner."

"Agreed," the king said.

"According to the Welsh prince, his daughter was declared dead. That oversight can be rectified immediately, but the rest will have to wait until we can hear a fuller story from both sides in this dispute."

Again the king nodded his agreement. His wife took a cool cloth and wiped his forehead, which was beaded with perspiration. Henry grew weaker each day, and every small task he must perform was difficult for him now. She had recently heard from their son Edward. He had only narrowly escaped an assassination attempt in Acre, and he was discouraged. The crusade had literally fallen into disarray. Mounting an expedition to retake Jerusalem was proving impossible. He was, Edward wrote, planning to return home with his wife shortly, after Eleanor recovered from the rigors of her recent childbirth. The baby, a little girl who had already been baptized Joan, was strong and healthy, unlike the infant who had been born and died the year before. They would come via Sicily and Provence, visiting relatives along the way. The queen was relieved, for while she knew she could hold England for her son, once Henry died her life would have little meaning. She was of a mind to retire to the Benedictine convent in Amesbury for the remainder of her life.

"I will send off messages to both Edward de Beaulieu at Haven Castle and to the lady Rhonwyn, who is with her aunt, the abbess of Mercy Abbey, in Wales," the queen told her husband, and again he nodded his assent.

Edward de Beaulieu was outraged to receive the royal summons to Westminster. "How dare the vixen complain to the king!" he said angrily.

"What did you expect?" his brother-in-law Rafe said. "While I am delighted that Katherine is your wife and the mother of your heir, you did marry her in some haste, cousin."

"I do not recall hearing you complain about my haste at the time," Edward replied dryly. "You could hardly wait for your sister to become the lady of Haven Castle."

"Our families have always hoped for the union," Rafe responded. "I was pleased that it was to be a reality at long last. You did not say how the lady Rhonwyn *died*, Edward. I did not press the issue because I believed her loss pained you or that possibly you had killed her yourself for her high spiritedness. Only the fact that the lady is generous has prevented my sister from being burdened with a terrible shame. What if Lady Rhonwyn demanded from the church that your marriage to Kate be declared null and void under the circumstances? Your son would then have been declared a bastard. A vindictive woman would have taken great delight in revenging herself on you for what you did."

"She cannot appeal to the church under the circumstances of her adventures," Edward said in assured tones. "Do you think the church would restore her to my side when she so merrily whored for another man? *An infidel?* When I expose her perfidy, she will be lucky they do not burn her at the stake for her adultery."

Rafe de Beaulieu looked closely at his cousin. "Do you love her then so much that you would destroy her, cousin?"

"I do not love her," Edward said honestly.

"Do you love my sister?" Rafe probed.

"Aye, I do. Kate is the perfect wife for me. I want no other," he said. "She is sweet natured and obedient to my will, as well as a good breeder. Look at our wee Neddie. What a fine lad he is."

"If you are happy with Kate," her brother replied, "then why does your anger burn so hot toward the lady Rhonwyn?"

"Because she betrayed me!" he said coldly. "Because she would destroy the happiness I now have."

"She believes you betrayed her," Rafe countered. " 'Tis an interesting conundrum, Edward. I will go with you to Westminster in order that you do not cost my sister and her child too much by your ire."

"I will tell the king the truth," de Beaulieu said stonily.

"You must tell the king the entire truth," the abbess counseled her niece. "It will not be easy, but it will save you from Edward's outrage. In the end it will all boil down to the fact that while you struggled to overcome great odds and return home to your husband, your husband hurried home and contracted another marriage."

" You cannot believe that my judges will overlook the fact I spent over a year in the harem of the caliph of Cinnebar," Rhonwyn replied in practical tones.

"Nay, they will not. They will declare great shock and indignation that a good Christian noblewoman, a prince's daughter, could have found herself in such a position and not ended it all in the name of our dear Lord Jesus," the abbess said dryly. "But you did not have to return home, yet you did. That will be what confounds them, my child, and that will be what gains you redress from Edward de Beaulieu. I will be by your side, speaking in your defense if necessary, Rhonwyn. Unless the archbishop of Canterbury himself speaks for de Beaulieu, and as there is no profit in it, Boniface will not, we will win."

"You are so damned worldly for an abbess," Rhonwyn noted, and then she laughed. "Aunt, I should rather have you on my side than all of God's good angels!"

"The angels are in heaven, my child," the abbess answered her. "*I am here.*"

They departed for Westminster on a warm and hazy summer's day. The prince of the Welsh had sent a fully mounted and armed troop to escort his sister and his daughter into England. Oth and Dewi were by Rhonwyn's side, as was Glynn ap Llywelyn, who would testify to his part in the affair. The trip had been carefully planned, and each night they sheltered at either a convent or a monastery. Their progress was slow but steady, and on the thirty-first of July they arrived in London, where the two women were welcomed at the convent of St. Mary's-in-the-Fields, near the palace of Westminster. The men were invited to make their encampment in a meadow outside the convent walls.

Rhonwyn and her aunt had, in the weeks they were together at Mercy Abbey, worked to sew a gown worthy of a prince's daughter. The gown, or cotte, fell gracefully to the floor. It had long tight sleeves. It was made of fine silk and was a spring green in color. Her over-robe, which was sleeveless, was fashioned from cloth-of-gold on darker green silk brocade. The gilt girdle, which sat just below Rhonwyn's narrow waist, was made of small rounds, decorated with a swirl of Celtic design.

Rhonwyn's hair had been parted in the center, two delicate plaits braided with cloth-of-gold ribbons and strands of tiny pearls and falling on either side of her face, with the main mass of her hair flowing behind her, amid strands of pearls. Atop her head a delicate filigreed circle held her sheer cloth-of-gold gauze veil. Her only jewelry was a brooch of emeralds set in Irish red gold.

Her shoes did not show, but they followed the shape of her foot and were of gilded leather.

"You are magnificent," her aunt said quietly as she looked over their handiwork. "You are every inch the prince of the Welsh's daughter, my child."

"I have never had anything quite this fine," Rhonwyn admitted.

"You are regal, but have not the look of a worldly woman," said the abbess. "That is the effect we have been striving for, Rhonwyn. Some ladies of the court paint their faces and dye their hair. You are fresh looking. Even though you will admit to your indiscretions, your appearance is one of innocence. The church will condemn you, but they will find it impossible to believe you willingly betrayed your husband." Gwynllian smiled, well pleased. "You must remember not to lose your temper with de Beaulieu. Let him rant and rave. You will weep, and that will cause the hardest heart to soften toward you."

"Is that not dishonest, aunt?" Rhonwyn said mischievously.

"This, child, is war. The object of a battle is to win it," the abbess advised with a twinkle in her brown eyes. "That is what your father would do. Will you allow yourself to be beaten by these English? Do not let it ever be said that ap Gruffydd's daughter was not as brave as he."

"I should far rather challenge Edward to trial by combat," Rhonwyn answered. "There I could absolutely beat him."

"I am certain of it," the abbess responded, "but it would certainly shock the king and give credence to de Beaulieu's charges. Come, it is time for us to go now. Mother Superior Margaret Joseph and a half a dozen of her sisters will escort us to the palace. It is but a short walk."

"I am to be surrounded by a bevy of nuns?" Rhonwyn laughed. "Oh, aunt, you are shameless."

The abbess chuckled, but did not reply.

The king's hall in Westminster Palace was very beautiful. The floor was set with wide square tiles. The walls were painted in red, blue, and gold. The windows soared high, allowing in the light. Henry III had made the effort to personally appear at the hearing. He was a shell of the man he once was, but his white hair and beard were neat. His blue eyes looked interested, though he slumped pale upon his throne, his queen at his side. On his right, sitting on a row of benches, were the clergy. The de Beaulieus and Rhonwyn's party sat on the left, carefully separated by several men-at-arms. The hearing, set for the hour immediately following the office of Tierce, began most promptly.

"Tell us your side of this dispute, Edward de Beaulieu, lord of Haven Castle," the king said in a stronger voice than his appearance would have represented.

"The woman given to me as a wife, Rhonwyn uerch Llywelyn, was never a true wife to me," Edward began.

The abbess squeezed her niece's hand hard.

"She denied me my husbandly rights except on rare occasions. She preferred the company of soldiers and playing with arms to being a good chatelaine. At her insistence I allowed her to accompany me on crusade. At Carthage, where we were encamped, many, including myself, grew ill with fever and dysentery. It was during my illness that my wife raced off into battle, deserting me. Of course she was taken prisoner. I sought for her for some days, but found no trace at all of either her or my knight who had followed after her in a brave attempt at rescue. I finally traveled to Acre, but the illness that had lain me low in Carthage returned, never having really been cured. Prince Edward sent me home.

"I am not a young man, sire. I had no legitimate heirs of my body. When you chose me to husband the prince of the Welsh's daughter, I had no previous commitments, although my family had always hoped I would wed my cousin Katherine. Now believing myself widowed, I wed her. Within ten months of our marriage, Katherine, who is dutiful, gave me a son. Just before he was born, Rhonwyn uerch Llywelyn appeared at Haven as if nothing was amiss. She claimed to have been imprisoned within a harem and boasted of how another man had unleashed her passions as I never had. When she saw how it was, she threatened me and left Haven. I am outraged that she should demand redress from me. *For what?* 'Tis she who should make amends to me for her desertion and her bold adultery." Edward de Beaulieu bowed to the royal couple and then the clergy before sitting back down again.

There was a silence, and then the king said, "Rhonwyn uerch Llywelyn, come forward and tell us your side of this controversy."

Rhonwyn arose slowly and stood before the king. She bowed, then turned to the clergy and bowed again. Thereupon she spoke in a voice so soft they all had to lean forward to hear. "Sire, my lords, I come before you today to beg for justice in this unfortunate matter. Edward de Beaulieu claims I was a bad wife to him, and in part, that is true. When my mother died my father took me and my brother, Glynn, to a fortress in the Welshry where we were raised. There were no women there to guide me. When my father returned ten years later to announce I was to be wed, he was horrified, though why it was a surprise to him I do not know, to discover his daughter was more a lad than a lass."

The king and the clergymen chuckled at her astute observation.

Rhonwyn continued. "I was then taken to my aunt's abbey, where for the next six months I learned all I could about being a female. My aunt, of course, had me baptized immediately, and I was enlightened in our faith. When I finally arrived at Haven Castle to be married, I was enough of a lass to be presentable, but I still had much to learn, and I endeavored to do so. I see that the castle priest, Father John, is here at this assembly. Good Father, did I become an acceptable chatelaine for Haven?"

"You did, lady," the priest answered honestly.

Rhonwyn sighed deeply. "My lords, where I failed my husband was in the bedchamber. On our wedding night he cruelly forced me to his will, claiming that you, sire, had said he must. I did not believe such a thing then, and I certainly do not now. It was his lust that drove him to rape. After that I was always afraid of his advances. I knew I should not have been, but I was. There was no lady of my own station with whom I might speak in order to calm my fears. Then Prince Edward came to Haven with his talk of a crusade. I was enthusiastic! His princess wife was going. I saw no reason why I could not go. Perhaps if I fought for our good Lord, he would help me to overcome my fears.

"In Carthage, I nursed my husband devotedly during his illness. He is wrong to say I neglected him. It is not true! It was he, himself, who invited me to go off with his knight Sir Fulk to practice with my sword on that terrible day. He even insisted I garb myself in protective gear, and helped me to dress. Then the daily skirmish with the infidels began while we practiced. Foolishly—oh, how I regret it!—I ran off to join the fray. Sir Fulk came after me. My lords! The battle was grand! We won it in our Lord Christ's name! I, however, foolishly allowed myself to be cut off. I am not, after all, really a soldier, just a woman.

While I may have a talent for the sword, I would, it seems, have none for tactics."

Rafe de Beaulieu, seated by his cousin's side, almost laughed aloud. She had more flare for tactics than any of them realized. All present sat spellbound by Rhonwyn's tale. The Celtic witch had them in the palm of her hand, and it was surely going to cost his cousin.

"Sir Fulk," Rhonwyn continued, "God assoil his loyal soul—" She crossed herself. "—rode after me. He kept my captors from discovering that I was a female until we reached Cinnebar. In the battle I had killed the caliph of that place's brother. They brought me before this ruler for punishment. When he discovered I was a woman he had me placed within his harem. Fair women are much prized among the Arabs. Sir Fulk was executed in my place." She crossed herself again.

"The caliph, his name is Rashid al Ahmet, took me as his second wife. He taught me not to fear passion, and he loved me, my lords, but all the while he held me in captivity I desired only one thing: to return to my husband, Edward de Beaulieu. I hoped, and I prayed, and finally God answered my prayers. My little brother, Glynn, came to Cinnebar, seeking me. His fame as a poet and a minstrel attracted the attention of the caliph's head eunuch, a man called Baba Haroun.

"My brother was invited to the palace to entertain. The first song he sang was in the Welsh tongue, inquiring if I were in this place. He had sung this tune many times over the months as he sought me out. This night, however, his search was ended." She sighed deeply.

Tears filled her eyes, and she swallowed them back bravely, then continued. "At that point in time, my lords, the caliph decided he wanted a child of my body. Harem women are kept sterile by means of herbs unless children are desired of them. Baba Haroun believed that any child of mine could compromise the position of the first wife's son, Prince Mohammed. He said so quite bluntly. It was then I took the chance that he might help me to escape. He did, my lords. We feigned my death, and with Baba Haroun's aid I left Cinnebar.

"Over the next few months my brother and our two faithful men-at-arms, Oth and Dewi, traveled back to England. It was a difficult journey, as you well may imagine. When I arrived at Haven, Father John told me that my husband had had me declared dead and remarried. Then the lady Katherine appeared. I saw how far gone she was with child. It was then I realized, my lords, that I had lost Edward de Beaulieu." A line of tears ran down her pale cheeks.

"My brother had told him in Acre that he was certain I lived, but Edward, alas, had no faith. He abandoned me, and now I beg you, sire, to give me justice. I seek the return of my dower and a forfeit from this man for the stain he has placed upon my father, upon me, and upon our family." She bowed her head.

"My lady," the archbishop of Canterbury said, "why is it you did not escape your shameful captivity in death?"

"My lord, I was taught it was wrong to take one's life, but even if I had been of a mind to do so, there was no way in which I might accomplish it. The women of the harem are watched constantly by a band of eunuchs. We are never alone. Our food is cut for us. We were required to eat with our fingers as no implements were allowed. Our garments are few, and there are no sashes or other loose girdles."

The bishop of Winchester spoke. "Did you tell your husband, my lady, that this caliph person had taught you passion?"

"I did, my lord," Rhonwyn answered. "Edward had been so unhappy with my coldness that I wanted him to know I had been freed of my irrational fears. That I could love him at last and was eager to give him children. I was too late. Another had taken my place. I accept that. It is my punishment for not being the proper kind of wife. I have always liked the lady Katherine, and I wish her no harm. I am glad that Edward has a son and an heir. But, my lords, what is to happen to me now? I fought with all my might to come home. I might have remained where I was in Cinnebar, beloved of another man. A powerful man, and a great ruler. In my heart, however, was a memory of the love I had for Edward de Beaulieu. *I had to come back to England.*

"I expected his anger, my lords, and I expected his scorn, to be sure. I did not expect that he should have held me in so little esteem that he had replaced me within a year of my alleged demise. I had hoped that I should be able to win back his love and his trust. I obviously never had it, and that, my lords, is my mistake. But again I ask you for justice. I was a faithful wife, if not with my body, in my heart and my soul. Edward de Beaulieu was not a faithful husband."

Her testimony concluded, Rhonwyn bowed once more to her judges and stepped back. Glynn ap Llywelyn was then called before the court. He described how he had learned of his sister's disappearance and his shock to discover Edward had written a letter to Rafe de Beaulieu less than two months after Rhonwyn had gone missing. How he had left his studies and traveled with as much haste as possible to Acre to plead with his brother-in-law to wait before remarrying. How Edward had summarily dismissed him.

"Following the example of King Richard's minstrel, Blondell, my lords, I traveled the region singing my songs until, as my sister has told you, I found her." He bowed

to them and then stepped back to his place by Rhonwyn's side.

"The lady Rhonwyn, her party, and the de Beaulieus
will leave the chamber," the king said. "We must discuss
this matter in private."

Accompanied by her brother and the nuns, Rhonwyn
glided from the hall. Behind her she could hear the de
Beaulieus stamping along. The king's steward came and
led them to a small waiting chamber where wine and biscuits had been set out. The men quaffed the wine thirstily.
Rhonwyn sat silently, a rosary in her hands.

"How meek and forlorn you appear," Rafe de Beaulieu
said softly as he came to stand by her side.

She ignored him.

He chuckled. "You say you are no tactician, lady, but I
think you would be a dangerous foe in battle. Despite
your own behavior your splendid performance will cost
poor Edward dearly, I am quite certain."

Unable to help herself, Rhonwyn looked up. "You are
despicable."

"Lady, 'tis a compliment I offer you, not a rebuke," he
replied. "I admire a clever woman, and you are very
clever, although perhaps not very wise. You should have
remained in Cinnebar. Did you not realize that it would
be impossible for Edward to take you back even if he had
had no new wife by his side?"

"If he had loved me, nothing would have been impossible!" Rhonwyn burst out angrily. She still found it difficult to accept the haste with which Edward had acted.

"*Love?* Love is for children, lady. Marriages should be
made for more practical reasons. Your marriage to Edward was part of a treaty between Wales and England.
How could you have believed there was any love involved in it?"

"Perhaps because I am not very wise," Rhonwyn

replied mockingly. "You are wrong, Rafe de Beaulieu. Love can exist between a married couple. I thought it had begun to bloom with Edward. He had, after all, said he loved me. Was I to think he lied?"

"A man will say many things when he is between a woman's legs" was the harsh response.

Rhonwyn's head snapped up, and she glared at him. "You really are despicable. *Go away!* Why do you find it necessary to torment me?"

He smiled down at her, and she was startled by the sudden realization that he was very handsome. The silver blue eyes mocked her. "I don't want to torment you, Rhonwyn," he said in a voice so low that only she could have heard him. *"I want to make love to you."*

She grew pale. She could have sworn that her heart had stopped beating in her chest. She could not speak for a long moment. Finally she said, "If you ever approach me again, I will find a way to kill you, I promise." Then she lowered her head again and began counting her rosary beads.

"You are very bold," the abbess said to Rafe, and she laughed when he flushed. "Aye, I heard you, sir. My hearing is acute. It has to be if I am to keep strict order within my abbey's walls."

"She will be like you when she is old," he said.

"Probably," the abbess answered dryly. "Now go back with your cousin, Rafe de Beaulieu, and leave my niece be."

They waited. Finally the door to the room opened, and the royal chamberlain stood, beckoning them. Returning to the hall, they saw that the king was gone. The queen and the clergy remained.

"The king," Queen Eleanor said, "was exhausted by this morning's events. He has left me to render his judgment. You acted in haste, Edward de Beaulieu, when you remarried without truly knowing if your first wife was dead. However, by having her declared officially dead, your marriage to Lady Katherine is declared legal by the church, and your son, legitimate. It is not believed that you acted with any malice, but rather from the honest conviction that Rhonwyn uerch Llywelyn was really dead. When you learned she was not, though, you acted with total disregard for her honor and her family's honor. For this you shall pay a forfeit, and you shall return her dower portion to her. Is that understood, my lord?"

Edward de Beaulieu bowed and said grudgingly, "Aye, my lady."

"As for you, Rhonwyn uerch Llywelyn, you have condemned yourself by your own words. However, you would appear truly repentant of your sins. The church has taken into consideration the absence of God in your life during most of your life. Your future, though, presents us with a difficult problem. Your lascivious behavior makes you, even penitent, unfit for the church. It will also make it difficult to find a husband for you, and you must have a husband, my dear. You are a lady of noble family who is obviously in need of strong husbandly guidance. But under the circumstances of your recent adventures, who will have you?" the queen said, troubled.

"I will have her."

Rhonwyn turned to stare, surprised, at Rafe de Beaulieu, and then she lost her temper. *"Never!"* she shouted at him. *"Never!"* She held out her hands in appeal to the queen. "Madame, surely you will not take this man seriously? Besides, there must be some consanguinity between us because of my marriage to Edward de Beaulieu."

Queen Eleanor looked to the assembled clergymen. "My lords?"

The archbishop and bishops put their heads together, and the hum of their voices could be heard murmuring in debate over the question. Finally the archbishop of Canterbury spoke.

"There is no blood tie between Rhonwyn uerch Llywelyn and Rafe de Beaulieu," he said. "If the lady had given Edward de Beaulieu a child, then the tie would be there, but it is not. He is free to take her as his wife. It is our opinion that this is the best solution to the matter at hand, my lady."

"*I will not have him!*" Rhonwyn said firmly.

"The choice, my dear," the queen replied, "is not yours. You must have a husband, and he is willing to have you despite all your faults."

"*No!*" Unable to help herself and in utter frustration, Rhonwyn stamped her foot at Eleanor of Provence.

The queen ignored Rhonwyn's protest and turned to her aunt. "My lady abbess, are you delegated by the prince of the Welsh to act in the matter of your niece?"

"I am," the abbess replied.

"What say you?" the queen queried.

"I would know first what kind of a home and hearth this man has to offer my niece. 'Tis not a castle, I am certain, and my niece is of noble blood. Even her mother, God assoil her, was lawfully born into a noble house. We are anxious that Rhonwyn be re-wed, but we will not act in haste and place our child in a difficult situation or one not suited to her station."

"Of course," the queen agreed, smoothing a wrinkle from her royal purple gown. She looked at Rafe de Beaulieu. "Sir, what have you to say to the abbess's query?"

"Through my maternal grandfather who had no other heirs, I hold the title of Baron Bradburn of Ardley," Rafe said. "My manor is small in land, but I have a fine house, servants, and ten serfs to work my fields. My cousin, Edward, has a piece of land, separate from his other holdings, that matches with my land. If you will give me the lady Rhonwyn for a wife, this land could serve as my cousin's forfeit to the lady, and my holdings would thereby be measurably increased. I have cattle and I have sheep among my possessions as well. I am not a very wealthy man but I am comfortable and my wife will not lack. I am not a powerful man, but my blood is as noble as hers. I will not hold the past against her. I will take her to wife despite her adventures and her bad temper."

Rhonwyn threw her rosary beads at his head, shouting, "You will have me in exchange for Edward's land, you bastard? *Never!* I would sooner spend the rest of my days in a windowless dungeon than have you for a husband!"

"The choice is not yours, my child," the abbess repeated quietly.

"Aunt . . ."

"Listen to me, Rhonwyn," the abbess spoke in the Welsh, "they will marry you off whether you will or no. At least you know this man. You may not like him, but you know him. What other will have you? Perhaps some lecherous old lordling who will use you and beat you and squander your dower portion? Rafe de Beaulieu is young. He will give you children. And, I suspect, in time you will come to an arrangement that pleases you both. I have the power to make this match, and I intend to do so. I would prefer, however, that you agree to it also. Not willingly, I know, but I beg you to agree, Rhonwyn."

"I feel like an animal caught in a trap," Rhonwyn said in her childhood tongue. "I hate it!"

"I know," the abbess sympathized, "and I do understand, my child."

"Why must I wed again?" Rhonwyn demanded angrily, but even as she asked the question she knew she was beaten. How in hell could she hope to prevail against the queen and the church? She couldn't. No one was going to come to her aid. Her brother stood silently, his gaze averted. She could see Oth and Dewi at the end of the hall, but she knew as much as they loved her, they would not act against what they knew her father and her aunt would want for her.

"Rhonwyn?" Her aunt's voice gently pressed her.

"I will marry him, but not willingly," she said, once more using the Norman tongue.

"Excellent," Queen Eleanor replied, well pleased.

"I shall marry them myself, here and now," the archbishop of Canterbury announced beneficently, a broad smile upon his face.

"You honor our family, my lord archbishop," the abbess said smoothly, "but I know I should feel more comfortable if all the legalities were tended to first."

"An excellent suggestion," the queen agreed. "They shall be wed late this afternoon, and if the king is better, he will come and give our beautiful bride away. My dear, I did not mention it before, but green becomes you well."

"I shall take my niece back to the convent, gracious queen, until the documents are ready for signature," the abbess replied.

The queen nodded. "I shall send my own page to fetch you."

The abbess and her escort turned to shepherd their charge from the hall. Rhonwyn was seething with anger. Edward de Beaulieu would not look at her, but Rafe stepped forward, taking her hand up and kissing it. His eyes met hers mockingly.

"You will regret your impetuosity, my lord," she snarled at him.

"I think not, Rhonwyn mine," he answered her.

"I will never be yours!" she cried heatedly, and the abbess took her niece's arm and hustled her off before the now affianced pair came to blows.

"Do not cause a scene!" the abbess snapped.

"I hate him! I hate him!" Rhonwyn said heatedly. Her pale skin was flushed with her ire, and the color made her features even more attractive than they usually were.

"You are fortunate," her brother said, coming to her side.

"*What?* Are you on his side, too?" Rhonwyn complained.

"You had to have another husband," Glynn said.

"Why does everyone keep saying that?" she demanded.

"Look on the brighter side of the situation," Glynn said. "Ardley is far nearer to Shrewsbury than Haven. We shall see each other often."

"I don't know why he wants to wed me," Rhonwyn replied, ignoring her brother's comforting words.

"He lusts after you," Glynn said with a chuckle.

"A man who is devoting his life to God should not say such things," she scolded him roundly.

"Had I not had as full a life as I have and known my share of women, sister, I should not be able to give up my life to God so easily," her brother told her with a smile. "Chasing after you and my time in Acre proved quite enlightening."

The abbess chuckled. "You are much your father's son, Glynn. I find it amazing that you can speak of giving up the world so cheerfully. The religious life is a hard life, nephew."

"I know," he said. "In my time in the abbey school I saw how difficult it could be sometimes, but it is also joyous and meaningful as well, my lady abbess. I will be happy at Shrewsbury."

"Then God bless you, Glynn ap Llywelyn," she said. The abbess turned to her niece. "You must rest, Rhonwyn, for you are certainly exhausted in body and spirit after these last few weeks."

Rhonwyn didn't argue with the older woman as they reentered the convent, allowing her aunt to help her from her beautiful gown so she might lay down in her chemise.

"Now listen to me, my child," the abbess said. "After the marriage ceremony I shall announce that we are all leaving immediately. That your father's men-at-arms will want to escort you to your new home, and as we yet have several hours of daylight, we shall leave right away. No one, not even your new husband, will gainsay me, I promise you. We can travel at least five miles tonight before darkness sets in. There is a small religious house just that distance away. It is there we shall shelter tonight. As you know, there will be no accommodations for a newly wed couple. You and your husband will be forced to sleep in separate quarters. Tomorrow we can retrace our route exactly, sheltering at the various convents and monasteries that we sheltered in on our way to Westminster. Until we reach your new home I can protect you from Rafe de Beaulieu's eagerness. Use that time, Rhonwyn, to know him better. You are not the frightened girl who married his cousin. You are a woman, and you know what is expected of you. I have never known a man, but I have heard it said the experience is pleasanter if the couple at least likes each other. There must be something you can learn to like in him."

Rhonwyn shook her head, but she was smiling slightly. "Aunt, I wish I had a predilection for the religious life, for I should enjoy being with you for the rest of my days. I do not think I shall enjoy that same pleasure with Rafe de Beaulieu. I am certainly being punished for my foolish ways."

"Tell me something," the abbess said, turning the subject. "How exactly did Sir Fulk die? You have never been particularly forthcoming in that matter. Do you feel such guilt for his death?"

"He did not die," Rhonwyn said. "I wanted him to return home with me, but he would not. He had been put in charge of Prince Mohammed's military training. The prince is but two years younger than Glynn and just a few years younger than Sir Fulk. They liked one another, and Fulk felt his opportunities would be greater in Cinnebar. He did not believe, however, that his family would understand his remaining with the infidels."

"Could he give up his faith so easily?" The abbess looked disturbed.

"Nay, he did not give up his faith, Aunt. In Cinnebar all faiths are permitted to worship freely," Rhonwyn told her.

"Indeed," the abbess said. "It must have been a very odd place."

When her aunt had left the tiny cell where she was housed, Rhonwyn slept. When she was awakened in the early part of the late afternoon, a bowl of lavender-scented water and a cloth were brought to her. She washed herself and dressed again in her lovely green gown. Her hair was unbraided and then replaited as it had been earlier, the mass in the rear of her head being brushed until it shone. A cup of wine and some biscuits were offered, and she ate with a good appetite, for she had had nothing since early morning.

"Are the documents ready for signature?" she asked the abbess when the older woman came to escort her.

"Aye. We are to go back to the palace now. Glynn and the others are awaiting us outside the convent walls. I have made our good-byes to the mother superior and given her one of your gold marks, niece, in thanksgiving for your marriage."

"A waste of a good coin, although I do not begrudge this convent my gold. The chapel roof, I noted, leaks."

Escorted by the queen's page, they walked the brief distance from St. Mary's to Westminster Palace. The king's chamberlain led them to a small room where Rafe de Beaulieu and Edward awaited them. The documents were laid out upon a large oak table.

"The de Beaulieus have already signed, my ladies," the chamberlain said. "Will you now sign, my lady abbess, here, and here, and here again."

The abbess scanned the parchments before her, and then she said, "My niece is quite capable of signing herself, my lords. Rhonwyn?"

"Traitor!" Rhonwyn whispered.

"You will thank me one day, my child," the abbess said calmly.

"I think not, Aunt," Rhonwyn countered, but she took up the quill and signed her name in the places designated.

"You can write," Rafe observed.

She glared at him, and he could not help but laugh. Her look was so deliciously outraged. Her beauty had overwhelmed all other considerations when he had so boldly proclaimed he would have her to wife. If she had been outraged by his offer, his cousin Edward had been equally so. He had calmed Edward by telling him it was better to keep the Welsh girl in the family where they could control her than to let her marry another man who might be cajoled by her beauty into an act of revenge against the de Beaulieus. Edward had reluctantly acquiesced.

The chamberlain stamped the royal seal into the wax that his assistant had dripped onto each document. Then rolling them up, he handed them to Rafe de Beaulieu. "The archbishop is waiting," he said.

For a brief moment Rhonwyn looked as if she were going to bolt from the chamber.

Then Rafe de Beaulieu took her arm, murmuring low, "Certainly ap Gruffydd's daughter is no coward, lady."

Fury blazed in Rhonwyn's emerald green eyes. "You shall soon learn just what ap Gruffydd's daughter is capable of, my lord!"

"Lady, have mercy. My appetite for you is already well honed," he said.

"I should like to hone my sword against your head," she replied angrily.

"I should far rather lodge my sword within your sheath," he teased her.

Her cheeks flamed pink at the randy reference.

"What? No sharp retort?" he taunted her.

She raised her hand to hit him. He caught the hand and, turning it, kissed her palm. Their eyes met, and she was almost staggered physically by the lightning she felt shoot between them. Rhonwyn snatched her hand back, her heart hammering with shock.

"How long has it been?" he murmured softly. His fingers brushed over her lips.

"Go to hell!" she hissed as softly as they entered the royal chapel where the king and queen awaited them.

The king was wan, his left eyelid drooping, but his look was a kind one. He smiled at Rhonwyn, coming slowly to her side as she and Rafe reached the altar where Archbishop Boniface awaited them. Rhonwyn noted the queen's worried expression as the king stood on shaky legs beside the reluctant bride. Poor man, she thought, and gave him a dazzling smile.

"You truly honor me, sire, and I thank you for it," she told the monarch, taking his arm to steady him.

"You will be happy, I promise," the king said to her, and he patted her hand. "A woman is happiest when she is well wed."

"I will remember your words, my lord," she promised him.

Then in his elegant Latin, Archbishop Boniface began the ancient words to the marriage sacrament.

Chapter Fifteen

Rafe de Beaulieu was more amused than angry when he realized he would not be able to consummate his marriage until they reached his estates. While he enjoyed female flesh, he had never been a man to casually bed a woman. The abbess made certain her niece rode by his side each day of their journey. He knew that she was attempting to foster some sort of a rapport between bride and bridegroom, but Rhonwyn was not feeling particularly cooperative. Each day he would attempt to engage her in conversation. She answered him in monosyllables. He gained far more out of her when he taunted her. She would erupt and excoriate him angrily until she realized just what it was he was doing. Then she would grow grimly silent, her lips pressed together tightly in a narrow line.

Finally one day he asked her bluntly, "Why is it that you are angry with me, Rhonwyn? I am not the one who betrayed you."

"You are a de Beaulieu," she answered him.

"So are you," he replied.

A strange look passed over her features, and then she laughed bitterly. "So I am. Twice, by marriage, I vow." Then she asked him, "Why did you wed me, Rafe?"

"For the land, of course, lady," he answered.

"And?"

"Because anyone else who might have you would have mistreated you" was the surprising reply.

"You felt sorry for me?" Her tone bordered on outrage.

"Aye," he readily agreed, "but I also lusted after you. You know how very beautiful you are. I think one reason Edward was angry at me for offering for you is that he, too, sees how lush and ripe you have become. You are no longer the avid little lass who so eagerly sought to go on crusade, Rhonwyn. You are a very desirable woman, *and now you are mine.*"

"Edward thinks I am desirable?" she said, a small smile on her lips. Her green eyes were thoughtful.

"Could you not see the hunger for you in his eyes?" Rafe replied. "He loves my sister, make no mistake, Rhonwyn, but desire you, even briefly, he did. And the secret knowledge of it rendered him full of guilty rage. He directed that anger at you, you will recall."

"I did not see it," she said. "I was too busy defending myself from his cruel charges and half truths, my lord."

"And what do you feel for him?" Rafe asked, attempting to keep the jealousy in his voice from her.

"What should I feel for him?" she countered.

He closed his eyes a moment, and then opening them, said, "You will drive me to murder one day, lady."

"But I suspect not, my lord, before you have plundered my body and gained the pleasures that I can give you," she taunted him.

"What of the pleasures I can give you?" he returned.

"Can you?" she replied coolly. "We shall see, my lord. It is to be hoped you are more skilled in the amatory arts than Edward was. There was very little he aroused in me but a desire to have it over and done with as quickly as possible." That, Rhonwyn knew even as she spoke the

words, was not entirely true, but her heart still hurt from the brutal rejection.

"You will find I am an entirely different man than my cousin," Rafe promised her. "You will long for more in my arms, and not less."

" 'Tis to be hoped your actions match or even exceed your boasting, my lord," Rhonwyn mocked him gently.

"As your aunt has so skillfully arranged our daily accommodations, lady, it will be a while longer before I may make good my gasconade," he said with an amused chuckle.

Rhonwyn was forced to laugh. "Passion is the better for the waiting," she advised him, her emerald eyes twinkling. Perhaps this marriage would not be as bad as she thought. To her surprise Rafe de Beaulieu was a humorous man, and she certainly admired his loyalty and devotion to his sister, Katherine.

"Shall I tell you how I intend to make love to you the first time I bed you?" he said, his silvery blue eyes making contact with hers.

Rhonwyn felt her cheeks grow warm. "You are indelicate, my lord." Was her voice shaking? Her knees suddenly felt weak as she bestrode her horse. She gripped her reins more tightly and hoped he didn't notice.

His laughter was low and insinuating. "I shall have you naked," he began softly. "I want to see the candlelight and the firelight flickering over your body, Rhonwyn. I will kiss you. Not just upon the lips, but each tiny bit of your flesh will feel the touch of my mouth. You will be warm and yielding in my arms, Rhonwyn."

"How certain you are," she said, laughing.

"Aye, I am certain!" he said with a smile.

"What will you do when you have finished kissing me?" she demanded.

Now he laughed. He liked her boldness as long as it

was reserved only for him. "I shall fondle those sweet breasts of yours and suckle upon their nipples until the flesh is swollen and aching with desire. I shall caress you until you are weak with longing."

Rhonwyn felt a small tingling beginning in her nether regions. She shifted nervously in her saddle.

He saw the motion and grinned wickedly at her. "I shall find your sweet jewel and torture it until you are creamy with your own sweet essence. Then I shall cover you with my body and enter you slowly, slowly, *slowly*. You shall feel me hard and throbbing my desire inside your sweet sheath, Rhonwyn. You will melt with pleasure within my arms, my beautiful bride, because, Rhonwyn, you are a woman who was meant to be loved, and there is no man on this earth who will love you as I do. And I will not be satisfied until you love me. Not make love, but *love*. Do you understand what it is I am saying to you?"

Her eyes were closed. Her breathing was shallow. His words aroused her in a way no man ever had. The tingle mushroomed until it shattered itself, and she sighed deeply. Then hearing his words, her eyes flew open, her look startled, her cheeks blushing guiltily.

"By the rood!" he swore softly, realizing what had happened to her. "Lady, it is all I can do not to stop this caravan and take you into the woods. My God, how you whet my appetites! Others might call you shameless. I will not, provided you keep your passion for me in the future. Praise God we shall reach Ardley tomorrow!"

"So soon?" she whispered. She was both astounded and distressed by the effect he had had on her with his wicked words.

"Not soon enough, lady," he told her frankly.

She kicked her horse into a loping canter and rode ahead of their train, the cool wind soothing the heat in her face. What had just happened was truly disturbing, and such a thing had certainly never happened to her before. I do not understand, she thought, confused. Why should this man have such an effect upon me? How can my body desire him when I do not? She shook her head, suddenly irritated. I am tired, Rhonwyn thought, of being controlled by men. First my father. Then Edward. Then the caliph, and now Rafe de Beaulieu. Why can a woman not live her own life without the interference of men?

She had surely asked the question over and over again, but had never received a proper answer to it. Glynn had said respectable women didn't run their own lives, but he had not explained why that had to be.

Only women like her aunt had a certain measure of autonomy, it seemed, but then even Gwynllian was answerable to her bishop, a man, of course. A queen could rule in her husband's absence or in her own right in certain cases, but her counselors were always men. Why not women? Why just men? Suddenly she laughed aloud at herself. She was asking questions to which there were obviously no answers. Men ruled the world, and that was all there was to it. She was married to Rafe de Beaulieu, and for better or for worse, she was going to have to make the best of it, but she didn't intend to be a docile and gentle creature like her sister-in-law, Katherine. As Rafe was now stuck with her, he would have to accept that Rhonwyn uerch Llywelyn was who she was, and there would be no changing her!

Early the following afternoon they reached Ardley. Rhonwyn had to admit she was impressed by the house. Rafe always referred to his branch of the family as poor relations, but his house was hardly a humble dwelling. It was constructed of stone with a slate roof and, to her surprise, fortified with a small moat that encircled the main building.

"They got royal permission for that somewhere along the line," the abbess Gwynllian noted. "Undoubtedly it is because we are so close to Wales here. The land looks prosperous, niece. You should be happy here, and it is more manageable than Haven."

"You will remain the night?" Rafe de Beaulieu asked politely.

The abbess chuckled. "Alas, sir, we cannot. I will, of course, want to satisfy my curiosity and see the inside. Afterward, however, we must be on our way. They are expecting us at St. Hilda's tonight."

There was a small wooden bridge that led across the narrow watercourse to a gravel path. They entered the house by means of a stone porch. Carved wooden screens were set on either side of the opening into the hall, which was to their left.

"The kitchen, the buttery, the pantry are on the right," Rafe said. "I have a library behind the hall where I do the estate business."

At the far end of the hall the abbess noted two oriels, one on either side of the room, that allowed much light into the room. There was a fine large fireplace on the right. The high board was set on a low but elevated dais. The table was of well-polished oak. There were herbs sprinkled upon the floor. The house had a well-kept look about it.

"The staircase to the bedchambers and the solar come down by the left oriel window," he explained. "Would you like to see the upstairs, my lady abbess?"

"Aye, I will admit to being curious." She smiled at him.

At that moment, however, Katherine de Beaulieu came down the stairs and entered into the hall. "Rafe!" she called, her voice sweet and welcoming.

"Edward came home several days ago and told me you had taken the lady Rhonwyn for your wife. I hope you will both be very happy." She hugged her brother, and the abbess saw her look was loving. She turned to Rhonwyn. "Welcome to Ardley, Rhonwyn. May you be content within these walls. My mother was, and the women who came before her." She embraced her somewhat startled sister-in-law, behaving as if the marriage between her brother and Rhonwyn was a wonderful thing. "I have brought you a gift, Rhonwyn. She is waiting upstairs for you."

For a moment Rhonwyn looked puzzled, and then suddenly she said, *"Enit?"*, and when Katherine nodded with a smile, Rhonwyn could not keep herself from hugging Edward's wife. "Oh, thank you, Katherine!"

"Her loyalty is to you alone. Once she knew you were alive, I knew I could not keep her from you," Katherine said. "Would you like me to give you a tour of the house? I know it far better than my brother, who only knows where to go to sleep, to eat, and to pee," Katherine laughed.

"Please," Rhonwyn said. Then she and the abbess followed after Katherine as she led them upstairs. Rafe watched them go, and when he knew he would not be observed, he smiled. When he had first seen his sister he feared that Rhonwyn would be unkind, but before she could even get her bearings, Kate had won her over with her natural sweetness. The abbess, he had noted, was equally relieved. He took the cup of wine offered by an attentive servant and sat down by his fire.

Upstairs Katherine showed her new sister-in-law the master chamber with its sunny solar and garderobe. There were also two smaller chambers. Each of the rooms, Katherine proudly pointed out, had its own fireplace. "The house is very tight," she said, "and the windows face south and west. Even in our awful Shropshire winters these rooms are toasty warm. My mother far preferred her solar on a winter's day to the hall below."

At the sound of the voices Enit hurried from the master chamber. "Oh, my lady, my lady!" Then she burst into tears.

Touched, Rhonwyn embraced her serving woman. "It's all right now, Enit. I'm here, and we have a fine new home, don't we?"

"Yes, my lady," the young woman sniffed.

"My lady abbess," Katherine said, "will you allow me to travel with you as far as Haven? At this hour I cannot hope to reach home by sunset, but I should be grateful to be somewhat nearer there by evening."

"Will your husband worry, my dear?" the abbess inquired.

"Nay. I told him I should travel with you and he would probably not see me until the morrow sometime. I have half a dozen men-at-arms with me, and your road is but a mile away from Haven."

"Of course, child, you are welcome to travel with me," the abbess said.

Suddenly there was the sound of a child crying, and Rhonwyn realized that there was a cradle by the solar fireplace. Walking over, she saw a swaddled infant lying in it. The baby looked up at her, and Rhonwyn jumped back. The child had Edward de Beaulieu's eyes and looked at Rhonwyn in the same way.

"Oh," Katherine said. "Neddie has startled you. I am so sorry. He is just two months old, and I certainly couldn't leave him behind at Haven."

"Why not?" Rhonwyn demanded. Had Katherine brought the child to torture her?

"He would have starved," Katherine said softly. "I do not believe in wet nurses. There was no danger in bringing him to my brother's house. Come and meet your nephew now. He will grow up with the children that you and Rafe have. Is that not wonderful?" She picked up the infant and handed him to Rhonwyn before her sister-in-law might demur.

The abbess almost laughed aloud at the look of terror on her niece's face. "Cuddle him, child," she said in her Welsh tongue. "He will not bite you. You do not smell of milk as his mother does."

Rhonwyn nestled the baby boy in her arms, her terror replaced by a feeling of amazement and wonder. "He really looks just like Edward," she finally said.

"Doesn't he?" Katherine crowed proudly. "I hope your first son is his father's mirror image. Men are so vain over these things, and Rafe in particular."

"Perhaps my first child will be a daughter," Rhonwyn ventured.

"Then I hope she looks like you, sister!" was the sweet reply. "You are truly the most beautiful woman I ever saw. My brother is a fortunate man. I hope you will eventually learn to love him as I love Edward. Do not think me insensitive, Rhonwyn, for I am not. I suspect you cared deeply for Edward. He is a difficult man, but I have known him my whole life long, and I know I am the better wife for him. You are impulsive and slightly reckless, like Rafe. You do not realize it yet, but you are strangely well matched, though you, I think, are the stronger. Be kind to my brother." She took her son from Rhonwyn. "You will want to refresh yourself, my lady abbess, before we are on the road again. I will leave you and go down to visit with my brother for a few minutes. I am ready when you are." Her son in her arms, Katherine de Beaulieu hurried from the solar.

Rhonwyn sat down heavily.

Joining her, her aunt said, "I have never known you to be this quiet, my child. What is it?"

Rhonwyn was silent for a long moment, and then she said, "I really am remarried, aunt. I have a new husband. A new house. A sister-in-law whom I should hate, but cannot. And I am expected to have babies!"

"You are no longer a child, Rhonwyn," the abbess said gently. "You are a grown and experienced woman of noble birth. It is indeed past time you had children. This is the life you will live now. Make your peace with it, my child. You are very fortunate to have been rescued by Rafe de Beaulieu. He is, I believe, a far better man than his cousin."

Rhonwyn nodded. "I know," she agreed, "but he is just so annoying, aunt! Part of me wants to accept my new life. Another part of me wants to fight with Rafe for daring to marry me! What am I to do?"

"My dear niece, in the never-ending battle between men and women, I have absolutely no experience, but I very much believe that you and that handsome husband of yours will eventually come to an understanding before one of you kills the other." She arose. "Now, call Enit and show me to the garderobe before I must be on my way. I will join you downstairs, my child."

In the hall Rhonwyn found her brother had joined Rafe and Katherine. They were laughing as they shared wine and biscuits. "What is your cause for such humor?" she asked as she came to Glynn's side.

"Rafe and I are comparing stories of growing up with a sister," Glynn said with a chuckle.

"And what have you discovered?" she asked him with a smile.

"That girls are all alike," he laughed.

"You will miss me when you are in your cold cell, subsisting on salt fish, bread, and bad wine," Rhonwyn predicted.

"Aye," Glynn agreed. "I will miss you, Rhonwyn."

Tears sprang to her eyes. "Damn you, little brother," she said softly. "You are the only person I know who can make me cry."

He embraced her tenderly. "Be content, sister, and be happy with this new life, this other chance you have been given. I know that I am glad to be returning to Shrewsbury Abbey where my life awaits me."

"And what will poor Oth and Dewi do without you, brother?" she asked him.

"They want to remain with you, Rhonwyn. I have already gained Rafe's permission in the matter. He is glad to have them. He knows it will make you happy." Glynn lowered his voice. "He is a good man, sister. Do not take him lightly."

"I won't," she promised.

The abbess came downstairs, accompanied by Enit. "Give me a sip of wine, nephew Rafe, and then I shall be on my way," she said.

When the wine had been consumed, the abbess, Katherine de Beaulieu, her infant, and Glynn ap Llywelyn took their leave of Rafe and Rhonwyn. Rhonwyn watched them go. Even though her brother had promised to visit when the abbott permitted him to come, she was already lonely, and only God knew if she would ever see her aunt again. When Rafe's arm went about her shoulder, she did not shrug it off.

"Come," he said when their guests had at last disappeared from sight. "You have not met your servants, wife. Do you like the house?"

She nodded. "It is a fine house," she told him.

"But not a castle," he remarked.

"I was not raised in a castle, my lord."

"Nor is it a caliph's luxurious palace," he noted.

"I was not raised in a palace, either," she replied. "Why do you seek to quarrel with me, my lord?"

"What, Rhonwyn, will you not fight with me?" he teased her. "Pray God you do not turn into a meek and mild creature like my sweet sister, Kate. Such decorum in a sister is fine, but 'tis deadly dull in a wife, I fear."

"How would you know, sir? Have you ever had a wife before?" she snapped back at him.

He chortled. "That is better, and in answer to your question, nay, I have never had a wife before, but I think I may enjoy one." The silver blue eyes danced wickedly at her.

"You are impossible," she fumed.

" 'Tis true, lady, but are you yet sad over the departure of your aunt and your brother now?" he queried.

Suddenly Rhonwyn laughed. "You are clever, my lord, perhaps too clever, I fear, for a simple lass raised in a fortress in the Welshry," she murmured. Now her eyes were dancing wickedly.

"*Simple lass?*" he scoffed disbelieving. "Your *simplicity* has gained me over three hundred acres, Rhonwyn. My father tried his whole life to get that land from his brother, Edward's father, but to no avail. Now, at last, thanks to you, we have it!" He gave her a hug as they entered the house again.

"Did it belong to Ardley originally?" she asked him.

"My grandfather, and Edward's, purchased Ardley for my father so he would have his own lands, but our grandsire retained the acreage in question because he felt it added to Haven's prestige to have more land. When Edward's father inherited it, my father attempted to purchase it from him, but my uncle would not sell it. It always galled my father that his own brother would not give him back the land that rightfully belonged to Ardley. When the queen's counselors asked what forfeit I would have for you, I chose this land. It was not so great a parcel that would make us appear greedy, and it matched

my lands. It was to all the obvious choice. Edward dared
not refuse me, although I know he was angered," Rafe
chuckled. "It truly pained him to release those acres to
me. Fortunately he had no other option."

"So you really did marry me for the land," she said almost irritably.

"Of course," he replied. "You are the first woman that
I ever considered who had a respectable dower portion."

"*Beast!*" She hit him on the arm, and he laughed.

"Surely you are not a romantic, Rhonwyn? You know
as well as I do that marriage is an arrangement between
families, mutually acceptable to them both. You were
married to Edward to seal a treaty between England and
Wales. You have been married to me because I saw an
opportunity to regain what was mine. You have profited
as well, wife. Shameless hussy that you are, you have
made a second respectable marriage and saved both your
honor and your father's good name." Rafe surveyed her,
curious as to how she would react to his speech.

Rhonwyn's look, however, was carefully masked. She
had not forgotten the words he had spoken to her the
day before. *And I will not be satisfied until you love me.*
Then she smiled a wicked smile. "You have done quite
well for yourself, Rafe. Not only have you gained back
the land your family lost, but you have wed above your
station by marrying the prince of the Welsh's daughter."

He chuckled. "You will not be easy to live with, I can
see it even now. Come, wife, the servants await. Kate was
so busy being house proud that she did not introduce
you as she should have." He took her hand, leading her
back into the house where she met Browne, the steward;
Albert and his wife, Albertina, who divided the cooking
and baking chores between them; and the three maidservants, Dilys, Mavis, and Annie. There was a kitchen
boy, Tam, who scrubbed pots, turned the spit, and edged

the knives. Lizzie and her sister, Rosie, were in charge of the laundry. There was Peterman, the bailiff, several grooms for the stables, and a hayward who kept the hedges trimmed. Rafe, Rhonwyn learned, kept his own accounts and ordered what supplies the estate could not grow or manufacture.

The servants were friendly but polite. They seemed to be pleased to have a new mistress. She thanked them for their greeting, and then said, "You have met my Enit and will welcome her as warmly, I hope." Then Rhonwyn smiled at them.

"Aye, my lady," Browne replied. "A good worker your Enit is, we already know. She has prepared your chamber for you and earlier unpacked your possessions that she and Lady Katherine brought from Haven."

For a moment Rhonwyn was tempted to say she wanted nothing from Haven, but she swallowed back the urge. She wasn't a wealthy woman, nor was her husband a rich man. She needed everything she had, and her pride would have to accept that fact.

"Come," Rafe said softly to her. "I will take you to our chamber, wife." His fingers closed about her arm.

"Our chamber?"

" 'Tis a small house," he murmured low. "The custom here is that the master and the mistress share a bed. 'Tis not like my cousin's fine castle where the lady has her own apartments and the lord his." He half dragged her up the narrow staircase and into the solar. "Go down to the hall, girl," he told Enit, who scurried out at his command. "Now, wife, we will talk," Rafe de Beaulieu said.

Rhonwyn sat herself in a high-backed oak chair by the fire. "What shall we talk about, my lord?" she asked him sweetly.

"You realize that I positively lust after you, Rhonwyn,

don't you? I have said it before," he remarked frankly as he stood before her.

"Aye," she managed to respond, looking directly up at him. Why did he have to be so damned handsome, she thought, admitting to herself that she could feel her own lust being engaged. It had been almost a year since she had lain in a man's arms, felt a man's weight on her, sighed with pleasure at a lover's eager entrance into her body.

He smiled, and she flushed, knowing he somehow read her randy thoughts. "Do you want me as much as I want you?" he asked her.

"I do not want you at all," she snapped, knowing it was a lie and knowing that he knew it was a lie.

"I have never forced a woman, Rhonwyn," he told her seriously. "I will not force you. You are my wife. Between us there will be respect and consideration until that time you wish us to enter into a true spousal state. We will, of course, share the bed in our chamber, for I am certain you do not wish the servants to know of our agreement. It would distress them to learn we were not doing all we could to make an heir for Ardley."

"*You don't want me?*" She was astounded.

"Nay, wife, as I have already said, I want you very much, but I will have no woman who does not want me," Rafe replied.

"That is ridiculous!"

"Do you enjoy being forced, then?" he demanded, his look leering. He tipped her face up to his.

Pulling away, Rhonwyn cried, "Nay! But you are my husband, and you have certain rights whether I will or no. Edward certainly never hesitated to claim his prerogatives."

"Edward was a fool who might have discovered the real reason for your fears had he not been so busy with his *claims*," Rafe said bluntly. "Your caliph obviously took the time to learn what it was that frightened you, Rhonwyn. Will you tell me?"

"Rashid al Ahmet said that the mind was a dangerous thing," Rhonwyn began. "He was patient and clever. Together we discovered that I hid a secret within the darkest recesses of my soul. Once, when I was a small girl and my brother barely out of infancy, a richly clad stranger came to our cottage and violated my mam. She never told ap Gruffydd and warned me not to, either. Glynn was too young to remember the incident. My mam told me I should never let a man do to me what the stranger had done to her. It somehow left the impression on my child's mind that I should not couple with a man. Once I was able to remember what had happened, my fears dissolved."

"Ah," Rafe said, and then he grinned at her. "And being fearless, wife, you went on to taste and experience all the pleasures of the flesh, did you not? I hope the caliph taught you well, for I am a man with a prodigious appetite for carnal delights."

"But you will not force me," Rhonwyn taunted him. "You have said it yourself, my lord, that until I desire you, you will not have me." Her fingers reached up and caressed his cheek, sliding down the curve of his visage and trailing across his lips.

He caught her hand and shoved her fingers into his mouth, sucking upon them vigorously, his eyes meeting hers in a silent challenge.

"You said you would not force me," she quickly reminded him.

He licked her fingers dry and kissed the tips of the digits before releasing them. "I said, lady, that I should not force you. I did not say I should not tease you, fondle you, caress you, or kiss you. *I said I would not force you.*"

"Is what you have said not coercion?" she demanded. Her fingers were tingling.

"You are proud, Rhonwyn, and you are a poor liar. You lust for me every bit as much as I lust after you, but you refuse to admit to it." Yanking her up, his arms closed about her. Their lips were dangerously close. "Tell me now that you do not want me!"

"I do not want you!" she cried.

"Liar!" he mocked her, and then he kissed her lips. They trembled beneath his, soft and yielding despite her protest. "Tell me you do not want me," he said once more.

"Bastard!" she hissed at him fiercely.

"Say the words, Rhonwyn," he pressed her.

"But you don't believe me," she half sobbed. Her heart was pounding wildly. Her legs felt like straw.

"Nay, wife, I don't. Edward was foisted upon you, as was your caliph. I am the first, the only man, whom you have ever truly desired with ever fiber of your being, Rhonwyn. Why do you deny so desperately what is so plain to me?" His mouth brushed hers again. "So proud. So fierce. So damnably sweet," he crooned low to her. "Do not fight it, lovely, I beg of you!"

She struggled against his grip. "You claim I am proud," she cried. "Your pride is far worse than mine, Rafe de Beaulieu. Let me be! You have promised not to force me, and I will not have you! Can you not understand me?"

He kissed her brow. "You will come to me sooner than later, wife," he told her as his grip loosened suddenly, and she almost fell.

Recovering, she stood facing him, her cheeks pink, her green eyes wide. "What makes you think I want you?" she demanded.

"I see it in your emerald eyes," he told her. "You trembled in my arms, and I felt the little nipples of your breasts hardening against my chest. Your mouth was sweet and did not deny me, Rhonwyn."

"I cannot remain here," she said desperately. "You are a devil, Rafe de Beaulieu! You confuse me with your wicked tongue!"

"Oh, my darling," he said, laughing, "you haven't begun to know the impact of my wicked tongue upon you, but you soon will."

She turned away from him. He was right, damn him! For the first time in her life she actually desired a man. She had almost desired Edward, and the caliph's passion had opened her eyes to the pleasures that could exist between a man and a woman, but she had never truly wanted a man as she wanted this one. *But it was wrong!* To give in to his wicked cajolery before they knew more about one another was not right. This was the man she would be married to until death. She wanted his respect, and if she was to have it, she must not yield to his taunts like some common whore of the streets. Drawing a deep breath, Rhonwyn turned herself about and looked directly at her husband.

"Aye, I do desire you," she admitted, "but I am not being coy when I ask you for a bit of time so we may know one another better. Because I have lived in a harem does not make me a loose woman, Rafe. Do you understand how I feel?"

He sighed. "Aye," he told her, "I do, but waiting will not make me want you any less, lovey."

Rhonwyn laughed. "I don't want you to desire me less, husband," she said. "I just want to know the man I am wed to better than I knew the last one. Perhaps we can learn to love one another in the romantic sense, but I seek your respect as well. Neither of us are children, Rafe, and we have both known passion. There is little that can surprise us, my lord, so let us be patient for now."

"You surprise me, Rhonwyn," he told her.

"Sometimes I surprise myself," she returned.

"If you had been Eve, and I, Adam," he said, "I believe we should still be within the Garden of Eden, wife."

Rhonwyn was unable to restrain her chuckle. "Perhaps," she said.

They stood awkwardly for a long moment, staring at one another, and then he said, "It is almost time for the meal, wife. Let us go down into the hall together. Tomorrow you must begin to learn the ways of this household. Browne will help you, I promise. He is a good man. It is he who trained Kate properly after our parents died."

The meal was simple. There was a broiled trout and a venison stew along with bread and cheese. They both ate with good appetites. Afterward they sat together by the fire in high-backed wooden chairs with tapestried cushions. A huge gray wolfhound with a rough coat came and put his large head in Rhonwyn's lap. Delighted, she stroked the beast until his dark eyes closed in obvious pleasure.

"His name is Flint," Rafe said. "I have never before seen him take to anyone. He has always been very aloof."

"He was but waiting for me," Rhonwyn told her husband, and as if to agree, Flint's eyes opened, and he barked.

They both laughed.

"So you like dogs, do you?" Rafe said.

"Cythraul had a small pack of them," she replied, "and there were animals at Haven, although none ever attached itself to me as this charming fellow has." Flint was now lying at her feet.

"Having done so, he'll guard you with his own life,"

Rafe told her seriously. "That is the way wolfhounds are if they attach themselves to any one person."

Flint ambled upstairs after them, and Rafe allowed him to sleep before the fire in the solar.

"Not our bedchamber?" Rhonwyn teased him.

"First he'd be on the floor, and then he'd push me right out of our bed," Rafe said. "Don't think I don't understand his tactics, wife."

Enit helped her mistress to wash and disrobe, then sought her bedspace in the solar. Rhonwyn climbed into the big bed with the dark green hangings. Turning on her side, she waited nervously for Rafe to join her, wondering if he would keep his promise. She found herself a little disappointed when he did, and when she awoke in the morning he had already gone.

Browne began guiding her through the business of being Ardley's new mistress.

The household was small and practically ran itself, but there were certain things done in season that were Rhonwyn's responsibility as mistress of the household.

"Most have been done for the year," Browne told his mistress, "for even though Lady Katherine is now at Haven, she would not allow her brother's household to falter. It will soon be time for the making of the October ale. The apples and pears are being harvested now and must be made into conserves or dried for winter use, and of course the pigs will need to be slaughtered for winter."

"I've never done such work," Rhonwyn admitted. "When I lived at Haven, these things were done by others."

"And so they will be here, my lady," Browne said in kindly tones, "but Ardley being a small manor, it will be up to its lady to oversee all these tasks. Do you know how to make salves and other medicines?"

"Aye, I was taught at the convent," Rhonwyn replied.

"It is a good time to seek out the berries, roots, and leaves you will need for that endeavor," Browne remarked. "Shall I call Enit and fetch a basket for you, my lady?"

"Yes," she told him. By the rood! She had missed what it was like to be a lady of the manor. Her time at Haven had been short, and in the harem she had done nothing more strenuous than gossip in the baths with Alia and the other women while beautifying herself for the caliph's visits. She had almost forgotten that a good English chatelaine's days were scheduled to match the march of the seasons. If they were to survive the winter, there was a great deal that would have to be done. Having lived at Haven, Rhonwyn remembered that Shropshire had the worst winters in all of England.

September and October flew by. The ale was made and sealed in barrels. The fruit was preserved by either drying or enclosing in jugs of honey and wine. Rhonwyn was delighted when her husband invited her to go hunting. Over the next few weeks they brought back several deer and a number of water fowl, which were hung in the larder. Rhonwyn purchased a barrel of cod and directed her servants to salt the fish in order to preserve it over the coming winter months.

At Martinmas they had goose, and Edward came in his wife's company to Ardley for the family feast. He could hardly wait to tell his brother-in-law and his former wife that Katherine was once again with child. It would be born next summer.

"You must not allow him to wear you out with childbearing," Rhonwyn scolded Kate. "This child will be born only thirteen months after its sibling. Go to Enit's mother afterward. She will help you to avoid conceiving again too soon."

"Such a thing is forbidden," Katherine said piously.

"Edward would be very angry should he ever learn of such a thing."

"He will be angrier if you die too soon. Do you want your babes raised by an uncaring stepmother? Be sensible, Kate. Rafe would certainly agree with me, I know," Rhonwyn told her sister-in-law.

"I do not need Rafe telling me what to do as he always did before I wed with Edward," Kate said heatedly.

"Doesn't Edward tell you what to do?" Rhonwyn asked.

"Edward is my husband," Kate answered with what she considerd perfect logic.

"What were you and my sister discussing so hotly?" Rafe asked her afterward when their guests had departed.

"Kate is sweet, but she is a dolt," Rhonwyn said bluntly, and told him of their conversation.

Rafe's visage grew concerned. "I will talk to her," he said firmly.

"Don't," Rhonwyn warned. "She will not listen. I will have Enit's mother conspire with her other daughter, who is Kate's maidservant. They will see Kate is protected from her foolishness."

"You are a good wife," Rafe said.

"Not yet, my lord, but soon, I promise," Rhonwyn told him. "Soon I will be the best wife you could ever have, Rafe."

Chapter Sixteen

The hall was practically silent. The fire crackled, and Flint snored contentedly, his massive head on his paws. The servants had disappeared, the meal having been cleared away an hour ago. Outside the windows a winter storm howled unrelentingly, the snow and ice beating against the windows as the shutters rattled with each windy blast. Rhonwyn and Rafe sat before the blazing fire, a chess table between them. They were well matched in skill, and the nightly battle between them was indicative of the other silent battle they fought.

Her fingers toyed with the carved ash-wood chess piece as she contemplated her next move. "Do you think the storm will be over by morning?" she wondered aloud, not even looking up as she finally moved her queen.

Rafe studied the outline of the chessboard now. "Nay, wife, this is a bad storm even for Shropshire. It may end by tomorrow's nightfall, but certainly not before." He checked her queen.

"By the rood!" Rhonwyn swore, surprised. She had not considered his clever move and felt a slight tingle of irritation as he removed her piece from the board.

He laughed. "Are you ready to concede this match, wife?"

Rhonwyn searched the chessboard for a way out, but finding none, she said, "I surmise I must. What forfeit will you have, my lord?"

"A kiss," he told her. "On the lips, wife."

Now it was Rhonwyn who laughed. "I did not expect you to kiss my hand, my lord," she told him and, standing, said, "Come, and receive your prize then."

Rising, he moved around the table and took her into his arms. His silver blue eyes searched her face, and to her chagrin, Rhonwyn blushed. His eyes asked her the one question that until now she was not ready to answer. She initiated the kiss, quickly pulling down his head to give him the answer he had been waiting for for the past five months, as their lips met tenderly in a sweet, but brief kiss.

"You are certain, wife?" His look challenged her.

Rhonwyn nodded. "There is only one way I may come to know you better, Rafe," she said softly. "We have waited long enough."

"Aye!" he agreed, and then he swept her up into his arms and carried her from the hall, up the narrow staircase, through the solar past a startled Enit, and into their bedchamber. He shut the door firmly behind them, and set her on her feet, taking both her hands in his. He turned them over and placed a hot kiss in the center of each palm. Not a word was spoken between them.

Retrieving her hands from his light grasp, she undid her girdle and lay it aside. Her eyes locked onto his as she drew her gown off and placed it with the cincture. Sitting upon the single chair in the chamber, she held out a leg to him. Kneeling, Rafe drew the soft house shoe from her foot, and slipped the garter holding her stocking up off her. Slowly, slowly he rolled the stocking down her slender leg, tossing it aside as his dark head bent to kiss first her slim foot, and then to run a succession of kisses up her leg, stopping at the soft flesh of her inner thigh.

"*Ummmmm,*" Rhonwyn murmured as a shiver ran down her back. "That is nice, husband." She offered him her other leg.

His fingers brushed the inside of her thigh teasingly, and then he repeated his previous actions with her second leg. This time, however, when he had finished his reverence he pushed her chemise up as far as it would go and parted her legs. He stared for a long moment at her plump, pink Venus mons. The shadowed slash between her nether lips beckoned him, and unable to contain himself, he ran a finger lightly down it, smiling as he felt her shiver. Opening her lips to his deeper view, he gazed upon the badge of her womanhood. It seemed to shimmer to his sight. "Jesu," he murmured low, "you are so beautiful there." Leaning forward, he kissed the moist flesh lightly.

"Oh, God!" Rhonwyn whispered, her voice ragged, and she shuddered at the touch of his tongue as it swept over her sensitive jewel.

Straightening, he closed her legs to his view. Taking her by the shoulders, he kissed her lips, his tongue plunging into the deep recess of her mouth to make contact with hers. She could taste her own salty muskiness as he teased at her. She almost swooned in his arms to her great surprise, for his desire was the most deeply sensual thing she had ever known. Hungrily she kissed him back, realizing very clearly how much she wanted to be loved by this man who was her husband. *Not simply made love to, but loved.*

Surprised by the intensity of her kiss, he released his grip on her shoulders and looked deeply into her eyes. "By the rood, wife!" he exclaimed, seeing the truth.

"If you gloat, Rafe, I swear I will slice your ears off!" she threatened him.

"I should be an odd sight then," he teased back gently, taking her hand in his and kissing the palm softly. "You are so damned proud, Rhonwyn uerch Llywelyn, and so I shall say it first. *I love you, wife.*"

"For how long?" she demanded, but her heart was hammering with the incredible joy overtaking her entire being. *He loved her!*

"From the first moment I saw you, and you were my cousin's wife and he did not really appreciate the magnificent creature he had in you. Edward didn't deserve you. I could plainly see that you were not the woman for him. *You were mine!*"

"Oh, Rafe," she said, her heart overflowing with her happiness.

"When they said you were dead I did what I had to do for my sister, but in the darkness of the night I cursed the fates that I had lost you. And then by some miracle you were restored to me, my darling! I can still remember all those pompous clerics sitting about with their pursed lips and disapproving looks, wondering who would have this fallen woman—this Magdalen who had lain in an infidel's arms and then had the temerity to return to England and admit it. I can still hear the angry sound my cousin made when I said that I should have you. It was a cross between a gasp and a curse, for while Edward knows Katherine is a better wife for him, he yet lusts after you."

"You delight in that knowledge," she accused him.

"Aye, I do," he freely admitted. "My cousin is a fool, but his witlessness has allowed me to have my heart's desire." His fingers began to unlace her chemise, pulling it down off her shoulders so that it finally puddled about her hips. He stared entranced at her breasts, shaking his head and murmuring, "So beautiful."

Rhonwyn took his face between her hands and looked into it. "I love you, Rafe," she told him. *"I love you!"* She kissed his mouth hard. "I said those words only once to Edward when he was ill, but never did I say them to Rashid al Ahmet. You hear this declaration from me because it is the truth. *I love you!"*

"I shall not be the fool that Edward was," he promised her.

"I know," she told him. "Now take your clothes off, Rafe, because I am hot to couple with you, my husband!" She pushed him from her and stood up from the chair, allowing the chemise to fall to her ankles. She stepped from the material and began undoing his sherte, her nimble fingers pulling the laces free as if by magic. She yanked the garment from him and then bent to cover his torso in kisses.

With a groan he pulled her up, drawing her against his bare chest with one hand while the other hand fumbled with his chausses. Both of them were breathing quickly in their eagerness. He cursed his awkwardness, and laughing softly, Rhonwyn aided him with sure hands until he was as naked as she. Stepping back, she viewed him as God had made him and smacked her lips in open approval.

He laughed aloud. "Shameless wench," he said, but his own eyes were sweeping over her admiringly.

Taking his hand, she led him to their bed and drew him down atop her. "Make love to me, husband," she said softly. "Have we both not waited long enough for this night?" Then Rhonwyn kissed him eagerly.

The warmth of her lips sent his senses reeling. He was already hard for her, but he had wanted more than a quick coupling the first time. Now he realized how desperate they both were for this first encounter. There would be more than enough time—years—for the tender passion that he believed should precede the event. Slowly, carefully, he entered her body, knowing how long it had been since she had last had a man. She was wet and hot, and she sighed deeply at his ingress. He groaned with the delight he felt at just possessing her. Leaning back slightly, he caressed her breasts.

Rhonwyn put her arms about his neck and drew him back down against her. "I am ashamed to be so eager," she confessed, "but, *please*!"

He smiled into her eyes, his lips gently kissing her face, and began to move upon her. Her eyes closed as she wrapped her slender limbs about him, her lithe body moving with his rhythm, encouraging him onward. His breath began to come in hot pants as his tempo quickened.

She half sobbed as she felt his great, thick length fill her. Neither of her previous lovers had been quite as well endowed as was Rafe. The beast throbbed within her love sheath, then it began to thrust and withdraw, thrust and withdraw, until she was mindless and wild with her passion. She clung hungrily to him, her nails digging into the muscles of his back and raking down the smooth flesh as her lust swelled. Finally they exploded in a starburst of satisfaction that they shared together before collapsing, replete with their shared pleasure.

"*Oh, husband,*" Rhonwyn breathed gustily.

"Wife, you should unman a satyr," he groaned happily.

"What is a satyr?" she demanded to know.

He laughed. "A creature that is half man, half goat, and incredibly lustful."

She smiled as she lay contented upon his smooth, damp chest. "Next time I shall make you feel like the randiest of satyrs," she promised.

"*Will you?*" he half taunted her.

"I will!" Rhonwyn raised her head and began to lick his nipples suggestively.

He closed his eyes for a long moment, very much enjoying her attentions, then he gently bid her cease. "While I should like you to believe I can be aroused almost immediately, wife, it is not possible, as we both realize."

"I bow to your husbandly wisdom," she said sweetly, arising from their bed and walking across the floor to the fireplace. There she took a pitcher of water from the coals and poured some into the small earthenware ewer that was set on the hearth along with a soft cloth. Returning to the bed, she set the ewer on the side table and began to bathe his masculine parts. He was very surprised, but she explained. "They do this in Cinnebar so that no pleasure has to be foregone the second, or third, or fourth time."

"Third or fourth time?" he queried her, swallowing hard.

"Aye," she replied, bathing her own female parts carefully before his eager eyes. "When this night is over, my lord husband, you will have even more reason to feel sorry for your cousin, Edward." And so saying she went to the window, opened the shutter, and threw out the water in the basin, laughing as the wind and snow blew into their chamber, and the fire blazed higher for a minute. Closing the shutter, she replaced the ewer and its cloth on the hearth and returned to the comfort of his arms.

"I know something Edward never knew about you," he told her. "You are a sorceress, my Welsh wife, and I am under your spell." Then he kissed her, softly at first, his lips tracing a path over her eyelids, cheeks, and nose. Then more fiercely their mouths fused together, their tongues playful and teasing. He was caught by surprise when she pushed him upon his back and bestrode him, her thighs holding him firmly.

Reaching up, she undid her hair, which was already half undone by their earlier love play. Tossing the pins carelessly aside, she let her tresses fall like a rich golden mantle about her. Then her hands reached out for him, and she began to smooth her palms in circles over his chest. "We must have scented oils in a basket by our bed," she told him. "I will rub them into your skin, husband, and it will give you great pleasure." Her center fingers began rubbing themselves over his sensitive nipples. Leaning forward briefly, she kissed him even as she pinched his nipples hard, catching his cry of surprise within her mouth. Then leaning back again, she nibbled thoughtfully upon a finger for a moment. Suddenly a wicked smile suffused her features, and Rhonwyn turned her body about upon his torso. Her fingers reached out for his manhood, which was showing definite signs of awakening.

"I learned this in the harem," she told him as she reached beneath him to press a finger against a sensitive spot that he had never even known existed.

"Jesu! Mary!" he groaned as fire began to pour through his veins and her hand tortured his twin jewels with teasing caresses.

Rhonwyn inclined her body forward, her fingers running up and down his stiffening manhood. Her pointed little tongue encircled the fiery head of his weapon several times, and then she took him into her mouth, suckling upon as much of his length as she could, rousing him into such a frenzy that he began to groan. When she determined that he had had as much as he could stand without spilling his seed, she ceased the sweet torment and turned her body back to face him.

His big hands fastened themselves about her narrow waist, and lifting her up, he lowered her again, delving deep into her hot softness. His hands fastened themselves about her round breasts, and he began to fondle them. Their eyes met suddenly, and she smiled at him, her hands bracing themselves as she began to ride him, slowly at first, and then with increasing vigor. His eyes closed, and he almost wept with the pleasure she was giving him.

Seeing him lost in his passion, Rhownyn's green eyes closed, too, and she gave herself to the moment. He was hard and strong. He filled her so completely that she sensed he was touching her womb. She tightened the muscles of her love sheath about him, and he cried out with his delight. Then without warning he released her breasts, took her by the shoulders, and rolled her beneath him. His hard thighs imprisoned her as he pushed himself deeper and deeper within her body. Her legs wrapped themselves about him, and she whimpered with the pleasure they were sharing. There seemed to be no real beginning or end to their heated encounter. She felt herself soaring higher and higher and higher; she knew he was with her and clung hard to him.

"I can't stop," he whispered desperately in her ear.

"I don't want you to," she responded. "Oh, Rafe! I have never known a lover like you, my darling!"

"Nor I," he answered. He wanted to go on and on forever with her, but then his body betrayed them, and his love juices gushed forth. He cried out in his anguish, but then the sound of her own pleasure reached his ears. She had released her own passion with his. His arms enfolded her tightly, half in comfort, half with his deep love for her.

They fell asleep, their bodies still locked together and intertwined. When they woke an hour or more later his manhood was hard once again as it rested within her lush body.

"You are amazing," she said softly, moving with him in the cadence of passionate lust.

"Only for you," he declared. *"Only for you, my wife."* His hard body pinioned her beneath him as he once again brought them to a sweet fulfillment, demanding to know afterward, "Was your caliph as passionate, wife?"

"Aye, and sometimes more so, but he did not really love me, Rafe. He only desired me. I was told passion is better shared by two people who love one another. Until now I did not know the wonder of it all. *Only with you, husband. Only with you!"*

From that moment on they were as one. During the snowiest winter in memory they spent a great deal of time making love to one another. There was, after all, little else to do until the spring. Rhonwyn realized she was happier than she had ever been in all of her life. Rafe found a peace unlike any he had ever known since he had found himself responsible for Ardley and his sister Katherine. It was so different with Rhonwyn, his beautiful wife with her exciting erotic erudition and her independent spirit.

She had taken up her weapons again, practicing with her two grizzled Welsh retainers, Oth and Dewi, in the snowy stableyards. He remembered Edward's complaints about such activities, but Rafe found his wife's skills fascinating. He didn't bother to ask where the alborium she used with such proficiency had come from, for he knew the answer would have really been no answer at all. He had absolutely no fear for her as she wielded her sword and a main gauche. She was to his eyes one hell of a fighter and certainly far better than he had ever been with weapons. Fortunately this knowledge did not disturb him at all. Edward, of course, had been less certain of himself, and Rhonwyn's nontraditional skills had been a great source of irritation to him despite his fondness for her. I am the better husband for Rhonwyn, Rafe thought.

The winter slowly disappeared, and there was a great deal of new life at Ardley. The ewe sheep had lambed well, and there were a goodly number of his cows who had calved. The offspring dotted the green hillsides. As the spring progressed the fields were plowed and the seed distributed for planting. Rhonwyn actually found herself busy with housewifely duties such as airing the feather-beds and picking violets to candy. They rode together and hunted rabbits. One day Glynn appeared in the brown robes of a Benedictine to tell them he had indeed joined the order at Shrewsbury Abbey, and while it would be a year or more before he took his final vows, he was happy.

"And your music, little brother? What of your music?" Rhonwyn asked him. "Are you allowed to sing and play?"

"Aye," he replied with a smile. "And the music I make now is to God's glory. It is the very best I have ever done!" Reaching out, he took his sister's hand in his. "You are happy, Rhonwyn. Really happy, and I am glad to see it."

"I love him," she said simply.

"He loves you," Glynn responded, "and that is another cause for my happiness. Now, I expect nephews and nieces in good order, sister."

She laughed. "If you do not get them it shall not be from want of trying on our part." Then she grew more serious. "You have not just come for the reasons you gave, brother. What is the truth?"

"Our kith and kin in Wales are causing difficulties once again, sister. We hear things more often in the abbey than outsiders would. Tad, it is said, attempts to wriggle out of his oaths to King Edward. Tad's enemies seek to unseat him, but this time they may have English aid in their endeavors. There are many who seek the king's favor and will do whatever they must to gain it. You are Llywelyn ap Gruffydd's daughter, and therefore you are vulnerable. Once the king has solidified his position he will turn an eye to Wales and the problems our father is causing. If I am recalled, I will be considered little threat in my abbey, but you, sister, may find yourself a pawn in this matter."

"How so, Glynn?" Rafe de Beaulieu asked his brother-in-law.

"It is not the English you need fear," Glynn answered. "Rhonwyn is your wife, and they will expect you to keep her in order." He smiled at them both, and there was a twinkle in his eye. "Not knowing my sister, of course. It is our Welsh brethren who could prove dangerous. Pray God you have no children right now. Tad's enemies will do whatever they must to harm him. Be vigilant."

Rafe nodded. "What of Oth and Dewi?" he asked Glynn.

"They are loyal to my sister and therefore to you as well."

"Even against their Welsh brothers?" Rafe said.

"We are their family first," Glynn responded. "They would not betray us to Tad's enemies."

"We will be watchful," Rafe assured Glynn, "and I thank you for your warning."

"When will I see you again?" Rhonwyn asked her brother.

"When you come to Shrewsbury, sister," he told her. "The abbot allowed me to come to Ardley only because he knows the truth of my identity and understood the seriousness of the situation."

"Now you see what marrying ap Gruffydd's daughter has gained you," Rhonwyn teased her husband later that night as they lay abed.

He took up a lock of her golden hair and kissed it. "Aye," he drawled softly. "You are a dangerous woman, wife."

"Our connection makes your position potentially hazardous, Rafe," she said seriously. "The Welsh are fierce fighters, and you know what is said of them. That they pray on their knees and their neighbors. I would not want to see Ardley destroyed because of me or my father."

"You worry too much," he told her, and let his fingers caress the nape of her neck. "Do not fret, dearling. I will protect you."

"Hah! I may very well have to protect you," she laughed, and he chuckled at her sly observation, not in the least offended.

"If it comes to that, I will welcome your fighting skills, wife, but for now it is your *other* skills I prefer." His hand tightened on her neck, and tilting her head back, he kissed her hungrily. His mouth was hard. His lips scorched her lips, wet and hot and eager.

"Devil," she murmured when he finally took his mouth from hers. She twisted her body subtly, rubbing against him teasingly.

"Witch!" he returned, attempting to hold her still. But she was quicker than he was and squirmed from his grip, turning her body and steadying herself as she straddled his torso, her tempting little bottom facing him, revealing her sex to him with its little jewel that peeped from beneath the coral flesh. He groaned with pleasure as she leaned forward and took his manhood into her mouth. Bending, he offered her the same service, his tongue finding her sensitivity and working her fiercely until she cried out, releasing his aching member that now longed to bury itself within her.

"Oh, Rafe!" she sighed as she rolled herself onto her back and held out her arms to him.

Sliding between her legs, he entered her hot wet love channel, filling her completely, and then he lay still for a moment atop her. Her breasts were soft beneath his chest. Her torso was silken. He could feel her fingers tangling in his dark hair, kneading at his scalp with her anticipation. Raising himself slightly on one hand, he pushed a finger into her mouth, and she sucked at it so hard he thought she would swallow it. He withdrew slightly, and then thrust hard into her again, and she whimpered with her desire. How often in the months since she had given herself to him had she controlled their passion with her wonderful and varied sexual games? Tonight, however, he wanted to be in charge. Pushing himself up, he sat upon her thighs, his throbbing member deep within her body.

"*Please!*" she whispered.

"I am not ready," he said softly, his hands reaching out to fondle her sweet round breasts.

"You are as hard as rock within me!" she half sobbed.

"Aye, and I would remain that way for now. Was your master, the caliph, always in such a hurry, wife?" He moved subtly on her. "Old men are frequently in haste lest they lose their ardor." He gently squeezed the soft twin mounds.

"He . . . c-complained as do y-you. Oh, God, I want it!" she cried desperately.

He reached out and took her little jewel between his thumb and his forefinger, pinching the sensitive flesh until she was half mad with the pleasure he was arousing within her. "There, wife, you see what delights can be attained when you are not so damnably eager?" He covered her body again with his and began to piston her in earnest, his torso meeting hers with a fierce force until they were both mindless with their shared lust and moaning with their fulfillment. When his love juices had filled her, however, he remained within her body. His lips met hers with gentle passion, and they kissed and kissed until he was once again hard with his desire for her.

She had always held a little bit of herself back, but this night Rhonwyn could not restrain her own passions and yielded every bit of her love to him without question. She felt both weak and strong at the same time. He overwhelmed her with his hunger for her, and yet she felt freer than she had ever felt in all of her life, and she was not afraid. Wrapping her legs about him, she encouraged his ardor until they were both weak again and replete with pleasure. Then she wept in his arms with her happiness, and Rafe de Beaulieu understood what it was that Rhonwyn had finally given him.

His arms tightened about her, and his big hand smoothed the tangle of her golden hair as he made unintelligible soothing noises to comfort her. Finally he whispered to her, "Wife, do you not know how much I love you? I have told you often enough."

"There has never been a love as sweet as ours!" she sobbed. "I wish I had been a virgin for you, my darling! Oh, I do!"

Rafe laughed. "Thank God you were not, Rhonwyn mine. I far prefer your skills and expertise in the arts of love to artless innocence."

"*Truly?*" She looked into his face anxiously, and her lashes were spikey wet clumps.

"Truly!" He nodded. "Edward, I suspect, did little for you, but your caliph was obviously a man of sophistication. He overcame your fears and taught you well how to please a husband. I am grateful to him, my love, but I am also very jealous. Should you ever turn a lustful eye on any man but me, I will kill you with my bare hands!"

"Truly?" she teased, her look wide-eyed and ingenuous.

He swiftly turned her over and spanked her bottom a loving smack. "Truly, you provocative witch!" he told her as she squealed with her surprise. Then he gave her another spank for emphasis.

Rhonwyn rolled over. "Oh, I think I like that," she said wickedly. "Would you like to spank me again, husband? I can be very naughty, you know."

He laughed and gave her a quick kiss. "Woman, you are quite wicked enough as it is. Now, let us get some rest. If I am to be alert to your wild Welsh kin, then I must sleep." He yanked the coverlet over them, wrapping his arms about her and falling asleep almost immediately.

Rhonwyn snuggled against him, breathing in the male scent of him. A small smile touched her lips. I wonder, she thought, if it is right to be so damned happy? Then she closed her eyes and slept.

The summer came, and with it a messenger from Haven Castle telling them that the lady Katherine had been safely delivered of a second son. Rafe and Rhonwyn were asked to come to Haven to stand as Henry de Beaulieu's godparents.

"Bless your sister," Rhonwyn chuckled. "She will have peace within the de Beaulieu family in spite of Edward. For all his bluster she rules him with a firm hand. I wonder that we were chosen wee Henry's godparents. It was certainly not Edward's choice."

"But we will go and please Kate," Rafe said, "and you and Edward will not snipe at one another."

"Do not be jealous, husband," she replied, stroking his cheek with her hand. "How could I feel anything for

Edward when I am so madly in love with you?" Then standing on tiptoes, she gave him a quick kiss.

"Do not think to cajole me so easily, wife," he said. "I am wise to your clever ways, Rhonwyn." He shook a warning finger at her.

"And you love them all as you do me," she taunted him. "Do you not, Rafe?" She gave him another quick kiss.

He laughed. "You are impossible, wife," he told her.

"Would you have me any other way, husband?"

"Nay, I would not," he admitted.

Haven Castle was a two days' ride from Ardley. How odd it was to be returning there, Rhonwyn thought as they approached it. She remembered the first time she had seen Haven as she came with her father to marry Edward de Beaulieu. How impressed she had been by the beauty of the castle. How frightened, and yet how hopeful her innocent heart had been when she met Edward. She had never been like other girls by the very nature of her upbringing. When he had demanded his marital rights, and she had bargained with him to gain custody of Glynn, Edward had been angry. She suspected he had never forgiven her.

How shocked he had been by her skill with weapons. Why could he not, like Rafe, have appreciated her expertise with the alborium and the sword? Perhaps that was why he had been so ready to declare her dead when she had been captured by the infidels. Rhonwyn smiled wryly to herself. Poor Edward. Kate was the better wife for him, and Rhonwyn was certainly the best wife for Rafe. This would be the second time since her marriage to Rafe that they had come together as a family. It had not been a successful meeting last Martinmas.

Kate greeted them joyously, coming slowly across the hall to meet them. "You have come! Mab, bring the baby so his godparents may view him. Come and sit with me, brother, Rhonwyn. Where is the wine for our guests?"

"You are pale," her brother said, a note of concern in his voice. He took her little hand in his and kissed it.

The baby was brought, and he looked exactly as his older brother had looked the previous year.

"He is your spit," Rhonwyn remarked cheerfully to the castle's lord.

"Aye!" Edward replied proudly. "Two fine sons in two years, and more to come, I promise you."

"Perhaps you will wait a bit before you make another," Rhonwyn said quietly. "Kate looks tired and should have a rest."

"Are you jealous then, lady, that I can get sons on Katherine so easily when I could not get them on you?" he said belligerently.

Rhonwyn swallowed hard. "I think of Kate, and so should you, Edward. It is not easy, I am told, to conceive and bear new life. If you love your wife, you will give her time to recover from this birth. Two sons in two years is hard on a woman. If, on the other hand, your pride in your randy cock and Kate's fertile womb are greater than your love for her, you will kill your wife sooner than later. But then you would take another wife as quickly as you could find one, would you not? That, it would seem, is your custom." She smiled sweetly.

Rafe held back his laughter, instead saying, "*Rhonwyn,*" in a warning tone. Secretly he agreed with his fiery wife.

"Outspoken as ever," Edward said meanly. "Rafe should beat you."

"He finds loving me works better," Rhonwyn snapped.

"What? You actually allow him between your legs, lady?"

"As often as he desires me, and that is quite often," she snarled.

"*Enough!*" Rafe said in a harsh voice.

"Oh, yes, please," Kate said. "Let there be peace between you two. We are a family and must be united."

"I apologize, Kate," Rhonwyn said softly. "I shall try and behave for your sake. When is the baptism?"

"Tomorrow," her sister-in-law said.

"Then we shall be able to return to Ardley afterward."

"Oh, will you not remain longer?" Kate pleaded.

"We cannot," Rafe spoke up quickly. "Rhonwyn is in the midst of making soap and conserves, and I must supervise the building of a new granary we must have before the harvest next month."

"Do you not have a bailiff to do such work?" Edward asked.

"Why should I hire a bailiff to do what I am capable of?" Rafe replied. "I am not the master of a castle, Edward. I have but a small manor."

"Greatly enriched by additional lands since your marriage," his cousin said sourly.

"Which reminds me," Rafe continued, "you have not yet repaid Rhonwyn's dower, and we will be wed a year next month."

"You will have to wait until I sell some cattle," Edward replied.

"I will take the cattle in exchange for the coin," Rafe said. "This is not a debt you want outstanding, Edward."

"What an excellent solution," Katherine de Beaulieu quickly spoke up. "Is it not, my lord? Now you may avoid all that fuss of driving the cattle to market and the haggling that goes with it."

"Indeed, my love, you are correct," Edward said with a smile at his pretty wife.

Kate smiled back, secretly relieved to have avoided any further argument. She was very tired and had not the strength to mediate between her husband, her brother, and Rhonwyn, who was so damned prickly, although she was trying not to be. Kate had had to give her elder son to a wet nurse as she could not nurse both children; but even so the new child had a healthy appetite that exhausted her. He persisted in nursing every two hours.

Henry John de Beaulieu was baptized the following day at midmorning. Afterward his family drank a toast to him in the great hall of Haven Castle. The baby had howled loudly as Father John had poured the holy water upon his fuzzy head, and everyone in the church had smiled. The infant's cries were an assurance that the devil was leaving him. Rhonwyn held her godson, and when he turned and nuzzled at her breast, she felt an odd sensation surge through her body. She continued to cradle Henry in the hall until finally his nurse took him away, but not before she had kissed his little downy head. Then and there she realized with surprise that she wanted a child of her own.

"So," Rafe said, coming to stand by her side, "I see in your eyes that you have decided to stop drinking that brew of yours each morning."

"*You knew?*" She was amazed, and quick tears filled her eyes. He had known she was preventing conception, yet he had not forbid her, even though it went against him and the church.

"You have been forced your whole life. Why would I make you have a child until you were ready? I know I am capable of making babies, for I have two bastards at Ardley. Besides, I am a selfish man, wife, and have been enjoying our shared passion. If you now want a babe, then we shall work very hard at making one." He kissed her forehead and brushed away the tears that slipped down her cheek.

"I do love you," she said softly to him.

"I know," he replied.

"Devil!" She smiled at him.

"Witch!" he rejoined.

Seeing them, a shadow crossed Edward de Beaulieu's handsome features. Why had Rhonwyn not loved him the way she obviously loved his cousin Rafe? He would never understand it, but he had at least been fortunate in his Katherine. He had no doubts regarding his sweet wife, and he knew he never would. Still, he could not help but envy the fire that so obviously burned hotly between Rhonwyn and Rafe. Why had not such a fire burned between him and Rhonwyn?

Over Katherine's gentle protests her brother and his wife departed for their own home, but not before Rafe had taken Edward aside.

"Rhonwyn is right," he told his cousin. "Kate is fragile, and she is now well worn with giving you two sons in so short a time. If you cannot contain your lust, find a willing serf upon which to slake your desires. You do not want to kill my sister with your loving, cousin."

"I know you are right, though it galls me to be chided by you," Edward replied. "Still, I do love Katherine, and I would not harm her. I will do as you advise . . . if I cannot contain my lust."

Rafe grinned. "Good," he said. "Then I shall not have to kill you, cousin."

Edward laughed, and the tension was broken between them. "Tell me," he said, "do you truly love Rhonwyn?"

"Aye," Rafe said, not in the least offended.

"And she loves you?"

"Aye," his cousin drawled. "Do not fret yourself wondering about all that has happened between us, Edward. Kate is the perfect wife for you, and Rhonwyn is the perfect wife for me. What came before doesn't matter. Let us both be content with what we have, and thank God."

Chapter Seventeen

They had been wed a year, and they celebrated the occasion on Lammastide as the early harvest began. It had been a good year, and the manor prospered as it never before had.

"You are good luck for Ardley," Rafe told his wife.

"The weather has been particularly favorable this summer," the more practical Rhonwyn said with a smile.

The grain was reaped and stored in the new stone granary. The apples and the pears were gathered. Cider was made from some of the fruit. The rest was stored in a cool stone cellar. Like the good chatelaine she was, Rhonwyn sat with the female serfs on the late summer days picking straw and other bits of dirt from the wool that had been sheared from the sheep earlier in the summer. It would have to be washed before it was carded, and then spun into cloth. It was a time-consuming labor, but it allowed her to get to know the women on the manor, and it permitted them to know her. It was soon decided that the master's wife was not just a pretty face, but a hard worker with no fancy pretentions. This decision having been made, the women were Rhonwyn's own from that moment on. No matter she played with weapons or was Welsh, she was a good lady.

The world about them seemed peaceful enough. They

had had no visitors since Glynn had come earlier in summer to warn them of ap Gruffydd's disobedience and
that his enemies were plotting with the English against
him. King Henry had died the previous November, and
King Edward, trusting in his mother's ability to maintain
order in England, was slowly wending his way back there.
He was not expected to return before next year, but when
he came, he would exert his authority over Prince Llywelyn and the Welsh, Rhonwyn knew. But perhaps, she
thought, her father just pressed the English while the
king was out of the country. Surely ap Gruffydd was wise
enough to know that when Edward returned, he must
give sway to the man to whom he had pledged his fealty.
It was his duty and the honorable thing to do. Duty and
honor were something that Rhonwyn knew her father
understood.

September passed, and then October. Rhonwyn loved
the autumn. It had always been her favorite time of year.
Now she and Rafe spent the daylight hours each day out
hunting with their men as they prepared for the long
winter to come. The deer were wonderfully fat that year,
and soon the winter's supply of meat was more than ample. Although Rafe would see his people were fed during
the cold months, he still allowed them to glean in the
fields, hunt for rabbits twice a month in his woods, and
fish in his streams one day a week. He was a generous
master, and his people were loyal to him because of it.

It was Enit who noticed that her mistress's link with
the moon had not been broken now in seven weeks. She
had also noticed that Rhonwyn's appetite was peckish.
"Lady," she said one morning as the two women were in
the garderobe going over Rhonwyn's gowns to see what
needed mending, "I think you may be with child. You
have had no show of blood in many weeks now, and your

food does not seem to agree with you. These are all signs of a breeding woman; I know this from my mother."

"Is it possible?" Rhonwyn wondered aloud.

"There is a midwife on the manor, lady. She is Maybel, the miller's wife. Perhaps you should go and see her."

"We'll go today, and you will come with me," Rhonwyn said. "If I am seen going alone, there will be gossip."

"There will be gossip anyway," Enit replied dryly, "but no matter. If you are with child, all will be joyous for you and the master."

They went to visit the miller's wife. She took one look at her mistress and nodded, saying, "Aye, you are with child, lady. God be praised!" Then she beamed a sweet smile at them.

"How can you tell by just looking at me?" Rhonwyn demanded. Surely there was more to it than that.

"Why, I can see it in your eyes, my lady," the miller's wife said. "And in your face. It glows with an inner radiance that only a breeding woman has. Still, I will listen to your symptoms."

"She ain't had a show of blood in seven and a half weeks now, and her food don't agree, even her favorite blankmanger," Enit said before her mistress might even open her mouth.

"Breasts tender?" Maybel asked bluntly.

Rhonwyn nodded.

"Belly feels swollen, but don't look it?"

"Oh, yes!" Rhonwyn said.

"Last show of blood?"

"Last week in August," Enit spoke up again.

"The child will be born in the beginning of June," Maybel pronounced, "and I will be here to deliver it for you, my lady. You need have no fears, for you are a healthy lass, but no galloping about the countryside from now on. A nice gentle walk or the cart for you, my lady, *and* no more battling with your sword with those two Welshmen of yours until after the birth. What if you had an accident, my lady?"

"I am too skilled for accidents," Rhonwyn said proudly.

"I shall tell the master," Maybel replied calmly.

"Oh, very well," Rhonwyn muttered irritably.

Both Maybel and Enit hid a smile.

"Not a word of this until I have told Rafe," Rhonwyn told them both. "I don't want it all over the manor until he knows. He will want time to crow and swagger," she chuckled, and her two companions laughed heartily, for they fully understood that their lord would behave as if he were the first man to father a child on his wife.

Wrapping her cloak about her, Rhonwyn left Enit and Maybel and walked out across the meadow. The sun was shining today, but the air was cool, the trees bereft of their leaves. *A baby.* Within her a new life was growing at this very moment as she walked. Was it a son she carried or a daughter? *A baby.* They were going to have a baby, and it had happened so quickly. She had ceased taking her secret brew only a few months ago. *A baby!* A new life to nurture. But what did she know about being a mother? And would what happened to her mother happen to her? Would she die in childbirth? Nay! She shook the frightening thought off. Vala had birthed both her daughter and her son easily. It had only been with that last child she had suffered, but then she had been so frightened that it was the child of her rape and not ap Gruffydd's. And in retrospect, Rhonwyn was never certain that her mother hadn't, in a moment of pure madness, tried to force that last child from her womb before its time and in doing so, caused her own demise.

I will pray, she thought. And I will ask my aunt to pray along with her entire abbey. Their prayers will surely keep me safe. *A baby.* Rafe and I are having a baby!

Rafe! She had to find her husband and tell him this marvelous news before he heard it elsewhere, for Rhonwyn had no doubt that the entire manor would know before long. Turning, she ran back across the meadow, the sheep scattering before her, her cloak flying in the breeze. "Rafe! Rafe! *Rafe!*"

He heard his name being called. Called with great urgency. It was Rhonwyn's voice! My God! Was it the Welsh? He dashed from the stables where he had been discussing several matters with the leathersmith and saw her racing toward him. He caught her in his arms, looking anxiously into her face. "What is it, Rhonwyn?"

"I am with child!" she cried, and then burst into tears.

His arms tightened about her. A huge, delighted grin split his handsome face. "*A baby?* We are having a baby, wife?"

She nodded, sniffling happily. "Aye, husband, we are."

"Since I took you for my wife," he said, "I did not think I could be any happier, but you have proved me wrong, Rhonwyn. My heart is so full that it is in danger of bursting with the joy your news has given me. How I love you, Rhonwyn, my wife. *How I love you!*" He kissed her hard upon the lips, and then kissed away the tears on her cheeks.

"But what if it is a girl and not a son?" she fretted.

"We shall call her Anghard, and she will look just like her beautiful mother," he replied gallantly. "I don't care if it's a girl, wife. My two bastards are daughters. When they are grown, they shall serve their half sister, eh?"

"You would give a daughter a Welsh name?" She was surprised.

"Her mother is a Welsh princess," he replied.

"Her mother was raised up in a fortress of men and treated no differently than any young lad. Princess indeed!" Rhonwyn laughed. Her palms rested flat against his chest. "I am nought but a simple lass," she told him teasingly.

He smiled down at her, his silver blue eyes warm with his love. "Nay, dearling, you are no simple lass, and well you know it, but I love you nonetheless. Now, when is this child of ours due?"

"Maybel says the beginning of June," Rhonwyn told him.

"No more swordplay with Oth and Dewi, wife," he said sternly.

"Yes, my lord," she replied.

"And no more hunting until after the child is born," he continued.

"Yes, my lord."

"I'm glad to see that being with child has at last rendered you a sensible woman," he mocked her, then ducked as she pulled away from him and hit his shoulder with her fist.

"I have always been sensible," she said indignantly.

Rafe de Beaulieu laughed heartily and happily, taking the little hand that assaulted him and kissing it. He was going to have a legitimate heir at last! "You, Rhonwyn my wife, are wonderful!" he told her with another smile, and then picked her up and carried her to the house while she laughed.

He had never lived with a breeding woman, and the experience was certainly unique, to say the least. Rhonwyn at first raced between great euphoria, when everything was simply perfect, and deep sorrow, when she would, for no visible reason, weep great sobs and tears. The tiniest thing could set her off, and it was usually when they made love, for Maybel had explained how they might without injuring the child. But most times she would shed tears as he entered her ripening body—tears of happiness, she always assured him, but it was extremely unnerving.

Finally in January she became peaceful and serene. Her breasts and her belly swelled with the evidence of the new life she was carrying and would nurture come the summer. She loved to have him stroke her expanding belly with his hands, for it seemed to soothe her greatly. He rubbed her back and elicited purrs of contentment. Her breasts, however, were so sensitive that she could not bear to have them touched for too long a time. It frustrated him, for he loved those sweet orbs, but he respected her wishes. A breeding woman must be catered to, his sister assured him, and to his surprise, his brother-in-law agreed.

There had been no deep snow at Candlemas, and so Kate and Edward had come for a visit. Almost at once the two women seated themselves by the fire, talking and laughing together.

Edward smiled a superior smile. "They get like that when they are with child," he said. "Congratulations. I did not think you would get a child on her, Rafe."

"She is not the woman you were wed to, cousin," Rafe replied. "Her caliph taught her to revel in and appreciate passion."

"How can you bear that another man knew her?" Edward demanded in a tight voice.

"It is as if she were a widow," Rafe responded. "Why are you so angry with her, Edward? She was faithful to you, and she is faithful to me. What more can a man want?"

"She was not faithful to me," Edward de Beaulieu said angrily. "She lay with this infidel and was shameless in admitting it."

"She was a captive, Edward. Would you have had her die rather than yield herself to this other man? You gave her up without even knowing if she were really dead. Within two months of her disappearance you wrote and asked to have Kate for your wife. At least Rhonwyn was faithful in her heart to you, Edward. You were certainly not faithful in your heart to her. You hurried home, wed my sister, and got her with child as quickly as you could. Rhonwyn plotted to avoid giving the caliph a child and planned her escape so she might return to you. Do not be angry because you lost the opportunity to know what she is really like. I shall tell you, cousin. She is warm and passionate and loving to me . . . *as my sister is to you.*"

The spring finally came, and with it Rhonwyn's moods turned again. This time she was waspish and shrewish as her body swelled, and it became difficult to both sit and walk.

"I am no better than an old sow," she grumbled.

"You are beautiful," he assured her.

"A beautiful fat sow about to litter," she groused.

"It will be all right, wife," he tried to soothe her.

She glared at him pityingly. "What on earth can a man know about having a baby inside of him, squirming and kicking? I can barely stand. I want to pee constantly. My navel has turned itself inside out, and you think it's going to be all right, Rafe? That is the stupidest thing I have ever heard any man say!"

He didn't know whether to laugh or scold her. Either one, he realized, would meet with the sharp edge of her tongue. He wisely remained silent.

And then on the first of June Rhonwyn went into labor, Maybel and Enit by her side. "If you ever do this to me again," his wife shrieked at him, "I will kill you! Ah-hhh! Ohhhh! God, I hate you!"

Rafe de Beaulieu fled the solar and wisely retreated outside, away from what was very obviously woman's work. From the open windows he could hear Rhonwyn cursing with her efforts. Finally as the sun was near to setting, and the day was prepared to melt into a long summer's twilight, Rafe de Beaulieu heard the cry of a child. The sound was strong and angry. He raced into the house and up the staircase, bursting into the solar to find Rhonwyn smiling and cradling an infant.

"You have a son, my lord," she told him cheerfully. She held out the baby, still bloody with the birth, and his father took him into his hands. "Welcome, Justin de Beaulieu," Rafe said softly, and then looking at Rhonwyn, he said, "Thank you, wife."

"Give him to Enit," she commanded, a maternal tone in her voice. "Why Justin?"

"Today 'tis Saint Justin's feast day, wife," he told her.

"I like it," Rhonwyn told him. " 'Tis a strong name, and he will not be like every Edward or Henry or John. I suppose we shall have to name the others with those names."

"You said you didn't want any others," he said, surprised.

"What? When did I ever say such a thing?" Rhonwyn said indignantly. "Of course we are going to have more children, Rafe. We must have at least two more sons, and a daughter or two for me. I promised a daughter to my aunt. The other must make a fine marriage. What foolishness! Who ever heard of just one child?" She laughed.

"Just take her at her word, my lord," Maybel murmured softly. "Women are strange in the last weeks of childbirth, but all is well once they have given birth to their babe."

Katherine and Edward were called from Haven to stand as Justin's godparents. Father John came with them. Kate cooed over the baby and said he was quite the handsomest little fellow she had ever seen, excluding her own two boys.

"Have you sent word to your father?" she asked Rhonwyn.

"Aye," Rhonwyn said shortly.

"And Brother Glynn?"

Rhonwyn smiled broadly. "I know he is excited for us, Kate. I only wish he might have been here, but he is not allowed to travel until next year, even to see us. When the next child comes he shall be its godparent. Perhaps we shall go to Shrewsbury before next winter and visit him at the abbey. I know that will be permitted."

"They say King Edward has come home. Soon we will have a coronation, although Edward and I shall not be invited. Only the great lords and those attempting to curry favor will go."

"Let them," Rhonwyn said. "I prefer my simple life here at Ardley, as you prefer your life at Haven. We are through with the powerful. At least until it comes time to marry off our children."

"I was hoping you would have a daughter for our little Ned," Kate said. "But he is only two, and there is plenty of time for you to have a little girl."

"I would like a daughter," Rhonwyn admitted.

"I am so glad you finally had a child," Kate told her sister-in-law. "I was so afraid that you were barren. Edward said you probably were because of your boyish activities. And you will be wed two years this Lammastide."

"I prayed to Saint Anne," Rhonwyn said piously, silently furious that her former husband, that betrayer, should have spoken of her so. If he weren't married to Rafe's sister, she thought, I would slice his ears off for that insult. Barren indeed!

In early September they took Justin to meet his uncle in Shrewsbury. Glynn was delighted by their visit, and the abbot freed him from his duties to spend time with his sister and her family. Justin was a fat and good-natured infant with his father's gray blue eyes and a fuzz of gold upon his mostly bald pate. He cooed, smiled, and

drooled for his uncle, who was mightily impressed and
said so as Justin grabbed Glynn's finger and attempted to
put it in his mouth—except he could not quite find his
mouth to match the finger with it.

They returned to Ardley, prepared to finish the harvest
and ready the manor for the coming winter. In Shrewsbury they had learned that the king had been crowned at
Westminster on August nineteenth. They planned to
share their gossip with Edward and Kate and were surprised to find Edward awaiting them.

"Where the hell have you been?" the lord of Haven
demanded of his cousin, ignoring Rhonwyn completely.
"I have been here for several hours. Your servants said
you were due back today, but they did not know when
you would come."

"We have been in Shrewsbury to see Glynn and show
him his nephew," Rafe replied. "What is the matter with
you, Edward?"

"Katherine has been kidnapped!"

"*What?*" Both Rafe and Rhonwyn spoke at once.

"My wife has been kidnapped!" He turned his gaze
upon Rhonwyn. "And it is all *your* fault, damn you!"

"*My fault?*" Rhonwyn was astounded. "Why should
it be my fault, Edward? I bear you and Kate no ill will."

"The Welsh have taken her," he half shouted. "They
thought she was you!"

"*Me?* Why would the Welsh want to kidnap me?"

"Not you. *Ap Gruffydd's daughter!*" he roared.

"Jesu!" Rafe exploded.

"Of course!" Rhonwyn exclaimed.

"*What is it?*" both men asked her at once.

"It could be any of several reasons," Rhonwyn explained. "It is possible someone wishes to curry favor
with King Edward and thinks to hold me hostage in exchange for my father's good behavior. Or it could be that

someone simply wants to topple Prince Llywelyn and means to do it by threatening him with his daughter's life. I would not expect my father to bargain for my life, and he knows that I comprehend him well enough to understand that. Had I been kidnapped, I should have attempted escape, but failing that I would fling myself from a battlement before I would allow my father's fate to be directed by such a dishonorable act. Either way they have the wrong woman, and we must find out where poor Kate is and mount a rescue."

"What a pity you did not think this same way when you were captured by the infidels," Edward said bitterly. Then he staggered back as Rhonwyn slapped him as hard as she might.

"How dare you preach to me, you pompous bastard!" she shouted. "This is an entirely different situation that Kate finds herself in than the one in which I found myself. I stayed alive to come home to you, Edward, but you did not care enough for me to wait. This, however, is not about you or about me. It is Kate we have to think of now."

"Agreed," Rafe said quietly, putting an arm about his wife. "Swallow your bruised pride, Edward, and finally accept that by acting in haste you lost Rhonwyn, but a merciful God allowed you to gain a good wife in my sister. Put her first, and let us decide how we are to proceed."

"Wine!" Rhonwyn called to her servants, and then she led them to the fireplace and motioned the two men to sit down even as she took the tapestried chair. "We must find out who has taken Kate and where they are. To this end I will send a messenger to my father telling him what has happened to her so he may be on his guard against any other betrayal. Where was Kate when she was taken, Edward, and where were you when it happened?"

"Word had come from my village of Ainslea that fever

had broken out among the children. Katherine, good chatelaine she is, packed up her medicines and herbs and rode off with her serving woman to minister to the sick. When she did not return by late the next day nor had sent any message, I went with a half dozen men-at-arms to learn why. I found the village burnt and looted. The women and children had been taken off as slaves and the men slain, but for one elderly man they left alive to tell me of what had happened. He said they told him to tell the lord of Haven Castle that the Welsh had stolen his wife, and that they wanted no ransom. They merely wanted possession of ap Gruffydd's daughter for a bit. She would be returned alive eventually if I made no effort to follow them."

Edward swallowed down the entire contents of his goblet, then flung the cup aside, his head in his hands. "Jesu! Jesu! What am I to do? My sweet Kate is not used to a rough life as you are, Rhonwyn. She will die for certain. I should have been able to protect her!"

"Kate is strong," Rafe said. "They believe she is ap Gruffydd's daughter, and so she will be safe, for they only want her person for leverage against the prince for one reason or another."

"But what if they learn she is not ap Gruffydd's daughter?"

"They are unlikely to," Rhonwyn said. "None but the men at Cythraul and the nuns at my aunt's abbey knew who I was nor what I looked like. Few of you English do either. Daughters of great men, particularly bastard daughters, are of no importance but for the marriages they make. These men who stole Kate away did not know that our marriage had been dissolved, Edward, and that you had remarried another. They thought Kate was me, and Kate is clever enough to keep them believing it. In this part of the world the English, if they cannot speak our tongue, at least undersand enough of it to get by." She looked to her husband. "Did Kate?"

"Aye. Actually she used to converse fairly well in your tongue-twisting language, wife," Rafe said with a small smile. "We had a Welsh nurse as children."

"Then having understood them from the first, Kate will continue to make them believe she is ap Gruffydd's daughter and be safe," Rhonwyn said. "Now we must learn just who has stolen her, and for that I will go into Wales and meet with my father. The messenger who finds him will tell him to come to Cythraul. It is the obvious place."

"Why should you go?" Edward demanded angrily. "I should go."

"Hah," Rhonwyn said mockingly. "Do you think my father will speak with you, Edward de Beaulieu, or give you his full cooperation? *After what you did to me?* Llywelyn ap Gruffydd is just as apt to kill you as speak with you. You mean nought to him. You have no blood tie with him. Go home and find a wet nurse for my godson, who will die without his mother if you do not. Rafe and I will go into Wales and retrieve Kate for you. There is no shame in your remaining with your sons, my lord."

"What of your son?"

"My milk was not rich enough for Justin, and he already has a wet nurse," Rhonwyn said sadly. "Go home, Edward, and wait for us to send word." She patted his hand in a kindly fashion, for the first time realizing that her bitterness toward him was now entirely gone. Then she said, "And, Edward, *please, I beg of you,* do not attempt to follow us or join us at Cythraul. It is likely that Kate's captors know you by sight. They will not know who Rafe and I are, however. *Trust us.*"

"I always trusted you, Rhonwyn," he said quietly.

She shook her head. "Nay, you did not, but that is

water beneath the bridge long past, Edward. My anger is gone, and I only wish to bring Kate home safely to you. Go now and watch over your sons. Kate would want that."

He nodded and then took up her gloved hand, kissing it. "Thank you," he said.

She nodded. "Not yet, my friend."

When Edward de Beaulieu had gone and they sat at their high board eating venison stew, Rafe said, "We'll need a good night's sleep if we are to start off tomorrow." He tore a chunk of bread from the cottage loaf and sopped up some of the stew's winey gravy before popping it into his mouth.

"Nay, we'll go the day after tomorrow," Rhonwyn answered him. "I want to send Oth off in the morning to find my father. He'll need a day's start. Then you, Dewi, and I will go to Cythraul."

"Just the three of us?" He was surprised.

"I have a fortress of men-at-arms who are loyal to my father. We will only attract attention if we ride out to Wales with a large party, Rafe. This is a battle that will be won with subtlety, not blunt force."

"I did not think your father was a man of subtlety," he said.

"He can be when necessary. You have never met ap Gruffydd. Do not prejudge him by the gossip you have heard. He is a great man for all our differences. He has welded together a country of petty princelings and lords, and held firm. Aye, he has enemies. Do not all powerful men, husband? Will you tell me that our own King Edward has no enemies among his subjects? That there are not those eager to do him a mischief, given the opportunity?"

"How did a little lass raised in a hill fort learn so much about the powerful?" he asked her.

"Men claim that women gossip, but they talk more. I

listened," she replied with a smile. "No one paid attention to a small child by the fireside, Rafe. They chattered and bragged and boasted, and I harvested their words for the truth. I did not learn how to weave or cook or sew at Cythraul. I did not learn manners, or about God, or how to play a musical instrument. I learned how to wield my alborium and my sword. I learned how men rule and what drives them to rule. For a woman it was a mostly useless education. Now, however, I will dredge up all the knowledge I gained at Cythraul, and it will help me to win your sister's freedom."

"I think," he said slowly, "that I should be afraid of you, Rhonwyn uerch Llywelyn. Of your mother there is naught said, but much is spoken of your father, and you are obviously very much Llywelyn's daughter."

"I know," she answered him. "It is something I have fought against my whole life, Rafe, but the truth is I very much like who I am. There is, they say, no escaping blood." Then she took his hand up and began to lick the gravy from his fingers. "We will be on the road for several nights and then at Cythraul, where there is, I promise you, no privacy." She began to suck on his forefinger.

Their eyes met, and then he pulled his hand from her sensual embrace. Taking up his goblet, he drew the potent wine into his mouth while pulling her head to him. As their lips met, he transferred the liquid from his mouth into hers, his tongue sliding past her teeth to meet with her tongue among the heady, hot fumes of the wine. As he broke the long, sweet kiss, Rafe murmured to her, "You are far too conventional, wife. There are places other than a bed where a man and a woman may take their pleasure. Come." He stood and took her by the hand, leading her before the hall fire.

Rhonwyn's green eyes widened. *"The servants!"* she

managed to gasp as he pulled her down to the sheepskin before the hearth.

"I see no servants," he murmured, his hand sliding beneath her skirts to caress her legs.

"*Flint!*" Her head motioned to the dog sleeping near them.

"Will understand perfectly," Rafe said softly, kissing her, his lean body pinioning her down.

"Thank God we have no priest here," she said. "Oh!" His fingers had found what they sought and began to tease at her sensitive flesh. "Rafe! We can't! *Not here!* Oh!" Holy Mary, this was so damnably exciting and dangerous. What if they were discovered?

" 'Tis our house, and we are the master and the mistress here," he said, divining her thoughts with accuracy. She was, he knew, despite her protests, enjoying every minute of their liaison, for she was already creamy with her love juices. He pushed her skirts above her waist and in a single smooth motion entered her body.

" 'Tis wicked!" she avowed, but faintly. Oh, God, he felt so good inside of her! With a deep sigh she let herself be carried away, her emerald eyes closing slowly in blissful anticipation of what was to come next. "*Oh, Rafe!*" Her arms tightened about him.

He grinned down at her. She was a wicked Welsh hussy, and he adored her with every fiber of his being. "Vixen," he said softly, his buttocks contracting and releasing as he pleasured them both.

"Devil," she murmured back, wrapping her legs about him so he might delve deeper into her eager flesh.

He could feel her body quivering as she reached the pinnacle of satisfaction, and as she shuddered over and over again with her release, he loosed his own passions with a gusty sigh. After several minutes he rolled away from her, drawing her skirts down as he pulled his tunic into a semblance of neatness.

"*That* was deliciously wicked and depraved," she said happily. Her eyes were still closed, savoring the remaining bits and pieces of their pleasure before it faded away entirely. "But we couldn't possibly do that at Cythraul, husband."

"Before we go," he promised her, "I shall show you what we can do at Cythraul, or anywhere else, for that matter, wife." Then rising to his feet, he drew her up. "Come on, my love, and let us find our bed now. I've plenty of energy yet left for you, and you won't have to fret about the servants. I saw how your concern prevented you from fully enjoying our little interlude, Rhonwyn."

She laughed, unable to contain herself. "You are a devil, Rafe de Beaulieu."

The following morning Oth was dispatched to find Prince Llywelyn.

"Tell him what has happened and that I will meet him at Cythraul. This threat must be contained immediately, and the lady Katherine rescued. He will argue with you, of course, and say that having little love for Edward de Beaulieu, he does not care what happens to his wife. Then you will tell him that I am begging this boon of him, for the lady Katherine is my husband's sister, and I love her right well. Niggle at him until he yields, Oth. You know him as I do."

"He'll come," Oth said. Then he added, "Send Dewi into Cythraul first to make certain that it is still your tad's and has not been taken over by strangers or enemies, lady."

"'Tis good advice. I will follow it," Rhonwyn told him. "I do not believe Tad would allow Cythraul out of his control, but if the worst has happened, we will wait for you by the ruin on the river near Cythraul, said to belong to the Fair Folk. I will be safe there for my mam's sake, I know. Now go, Oth, and God watch over you."

He kissed her hand and was gone from the hall.

Rhonwyn and Rafe spent the day as if nothing were amiss, each going about their duties. Browne, the steward, and Peterman, the bailiff, were both called into the hall so that Rafe might explain the situation to them.

"I will send word when we are to return," he assured his servants.

Rhonwyn told Enit of the venture. "You cannot come with me," she said. "I need you here to be certain Justin is well cared for in my absence. Bess is a good nurse to him, but sometimes she is absentminded. Watch her carefully, and see my son is safe. Do not allow the child or his nurse from the house except into the gardens with men-at-arms guarding them," she instructed both Enit and Browne. "If those holding Lady Katherine should learn of their mistake while I am gone, Justin could be in danger. Allow no stranger into the house, even a religious."

They nodded.

"With luck and Prince Llywelyn's aid, we shall not be gone for too long a time and will return in triumph with Kate," Rafe said.

"Amen, my lord!" Browne said fervently.

Rafe and Rhonwyn would take little but the clothing they wore and their weapons. They ate their evening meal early, and as they wanted to start just before dawn, they departed the hall almost immediately after eating. As they reached the landing of the second floor, Rafe pulled his wife aside and pushed her against the stone wall of the corridor.

"Fondle me," he growled in her ear, licking it and the side of her face. "I promised you I would show you that a man can take and give pleasure in almost any setting."

Then he groaned as her hands pushed through the fabric of his garments and began to stroke and play amid the badges of his sex. "Ah, witch!" he groaned as her skillful toying had the desired result. His hands were beneath her skirts in a trice, cupping her buttocks and raising her up to impale her upon his manhood. "Ah!" he sighed as he entered her wet, hot sheath. "You are always ready for me, wife, and how I love you for it!"

She gave herself over to the passion of the moment, and when they were both most thoroughly sated they stumbled to their bedchamber, where Enit was awaiting them in the solar with a large bath ready and steaming.

"Wonderful!" Rhonwyn enthused. "We shall not see such luxury for many a day, my lord. We must take advantage of it while we may." She began to pull her garments off, as did he.

Enit, not in the least disturbed, picked up the clothing as it was tossed, clucking and scolding them both at their haste.

"We'll wash each other, Enit," Rhonwyn said, and taking up the boar's-bristle brush, she began to scrub her husband's back vigorously.

"Then I'll take these wretched garments you have both worn to death to the laundress," Enit said.

"Take your time," Rafe called to her as the door shut. They heard Enit laugh as she hurried down the stairs.

"How long do you think we have?" he asked Rhonwyn.

"At least half an hour," she chuckled.

"Good!" He turned and cupped her full breasts in his two big hands. "Ah, I love these sweet fruits," he purred in her ear as he fondled them gently. He pressed his body against her suggestively. "I'm as randy as a billy goat tonight, wife," he warned.

She wiggled her bottom into his groin. "Then we shall be randy together, Rafe, my husband. The tiny interlude in the hallway was but a taste of what I want from you tonight. Oh, yes!"

"So you like that," he whispered in her ear as he rubbed his stiffening lance between the twin moons of her bottom.

"Ummmm," she answered him. "You are so quickly roused, husband."

"Because you are so damnably tempting, wife," he responded.

She turned about and kissed him slowly. "What a nice compliment, husband," she purred. Then she began licking his face and throat with broad, hot sweeps of her little tongue. "You are salty," she said.

"You are sweet," he countered, his tongue licking at her face, her chest, and, after he lifted her slightly, her full breasts.

They coupled once again, the water sloshing about them as their passion rose. When they had pleasured each other, they washed and exited the tub, Rhonwyn shaking her head at the puddles.

"Thank heavens the floor is stone," she remarked as she first dried him with a rough cloth, and then herself. "What will Enit think?"

"That her master and her mistress were as randy as two billy goats tonight," he chuckled, and took her hand. "Come, wife, to bed with you lest we both catch a chill. We are off on serious business come the morrow. Pray God my sister is yet safe."

"She will be safe, Rafe," Rhonwyn assured him. "Even if they learned she was not ap Gruffydd's child, they will ransom her to Edward. The Welsh have been called many things by you English, but never have we been called foolish. We know how to make a groat. Kate will be safe."

They climbed naked into their bed, and he cradled her in his arms. "I trust you, wife," he told her.

"I know," Rhonwyn said with a small smile. "That is one of the reasons I love you, Rafe de Beaulieu. You really do trust me."

"I love you," he said simply. "Now sleep, wife."

Rhonwyn smiled again to herself and closed her eyes.

Chapter Eighteen

It had been many years since Lady Katherine de Beaulieu had heard the Welsh tongue spoken. Now, however, she silently thanked God for her old Welsh nurse and her own linguistic abilities. At first it was all garble, but then gradually her mind focused, and she understood. The men who held her captive believed she was Rhonwyn. Her first instinct was to tell them they were wrong, but then she thought that they might kill her as they had so many in Ainslea village. Reaching out, she gently tugged the skirt of her servant Mab. The woman turned a frightened face to her mistress, and Kate put a finger to her lips, warning Mab to silence.

"They believe," she whispered softly, "that I am Rhonwyn. Address me as such else they kill us for their own error."

"What is it you say in that barbaric tongue, Rhonwyn uerch Llywelyn?" one of her captors asked roughly.

"I am calming my servant," Kate replied. "She is frightened by you and by what she has seen this day. These English are not strong."

"Strong enough when they choose," the man laughed.

"Who are you, and why have you done this?" Kate asked him.

"In time, Rhonwyn uerch Llywelyn" was the answer.

Almost all the male inhabitants of Ainslea had been slaughtered, but for those who had managed to flee. The women and the children, however, were herded together to be driven into Wales where they would be sold as slaves. One old man was left to tell the tale to any who came seeking the lady of Haven Castle. The village was then fired, and the Welsh rode off with their captives and their loot—for they had sacked whatever had value including several milk cows, the poultry, a team of oxen, and a small herd of sheep.

Late in the afternoon Kate and her servant were taken in a separate direction by four of their captors. Mab began to whimper again with fright, moaning that they were going to be ravaged and killed for certain.

"Be silent!" Kate said sharply. "If they intended such villainy they would not have brought us this distance. It is something else, and I am interested to learn what."

"They will kill us when they learn the truth," Mab sobbed. "You should have told them back in Ainslea, and surely they would have released us, lady."

"Nay," Kate said. "They would have killed us then for they could not allow me to alert my sister in law to their perfidy, whatever it may be. I must maintain this masquerade for the time being until I can learn what is afoot. Then perhaps I may speak the truth. Or mayhap not, Mab. Now, pull yourself together, lass. We will not show these Welsh that we are afraid."

"Are you, lady?" Mab quavered.

"Aye, I am," Kate replied. "I should be a fool not to be fearful, Mab." Then she reached out and patted her servant's hand in a gesture of comfort, giving her a small smile.

"My name is Ifan ap Daffydd," the leader of her captors said. "We will overnight at a small convent, lady. If you attempt to escape or try to tell the nuns who you are or that you are captive, my men and I will kill the holy women. Do you understand me?"

"Aye," Kate said, "I do."

"Tell your servant what I have said, and tell her if she continues to whimper and whine as she has been, I will personally slit her throat. There are good Welsh women at my brother's castle who can serve you. You do not need this English cow."

"Nonetheless, Ifan ap Daffydd, I will have her," Kate answered him. "She has been loyal to me since I arrived at Haven. Perhaps you do not value such traits in a servant, but I do. She is not used to seeing such slaughter as she has viewed this day. You will leave her be, for she is my responsibility."

"Your Welsh is odd," he said to her.

"I have been living among the English for several years now and have not spoken my own tongue. I am surprised that I can recall it at all," Kate told him blithely. "Besides, each end of Wales speaks a different dialect, Ifan ap Daffydd, yet we all manage to understand each other."

"Aye, we do, especially when it comes to your tad, Rhonwyn uerch Llywelyn," he replied, and then he laughed.

When he had ridden ahead again Kate explained to Mab what had been said, couching the Welshman's threats in gentler language. "You must not carry on any longer, Mab, for you are irritating these men, and they could punish us both for your behavior."

"I will try," Mab said.

"You must succeed," Kate said firmly.

"Where are they taking us?"

"To the castle of Ifan ap Daffydd's brother, whoever he may be," Kate said. "From what this Ifan has said, I suspect it has something to do with the Welsh prince, but what, I do not yet know."

When they reached the small convent where they were

to overnight, Ifan ap Daffydd explained to the porteress that he was escorting his sister to the castle of their brother, Rhys ap Daffydd, lord of Aberforth. They were welcomed and fed, and then offered pallets in the guest house. The nun apologized that they had but one space for guests and could not separate the sexes.

"I will sleep outside the guest-house door with my men so my sister may have her privacy," Ifan ap Daffydd said gallantly. "We are used to sleeping beneath the night sky, good sister." Having seen the interior of the place, Ifan ap Daffydd felt secure, for it had but one door and the two windows were too high for his captives to use for escape.

In the morning they attended Prime, and then they were given brown bread, a snip of cheese, and cider before they departed. Kate took a coin from her purse and pressed it into the hand of the porteress.

"Thank you, good sister," she said. "Will you pray for my sister-in-law, Katherine?"

"I will, my child," the nun said.

"What was that all about?" Ifan ap Daffydd demanded to know as they rode off.

"I gave the nun a coin from my purse. I doubt you thought to do it, Ifan ap Daffydd. Then I asked her to pray for my sister-in-law, Katherine. There was no harm in it. I spoke our tongue, and you were free to hear it. It is customary to pay for one's lodging if you can, and what with your boasting about taking your sister to your brother's castle, it would have been expected that you offer the nuns who sheltered us a small donation for our food and accommodation. You men have no sense of propriety."

He laughed. "I had heard that you were a firebrand."

"Had you?" she remarked dryly.

They rode all day and sheltered the second night in a dry cave, for there were no religious houses or villages along their route. Their supper and their breakfast the following morning was roasted rabbit, hot in the evening and cold in the morning. They slept, wrapped in their cloaks, on the dirt floor of the cave, a fire at its entrance to discourage any wildlife from entering. They rode all of the third day, finally coming to Aberforth Castle shortly after the early sunset of that autumn day. The castle before them was small but dark and forbidding. Kate shivered nervously, but then pulled herself together as they passed beneath the portcullis into the courtyard.

When they had dismounted they were led into the castle's great hall. There were no fireplaces, but rather a large stone fire pit in the center of the hall that blazed, heating the entire room. To Kate's surprise the stone walls were hung with beautiful tapestries, and there were fragrant herbs scattered upon the stone floor that gave off a sweet odor when stepped upon. Upon the dais was a high board, and seated there eating was a richly dressed black-bearded man with piercing dark brown eyes and black hair.

Ifan ap Daffydd hurried forth, bringing his prisoners with him. He bowed low, and then straightening, he said, "I have brought Rhonwyn uerch Llywelyn as you requested, my lord brother."

The lord of Aberforth looked up and perused Kate. "You do not look like your mother," he said in a rough voice. "Nor do you favor your tad particularly, lady. However, I see ap Gruffydd's mother in you. She had hair your color. Your mother had hair like gilt thistledown."

Kate was curious, and she realized she was expected to reply. "You knew my mother?" she said.

"Briefly, though intimately," he chuckled.

"Why, my lord, have you kidnapped me and had me brought here?" Kate demanded to know. "My husband will be most vexed. He is not a wealthy man and cannot be expected to pay you too exorbitant a ransom."

Rhys ap Daffydd laughed. "You have your father's overweening pride and your mother's spirit," he replied. "I want no ransom from your husband, lady. It is your father I have occasion to deal with, and as he will not listen to reason, I thought perhaps if I had custody of his daughter he might be more amenable to . . . ah, negotiation."

"You have a quarrel with Prince Llywelyn, and so you have kidnapped me?" Kate was both astounded and outraged. "You are a coward, my lord, if you cannot deal with ap Gruffydd without threatening a woman of his family! I will not help you."

"You do not understand, Rhonwyn uerch Llywelyn," Rhys said. "Your father has gained his title from the English, but nonetheless we have honored that title because it meant that Wales was left in peace by the English. Now your sire refuses to do fealty to King Edward, thus breaking his bond with England. Edward Longshanks is not an easy man and will not bear this insult. When he comes into Wales to punish your father, we will all suffer for our prince's misbehavior. I have friends in England who have requested that I reason with your father, for all our sakes. Since he has refused to grant me an audience, I must gain his attention in the only way I can, by bringing you here to Aberforth. Your father will not allow you to be harmed."

Kate remembered what Rhonwyn had said the few rare times she had spoken of her father. It was very unlikely that ap Gruffydd would come to his daughter's aid if it did not serve some good purpose for him. Kate could see that Rhys ap Daffydd was no true patriot. What he did he was doing for his own gain. She suspected he meant to attempt an assassination of Llywelyn ap Gruffydd when he came to rescue his daughter. She saw her own country's hand in such a plot. It was absolutely disgraceful and dishonorable. "Well, my lord, you can but try to reason with my tad," she told him, "but he never really cared greatly for me as I was not a son."

"What happened to the lad?" Rhys demanded.

"What lad?" she countered.

"Your little brother" was the reply.

"Glynn? Oh, he died when he was twelve of the pox," Kate said easily. She knew that if she said Glynn was a religious in the abbey at Shrewsbury, Glynn might very well find himself in danger, too.

"So," Rhys crowed triumphantly, "you are Llywelyn ap Gruffydd's only living heir. He will come for you, female or not."

"If you say so, my lord," Kate told him. "Now, I am hungry and I am chilled to the bone, as is my servant. Have me shown to my chamber and have hot food brought to me. I should not want to tell my tad that you were a poor host, Rhys ap Daffydd."

The lord of Aberforth laughed heartily. "They say you were raised roughly in the Welshry, lady, but you speak as if you were truly a princess born."

"*I am,*" Kate replied loftily. Then she followed a servant who led her to her chamber. When the door had closed behind them, she breathed a deep sigh of relief and said in her own English tongue, "It is obvious that none of these people have ever seen Rhonwyn, Mab. And I fooled them! I actually convinced them I was she."

"I couldn't understand a word you spoke, lady, but your manner was fearless and proud. What will happen to us now?"

"Our captor is Rhys ap Dafydd, and he is in league with some of our countrymen. I think he means to use the prince's daughter to lure ap Gruffydd here. Then, I believe, he will assassinate him if he can. This is to be done to curry favor with King Edward."

"And afterward?" Mab ventured.

"I don't know," Kate answered her servant honestly. "I don't think they will kill us. We are just the bait in the trap. And the prince's daughter is supposed to be wed to an English lord, and the marriage was part of a treaty between our two lands. I suspect they will return us back to England when they have accomplished their nefarious purposes."

"How do you know he means to kill the prince?" Mab asked.

"I do not, for certain," Kate replied, "but instinct tells me he lies, Mab."

"But when the prince comes and sees you are not his child," Mab fretted, "what will they do?"

"By then it will be too late," Kate said.

"Oh, mistress, I am so afraid!" Mab said.

Kate put comforting arms about her servant. "I know," she said, "and I am, too, but we cannot let these men see we are afraid. Edward and Rafe are already on our trail, I know it! They will find us and rescue us before long, Mab."

"*How?*" Mab now sobbed, totally unnerved. "How will they get into this fortress, and how will they get us out? It is hopeless, my lady. It is hopeless!" She began to weep.

"Nay, 'tis not hopeless," Kate reassured her, although she was not certain at all that Mab wasn't right. "Mab, think! What is the worst that can happen to us? We will be killed. But if our mortal bodies die, do we not live on in the spirit? To be with our blessed Mother would not be such a terrible fate, Mab."

"*But I haven't ever lived, lady!*" Mab hiccuped. "I am still a virgin. You at least know the joy of marriage and children."

"And so will you, Mab," Kate said firmly. The door to

their chamber opened, and she continued, "Look! Here is a nice hot supper for us. Things will seem much brighter after you have eaten."

"If it ain't poisoned," Mab said darkly.

"I don't think they brought us all the way from Haven just for the pleasure of poisoning us," Kate remarked. Then she turned to the servant who had brought the meal. "Tell your master I will require a hot bath tonight. I was nursing an infant when I was taken, and my bodice is soaked through with my milk. I shall also require a clean chemise and a gown. Are there women of rank here?"

"Lord Rhys's leman," the servant answered.

"Then my requirements can be satisfied certainly," Kate said.

"Yes, lady," the servant replied, and hurried out.

"You would wear the clothes of that bandit's whore?" Mab demanded.

"Aye," Kate admitted. "They are surely cleaner than what I am now wearing. Both my chemise and gown are sticking to my breasts. The smell on my clothing is not particularly pleasant. Oh, I hope Edward was wise enough to get wee Henry a wet nurse, Mab."

"If he wasn't, the other women will see to it," Mab, her courage now restored, comforted her mistress. Her eye went to the tray of food as she realized that she was very hungry. "Let us eat, lady. You sit, and I shall serve you." She began to ladle rabbit stew onto the trencher of bread. "How long do you think it will take Lord Edward to find us, my lady?"

"He is probably on his way now," Kate said, spooning the hot stew into her mouth. "Ummm, this is good. At least the cook is competent here, Mab. We shall not be starved. Aye, Edward is more than likely very near us, and my brother with him. Listen! Do you hear rain? Well, at least we were spared riding in a downpour."

Outside, the rain fell heavily, and at the convent where Kate's captors had stopped that first night, Rhonwyn was in earnest conversation with the mother superior, having introduced herself as the niece of the Abbess Gwynllian of Mercy Abbey. The convent's porteress was with them, waiting to be given permission to speak.

"We do not have many guests, being in such a distant locale," the mother superior said, "but several nights ago four men and two women sheltered with us. Sister Margaret can tell you more." She nodded to the porteress, giving her permission to add what she could.

"Did they tell you who they were?" Rhonwyn asked.

"The one who appeared to be their leader said the lady was his sister and the other her servant. He was taking them to his brother's castle, but he did not give his name or that of his brother. The two women were quiet except the next morning when they were leaving. The lady asked me to pray for her sister-in-law, Katherine. She gave me a coin, which is more than the man did."

"Do you remember what she looked like?" Rhonwyn gently probed the elderly nun's memory.

"Young and pretty," Sister Margaret replied. "She had beautiful light blue eyes, and although she wore a head covering, I could see a bit of her hair. It was a nice nut brown. She was well spoken, although her Welsh sounded a bit strange to my ear, as if it were not her native tongue. Her servant was ordinary and appeared frightened."

"Did the lady perhaps favor this gentleman with me?" Rhonwyn asked. She drew Rafe forward.

"*She did!*" Sister Margaret cried. "Indeed she did. Why, my lord, you could be sister and brother."

"We are," Rafe replied. "My sister Katherine was being

kidnapped, good sister. Are you certain you cannot recall hearing a place or a name? We must find her!"

"I am sorry, my lord," Sister Margaret said, but then she brightened. "I can tell you that when they departed the following morning they went north. Straight due north."

"What is in that direction?" he asked her, but she shrugged.

"There is only one place to the north," the mother superior told them. "It is a two days' ride, and there is nothing in between. Aberforth Castle would be the next inhabited place. There is nothing before it, and nothing in any other direction at all, my lord."

"Who is the lord of the castle?" Rhonwyn asked the nun.

"Rhys ap Daffydd, lady" was the response.

They sheltered the night in the convent guest house, and then the following morning they departed.

"We must go to Cythraul," Rhonwyn said as they turned west. "I want to speak to my father before we beard this Rhys ap Daffydd."

"How far are we?" Rafe asked her, and Dewi answered.

"We should be there by nightfall," he said.

"Do you know this Rhys?" Rhonwyn asked Dewi.

"Only by reputation, lady. He is an ambitious man, they say," Dewi replied, "and never your father's friend."

They rode that bright November day over the green hills of Wales, seeing no one. Finally, as the sun was setting, the ramparts of Cythraul appeared ahead of them.

"I will go ahead to be certain it is safe," Dewi said, and kicked his mount forward while Rhonwyn and Rafe drew their horses aside in a thicket to await Dewi's signal. When it came they rode quickly into the fortress. Looking about her, Rhonwyn wondered that she had been raised in such a rough place.

"Rhonwyn, welcome home!" Morgan ap Owen lifted her from her saddle. "Why have you come?"

"Is my father here yet?" she answered his question with a question. "Oth went for him some days ago."

"He hasn't come, but then neither has Oth. Come into the hall, lass. And who is this fellow who accompanies you?"

"This is my husband, Rafe de Beaulieu," she answered.

"I thought you wed Edward de Beaulieu," Morgan replied.

"I did, but then our marriage was dissolved, and I wed his cousin Rafe. Rafe's sister married Edward. That is why I am here, Morgan ap Owen. Several days ago some Welsh came over the border and kidnapped Lady Katherine, believing she was me. It obviously has something to do with my father. We have to find Kate before she is harmed, and she will be when they learn she isn't me. I needed to meet with ap Gruffydd in a location where we wouldn't be observed so I could learn from him just what is going on, old friend."

"I understand," her old mentor said. "Well, there is nothing for you to do but sit down with us in the hall until he comes."

The evening meal was served, and they sat at table with Morgan ap Owen as bread, venison, and trout were placed before them. At first the men who had raised her were shy of Rhonwyn, but gradually they realized that while her manner had softened and she was a grown woman, she was still *their* lass. The hall soon became noisy as they told Rafe tales of her childhood, and he joined in their uproarious laughter at her many adventures and misadventures.

"I suppose," said Lug ap Barris, "that you're no longer the fine soldier you once were. After all, you're a mam now."

"Would you like to go hand-to-hand with me, Lug?"
she asked him in a deceptively innocent voice.

He saw the look in her eye and chuckled. "Nay, Rhonwyn. 'Tis obvious I am mistaken."

"And who do you think will teach my son how to use
the alborium, Lug? Is there anyone in your memory who
can shoot as well as I?"

"Nay, Rhonwyn," he replied.

"You taught me well," she said softly, and he flushed
with pleasure that she would remember him now that
she was a lady.

Brenin, the ancient wolfhound, came and lay by her
side. "He is my first dog," she told Rafe as she leaned
over to stroke the old animal's head.

"Tell me of the laddie," Gwilym the cook said.

"He has joined the Benedictines in Shrewsbury,"
Rhonwyn said, "and is at the abbey. You would have
been proud of him. When he learned I had disappeared
while on crusade, he came to Palestine and sought me
out by doing what King Richard's minstrel, Blondell,
once did. He went about entertaining with song, singing
his first song always in our Welsh tongue, waiting for an
answer, and when he finally received it, he helped rescue
me." Then she told them of her adventures and the reason for the dissolution of her marriage to Edward.

When she had concluded her tale Morgan op Owen
spoke up for them all. "The Englishman was wrong to
remarry so hastily."

"He was fearful of dying without heirs," Rhonwyn
said, shrugging, "and he could hardly expect I would return to him. It was a miracle, but the other miracle was
that I have found real love with Rafe, my friends. I hold
no bitterness any longer toward Edward, and I love his
wife, Katherine. I must find her, Morgan. She is a gentle

woman, and she has two sons at Haven. One is yet new and at the breast."

"We'll help you, Rhonwyn," Morgan said. "You know you can count on the men of Cythraul."

They slept that night in the hall, cuddling in her old bed-space. Rafe fondled his wife's breasts, but after a purr of pleasure, she warned him off. "We cannot," she told him.

"Why not?" he murmured in her ear, licking softly at it.

"Would you embarrass the men who raised me by letting them hear the sounds of our passion, Rafe?"

In response he took her hand and placed it on his manhood, which was now rock hard. "You will owe me greatly for this enforced abstinence, lady," he told her, and then kissed her mouth sweetly.

"I always meet my debts, my lord," she responded with a smile.

In the late afternoon of the following day Llywelyn ap Gruffydd appeared in the company of Oth. "How is my grandson?" he asked.

"Thriving, and with your chin, my lord," she told him.

The prince turned and looked at Rafe sharply. "Is this the one they married you to after Edward de Beaulieu betrayed you?"

"Aye, and I love him, so there is no harm done," Rhonwyn quickly replied. "Rafe, come and give your hand in friendship to my sire."

Rafe held out his hand to Llywelyn ap Gruffydd. "My lord."

The prince grasped the hand and said, "If she is happy, then I will accept you, Rafe de Beaulieu. You look a better man than Edward."

"I am," Rafe replied without a moment's hesitation.

Ap Gruffydd stared hard at him a moment, and then he burst out laughing. "By the rood, Rhonwyn, here indeed is your match, and I thank God for it, for certainly I have done little enough for you, daughter."

"You are a great man, Tad, and have great things to do," she answered him with a small smile.

"Your mam always said that to me," he said, a cloud briefly flitting over his features.

"I know," Rhonwyn responded.

"Wine, my lord?" Gwilym was at his side with a large goblet.

"Aye," the prince said, taking it and gulping down a swallow. "Come, daughter, and let us sit by the fire while you tell me what it is you desire of me. I will grant it if it is in my power."

They sat, and she explained the unfortunate situation to him as he drank his wine and listened closely. When she had finished, he spoke.

"It will be Rhys ap Daffydd without a doubt who holds the lady Katherine hostage. He is a weasel of a man and a coward to boot. Long ago I caught him in a treacherous plot with the English. Few would have anything to do with him after I exposed him. You were just a wee lass then, Rhonwyn. He always said he would have his revenge upon me for it. Now he seeks to take advantage of my dispute with King Edward."

"I think he means to kill you," Rhonwyn said quietly.

"Aye, that would be his way. Then he would gain more favor with his English masters, and Wales would fall to them. I will not have it! We cannot, of course, storm Aberforth, for he might kill the lady Katherine. Yet we still might make him believe I am coming to the aid of my daughter without endangering her."

"First we must be certain Kate is there," Rhonwyn said. "Let us send Oth into Aberforth as your messenger with a date for your meeting with Rhys. Oth will insist upon seeing the hostage so he may return to you and tell you your daughter is being well cared for at Aberforth. Then Rafe, Dewi, and I shall enter the stronghold disguised as wandering entertainers. Such people are always welcome, and I have had experience enough as I worked my way back from Palestine with Glynn. Once inside Aberforth we shall rescue Kate."

"How?" the prince demanded.

"I shall kill Rhys," Rhonwyn said quietly.

"How?" the prince asked as quietly.

"With my alborium, Tad. I can do it, never fear," Rhonwyn told him. "This man has taken Kate from her family and means you harm. I have no qualms about killing him."

"So, daughter, you would do this for me, would you?" the prince said, rather surprised by her words.

"I was raised here, my lord, and I was taught duty to family and to Wales. I have an English husband whom I love, and I am content to recognize the English king as my overlord. But this business has little to do with England. It is Welsh business, my lord, and it must be concluded by the Welsh. This Rhys ap Daffydd is a man of guile and dishonor. Both he and his vile actions shame our race."

"And you, Englishman, you are content to allow your wife to do this thing?" ap Gruffydd asked Rafe.

"Aye," Rafe said. Then he continued, "My wife is not some delicate flower in need of my protection. She is a strong woman, and frankly at times I have been glad for her protection. If she believes she can do this, then I am content to let her. But know that if she should fail, I will, myself, see to this man's death for the temerity he has shown in taking my sister as his hostage."

The prince of the Welsh smiled slowly. "This time, daughter," he said, "you have married a *real* man. I do like you, Rafe de Beaulieu." He clapped his son-in-law upon the back in a friendly gesture.

It was decided that the prince, along with a troop of men-at-arms from Cythraul, would travel several hours behind the others. They would not enter Aberforth until signaled. Rhonwyn, Rafe, and Dewi would come to Rhys ap Daffydd's castle in their guise as traveling entertainers. Rhonwyn had decided to dress herself as a female in boy's garb, the better to entice the castle's master. Oth would leave Cythraul in the morning, Rhonwyn and her party would come two hours behind him, and the prince and his men would be four hours behind them.

The evening meal was served, and afterward Gwilym sang several ballads of ancient times. "But," he told them as he so often did, "my laddie, Glynn, has sung and played them better."

"Now he sings and plays for God," Rhonwyn said.

"My only son, a priest," the prince muttered, disgusted.

"He's happy," Rhonwyn said quietly. "Besides, when you can celebrate your marriage to de Montfort's daughter, get yourself a son on her. That child will be your legitimate heir."

"I've been betrothed to the wench for long enough, but she is hidden in a convent in France, and the English will not give her permission to travel through their lands so we may marry," ap Gruffydd groused. "Edward Longshanks is in fear of de Montfort's daughter, the fool."

"King Edward is scarcely a fool, my lord," Rhonwyn told her father. "It is you, I'm thinking, who is foolish. Why will you not pledge your fealty to him? If you did, perhaps your bride could come to Wales, and you would have many sons. But nay, you will niggle and haggle to gain an advantage you will never obtain from this king. He is a hard man like his grandfather King John, although he can be quite charming. Nonetheless, Tad, he will have his own way, and you and your allies will eventually cost Wales her freedom, I have not a doubt."

The prince looked extremely disgruntled by her words. "You still speak your own mind, Rhonwyn, I see," he said. "The English shall not have Wales as long as I live. I swear it on the true cross!"

"Words come easy to you, my lord, but 'tis actions that count," Rhonwyn said scathingly.

Rafe was fascinated by the combative relationship between father and daughter. He knew that ap Gruffydd had had next to nothing to do with her upbringing, but he had not realized before just how bitter Rhonwyn was toward the prince of the Welsh. Absently Rafe took her hand in his and, raising it to his lips, kissed each fingertip. "Let us retire, wife," he said low. "We will have a long day tomorrow."

Ap Gruffydd sipped on his wine thoughtfully, but when his daughter and her husband had crawled into their bedspace, he said to Morgan ap Owen, "He manages her well, and she does not even realize it. She must indeed love him, Morgan."

The captain of Cythraul smiled his reply.

Oth was gone before the dawn, and Rhonwyn and her party followed him two hours later. They had borrowed several of Gwilym's old instruments, for it was likely they would have to perform. Dewi and Rhonwyn were skilled in such arts, but Rafe was not. When they camped that night she taught him how to keep time with a tambourine and cymbalum, which were a type of bells. Dewi was adept on the pibau, or bagpipes, and the pibgorn, a reed instrument. Rhonwyn would play the Telyn—a Celtic harp—as well as the lute, and sing.

They traveled from dawn till dusk for two days. On the morning of the third day they reached Aberforth

Castle, meeting Oth but an hour after they sighted the castle, and they drew their mounts into a wooded area off the road to await him. Seeing them, he stopped.

"She's there," he said, "and in the dirty, stained gown they took her in, for the leman of the master will not loan her a clean garment. These are wicked people, my lady. Be careful. I shall ride on to meet with your father and tell him what I have learned."

"Into the lion's den," Rhonwyn said, and kicked her mount forward.

They rode down the road, across the heavy wooden drawbridge beneath the portcullis, and into the castle courtyard, asking for the steward when they stopped.

"You must go into the hall," the stable boy said. "He will not come out here, for who are you but a ragtag and itinerant bunch?"

"Will you watch our horses, you handsome fellow?" Rhonwyn said, favoring the lad with a broad smile and chucking him beneath the chin. She bent, allowing him a generous view of her breasts. "We'll make it worth your while," she purred.

The boy swallowed hard, scarcely able to look away from her bosom. Without a word he took the reins and nodded, blushing beet red when Rhonwyn pinched his cheek and blew him a kiss.

"Must you be so damned bold?" Rafe muttered as they mounted the steps to the porch and went through the door of the castle.

"Men like bold women, for they always assume that bold women are bad women," Rhonwyn told him. "I may have to do things that I would certainly not do otherwise, Rafe, but you must trust me."

"Aye, my lord, follow her lead," Dewi said. "She's a clever lass and more than once got us out of a scrape as we made our way home through France."

In the great hall they asked for the steward and were directed to his chamber. Knocking, they entered, and Rhonwyn immediately spoke up.

"Greetings, my lord steward. I am Anghard, and these are my two companions, Dewi and Rafe. We are musicians and thought perhaps that you might have a need of a night's entertainment."

"It is not often we get travelers in this place," the steward said, a hint of suspicion in his voice. "Where are you from and where are you bound for, Anghard?"

"We have no real home, my lord steward, but we have at last been in Shrewsbury and now make our way to Prince Llywelyn's stronghold, for we hear he is a lover of music and generous to boot. We have spent the last two nights out-of-doors and would welcome a night beneath a strong roof with a fire and some hot food." She smiled at him.

"I can save you a long trip," the steward said, "for the prince will be here in a few days' time. He is coming to visit my master, Rhys ap Daffydd, lord of this castle. We will give you a week or more of shelter, Anghard, and you and your companions will entertain us, eh?"

"With pleasure, my lord steward, and I thank you for your generosity," Rhonwyn said.

"Go into the hall," the steward told them. "You may sleep there and eat at the lord's tables below the salt. If you play well, there may be a little something else for you as well."

"Thank you, my lord steward," Rhonwyn said, bowing as she backed from the room.

"You are a devious woman," Rafe said as they returned to the hall. "I should have believed you myself did I not know you."

"We must find the perfect place," Rhonwyn said to Dewi, "and then you must make certain my alborium is

ready to be used. We'll watch for servants while you prepare it, for if it is learned we have brought weapons into
this lord's hall, we may be killed for our daring."

They found a niche in a dark corner and, drawing a
bench before it, shielded Dewi as he prepared Rhonwyn's bow for use when the proper time came. When all
was in readiness they rested, waiting for the main meal of
the day when they would certainly be asked to entertain.
In midafternoon the servants began to come into the hall
with platters and bowls. Rhys ap Daffydd, his leman, his
captain, his brother, Ifan, and Katherine came into the
great hall and took their places at the high board. The
tables below the salt began to fill, and Rhonwyn and her
companions found seats at the very last table.

At the high board a plethora of dishes was served, but
below the salt there was bread, a pottage, and some hard
cheese with only beer to drink. Rhonwyn looked toward
the dais, seeing that Katherine, while pale, was hardly
cowed by her captors. She has more courage and strength
than I believed, Rhonwyn thought proudly. She found,
though, that she was angered by the fact that Rhys ap
Daffydd had not had the decency to find his captive clean
clothing. Katherine wore, as Oth had told them, the
milk-stained gown she had been taken in. You shall soon
pay for all your wickedness and deceit, Rhonwyn silently
thought.

When the meal was over, the steward came forward
and said to his master, "My lord, three traveling musicians have asked leave to entertain you in exchange for
shelter and food. Anghard and troupe, come forward at
once!" He waved his hand in their direction.

Rhonwyn and her companions arose and came before
the high board, playing and singing as they gamboled
along. The men were dressed in spring green tunics that
came to just above their knees and chausses striped in

blue and green. Rhonwyn was garbed in a darker green tunic that was extraordinarily short, coming to just below the tops of her thighs. Her chausses were also striped, but in gold and green. She had loosed her hair, and it flowed down her back, hiding her alborium that was affixed there, the string of the bow hidden by the tunic's dark colors as it rode across her chest. In her hair were silk flowers of many hues. Her tunic had a bateau neckline, and she wore nothing beneath it. When she bobbed low her breasts were quite visible to all, and the length of the garment, or rather lack of it, offered a bold view of her tight, round buttocks. She was every bit the picture of an entertainer with an easy and loose virtue.

Rhys ap Daffydd leaned forward—much to his leman's annoyance—very interested in the beautiful musician who smiled most seductively at him, bowing low with her two companions and then standing once again.

"My lord, will you allow us to entertain you?" Rhonwyn purred in a smoky, seductive voice. "I am certain that we can please you if you will but let us." She smiled again at him, their eyes making contact, and Rhonwyn was appalled by the cruelty and the lust she saw in his gaze. This was indeed an evil man.

"You have my permission," Rhys said grandly. He had already decided to bed the wench later.

"Before we begin," Rhonwyn said, "may I know for whom we are performing? I enjoy making little personal songs for all if I but know their names, my lord."

"This is my brother, Ifan, my captain, Llwyd ap Nudd, my mistress, Iola; and my guest, Rhonwyn uerch Llywelyn, whose father is the prince of all the Welsh, or so say the English."

"And many of the Welsh as well," Rhonwyn replied, "or so I am told, Rhys ap Daffydd."

At first he wasn't certain if she had insulted him, but then he laughed. "You are bold, my pretty one."

"And you, my lord, are a fool," she replied easily.

There was an audible gasp in the great hall.

"Boldness is only amusing for a brief time, wench," Rhys said threateningly. "If you offend me again, I shall have your tongue torn out, and then how will you earn your living but upon your back?"

Rhonwyn laughed loudly. "You say your guest is the daughter of Prince Llywelyn, my lord, *but I tell you she is not.* If you wish to use ap Gruffydd's daughter against him, you will have no chance with this woman. She is Lady Katherine de Beaulieu of Haven Castle, wife of Lord Edward. His first marriage to ap Gruffydd's daughter was dissolved several years ago. Did you not know?"

"And how, you audacious and brazen wench, do you know?" Rhys ap Daffydd demanded angrily.

"Because, my lord, I am Rhonwyn uerch Llywelyn," Rhonwyn replied.

Rhys ap Daffydd stared hard at Rhonwyn, and then a cruel smile touched his mouth. "Yes," he said slowly. "Of course. Why did I not see it before when you first stood before me? You have her coloring, Rhonwyn uerch Llywelyn. While you are more ap Gruffydd's daughter in your features, you have Vala's coloring. Do you remember me, my pretty? Do you remember that night I visited your cottage and had my way with your mother? Ah, how she wept and pleaded with me; and you stood, wide-eyed, clutching your baby brother in your arms. How I enjoyed that night, and how I will enjoy this one. Will you give me as much pleasure as your mother gave me so long ago, Rhownyn uerch Llywelyn?" He grinned at her.

All in the silent hall heard the whining sound, but until the arrow buried itself deep into Rhys ap Daffydd's chest, they did not connect it with a weapon. As the lord of Aberforth fell face first into the remains of his meal, Rhonwyn loosed the two arrows that Rafe quickly handed her, one killing Ifan ap Daffydd and the other Rhys's captain, Llywd ap Nudd. Rhys's mistress began to scream in terror as the trio made their way to the high board. It was very necessary to gain control of the castle's inhabitants before they fully comprehended what had just happened.

"Do not be afraid," Dewi shouted to them all. "Prince Llywelyn is even now marching into Aberforth. Our quarrel was with your master and his ilk. It is not with you. Welcome the prince as loyal Welshmen, and you will be left in peace. Now go and open your gates for my master."

The hall virtually emptied at his words.

"I'll go and make certain they obey me," Dewi said.

"Be careful," Rhonwyn cautioned him. She turned to Rhys's mistress. "Stop howling, you silly woman! You are not hurt nor will you be unless, of course, you don't cease that unpleasant caterwauling."

"Oh, Rhonwyn, you are so brave!" Katherine said breathlessly, hugging her sister-in-law. "When I saw you all come before the high board, I could not believe my eyes. Gracious, brother, you do have a well-turned leg," she teased him as she released Rhonwyn.

"Thank God you are safe, Kate!" he said, hugging her hard.

"I didn't know what was going to happen," Kate admitted, "but thank heavens for our old nurse, Wynnifred. After a few minutes the language began to come back to me, and I quickly realized they thought I was you, Rhonwyn. I was afraid to say I wasn't for fear they would kill me, and I decided that since you had grown up in such an isolated location, it was unlikely they would know I wasn't you."

"It was cleverly done, Kate, and Edward will be proud when he learns how bravely you have conducted yourself." She turned to the woman Iola. "Selfish cow, you will regret your mean spirit. Lady Katherine's servant will pick a gown from among your possessions for her mistress, and come the morning you will go from Aberforth with only what you can carry. I am certain you will find another lordling to whore for soon enough. Leave us now!"

Iola scurried from the great hall.

When she had gone Rhonwyn turned to her husband and sister-in-law. "You heard Rhys ap Daffydd's words. Until he spoke I did not know him. Many years ago when I was a child he came in the dark of night to our cottage and raped my mother. She never told my father, and I do not want her memory fouled by the tale now. Dewi, I know, will say nothing."

"I understand," Katherine said. "You have my word that I will not repeat what I have heard this night."

Rafe put his arm about his wife, and as their eyes met he gave her his silent promise.

People were beginning to stream back into the great hall of Aberforth Castle. They could hear cheering. The sound of booted feet came marching toward them and into the chamber, Llywelyn ap Gruffydd at the soldiers' head upon his stallion, which he rode up to the dais, looking dispassionately at the three bodies draped across the high board.

"Well done, daughter," he praised her. "Well done!"

"And now, my lord tad," she replied, "you will thank Morgan ap Owen for raising me as he did."

"I do indeed thank him," the prince said, a small smile upon his lips. "But you get your eye for marksmanship from me, daughter." His look went next to Katherine de Beaulieu. "Lady Katherine, I apologize that one of my subjects should have mistreated you so. You are free to return to Haven with your brother and Rhonwyn."

"I thank you, my lord prince, for your timely rescue," Kate answered him graciously, and then she curtsied prettily.

"Remove the bodies and put them outside for the dogs," the prince said, dismounting his beast and ascending the dais to stand before the hall, which now erupted into cheers.

"How inconstant and capricious are men's loyalties," Rhonwyn murmured sardonically.

"Not mine for you," Rafe said softly.

"You are certain?" She was smiling at him.

"*Very certain,*" he assured her.

She sighed happily, laying her head upon his shoulder. Whatever memories she had once had—of love or evil— had been replaced in her heart and her mind by the reality of this man and his love for her. There could surely be no more than that in life. Looking up at Rafe, she smiled once again, saying, "Let us go home, my lord," and he nodded in agreement as he took her hand and they walked from the hall together.

Ap Gruffydd watched them go, and then he said, "Oth, Dewi. You belong to her as you always have, but before you return to Ardley, will you bring Lady Katherine home to her husband?"

"Aye, my lord," the two chorused, grinning.

He acknowledged them absently, his eyes taking in a last glimpse of his daughter. *Farewell, Rhonwyn uerch Llywelyn,* he said silently to himself. *Farewell!* And then to his surprise she turned, giving him a brilliant smile and raising her hand to him in salute.

"Farewell, Tad!" he heard her call, and then she was gone.

The prince of the Welsh felt his eyes moisten with tears. He blinked them back quickly lest anyone see his weakness. Now what the hell was he going to do with another castle? he thought.

An Afterword

The year between 1276 and 1277 was not a good one for the prince of the Welsh. Llywelyn ap Gruffydd had badly misjudged the new king, and Edward reacted fiercely to the man who would not fulfill his obligations as a vassal. He immediately declared war on the Welsh, which was concluded by an English victory at Aberconwy in 1277. As punishment Edward took most of ap Gruffydd's lands, leaving him with only Lesser Gwynedd and the overlordship of five lords. Finally chastened, ap Gruffydd was at last allowed to marry the daughter of Simon de Montfort, to whom he had been betrothed since 1265. It was hoped the marriage would settle ap Gruffydd down. The marriage took place in 1278.

Disputes did arise regarding the use of English or Welsh law in the prince's lands, but the peace held until 1282 when ap Gruffydd's younger brother, Daffydd, attacked Harwarden. The prince, bound first by family loyalty, was forced to go to his brother's aid and was killed at Builth. He was buried at Cwm Hir, a Cistercian monastery he favored. His wife was already dead in childbirth, and his only legitimate heir was a sickly daughter, named for his sister, Gwynllian. She was put into a convent where she lived out her life. Daffydd ap Gruffydd was finally captured and executed in 1283.

When the Welsh told King Edward that they would only accept a prince who spoke no English, he cleverly presented them with his infant son, Edward, who had been recently born at Llywelyn ap Gruffydd's former stronghold of Caernavon. Thus ended Wales's last attempt at political independence. *Until the year 1999.*

Don't miss this sizzling novel
by Bertrice Small!

TO LOVE AGAIN

*She would ride the fiery passions of her troubled
past to forge a magnificent destiny. . . .*

Legendary for her exotic novels of faraway places
teeming with adventure and intrigue, Bertrice
Small has written an extraordinary tale of passion
and history, sweeping readers back to fifth-century
Britain and Constantinople, where battles of love
and war are fought with abandon—and victory is
savored with sweetest pleasure. . . .

Published by Ivy Books.
Available wherever books are sold.

Don't miss this sizzling novel
by Bertrice Small!

THE INNOCENT

She lived within convent walls—
until destiny thrust her into the arms of passion.

With her brother's untimely death, Eleanore of
Ashlin becomes the heiress of an estate vital to
England's defenses. Now she is ordered by royal
command to wed one of the king's knights. Ranulf
de Glandeville is all too aware of his bride's innocence; yet his gentle hand and growing love for his
spirited young wife soon awaken Eleanore to passions she never knew. But their love will soon be
threatened by a depraved woman who will put
Eleanore's life in jeopardy—and the young bride's
love to its greatest test. . . .

"A tantalizing read . . .
This story of good versus evil will
captivate readers."
—*Literary Times*

Published by Ivy Books.
Available wherever books are sold.

Subscribe to the new Pillow Talk e-newsletter—and receive all these fabulous online features directly in your e-mail inbox:

♥ Exclusive essays and other features by major romance writers like Linda Howard, Kristin Hannah, Julie Garwood, and Suzanne Brockmann

♥ Exciting behind-the-scenes news from our romance editors

♥ Special offers, including contests to win signed romance books and other prizes

♥ Author tour information, and monthly announcements about the newest books on sale

♥ A Pillow Talk readers forum, featuring feedback from romance fans...like you!

Two easy ways to subscribe:
Go to **www.ballantinebooks.com/PillowTalk**
or send a blank e-mail to
join-PillowTalk@list.randomhouse.com.

Pillow Talk—
the romance e-newsletter brought to you by
Ballantine Books